THE MOONSTONE GIRLS

BROOKE SKIPSTONE

Skipstone
PUBLISHING

My life would be changed forever by a photo. And saved by a girl and a mountain.

— TRACY

PLAYLIST

Please visit this link to find all the songs mentioned in this book:
https://open.spotify.com/playlist/3FHQ6I55MRmqkIuFhA2mvD?si=f0b4e7f7b66141cb

The rock/pop songs are listed first, in order of appearance. The classical pieces appear at the end of the list.

Enjoy!

PROLOGUE

I should have been a boy. Even my older brother Spencer said so in the late 60s. Yet as I look now at the three Polaroid prints on my desk in Fairbanks, Alaska, it's hard to remember why. Taken fifty-three years ago and seen by only me and three others, the photos show two nude girls kissing and walking hand-in-hand without embarrassment in front of dozens. By then, we were MoonStone—a girl band eager for a new beginning.

I was seventeen when I traveled to Alaska dressed as a boy in the summer of 1968, leaving my parents in turmoil, full of anger and grief. How that happened is what I want to explain—to myself, my children, and grandchildren, who are themselves in turmoil for many of the same reasons.

In the late 60s, our country was at war with itself—war hawks vs doves, patriots vs antiwar demonstrators and draft card burners. It was much like today's battles over masking and vaccines, police shootings, and an election. I saw riots and marches for racial justice in my teens and now in my seventies.

What I didn't see back then, however, were Pride Marches.

Very few at that time wanted to be called a *queer*. Least of all my older brother Spencer, who'd already suffered insinuations, eye rolls, and tight-lipped head shakes from Dad. Why? Because he played piano instead of sports. Because his mannerisms were too effeminate, his emotions too affected. He was too soft.

Of course, we both suffered from rigid expectations of how a girl or boy at the time should look and act. We were Baby Boomers, the children of the Greatest Generation, who saved the world from Hitler and Tojo and weren't about to allow hippies, riots, student walkouts, and a sexual revolution destroy the world they had defended and preserved. And they were determined to prevent their children from losing a war against men wearing sandals and eating rice balls in Vietnam.

Our father had volunteered for WWII at seventeen and flown Hellcats and Avengers from aircraft carriers. After the war, he became a commercial pilot where he met Alice, a stewardess, who promptly became his housewife. They went to church, bought a house, had two children who attended Sunday School and rode bikes without helmets many blocks from home because the world was safe.

Then came the Beatles and the Stones, bleeding boys in jungles and body counts on the news every night, nudity in the movies, the pill, mini-skirts, marijuana, and flag burnings. But even with all this disruption, my parents and their friends could find solace in the basic truth of two separate genders—one who wore pants and another who wore skirts, slips, girdles, and pointy-tipped bras that lifted and separated. Boys and girls were meant for each other. Any other arrangement was unnatural and specifically condemned in the Bible.

At that time, *queer* was a slur, not a proud identity. Sodomy and homosexual behavior were illegal. Which explained my reluctance to look in the mirror and say, "Tracy, you're gay."

Spencer and I felt awkward inside our skin and wondered whether some mad scientist or prankster-god had messed with our chromosomes before birth. Maybe one day we'd awaken from that crazy dream, me in pants and him in a dress.

But, of course, that never happened.

We never awoke.

We had to face what we were and find a way to live as best we could.

On February 27, 2020, when the world hunkered down to stop a pandemic, I began to write this book as a gift of love and often brutal honesty to myself and to others.

From such a distance, it is difficult to know which events were causes and which were results. Can't every decision we make in the present be the result of a lifetime of events? Is there ever a real beginning?

Because of one critical moment—one I have regretted most of my life—I will start on the night of my brother's fall concert during his senior year in high school, November 11, 1967.

CHAPTER 1
JUMPING THE HUMP

I wrapped my arms around my chest and wished I could've worn a slick tux like Spencer, but no, I had to wear a puffy, frilly dress which did nothing to stop Jack Frost breathing up my legs. I leaned back against my car, shoulder to shoulder with my brother in the parking lot outside Trinity University's Music Center. Usually the weather in San Antonio was mild in November, but a cold front had started to blow through. Oak leaves rattled above us and acorns peppered the pavement. We'd run outside after Spencer's performance because he was upset with Dad and needed to smoke. I'd forgotten my coat in the rush.

I watched him inhale, holding the butt between his pointer and thumb, little finger raised, sucking the smoke through pursed, thick lips. He did everything with style and panache. He was as tall as me, but heavier and softer with a rounder face and a cute grin that Mom and the ladies at the Tuesday Musical Club adored. I was tall, lanky, with broad shoulders, muscular arms, shins that needed shaving twice a day, and small breasts. And I had what my friends called a handsome face—narrow, high cheekbones, strong nose, fuzz by my ears, and a widow's peak.

I don't remember anyone calling me cute.

I bumped against him and stomped my feet. "Hurry up and finish your cigarette so we can get in the car. I'm freezing." Our parents didn't know about his smoking, but he was eighteen, which made it legal back then. Some had accused me of smoking because of my low-pitched voice, but that was how I normally sounded.

He looked down at the asphalt, slid his shoe next to mine, and chuckled. "God, you have big feet!"

He'd done this comparison a hundred times, and I played along to cheer him up. I held out my shaking hand, fingers splayed. "Don't forget the hands. They're big too."

He put his hand on top of mine, his fingers shorter than mine by a knuckle. "If I had your hands, I wouldn't have to roll those opening chords."

"But now you have an excuse to be flamboyant." I smiled and leaned against him.

"Be *gay*, you mean." He dropped the butt and stepped on it.

I grabbed his hand and squeezed as my stomach dropped. What had Dad said to him?

Spencer had just performed the first movement of Tchaikovsky's Piano Concerto No.1 with the Youth Symphony, the final event of a celebration of Piano Guild winners, including me. He'd wanted to play that piece since we both saw Van Cliburn perform at the Coliseum in San Antonio the previous year. Our mother had bought tickets, hoping to inspire us both to dream of playing at Carnegie Hall in New York City. It was mostly just Mom's dream since she dragged us both to Mrs. Francis for piano lessons eight years ago. Spencer cried during Cliburn's performance and ran to the stage afterward, trying to meet the Texan who'd won the first Tchaikovsky competition in Moscow in 1958. From that moment, Cliburn was his idol. Neither of us knew he was gay. Or cared. Fortunately, Dad was off flying cargo to various countries as he did for more than half of every month, so he missed Spencer's emotional outburst in the car driving home. He said Cliburn had smiled directly at him.

If Dad were driving that night instead of Mom, he would've glared at his son through the rearview mirror and shaken his head. We'd both seen this reaction before and many times since.

That night in '67, Spencer played with more flair and confidence than I had ever seen. He almost pranced to the piano before his big bow. At times, he lifted his eyes to the ceiling, his body swooning to the heartbreakingly beautiful melodies, face sagging in sorrow or beaming in joy. At the triumphant conclusion, he leapt from the bench, sweat dripping down his face. The crowd stood and roared.

"Bravo! Bravo!"

Spencer clasped his heart and blew kisses to everyone. Several handed him roses, which he sniffed deeply, his eyes upraised, his face entranced. Then tears flowed and the din somehow grew louder. He shook hands with the conductor, who pulled him in and slapped his back. Spencer raised his arms toward the orchestra, asking them to stand. Once they did, he bowed deeply in appreciation.

Our mother furiously clapped her tiny hands. Dad kept a stiff smile on his face as he applauded steadily. Mom grabbed his hand then pulled him to the stage and up the side stairs. When Spence saw Mom rushing toward him, he opened his arms wide to receive her hug then gave her the flowers and a kiss on her cheek. Spence threw out his arms for a hug from Dad, who then stuck out his hand, keeping a distance.

I saw my brother deflate just as I stepped onto the stage. I ran toward him, pulled him away from Dad, and gave him the biggest hug of my life, lifting him off the ground. The crowd laughed, we waved, and I hurried him outside.

He lit another cigarette as we stood in the dark parking lot, facing the trees.

"You know what he said?" asked Spence with a squeaky voice before taking another drag.

"You were too dramatic?"

He barked a bitter laugh. "If only. He said, 'Why are you being so prissy in front of all these people?'"

"For real? Prissy? That means the opposite."

"Yeah. Never known for his vocab skills," he scoffed. "All he knows is it's an insult for a girl." He flicked his ash then sucked smoke deep into his lungs. "Would it have killed him to hug me? I totaled that piece. The best I've ever played." He tossed the butt, ground it with a grunt, and narrowed his eyes at me. "If I had announced tonight that I'd decided to be a pilot, he would have flipped out. He would've hugged me then. And been so proud!" He shook his head and tightened his lips. "I hate him." His eyes blinked back tears. "I fucking hate him."

My hands found his face and wiped his tears. "Don't. Just ignore him. What does it matter what he thinks?"

"Because he's my father, and I'd like him to be proud of something about me." He turned around.

I saw his back heave as he cried. I wrapped my arms around him. "I'm proud of you, Spence."

He clutched my hands against his stomach, sniffed, and cleared his throat. "I know, Sis." He took a deep breath. "We should go back. Dad made a dinner reservation at Christie's."

"Why don't we drive somewhere? I'll go back to fetch my coat and tell them you want a hamburger. Maybe see a movie?"

He turned toward me and nodded, holding my hands. "Okay. You played really well tonight. I've never heard a more exquisite Chopin."

My face warmed despite the chilly air. "That's high praise coming from the king of the Piano Guild."

"King only because you let me. You'd be the best if you practiced more. Why do you hold back?"

A familiar ache settled below my sternum. "It's a man's game, isn't it?"

He frowned.

I raised my brows. "Name one female pianist."

His mouth dropped open while his eyes searched above my head for an answer.

"Name one piece we've ever played composed by a woman."

He shook his head.

"Why devote my life to playing dead white men's music just so I can end up like Mrs. Francis, teaching piano to children of ambitious mothers? Frankly, I'd rather learn guitar and write my own music. Like Judy Collins and Grace Slick and Joni Mitchell."

He rolled his eyes. "Have you mentioned that to Mom?"

"Not yet. Here." I gave him the keys to my Mustang, a basic model I'd bought three months ago after working at Frost Brothers selling shoes all summer. "Warm it up. I'll only be a minute."

"I can't drive a stick shift."

"You don't have to drive it. Just push in the clutch and turn it on."

He raised his hands and backed away. "Not gonna do it. I'll just sit inside and wait for you."

"Suit yourself." I turned and walked two steps before I heard the car door open then shut. Spencer grabbed my arm.

"I should go with you. Otherwise, he'll call me a wuss."

We hurried toward the auditorium entrance. "You have to stop worrying about his comments. Who cares what he thinks?"

"You do. You argue with him all the time about politics and the war."

I kicked acorns across the sidewalk. "Yeah, well, boys are dying because of him and others like him. Almost 11,000 so far this year. I have to say something."

We opened the doors and walked into a warm lobby full of elegant people, dressed to the nines. Somebody yelled, "Oh, Spencer! You were magnificent tonight."

He stopped, put his right hand to his chest, held his left out then bowed.

"Where have you two been?" shouted Dad, standing near the women's bathroom. My coat and Mom's ermine wrap were draped over his arm. His eyes darted around to see who might hear or see him while his feet couldn't keep still.

Spencer smiled at his fan and threw up his hands as if to say, "What can I do?" Then whispered, "This will be fun," as we walked toward our father.

Somehow, both Spencer and I were taller than Dad. Though he never said anything, I knew that difference bothered him. One of his uncles and his brother were tall, so he had the genes to give to us. To compensate, he'd told stories of having to fight his way to school and even defend his older brother, so being tough was important to him. Maybe he would've been more tolerant and empathetic if he'd been six inches taller and not grown up having to prove his manhood every day during the Great Depression.

He had the more handsome version of my face with blue eyes and deep dimples. Mine and Spencer's were brown like Mom's. Right then, however, he was just an angry forty-three year-old pilot—Captain Arthur Franks, Jr., known as Art to his friends—not Arty. That was his father's nickname, and Dad damn well didn't want to be mistaken for his father. The irony of his relationship with his dad and the one he'd built with us had always escaped him.

I reached for my coat.

He tightened his grip and glared at both of us. "You upset your mother by running off."

"But not you?" I asked, my neck stiffening with anger. "You must've been relieved that your prissy son left."

Spencer flinched.

Dad tightened eyes at Spencer then looked at me, snarling. "Why do you always —"

"Because you always do your best to hurt him."

He scrunched his forehead and shifted the coats to his other arm. "My God, if he gets hurt that easily . . ."

"What?" I asked. "He can't be a man?"

We glared at each other. I'd decided long ago to never let him hurt me and to never back down. If I did, he'd be a shark with blood in the water.

He clenched his jaw several times then took a breath. "How did I hurt him?"

"Give him a hug."

"What?"

"Tracy, don't," said Spencer, hunching down and turning away.

I stomped my foot. "A hug. Here, now, in front of everyone. Your son brought the entire auditorium to its feet. They would have loved to see you hug him like Mom did, but no, you couldn't do it."

Dad stared at Spencer like he was an alien, glanced around to see if anyone was listening, then spit his words: "You were upset because I didn't hug you? We shook hands. That's what men do." He flattened his lips against his teeth. "If I had asked my old man for a hug, he would've . . . hell, I don't know what he would've done." He hissed, "This genera-tion." He opened his arms like a wrestler wanting to crush his opponent. "Okay, Spencer, you want a hug, I'll give you a hug." He took two steps forward before Spencer bolted away.

I pulled my coat from Dad's arm.

"What's wrong with him?" he barked then checked if anyone heard.

"You. I'll drive him home." I took a step then turned around. "When do you fly out?"

"Tomorrow."

"Good." I hurried after my brother, ignoring Dad yelling after me. After all, what could he have done to me besides yell? I caught up to Spence at my car.

He wiped his face. "Now he's going to tease me forever. You shouldn't have said anything."

I unlocked the door, and we both got in. "You shouldn't have run away."

"Yeah? What would you have done?"

I pulled my door hard. "Put out my hand to stop his hug and said, 'Not until you beg me. And even then I won't let you.'"

"Really?"

"Damn right." I crushed the clutch, flipped the key, shoved the stick into reverse, and raced backward into a ninety-degree turn before spinning my tires forward on the pavement.

"How can you be so tough?"

"That's the only way to treat men like that. Show them any weakness, and they take advantage. That's how he was raised. Make yourself hide your emotions." I pulled into traffic on Stadium Drive and headed toward Woodlawn Ave. "Like Iago: '*When my outward action doth demonstrate the native act and figure of my heart . . .*'"

"'*I will wear my heart upon my sleeve for daws to peck at.*' Dad is like a flock of crows, ready to pounce."

I turned my face and smiled at him. "I just finished *Othello* in class. You still remember from last year?"

He nodded and smiled. "I never forget. I can still play every piece I ever learned."

Like a stoner, I said, "Wow, man," dragging out my vowels, hoping he would play our game of slang.

"For real."

"That was lame. Put some feeling into it. Far out, man."

Spence laughed and finally copied my accent. "Groovy."

"Such a gas."

"That's boss."

"Righteous, Bro."

"Uh, for real."

I slammed the horn. "You lose. Already used 'for real.'"

"When?"

I jutted out my chin. "Says the man who never forgets."

"With things that matter. Stupid slang doesn't matter."

"Don't be square!" I laughed.

"Okay, you win."

"Of course, I do. Our generation has the best slang." My eyes widened when I saw the train track hump on Woodlawn Avenue. "Guess what I'm going to do?" I downshifted and sped up, blood surging to my neck and face.

Spence's eyes bulged when he saw the tracks. "Tracy! Don't!"

I raced down the hill toward a slower car. "Guess I'll have to pass."

"Please!" Spencer lifted his knees and covered his face with his arms.

I jerked the wheel to the left and raced past a sedan just as it crawled across the tracks. I caught air, landed with a satisfying thud, and whipped the wheel back to the right just before running into the dividing curb where palm trees grew in single file between lanes. "Yee haw! Loosen up, Spencer. Get it together! That was so bad!"

Spencer unfolded and sat up in his seat. "Are we still alive?"

"I caught more air than Dad ever did. That was righteous."

Spencer slammed his hand on my dash and made a buzzer sound. "You lose. I already used righteous."

"I know. I wanted to see if your brain still worked."

"Promise me you'll never do that again with me in the car."

"Okay, but promise me you'll do that yourself one day. Just catch a little air. That's the only way you'll throw him off your back. Every day he drove us to school in his VW Bug, he'd race over that hump."

"Why? I could never understand why he enjoyed scaring us."

"He was pushing our buttons, trying to toughen us up. As long as we screamed, he kept doing it. When I laughed and said, 'Higher, Daddy,' he told me, 'Good girl,' and stopped. You weren't there the first time I drove his Bug to school. He wanted me to prove I could drive before letting me do it myself. I raced over the hump faster than he ever had. And you know what he did?"

"What?"

"He screamed, 'Shit, Tracy, slow down!' I laughed and slapped my wheel. 'Got you back, didn't I, Dad?'"

"And your point?"

"You never got him back, Spence. You just stopped screaming, but he always knew it bothered you. Jump it yourself once then do it with him in the car. You'll feel so much better."

"That's easy for you to say."

I stopped at the light before turning onto the expressway. "Just a little jump. Please. You'll love it. Trust me."

"Okay. Someday I'll do it." He held up his thumb and pointer finger separated by half an inch. "A teeny jump."

"Cool." I smiled at him then merged onto IH10, heading home.

He did do it someday, and never came back.

He caught more air than all of us.

CHAPTER 2
ITSY BITSY GLASSES

Spencer! Come watch the Cowboys with me!" Dad's voice boomed as he turned on the television for the Thanksgiving contest between Dallas and St. Louis. He leaned back in his recliner, feet up, hands clasped behind his head. Spencer started the opening trill of Debussy's *L' isle Joyeuse*, a beautiful piece he would play later that afternoon. The sound drifting from the living room was so exotic—notes dancing on high then falling, only to rise again. Spencer's version of this piece was beautifully expressive, almost improvisational in tempo and tone.

As I carried the leftovers of our Thanksgiving lunch back to the kitchen, I saw Dad grit his teeth, get out of his chair to turn up the volume, then look back toward the living room where Spencer played with eyes closed behind the raised lid of our Steinway Grand Piano. "Five thousand dollars and no volume control," Dad growled. He marched out of the den toward my brother. "Spencer! The Cowboys are on. Watch with me."

Spencer stopped. "I'm supposed to go to Dr. Sorel's later and play this for him," he pleaded.

"It's Thanksgiving. Take a break, for God's sake," he shouted. "You don't want to miss the kick-off."

"Dad, please. I'm supposed to meet another pianist from Mexico. I need to practice."

"At least put the damn lid down."

I heard a thump as I wiped the dining room table. Then the front door opened and closed.

Dad huffed his way back into the den and stood with his hands jingling keys and coins in his pockets.

Mom exited her bedroom, wearing a plain housedress, rubbing lotion on her hands. She stopped in the foyer. "Did Spencer leave? What was all that yelling about?"

"Dad wanted to watch football," I said while twisting the cloth around my hand. "Spence wanted to practice. Dad won."

Dad threw his hands into the air. "It's tradition to watch football on Thanksgiving Day. Millions of people are doing it right now. And most of them don't have to deal with a Steinway Grand drowning out Frank Gifford's commentary." He plopped into his chair.

I threw the cloth into the kitchen sink. "You mean only one of them had the privilege of listening to Spencer's version of *The Isle of Joy*. There's a high school pianist visiting Dr. Sorel from Mexico. Spencer was invited to play for him. Pablo is supposed to be very good. He's also applying to Juilliard, so they'll be competing against each other at the auditions. It's the first time Spencer has met anyone as good as he is."

Grumbling, Dad cranked the lever to recline his chair. "He could've watched a game with me then practiced."

"He doesn't like football."

He slapped the Naugahyde covering. "I'm gone from this house over half of every month. When I'm home, I'd like to spend time with him and you . . ."

I stood between him and the television. "Doing what *you* want to do? Dad, we're not little kids anymore. Most of our lives are spent without you around. We can't just drop everything we're doing and planning because you're home."

"One game!" His voice shook. "That's all I'm asking." He slapped the arm of his chair with each word. "One. Stinking. Game!" He jerked his head left and right, trying to see around me as a thunderous cheer rose from the TV. "Move! Move!"

Mom sat on the sofa. "I'll watch it with you, Art. Tracy, could you . . ."

A sour tang filled my mouth. "Sure." Mollifying Dad was more important than comforting her son. I grabbed my jacket and walked outside.

Dad flew for Jupiter Airways, a charter company that moved freight and people all around the globe. As a child, I remember feeling sad when Dad had to leave the house for days at a time, often weeks. Tree houses and science projects were started but never finished. Vacations were interrupted or postponed. The rhythm of life jerked and lurched from heartache to disappointment to apathy.

Somewhere between preteen and teen, both Spence and I noticed everyone felt more awkward when he was home. He was like a distant relative who dropped in randomly and expected to be treated as the king of the house.

I saw Spencer walking down our street toward Shallimar where he could round the corner and smoke. When I caught up to him, he flicked his butt into a culvert.

"Don't be a litterbug, Bro."

He leaned on the metal railing separating the sidewalk from the ditch. "Want me to climb down there and fetch it? I'm afraid if I do, I won't want to come out."

I shuddered. "You don't mean that."

He turned his moist eyes toward me. "You sure?"

My skin turned clammy. "No." I hooked his arm and leaned my head against his shoulder. My pulse raced. "Come out, as in stay alive . . . or reveal a secret?"

He breathed heavily, staring hard at the concrete. "Could be both. Or one could cause the other."

My brain swirled. I hadn't expected this. "Maybe your secret isn't as big as you think." My heart pounded. *Should I push this?* "Maybe it's something we share." I watched a single tear ooze out of the corner of his eye.

He turned to me. "Your eyes are dry. Mine are wet like a girl's."

"Lots of boys cry."

He pulled his arm away and wiped his face. "Not like me. I've always been emotional. But you. . . It's been a long time since I've seen you cry. You always manage to suck it up."

"Like a man?"

"Exactly."

I stared out, following the culvert to a larger one between the elementary school and the residential area. My throat ached, and I tried to swallow. "I cry sometimes at night when I can't . . . when I can't stop thinking about why . . ."

Almost as a whisper, he said, "Why your body should be different?"

I nodded. "Yeah. I look pretty much like a boy anyway. It wouldn't take much to fool anyone. Besides, I act more like a boy than a girl." I hocked up a big loogie and spit it into the ditch.

Spencer backed away from the rail. "Jesus."

I laughed. "That is so cool! You don't like to?"

His body shook. "Promise me you'll never do that when anyone else is around us. You should watch the game with Dad. Spread your legs and smack gum and throw your fist into the air with a whoop when Dallas scores."

I felt a surge of blood race up my neck. "Sometimes I want to be loud and gross and scratch my privates."

"Gag! And I don't want any part of that. Or towel popping in the dressing room."

I clapped my hands. "I'd love to do that!"

"It fuckin' hurts."

"You're supposed to pop someone else. Not *be* popped."

He grimaced and turned away from the rail. "You scare me sometimes."

"Just go inside, sit down, and watch the game."

He shook his head. "I'd have to act like I care for two hours. Sounds like you know what to do without even trying."

"But you're his son. That's what he expects from you."

He kicked a rock against the curb. "That's bullshit."

"Yes, it is, but that's the sexist world we live in. You notice he didn't ask me to watch with him."

He hooked my arm and started a slow walk. "You know football is a rape simulation, don't you?"

I coughed a laugh. "I've never thought of that."

"Sure, it is. Those beefy guys bang heads, trying to *penetrate* that line. Their family jewels bulging through their light blue shiny pants. So much of the terminology is sexual, like 'scoring.' And the football is a. . ."

"Sperm! It is! And the end zone is the egg."

"And you have to kick it through a *narrow* opening."

I laughed. "You should tell that to Dad."

"He'd just scream at me." He imitated Dad's voice, "'How dare you make fun of the Cowboys. They're not rapists!'" We neared our house. "That's the second time he's touched the piano—when he dropped the lid. The first time was in Alamo Music when the salesman told him the price. 'Is it made of gold?' he asked. Not once has he sat down in the living room while I played or asked me anything about the music."

I sighed. "Mom told him that would be the last piece of furniture he'd ever have to buy, which is why our house is so bare."

We stopped, looking at our large, two-story, inconspicuous brick house with two oak trees in front.

Spencer shook his head. "Empty, you mean. No pictures, no knick-knacks. Just a big, brick rectangle with blank walls and a grand piano."

"So we don't have much to move when we have dances. Does he know about our party tomorrow night?"

"Nope," he said. "He's never seen me dance with Ava. Can't imagine what he'll say."

I squeezed his arm. "Maybe he'll cheer like the rest of us."

"Fat chance. Tell me some names on the team, so I don't sound like an idiot."

We turned into our walkway from the sidewalk. "Don Meredith is quarterback. Dan Reeves and Don Perkins are running backs. And don't forget Bob Hayes . . ."

"The fastest man in the world. I remember him."

After we opened the door and walked inside, Spencer bellowed in his best Texas accent, "Are we ahead? Has Dandy Don thrown a touchdown yet?"

Dad turned around, beaming. "Yes! Cowboys lead 7 – 0." He thrust his fist above his head.

"Hot damn!" Spencer jumped into the sofa next to Mom and spread his legs as wide as he could. I caught his eye as I walked toward the kitchen. He saw me discreetly scratch my privates and grinned.

At the end of the third quarter, Spencer excused himself and headed for Dr. Sorel's house.

Hours later, after I'd practiced piano, had a few arguments about the war at dinner, and listened to complaints from Mom about Spencer's continued absence, I slipped into my pajamas and tried to stay awake, listening to "19th Nervous Breakdown" from the Stones' *Big Hits* album.

Something stumbled against my door. I heard Spencer cuss. I ran to the door and yanked it open just as my very drunk brother rapped his knuckles against the air.

"Whoa," he said. "Where'd the door go? Hey, Sis."

He wobbled just outside my room with a lopsided grin on his face then put his finger to his lips. "Shhhh. Don't tell anyone, but I'm drunk." He giggled.

"No shit." I put his arm over my shoulder and turned him around. "Let's get you to bed."

"Whaa . . . No." He jerked his arm away and banged it into the wall. "Ouch. Why'd you hit me?"

"You hit the wall, Spencer. Get to bed before you wake up Mom and Dad."

He put his hands on my shoulders and his face an inch from mine. "You need to meet Pablo. He's outside."

"He drove you home?"

"Yeah. He thought I was too drunk to drive." He breathed and giggled. "He's a really nice guy. We had a good time."

I laughed, trying not to pass out from the alcohol fumes. "Evidently." I had never seen Spencer drunk. Dad would let us drink wine at dinner sometimes. Maybe share a beer between us. But Spencer was never that interested. Probably because Dad said a man's got to learn how to hold his liquor. "What did you drink?"

His eyes crossed. "Tequila. Oh, that's the best. From itsy bitsy glasses."

"A shot glass?"

He held his hand like a pistol. "Bang. Bang. Shot after shot. C'mon, you need to meet him."

I helped him down the stairs. He tiptoed to the foyer then grabbed the front door handle. Red lights flashed through the glass at the top of the door.

"Cops?" I helped him open the door, and we both stared at a policeman with his foot on the back of a young man, spread-eagled in our yard.

"Don't you move, son," yelled the officer.

Spencer's eyes bulged as he screamed, "What are you doing?" He ran toward the officer.

Somebody's going to get shot! I followed. "Spencer! Stop!"

"He's my friend!" He pushed the cop nearly to the ground then bent down to help Pablo.

I ran to the officer whose hand moved toward his holster. "That's my brother's friend. He drove my brother home and was waiting to meet me." I stood between him and the boys, holding my arms up, gasping for breath.

The man looked at me. "You live here?"

"Yes, with Spencer and my parents."

Pablo was on his knees crying. "I thought he was going to kill me."

Spencer knelt and pulled Pablo to his chest. "You're safe. You're safe." He bent down to pick up Pablo's white beret, brushed it off, and set it on his head.

Pablo was thin and shorter than Spencer. His mouth hung open as he gasped for breath; his face was wet with tears.

Spencer clutched the boy against his chest and glared at the cop. "What did he do?"

"He was a Mexican outside our house at midnight," I said. "Right, Officer?"

The man tightened his eyes at me. "I've never seen him in this neighborhood. He looked suspicious."

"Suspiciously brown?" I barked.

"That's enough, Tracy," said Dad, tying his robe, as he strode down our walkway. "I'm Arthur Franks. This is my house. Did the boy do anything wrong?"

"He looked like he was trying to get inside that car, and I knew it wasn't his."

Pablo's voice cracked. "I wanted my cigarettes. I just wanted to smoke a cigarette. ¿Qué carajo?"

I hoped the cop didn't speak Spanish because Pablo had just said "What the fuck?"

"Are we done?" I asked.

The officer rested his hand on his pistol. "You sure you want this kid in your yard, Mr. Franks?"

"No, I'm not, but he'll be gone soon. We'll take it from here, Officer."

"Okay, but if you need anything, just call dispatch. I can be back here quick." He shot Pablo one last glare before sliding into his Castle Hills patrol car and drove away.

"Where have you been, Spencer?" Dad growled. "And do I smell alcohol on you?"

"If your nose works," Spencer giggled. "We stayed at Dr. Sorel's for a while then went to Pablo's cousin's house. I think I had one too many shots of tequila." He giggled again.

"Maybe two too many," laughed Pablo with a thick accent.

"You said tutu!" Spencer laughed.

"No, I said two too," laughed Pablo as he playfully patted Spencer's face.

"Jesus," Dad muttered as he folded his arms and glared at the two boys.

With his arm around Spencer's shoulder, Pablo faced me and Dad. "Hello, my name is Pablo Gutiérrez Delgado. I drove Spencer home because he's not used to tequila, and I wanted to make sure he arrived safely. He wanted me to meet his sister, Tracy, so I waited outside while he brought her down."

"Thanks for driving him home, Pablo," I said, shaking his hand. "And I'm very pleased to meet you." Dark skin framed his big brown eyes and beautiful mouth.

"El placer es todo mío. Sometime you should play for me. Spencer says you are very good."

"I'd love to, but maybe not tonight."

He laughed. "No, it's late. Yes?"

"How are you getting home, Pablo?" asked Dad, his voice stern and cold.

"He can drive my car," said Spencer. "Tracy can take me to his cousin's tomorrow or the next day." He gave Pablo the keys. "Drive safely." Spencer grabbed Pablo and hugged him fiercely. "Thanks for tonight."

He kissed Pablo's right cheek as Pablo kissed his.

Dad's eyes widened. He shook his head stiffly, a snarl on his lips. Fearing a confrontation, I reached for Pablo's hand. "Good night, Pablo." Then I leaned in and kissed his cheek. He kissed mine. "We'll see each other again."

He nodded and smiled. "I will look forward to that time. Good night, Mr. Franks." He sat in the car, waved through the windshield then pulled away.

"Was all this necessary, Spencer?" barked Dad, his eyes darting up and down the street, obviously checking for onlookers.

"Absolutely. This was the best night of my life!" He grabbed me by the waist and tried to lift me off the ground. "Ugh! You've gained weight, Sis."

Laughing, I said, "Or possibly you are slightly impaired." I grabbed his hand. Dad was going to blow up any second. "Come inside and tell me everything."

As we passed Dad on the walkway, he hissed, "What's with the kissing? It's bad enough the neighbors have to see a policeman and my drunken son on my front yard. You don't have to compound it by kissing a boy." The porch light revealed his blood-red face and clenched fist.

I stopped and glared at him. "It's considered a cultural courtesy in Mexico. On the right cheek."

"That's bullshit." Spit flew out of his mouth as he jabbed the air with his finger. "I've known hundreds of Mexicans, and I've never seen them kiss each other or try to kiss me."

"It was just a friendly peck on the cheek," Spencer whined. "We had a good time tonight."

"Is he your boyfriend?" sneered our father.

Spencer's mouth dropped open. "We played piano, told jokes, and drank a little. Why does that make him my boyfriend?" His chin quivered. "C'mon, Dad. Why do you have to ruin everything?"

"Me? *You're* the one ruining your life with this pansy bullshit. And I guarantee you it will ruin your life."

I let go of Spencer's fingers and folded my arms. "Actually, Pablo asked me if he could call tomorrow, so I think he's interested in me."

Dad shook his head. "You two are thick as thieves." He spit into the grass. "What a great pair of kids I raised."

"Why thanks Daddy." I almost jumped with fake joy. "That's the first time you've complimented us both since . . . since when Spencer?"

"Since who gives a fuck?" Crying, he stumbled into the house, ignoring our scared mother who had been peeking around the door.

Both of my hands clenched, I stood between Dad and the door. "What's ruining his life is you! Everything he does is wrong. You're killing him!"

He stepped forward. "How much more do you want our neighbors to see?"

"That's all you care about. Such a kind and loving father!" I moved inside and bolted up the stairs. As I passed the bathroom, I heard Spencer retching into the toilet, crying, and banging his fist against the wall.

CHAPTER 3

AVA AND THE LIFESAVER

The next day, just before 7:00 pm when our party would start, Spencer and I carried a bucket of grapefruit, oranges, and golf balls to the back porch. We planned to make two teams pass the objects from neck to neck. We also had toothpicks and cherry Lifesavers in reserve for a mouth-to-mouth relay if there was interest. Passing a candy from one set of lips armed with a toothpick to another was fun and a little dangerous.

House parties were fairly tame back then for us. No spiked punch, no marijuana, no real sex. Most of our friends were excited about the relays, though some said they were lame, a cool response to avoid revealing one's insecurities. Some of the girls planned to line up in front or behind specific boys and maybe sneak a kiss. I'm sure guys thought in similar ways. The winning team members would receive a set of love beads.

I had brought my record player, speakers, a microphone, and albums down from my room and set them on the built-in shelves in the den. My collection was larger than most, so kids knew they didn't have to bring their own records. Both of us played DJ during our parties, with Spencer adding the most commentary.

We set up a few plastic chairs along one wall and hung colorful beads across every entrance to the den. Our dance floor was an open expanse of terrazzo—easy to dance on. Neither of us wanted helium-filled balloons floating against the ceiling, but Mom had insisted. She wanted a festive look. At our last party, a couple of guys sucked on balloons and talked like "homos," complete with limp wrists. But Mom was in the kitchen at the time and had heard only pops, not the talking and laughing afterward. We inflated just a few for tonight.

I had just started the Beatles' *Sgt. Pepper's Lonely Hearts Club Band* album to set the mood when Dad came out of the dining room, munching on a sandwich. We'd spent most of the day avoiding each other. Spencer had slept past noon, nursing a hangover, telling me later he'd lain in his bed awake the last hour, worried that Dad would barge in and call him a queer.

Mom must have told him to not start a fight before our party, because he hadn't mentioned the previous night at all.

"Y'all are dressed up," he said. "I thought parties were more casual now." He finished his sandwich.

I crossed my arms and tried to keep my anger from rising. "Is that a criticism or an attempt to pretend nothing happened yesterday?"

He stopped chewing and swallowed. "Just trying to make conversation." He paused, looking at each of us. "That's quite a tie."

"Mom liked it," Spencer said, looking anywhere but back at Dad.

I held the purple paisley tie away from my brother's shirt. "'Quite a tie' as in great and beautiful or too loud or . . . too flowery, perhaps?"

Dad clamped his jaw, forcing facial muscles to knot.

I spread my dress hem and swayed. "And is this *quite* a dress?"

Dad raised his brows. "Quite a short dress."

"I wanted to wear pants, but Mom said no. She's right, however." I sighed and pouted my lips. "How else am I to attract a boy? I have few attributes except my long legs. Got to get a boyfriend soon or people will talk."

Spencer stifled a laugh.

Dad glared at both of us. "We can always cancel this party."

"*You* can," I said. "Mom likes our parties."

The doorbell rang.

Mom came out of the kitchen wearing her full bow apron and looked at us. "Will one of you answer the door?"

I flashed a smug smile at Dad. "I will." I almost skipped toward the foyer.

"Tell them I have tamales and queso in the kitchen," said Mom.

"Will do." I opened the door and found two freshmen with parents. "Hey, Buddy. Mary. Come on in." With a flourish, I raised my arm toward Dad. "Meet my father, Art Franks."

Dad smiled and shook hands. "Follow me for food and fun."

Ava stepped through the door followed by her father. I tried not to gasp, but still let out a tiny cough. "Hey, Ava." I'd always thought she was gorgeous. Her father hadn't taken her to a party since she got her license at fourteen—the same age we all did. We played basketball together and were friends.

Ava cocked a brow. "I got a speeding ticket today, so Daddy was kind enough to supplement my driving instruction." She rolled her eyes.

"Okay. Hello, Mr. Blunt. Just toss your coat on the sofa, Ava." I gestured toward the living room. Ava removed her jacket to reveal an orange chiffon sleeveless, backless dress with a plunging neckline held up by a loop around her neck. I couldn't help but stare.

She twirled around. "You like?" she asked. Mr. Blunt's eyes bulged.

"Love it. And those earrings are perfect."

She jiggled her large, gold hoops. "Of course, they are. Daddy, the kitchen and food are at the end of the den." She waved her hand. "Go. Go. I don't want to be hovered over."

He shook his head and sighed. "Excuse me, Tracy." He walked away.

"That's the first time he saw the dress?" I asked.

She nodded and laughed.

Ava was almost as tall as me with short red hair and green eyes. And a much fuller figure than mine, which was great for clearing space under the backboard, trying to snag rebounds. She played defense and I played offense for the Lady Wolves, which kept us on opposite ends of the court back then. Girls couldn't possibly run the entire eighty-four feet or learn both offense and defense, after all. It made me sick.

I touched the material below her waist. "It's so pretty."

"Thanks. It was on sale at Ward's. But I couldn't find a bra." She shook her torso slightly. "Do you think anyone will notice?"

I clasped my hands to my mouth and tried not to laugh. Her jiggling boobs were obvious. "Maybe if you stay in the dark. Don't get food. If you want something, tell me, and I'll get it for you." Was she flirting with me or just being Ava—loud, unreserved, and funny?

She tilted her head and grinned. "Tracy, you're staring." She shook a little more.

I pulled my eyes away from her breasts to her face, but couldn't keep them there. "I have a thin white shawl. You can drape it over your shoulders."

"Show me." She flipped her shoes into the living room and ran up the stairs. I followed. My bedroom was near the bathroom that kids could use during the party. I'd cleaned up my stuff in case someone peeked inside. Ava had been there before, during other parties and a sleepover for the basketball team last year. She loved to laugh and was definitely not shy. The only girl to take a shower after PE or games, she'd emerge from the little bathroom wrapped in a towel, face her locker, pull her panties up, then drop the towel and put on her bra. Most girls rolled their eyes and turned away, but my locker was right next to hers. I couldn't help but see her, unless I turned my head to the wall on my right side, but I didn't want to make a scene.

Besides, I didn't mind catching glimpses. And I'm sure she'd caught me a few times.

She opened my door and walked in. "When are you going to have another sleepover?"

"For the team?"

"Or just me. Girls can have sleepovers, you know."

A thought slithered into my brain—was Ava gay? Was she trying to tell me?

My heart skipped. Could I? No. I could see Mom's face if I'd asked. And Dad would've freaked. "Kinda weird to invite just one girl. We're seventeen, not ten. Could you?"

She shook her head and looked at my posters. "You really like Grace Slick, don't you?"

"I love her. Voice. Music."

"Looks?"

I nodded. "She's very pretty."

"Do you still have the one where she shoots the finger?" She opened my closet door to see the poster hidden behind a few shawls and scarves. "Yup. You do."

"That's the shawl, by the way." I reached for it.

"Wow, your dress is short. I love it."

My heart raced as I draped the shawl around her neck so the ends covered her chest. "There. Now you can flash people if you want or hide when necessary."

She lifted the shawl ends from her chest and shook. Blood rushed to my face as I grabbed her shoulders. "Stop. Please."

"Okay, but who cares what I do up here? You obviously like looking, and I don't mind. It's kinda fun."

I shook my head. "I don't *like* looking. It's just hard . . . not to."

"It's okay if you do. What's the harm?"

My chest tightened and I looked away. "People talking."

"They can't talk about things they don't know."

I tried to breathe. "But what if they find out?"

She put her face right in front of mine, her eyes wandering over my features. "Tell them to go fuck themselves. Girls can have fun too. There's no law against it." She licked her lips and backed up to my door.

"But there is."

She held the door knob and grinned. "And you never break the law? You never speed?"

"Sometimes. But I think they'd do more than hand out tickets . . . for that."

"Life's too short to fret the details. What we do stays between us. You dig?"

I bit my lip and nodded, feeling a wave of possibilities swirl in my stomach.

"C'mon, let's party." She ran down the stairs, me following at her heels.

During the next ten minutes, our front door was open more often than closed. A few more parents arrived with eighth and ninth graders. Most everyone else drove themselves. By 7:30, both sides of our street were full of cars, and our den was full of teens.

Adults usually stayed in the kitchen where we had a large, round breakfast table. Mom made great deviled eggs and cocktail sandwiches full of pimento cheese or chicken salad, crust removed, of course. And lots of chips and dips.

I turned on two large lava lamps at each end of the room. Somebody yelled, "Groovy." The blobs of orange and red reflected off the walls and ceiling. Spencer grabbed the mic and howled. "Owoooooooo! Greetings from your DJ for the evening. I am not a big bad wolf. Owooo, I mean baaaa. Time to turn off the lights and turn on the dance moves."

I flicked off the lights just as Dad slid open the kitchen door, throwing a glowing shaft across the floor.

Spencer howled again, "Owoooo! It's supposed to be dark in these spooky woods." He started "Lil' Red Riding Hood" by Sam the Sham. "Either close the door or kill the kitchen lights."

I moved to the door, reached around the jam, and flicked the kitchen switch. Then I danced out to the middle of the floor. "Somebody dance with me." I'd been practicing my moves while watching *American Bandstand*, just like most of us had learned to dance. This song had a slow, steady beat, so it was easy to sway hips and arms without looking stupid. A few couples moved toward me then Ava literally jumped out of the darkness.

I yelped a little then smiled. "Hey, Ava. Are you playing wolf tonight?"

"You want me to? By the way, I love your dress."

I twirled. "Thanks." *Okay, she's definitely flirting. And I love it.*

She turned the shawl around so the ends hung over her back then raised her arms above her head. "Do what I do," she flashed a mischievous smile then shook her boobs.

I shook my chest. "Doesn't have the same effect for you, I'm sure."

"You never know." She stared at my chest. "I'll do other moves."

"Okay, but keep them simple." I raised my hands and swayed my arms with hers.

She looked at my legs. "Oh, my! That hem is pretty high."

I looked down and saw my dress hiked up most of my thigh. "Lucky it's dark." I glanced around to see if anyone else was watching me.

"I can see just fine." She reached higher and side-shuffled, leading with her hips a few steps left then right.

I followed her, taking some awkward steps, my legs separating.

She laughed, and I pulled my dress down. She leaned close. "Pink panties?"

My eyes bulged. "You saw?" The funny thing was I didn't feel embarrassment as much as excitement.

She moved closer. "Just a flash."

"Do you think anyone else —"

"Just me. We'll have to do this again sometime." She winked, turned her shawl around, and moved over to Spencer just as he set the needle down for "Along Comes Mary" by The Association.

"Mary Ford, this song is for you," announced Spencer as he pointed to Larry. "She needs a partner. You're the man."

Some of the girls pushed and pulled Mary onto the floor while guys on the basketball team walked Larry out to her. He was the back-up point guard, shy with girls but a little general on the court.

Travis, the speech contest king with hair reaching close to his collar —the limit permitted at school—tapped my shoulder and we danced. He liked to tuck his arms close against his torso with clenched fists as he bent over and shuffled with this feet. His face grimaced and jutted, as in, *I'm so tough, so cool, don't you think so?* He tried to twirl me around, but he was shorter than me, and my head hit his arm. But it was fun.

Most of the girls' hairdos were short, various beehives and bobs. Some had long hair pulled back with stretch headbands. A few had hippie hair, including me. I'd clipped two daisies on the side. Boys' side-burns were just beginning to lengthen, but none past the ear hole— school rules. A few had pulled their shirttails out, perhaps in a silent protest of the school's tucked policy. Tommy, the sophomore class president, wore a pair of bell bottom jeans he'd bought in New York City, as well as a silver peace symbol on a leather loop around his neck.

"Find your honey," Spencer crooned. "This one is slowwww." He dropped the needle on "Scarborough Fair" by Simon & Garfunkel. This plus "Sound of Silence," and "Cherish," and "When a Man Loves a Woman," were stand-and-hug songs. Guys who refused to fast dance would volunteer for these because all you had to do was wrap your arms around each other and sway or shuffle in a circle.

I was about to leave the floor and get something to drink when I felt a tap.

Charles gave a slight bow. "I don't think we've ever danced, Tracy." He held out his arms. "Would you?"

Charles was the star basketball player—tall, handsome, slicked hair, and very full of himself. Several girls in my class would nearly faint if he smiled at them. "Certainly, Charles. I'd love to." I'd danced close with boys before and tried to like it, but had always felt the urge to push away. I'd thought maybe I was shy, that I'd grow out of my aversion. But that never happened.

Since this was our first time, I expected him to put his hands on my waist and keep some distance between us. But he wrapped his arms around my back, one hand just above my butt. He groaned as he pressed his cheek against mine. I nearly gagged on the scents of Dentyne, Brylcreem, and Old Spice. I tensed and nearly pushed him away, but I forced myself to calm down. Maybe I could do this.

He groaned. "I've always wanted to dance with a tall girl."

"Why?"

"So everything would fit better."

I leaned back. "Fit what?"

He pulled my lower body closer to his. "I don't have to lean over. I can stand up straight and feel every bit of you. And you feel very good." His other hand rubbed up and down my back slowly. "You are so warm," he whispered.

Panic shot up my neck. I was just about to push away when I felt his boner against my pubis. He pressed it ever-so-slightly against me. My stomach clenched, and a bitter tang filled my mouth.

"You see, everything fits."

I almost hit him but then I thought, *A guy can do this and get away with it.* My skin tingled as my body temperature soared.

He slowly pushed it higher and moaned.

I pulled my head back and looked at his closed eyes. "You've got to be kidding me."

He opened his blue eyes and half-smiled. "Whatever are you referring to?" He pulled it down then pushed slowly up.

My stomach tensed. I had an overwhelming urge to lift my knee into his groin. *What a fucking prick!* "How do most girls react when you . . . do this?"

"Most say nothing. Their hearts beat faster, they breathe fast or hold their breath."

"Then what?"

"When the song ends, I ask them if they want to go outside for a walk. Do you want to?"

Okay. Time to teach this asshole a lesson. I pushed my fingers through his hair above his ear and nearly touched his nose with mine. "Why don't we just go upstairs to my bedroom?"

His eyes widened and he leaned back. "Whoa. For real?"

I tightened my fingers around his hair as I looked directly into his eyes. "So what you do is push your boner into girls' stomachs. They freeze because they don't know whether you're doing it on purpose. You hump them a little and groan, which makes them more uncomfortable. Then you get them outside and, what, kiss them, push it against them again, and maybe you get a hand job, or better?"

He tried to back away, but I yanked both arms and pulled him closer. "What if a girl pulled you close so that one of your legs was between hers. Like this." I straddled his thigh and hip then slowly humped. I moaned. "Babe, you fit so perfectly."

He tried to push back, but I clamped onto him. "You don't like it?"

The song ended.

"I think you're a little crazy." He squirmed and gasped.

"But I'm doing the same to you as you do to girls," I taunted. "And you get away with it all the time. Because you're a guy, and the world is so fucked up." I let go of him and stomped over to Spencer. "I think it's time for Grace."

Dad came toward us, his lips tight and eyebrows scrunched.

"Oh fun," I said.

"Maybe he has a request," said Spencer.

"Weren't you dancing a little close to that boy?" he growled.

"Were you spying on me?" I so wanted to tell him what Charles had done, but I knew Dad would freak out. Most likely at me, not at Charles. My fists clenched at my sides.

"That's not an answer," he snapped.

"Yes, I was dancing close, but I didn't have a choice."

"You always have a choice, young lady. Just say, 'No thanks,' and walk away."

I smiled. "What great advice. Why didn't I think of it? That must be what Dads are for." *Of course, it's always the girl's fault. Boys are naturally horny, so it's solely up to girls to keep them at first base. Any farther and the girl must be a slut. So. Fucking. Sick.*

He shook his head at me then turned to Spencer. "Do you ever dance?"

Spencer cocked his head and smiled. "Why, yes I do."

"Really? I haven't seen you once. Did I miss something?"

I saw Ava sitting on the brick ledge in front of the fireplace, drinking from a cup. "Your dance queen is over there." I pointed.

"You miss almost everything, Dad." Spencer took off toward Ava.

I grabbed the Jefferson Airplane album and found the mic. "I think it's time for some psychedelic rock, a little acid group from San Francisco and my favorite singer, Grace Slick." I didn't use drugs, but I loved the raw power of her voice and the image of her leading six guys like the queen she was. "So hug one of the lava lamps or find somebody to love." I put the needle down, and "Somebody to Love" pounded through the speakers.

Spencer and Ava held hands above their shoulders and calmly walked to the center of the room before both their bodies bucked and whipped to the beat. The difference between Spencer's movements and every other guy's was commitment. When he moved his pelvis, he thrust it. No holds barred. When his torso undulated, I wondered how his bones stayed attached. He commanded space. He and Ava had some kind of weird connection. They never seemed to look at each other but always knew what the other was doing. When one held out a hand, the other immediately grabbed it for a twirl or a pull-in. When Grace pounded her syncopation lyrics, both circled the other, grinding to the rhythm, like perfect counterpoints in space. And always at the end, he spun her into a lay-back on his knee, one of her feet kicked up.

The applause was immediate and loud. They both popped up and bowed, Spencer throwing out his left arm and flicking his wrist. As they walked toward Dad and me, others filled the dance floor in their wake as I let the next track play.

I hugged Spencer then Ava. "That's the best you two have ever danced." And I'd meant it.

"Aren't you going to introduce me to your girlfriend?" Dad asked.

Spencer rolled his eyes at me.

Ava stuck out her hand. "Hi, Mr. Franks. I'm Ava. I play with Tracy on the basketball team." She side-glanced me. "We've met before."

"Oh, that's right. How long have you and Spencer been together?"

Spencer smiled. "Ava, how long have we been, you know, doing it?"

Ava barked a laugh.

"They've been dancing together since last year," I said. "So what'd you think?"

"Oh, they were good," said Dad, nodding at both of them. "I didn't know you could be so loosey-goosey, Spencer." He chuckled.

"Loosey-goosey?" Spencer asked, scrunching his forehead. "That means relax. Jim's girlfriend yells that out before he shoots a free throw."

"Well, I meant flexible." Dad smiled and tried to move his arms and torso, doing a poor imitation of Spencer's moves.

Was he mocking? Or trying to find a way to say something nice but screwing up, as always? I could see the hurt in Spencer's eyes as they looked down at Dad, still waving his arms.

Dad pointed at a couple dancing nearby. "They're doing great."

I shook my head and grabbed the mic. "It's time for relays! The winning team gets hippie love beads. You can put them on and say, 'Far out, man,' and everyone will think you're stoned."

Dad frowned at me. I covered the mic and whispered, "Just a joke. Be cool, Dad. Please."

"Everyone who wants to participate or watch, exit this door." I pointed onto our back porch. "I'm going to put on The Turtles' *Golden Hits* album and let it run for all you deadbeats who don't know how to have fun." I turned off the mic and started the record.

"Lead the way, Bro," I said. "Why don't you run this show?"

"Sure." He looked back at Dad and shook his head. I heard him mutter, "Such a dick."

Over half the teens and a few parents gathered on the porch.

Spencer lifted both arms. "Okay. Two teams form a line on my left and right."

Kids scurried to get into lines, alternating boy/girl, leading from the back porch into the grass, beyond the halo of light. Ava sauntered to the back of one line.

"Everybody settled?" Spencer asked. "Tracy, check the numbers."

I moved down both lines, counting sixteen in one and fifteen in Ava's. "We need another boy behind Ava."

"Another boy," Spencer shouted. No one moved.

I pointed at Spencer and signaled him to take the spot while I ran the race. He shook his head.

"Tracy, you're better than all the boys anyway," Spencer said.

He wanted me to stand behind Ava. A tongue of excitement flicked up my legs.

"The last person in line is the most important because they have to carry the object under their necks using NO hands and drop it in this bucket. Does everybody understand?"

Kids nodded and murmured their agreement.

"We'll start with grapefruit." He held two up. "Your hands must be on the other person's waist. If you drop it or touch it with your hands, the grapefruit goes back to the head of the line, and you start over. If the last runner drops it, you start over. Questions?"

Somebody yelled, "Start already!"

I moved behind Ava, my feet fidgeting as my stomach fluttered.

She turned and smiled. "We got this, girl."

I got lost in her eyes and smiled.

"Your father is a dork," she said.

"Among other things."

Spencer placed both grapefruits between the chin and chest of Charles and Travis who headed each line. "Go!"

The two guys spun around and bent until the girls behind them could reach up to snag the fruit.

"No kissing!" yelled somebody.

A jolt of excitement slashed through me. I'd be grabbing and hugging Ava in front of everyone. Luckily, we were at the end of the line out in the grass where the light faded.

Each line moved in sync, passing without difficulty. When Ava turned, she grabbed my waist and pulled me against her. Our cheeks touched, and I gasped.

"Sorry," she said. "Did I grab you too hard?"

"No. Hurry." I clasped the fruit and ran, head hunched, alongside Buddy from the other line. Spencer held out the bucket. Buddy and I released our fruits. They both got stuck against each other inside the rim.

"That, my friends, is a tie!" said Spencer.

Some yelled, "No way!"

Spencer carried the bucket down the line to show the two fruits wedged together.

"So each team has a point. Looks like we might need the toothpicks and Lifesavers, after all."

He held out two oranges for Charles and Travis to put under their chins. "Go!"

The flurry of turning and bending moved down the line until someone yelled, "Shit!"

I leaned forward to see what had happened and soon felt Ava's butt against my thighs. "Sorry," I said, but before I could back up, she reached her arm behind her and pulled me close.

"Sorry, my ass," she whispered. "You did that on purpose." Her arm still held me.

"I swear I didn't." My heart danced in my chest.

She whipped around so that our fronts touched. "I think you're blushing," she whispered, her lips close to mine.

"You're so warm," I stammered.

She smiled and turned around, making sure her butt still touched me.

"Back to the front," said Spencer.

Someone in my line had dropped the orange. The other line was still moving, but when they got to the end, Buddy dropped it during his run.

"Back to the front," said Spencer, amidst groans.

Twenty seconds later, Ava turned around with the orange in her neck. I bent my head to clasp on and did, but she wouldn't let go.

"Let go, Ava," I whispered, my pulse surging.

"I like you here," said Ava. "You'll have to pull it from me," she giggled.

I pushed closer and forced my chin into her neck. I could smell the orange squeezing.

"What are they doing?" asked a girl in the other line.

Ava laughed as she clenched tighter.

With another push, I forced her chin up and grabbed the orange with a grunt. The other team was about halfway through, so I sauntered and twirled as I moved to Spencer. Several on my team screamed at me. "Hurry!"

I stood next to Spencer and watched Buddy start his run then I lifted my chin and dropped the orange slowly into the bucket.

"The winner!" yelled Spencer.

During the next round, our team couldn't get the golf ball to Ava because of multiple drops. Once when I leaned forward to see what was going on, Ava quickly turned around, our chests touching, and her lips just below mine. "There you go again," she said. "Are you hitting on me?"

My mind screamed, Yes! but I couldn't speak. I panted and couldn't move my eyes away from her lips. Finally, I said, "Someone will see."

"Who? It's dark back here." She licked her lips.

Spencer declared the other team the winner of that round. I had to bite the inside of my cheek to keep myself from kissing her. With a groan, I grabbed her waist and twisted. "Turn. It's the candy race."

Spencer raised his arms. "The candy must be an intact circle when it's dropped into the bucket. Dropping a toothpick is okay. The only thing that matters is the Lifesaver."

He handed everyone a toothpick.

As he walked back to the bucket, Ava turned and leaned into my ear. "I won't give it to you if you have a toothpick between your lips."

I gulped. "Then how . . ."

"From my lips to yours," she whispered.

My head seemed to float above my body, every hair prickling my scalp.

Spencer placed the candy onto Charles and Travis' toothpicks then yelled, "Go!"

After a few passes, someone yelled, "Ow! You poked me."

"Sorry!"

I heard a candy shatter on the concrete. Then more grunting and yelling until finally Ava turned to me and pulled her toothpick from her lips.

"Where's the candy?" I gasped.

She opened her lips, revealing the red cherry Lifesaver between her teeth. She flashed her brows. "Come get it."

My heart fluttered then pounded. I glanced at the other line. They were three from the end. Then I saw Ava's father standing by the back door with his arms folded, squinting at us. Could he see? I looked at Ava and nodded toward him.

"We're in the dark," she said. She slowly pulled me close, touched my lips with hers, and pushed the Lifesaver into my mouth followed by her tongue. Heat exploded in my mouth. I touched her tongue with mine then pushed it hard into her mouth.

She pulled back slightly with a grin. "Wow. Now go."

I broke away and ran toward my brother. I bent over the bucket and dropped the Lifesaver I most wanted to keep.

"The winner!" yelled Spencer.

My team erupted in shouts and applause. I turned to find Ava and saw her father pulling her into the house. I pushed my way through my cheering teammates and found Ava putting on her shoes in my living room.

"What's wrong?" I asked, my stomach twisting into a knot.

She turned to me with red, teary eyes. "Him!" She blew out a breath. "I just had to get a ticket today."

"Let's go, Ava." Mr. Blunt opened the front door. "Now!"

"I need to give her this," Ava barked.

She reached out her hand with my shawl. As I took it from her, she squeezed my fingers and kissed the air between us. Her father grabbed her arm and pulled her outside.

We weren't done yet, I'd make sure. I'd had a taste of freedom to be who I was, to touch who I wanted.

I was determined to do it again.

CHAPTER 4

SHARED SECRETS & SCARED PARENTS

After everyone had left and we'd cleaned up, I went to my room to replay every moment I'd had with Ava. I knew if she had pushed her leg between mine during our kiss, I would have cum. Breathless, I lay back on my bed and moved my hand down my stomach.

Spencer knocked. "Tracy, can we talk?"

I jerked up and tried to calm down. "Sure."

He came in and closed my door behind him before sitting stiffly in my chair. "What happened between you and Ava? After she left, I heard some talk about what you two were doing in line."

Nerves fluttered in my neck. How would Spencer respond? "Which is why you're going to start dating Ava."

"What?" He moved the chair closer, scrunching his brows.

"Not for real. Just to kill the rumors for both of us and so Ava and I can . . ." I stopped and wondered how he would react. Laugh? Think it's cool? Warn me to stop? What? "So we can have some time together."

"Whoa, Sis." He swallowed and lowered his voice. "Are you serious?"

"Totally. Maybe we can make plans tomorrow?"

A smile tugged at his lips. "You like her?"

I felt my face blush and wondered whether I should say yes or pretend I was kidding. He could've said, 'That's obvious,' but he didn't. I thought, *Go for it!* "Yes. Does that shock you?"

"No. Were you surprised about me and Pablo?"

"No. And you had more time with him in private than I did with Ava." I smiled and wiggled my eyebrows. "Looked like you got to know each other very well."

He nodded and blushed then tried to hide his widening grin. "Yeah. Really well." He covered his face with his hands. His embarrassment was so cute.

"And I'm sure the tequila helped break the ice, so to speak."

He coughed a laugh and looked to the ceiling. "Yeah, it pretty much melted on the spot. Like, Boom! An explosion." He hid his face again. "Several, actually."

My neck burned, and I wanted to cover my eyes. "Maybe you shouldn't go into details."

His ears were blood red. "No. I think we should change the topic."

We tried to avoid looking at each other, but inevitably our eyes locked, and we burst into laughter. Finally, we both calmed. I asked, "How long have you known about me?"

"I'd always suspected," he said, "but then I saw you dancing with Charles, and that threw me."

I grabbed my pillow and pulled it against my stomach. "He was trying to rape me through my clothes. I was trying to teach him a lesson."

"I don't think he's capable of learning. He's got the biggest dick in school. That's all he cares about."

I folded my arms and smiled. "His boner did seem large. Tell me about his big dick. How do you know? Hmm?" I raised my brows several times until his face turned blood red.

He scratched his head and stood. "I know because of what happens in the boys' locker room after PE. We have gang showers where ten naked guys at a time stand under random shower heads. He actually goes around comparing length. Most guys try to keep their eyes chest-high to avoid being called a homo, but he goes up to Buddy and says, 'Such a little thing, Buddy. You need to feed it more.' And everyone laughs. It's insane."

I choked and coughed. Finally, my spasm ended. "Have you seen it?"

"No way. I don't go near the showers. I could never . . . never take a shower like that. Why do guys' toilets and urinals have no barriers between them, yet girls always have stalls and individual curtains?"

"They want boys to shower and crap in public to prove they're not gay," I said. "If you stay limp among all those wet, soapy guys, you're good to go. Girls get stalls to ensure they don't become gay."

"Like it's a disease. The gay plague." He looked up to the ceiling and slowly shook his head.

"Maybe there's a treatment."

"If there were, would you take it?"

I smiled and winked. "Ask me after I've been alone with Ava. Would you?" For the first time in my life, I felt excited about being gay, rather than confused and scared.

"God, yes. In a heartbeat." He paused. "Even though I loved every minute with Pablo, I wish I could have the same pleasure with a Pauline. It would sure make life easier."

I had hoped for more enthusiasm to reinforce my hope I could feel normal being with Ava, rather than awkward and worried. I surely didn't wish to trade my experience with her for being Charles' humping post.

He turned to leave my room then stopped, tapped his fingers against the wall, and turned his face toward me, softening, but flicking his eyes away. "Hey, thanks for . . . telling me about Ava. I'm glad we can share stuff like that with each other." He looked directly at me and nodded.

"Make sure we keep sharing. Otherwise, we'll go ape. You gonna hit the hay now?" I smiled at him, hoping he'd take the bait.

"Time for me to book it."

I stood and put my hands on my hips. "So you're bugging out?"

"Yeah. Don't have a cow."

"Nah, I won't sweat it."

"You look bummed."

"Nope," I said. "Everything's groovy."

"Peace out, Sis."

"Peace, Bro. You win."

· · ·

After lunch the next day, Spencer challenged me to a game of HORSE.

"Sure. Should I tie one hand behind my back or two?"

"One hand and one eye closed."

"Deal."

We went outside and grabbed a ball from the garage. The one project Dad completed for us a few years ago was installing a pole next to the driveway and a backboard with rim.

Spencer made both free throws after I'd missed one (on purpose) so he shot first. Our rules were no running or dribbling. Just set shots and we had to call banks. He stood in the grass about twenty feet away and swished it. I did the same. We shot a few more times until each of us had an H.

Spencer walked to the corner of the open garage and banked it in.

"Good shot," said Dad from behind.

Spencer flinched and muttered, "Shit."

Neither of us had seen Dad walk outside.

I moved to the same spot and missed.

Spencer stood in the grass at what would be a few feet beyond the corner of the key and swished it. I followed with the same.

"Why don't you play basketball, Spencer?" asked Dad. "You have a great shot."

Spencer glanced at me, and I knew what he was thinking. Dad could've said, "Your dancing was great," last night. And, "You played great," after his concert. But he didn't because those activities were for sissies. Basketball, however, was a manly activity—not as good as football, but a sport all the same.

Spencer held the ball. "I don't play because I can't afford a sprained ankle or a jammed finger. I have auditions and contests coming up which are more important to me than basketball." He shot and missed.

I made it. "HO to HO," I said.

Dad cleared his throat then pursed his lips. "I got a call from Mr. Blunt this morning."

My stomach churned. "And?"

Spencer sank a free throw then tossed me the ball.

"He told me what he saw during the relays and explained why he took Ava home."

I tried to hide the panic welling up from my chest. "I wish he had explained it to me before he yanked her out our door." I shot and banked it in. I caught Spencer's eyes.

"I heard you call it," he said with a smile.

Dad continued. "He said Ava forced you to kiss her."

"She didn't force me to do anything. We were both being silly."

"He said she wouldn't give you the orange, so you had to neck with her. Then she forced the Lifesaver into your mouth with her lips." He grimaced. "Is that true?"

I chuckled and shook my head, trying to keep my arms from shaking. "What are you worried about, Dad?"

"*Should* I be worried?"

I fixed my eyes on his. "Ava was pissed he drove her to the party. She's used to her freedom, and he was hovering over her. He'd been watching her the entire time. After she passed the grapefruit, she saw him on the porch, glaring at her. So she said, 'Wanna freak him out?' And I said, 'Sure.' So she did." I crossed my arms. "Is he worried Ava is gay?"

He scratched his neck. "Certainly. Why wouldn't he be, given what he saw? He wanted to know if I'd noticed *you* exhibiting any . . . odd behavior."

I forced myself to flash a smug smile. "Odd, as in gay?"

He swallowed and pursed his lips. "Yes."

"And you said?" I waited for the punch in my gut.

"No. In fact, I had to scold you for inappropriate dancing with whoever that boy was."

I harrumphed. "Yeah, I was climbing all over Charles. I hope I didn't scar him for life."

Dad shook his head. "Do you always have to be a smart ass?"

"Better than being a dumb ass."

Spencer snorted a laugh.

Mom opened the front door. "Tracy, you have a phone call."

"Coming." I took a few steps then stopped and turned around. "Maybe it's Charles. Now I can apologize," I said with false glee. "Cool beans."

I walked into the foyer.

Mom said, "It's Ava." Her eyes searched mine.

I hitched a breath as my heart skipped in my chest. "Did Dad tell you—"

"Yes. Tracy . . . are you all right?" She sucked in her bottom lip.

"I'm trying to be."

"I hope you feel you can talk to me. Especially when your father is away."

She was always easier to talk to when Dad was gone. "Thanks, Mom. I'll take it in my room."

Many of my friends had one phone in the house so every conversation was public. Spencer and I had chipped in for another phone and a long cord so we could pull it into our rooms for privacy. I bolted up the stairs, grabbed the phone, and ran down the hall. I spoke into the handset. "Okay, Mom. I've got it," then closed my door.

"Okay, dear." She hung up.

My heart pounded. "Ava? Can you talk?"

"Just for a few minutes. We're at Earl Abel's. I told my parents I had to use the restroom. I'm using a pay phone."

I swallowed and tried to slow my pulse. *Is she calling to apologize? Please no.* "Your father called my father this morning. He's worried you're gay." My heart pounded in my ears.

After a long pause, Ava whispered, "So am I."

I breathed several times into the phone. My hands and forehead were sweaty. "What we do stays between us."

"Always."

I sucked in a breath and held it, trying to boost my courage. I knew what I was about to say could never be taken back. "So am I," I whispered, leaning against my wall, my legs wobbly.

"Cool."

I heard her breathe rapidly for a few seconds. "I was worried . . . you'd be mad at me."

"I loved it." I pulled open my door to check if anyone was listening.

"You think maybe we ought to make sure?"

"Yeah, but how?"

"I don't know." She blew out a breath. "He's pulling me off the team."

My head pounded. "Why?"

"Because we have a tournament in Medina in two weeks, and we have to spend the night. He doesn't want me in a hotel room sleeping with a bunch of girls."

I closed my door and lay on my bed. "He's not worried about you. He's worried about rumors affecting him. Why can't he drive you both days?" The team only had six girls, and six were needed to play.

"I don't know."

"Did he ask you about being gay or just accuse you?"

"Both."

"And you said?"

Ava sighed. "That we were being silly. That he grew up with brothers and has no idea how girls act."

"I told Dad you were trying to piss him off because he was hovering over you."

She laughed. "I said the same thing! Hey, I better go soon."

I sat up. "Listen. You need to convince him you're straight."

"How?"

"Go out with a boy. Like Spencer."

"Why would Spencer date me?" She lowered her voice. "I think he's gay."

I know he is, I wanted to say. "Does anyone else think that?" My shoulders tensed.

"Haven't heard anyone say anything."

Good. My muscles relaxed.

"If he takes you out, then no one will know about either of you. I'll talk to him. He can pick you up, and we can meet."

"Will he do that?"

I sat up. "I know he will. One way or another I'm going to find a way for us to be together."

She laughed. "I knew you'd break the law."

Tingles fluttered up my legs. "That was the best Lifesaver I ever had."

"I've got more . . . if you want."

"Only if you share." My body flushed with heat, and I stood, my muscles tight and ready for anything. I could still see the shiny, wet candy between her teeth and taste her warm, salty tongue. I'd never been that excited about anyone or anything. I wanted another taste.

"I'll see you Monday, unless they put me in a convent. I've got to go. Bye."

She hung up.

I stared at the phone and thought, *Can parents force their girls into convents? In 1967?*

Beethoven's "Pathétique" Sonata pummeled my floor which sat above the living room. Spencer was practicing then abruptly stopped. I heard Dad's angry voice and ran downstairs.

"I never said Ava was my girlfriend," Spencer shouted.

Dad slapped the piano. "I believe your exact words were, 'How long have we been doing it?'"

"He meant dancing," I said, my pulse throbbing in my neck. "What's your problem?"

He turned his beady eyes to me. "My problem is both of you lie like you breathe."

"How did we lie?" I asked.

His finger stabbed the air. "You purposely led me to believe Spencer and Ava were a number."

"A *number*?" asked Spencer. "What the hell does that even mean?"

"Going steady, for chrissakes!" He stomped his foot. "You were trying to make me forget about you kissing Pablo in our front yard. And you!" He turned his purple face to me. "You set it up so you and Ava could make out during that stupid game."

"How did we get such a brilliant father?" I asked. "Just when we thought we were getting away with it, Mr Genius here figures it out." I applauded slowly. "Nothing gets past you, Daddy. I'm so impressed."

"If it was up to me," he snarled, "you both would be out of here."

I smiled and asked politely, "Would you like us to leave now?"

"No, you both are grounded for the rest of the holidays."

"I need my car!" whined Spencer.

"Not if you're grounded. Now I'm going back to the TV to watch football, and I don't want to hear that piano. So find something else to do."

Dad left before I could say anything back to him.

Spencer covered his face with his hands, his chest heaving. "Pablo and I had plans for tonight. Dammit!" He banged his fists on the keyboard then yanked them up, trying to make the sound disappear. He craned his neck toward the living room then bolted upstairs.

Shit! We'd have to wait until Monday to hook up with Pablo and Ava, after Dad flew out. Technically, he couldn't ground me because the car was mine, and I paid for my gas. But Spencer would never stand up to him, so a double-date would have to wait.

I calmly walked through the living room where Dad yelled at the referees about a missed call. I saw the Saturday paper on the kitchen table, already picked through by anyone who was interested. I heard Mom in the utility room and slid the kitchen door closed.

She took clothes out of the washer and placed them into the new dryer Dad had installed last week. "Do you miss hanging up everything?" I asked.

"Nope. Though I still don't trust this beast. Just experimenting for now." She closed the dryer door, pressed a button, and walked back into the kitchen. "How did your conversation with Ava go?"

I sat at the table and pulled the newspaper toward me. "She's worried her parents are going to pull her from the team and maybe school."

She sat down. "I'm sure they're scared."

I looked into her face—big brown eyes, high cheekbones, wavy brown hair to her shoulders, full lips that rarely smiled. "Why?"

"I think most parents are scared nowadays. All the race riots this summer . . ."

I rolled my eyes. "If I were black, I'd probably riot too. The cops treat them like animals."

"Yes, but still." She folded her hands on the table. "They loot and burn their own neighborhoods. I don't believe you'd do that to Castle Hills."

I chuckled and shook my head. "Mom they live in tiny, un-aircondi-tioned apartments in downtowns which are run down because all the whites fled to the suburbs, like Castle Hills. What do the riots have to do with Ava's parents?"

She rubbed at dark spots on her hands. "Everything is moving so fast —drugs, hippies, sex everywhere, your music."

"My music?"

"You have posters of a drug addict on your wall. She takes LSD. And what's 'White Rabbit' about? Feeding your head with who knows what? You love her music and yet you say you have no interest in drugs."

"I don't."

"I believe you, dear. But that's what parents worry about. Ava's father saw you kissing. Why shouldn't that worry him? It worries me."

I tried to ignore my heart skipping beats and smiled at her. "We were in a relay race. She passed me the Lifesaver."

Mom sighed and leaned back in her chair. "That's an old game, Tracy. Even I played it."

"Really?" I couldn't believe my mother played that game. She always seemed so reserved, in control. "Did anyone ever kiss accidentally?"

"Certainly. A boy and a girl. But not two girls. I can't imagine what my mother would have said if she'd seen me —"

"Did you see us?"

"Yes." She sighed then added sadly, "I was looking through the curtains."

I leaned back and pushed my fingers through my hair. "We were just being silly. It was a spontaneous moment."

She raised her brows and lowered her chin. "Those are the most dangerous moments when girls can lose their reputations. Tracy, you are strong-willed, which I love. You're smart and determined and talented. But you have to pay attention to rules. You can't always do what you want because it feels good or makes you happy. You have to learn to wait and consider the consequences."

"Delayed gratification," I said as I shook my head. "Suffer now for a greater reward later. The question I ask myself is what's this greater reward I'm told about? Is it worth waiting for?" I fixed onto her now frightened eyes. "Mom, is it? Are you telling me you don't regret all the delays you made in the past, all the decisions not to do what you wanted at the time?"

She stared for several seconds then lowered her eyes. "Everyone has regrets. But my great reward was having you and Spencer. And I want the best for both of you."

"If not kissing Ava meant I would sooner be a housewife with an absent husband and two kids who will soon leave home, I think I'd kiss her twice." I stood up.

Mom's eyes widened as her mouth dropped open.

"I'm sorry, Mom. I know you had a hard childhood, growing up in The Depression and then the war, but I have to do more with my life than get married and have kids. We wouldn't be having this conversation if I were a boy."

Mom stood. "But you're not."

I leaned back against the table. "People shouldn't freak out because two girls were having fun and happened to touch lips."

"They wouldn't if it was accidental. The problem is that you both liked it."

I blew out a breath. I probably should have laughed and denied what she said. But I didn't. "That's a problem?"

She moved closer. "Have you kissed a boy?"

A quick memory of sitting on Jimmy's lap during a freshman party flashed through my brain. We "made out" for about five minutes behind a tree before the party's sponsors caught us. "Yes, I've kissed a boy."

"Did you like it?"

I swallowed a few times as we locked eyes. I wanted so badly to say, "No." But I couldn't force the word out of my mouth.

Still, I knew she heard it.

CHAPTER 5

LUNCH DATES AND A NEW IDEA

When Spencer and I left the house for school on Monday, we felt like prisoners released from the dungeon. The sun shone bright in a clear blue sky as we waved to Mom driving Dad to the airport.

The radio played Aretha Franklin's "Respect." We both juked to the beat, Spencer singing along.

At an intersection while ads played, I asked, "How much of his bullshit did you have to endure yesterday?"

Spencer slumped in his seat. "All together? Probably three hours. He'd leave then remember something he forgot to say and come back again. How about you?"

"Not once."

"Why?"

"Because he knows I'll fight back," I said. "If you'd stand up to him, he'd leave you alone too."

"So you think I'm a wuss too." He turned toward the window. "Great."

"You're a kind, smart, beautiful human being. Not a wuss or whatever else he called you. I'm a bitch when I need to be. I won't let him win." The light turned, and I sped through the intersection. "We're taking Pablo and Ava to lunch today."

"What?" Spencer sat up. "Do they know?"

"Not yet. You're dating Ava, and I'm with Pablo." I parked in front of our high school building. "You need to talk to her in the hallway and sit by her in class. You two are in love."

Spencer squirmed in his seat. "How do you know she'll agree to this?"

"Because I'm going to talk to her in a few minutes. And I'll start talking about Pablo. By the end of today, everyone in school is going to know I have a boyfriend and you have a girlfriend. And don't forget to call Pablo this morning."

"Got it." He climbed out of my car then stuck his head back in, his face tense with worry. "You don't think anyone's going to be suspicious after what they saw Friday night?"

"Maybe they will," I replied, "which is why we're going to eat lunch together many times. Go, Spence."

He sucked in his lips. "Okay." He headed for the cafeteria where a pay phone was available.

We attended a small, private K - 12 school in an historic section of San Antonio comprised of old brick and stucco mansions, carriage houses, and a former apartment building. Adler School offered an accelerated curriculum and small class sizes. Parents thought their kids were safer from drugs and "bad" influences there than the larger public schools, and the tuition was low enough to allow a diverse group of students. Most other private schools were much more expensive or religiously affiliated or both. From Dad's perspective, it was cheap and not Catholic.

Students had more freedoms there than in other schools. We could drive off campus during lunch. Upperclassmen usually had at least one free period when we could hang out—in the locker room, outside under an oak or pecan tree, or anywhere we could drive and be back within fifty minutes. I'd bought old books, records, and clothes from a nearby head shop, or ice cream from the pharmacy behind the school, which is where we planned to eat lunch today—Pablo and I on one side of the booth; Spencer and Ava on the other.

I found Ava sitting on the small rock wall between the main building and the science lab. Both of us wore our red and white letterman jackets. She offered me an open package of cherry Lifesavers when I stood next to her.

"Want one?" she asked. Her eyes sparkled with mirth as she put a candy between her lips and wiggled it.

"You're such a devil." My fingers ached to touch her.

She sucked the Lifesaver into her mouth with a slurp. "You had your chance."

"I'll get another later today." I started to sit down, but just before my butt touched the wall, she slipped her hand under me.

"Oh my," she said, wiggling her fingers dangerously close to my crack. "You're sitting on my hand."

I lifted my left cheek and lowered my voice. "Ava, pull it out."

Her face turned red. "How many boys have you said that to?"

We both blurted laughs. She squeezed my butt before removing her hand. I squealed and jumped off the wall.

"What is wrong with you two?" asked Judy from behind. She was on our basketball team and the head cheerleader.

"There was a big spider on the wall!" I exclaimed.

Ava spread her fingers. "Yes, it was as big as my hand." She jumped up, her face red, pointing behind Judy.

"What?" Judy lifted one foot and craned her neck to see behind her.

"It ran into the grass!" shouted Ava.

Judy backed away, turned, lifted each foot, looking for the spider. Her chest heaving, her black hair flip bouncing off her back, she looked at both girls with wide eyes and an open mouth before running toward the high school building.

Ava and I coughed laughs.

"As big as your hand?" I asked.

She blinked her long lashes a few times and said with total innocence, "Well, it was." She sat down and patted the wall next to her. "Here, come sit. You had more to tell me."

I approached her warily, both of us stifling laughter behind clenched lips, and began to sit. Just as I thought, she slipped her hand over. I swung my butt away and sat a foot from her.

"Coward," she said.

"I'll get you later."

"Promises, promises."

"Here's the plan," I said.

"We have a plan?" She stared at my lips.

"A good one." Every nerve ending vibrated. "Don't do that."

"What?"

"Don't look at my lips."

"You're looking at mine." Her tongue touched her top teeth.

I forced myself to turn away and watch Rudy, the starting center for the Wolves, as he plodded up the driveway, carrying his big briefcase. But I still saw Ava's mouth in my mind. "Find someone to look at while we talk."

"Okay. I'm watching Susan flirt with Gene. What's the plan?"

Leaves skittered across the grounds, pushed by a cool breeze. "You and Spencer are madly in love. He's going to talk to you and sit by you in class. Help him out if he gets nervous. I met my new boyfriend Thanksgiving night after Spencer brought him home. His name is Pablo Gutiérrez Delgado from Mexico. He and Spencer got drunk so Pablo drove him home and kept Spencer's car. We're going to fetch it during lunch then all of us are going to the pharmacy. We'll do this a few times this week. Spencer's taking you to a drive-in movie on Friday, the same movie Pablo and I will see. We'll take turns necking in the back seat." I hoped Ava wouldn't laugh.

"You and Pablo?" she teased.

"No. You and me."

"You and I." She scooted over and bumped her shoulder into mine.

"I don't think I'll be looking for the correct pronoun."

Lowering her voice, sounding sexy, "What will you look for?"

"Hidden lifesavers."

"Cool. A scavenger hunt in the back seat. What else is on the list?" She crossed her legs, brushing her shoe against my shin.

My mouth flooded with saliva as I pushed my leg back against her shoe. "Buttons. Zippers. Little hooks."

"Pink panties?"

The air turned hot, and I could feel electricity about to spark between us. "Definitely. I can feel you looking at me, Ava. You need to turn your face away."

"Done. Spencer's walking toward us."

"Good for him. Meet us at my car at noon." I quickly touched her hand with my fingers as I stood. "Be nice to Spencer. He had a very difficult holiday." I walked away. Just before I entered the high school building, I glanced back to see Ava leaning against Spencer, both laughing as they sat on the wall.

Such a normal scene. All I had to do was give the same performance with Pablo, and we'd be home free.

Free to do what we wanted only in secret.

Later, at noon, I pulled away from the curb with Spencer and Ava sitting in my back seat. They actually held hands walking down the driveway toward my car.

"You guys sure looked cute this morning," I said.

"My cheeks are cramped from smiling so much," said Ava. "Maybe we're going overboard."

"Better to do too much than too little," I answered. "Spencer, remember to put your arm around her in the booth."

"Yeah, but don't leave it there forever," Ava said as she leaned forward and put her head right above my shoulder. "Remember when Gene put his arm around Susan and then tried to eat his whole burger with his left hand?" She laughed. "All the guts fell out on his plate, and he still wouldn't move it. He grabbed napkins to wipe his messy hand, but how do you wipe with one hand?"

"So what happened?" I asked.

"Susan wiped his hand and his mouth. It was the cutest and silliest thing I ever saw. And when they left, he rubbed his right shoulder the entire walk back to school because he had a cramp. Such a dork."

"I feel sorry for him," said Spencer. "Just don't laugh at me if I screw up."

I stopped at a light. "We would never laugh at you, Bro."

Ava purred behind my ear. "Want a lifesaver?"

I turned my head and found her lips an inch from mine. "Where is it?"

"You know." She opened her lips slightly to reveal the cherry candy.

I checked my mirrors and out the windows, looking for voyeurs then brushed her lips with mine. "Are you going to give it to me?"

She tilted her head and lifted one brow. "You have to find it."

I reached back to her neck and pulled her closer as I explored her mouth with my tongue. Heat filled my mouth and rolled up my neck in waves. I found the candy nestled between her back molar and cheek. The car behind me honked. Only my tongue moved.

"Go," said Spencer, "before someone sees you."

I turned around, shifted into first, and took off. Ava played with my hair as I drove down McCullough then turned onto Rosewood. Most cars did not have seat belts for the back row, and the leg room in my back seat was minimal. All Ava had to do was scoot forward a few inches to reach me.

I had an idea. "We can leave my car at Pablo's and all ride together to the pharmacy. Ava and me in the back, and you two guys in the front. You'd have more leg room, Spencer. What do you think?"

"I vote yes!" squealed Ava.

"No," said Spencer. "I don't want to hear my sister making out behind me. Besides, you two need to be careful. Someone will see you and what then? This whole plan goes to hell. You have to show more restraint."

"Like you did Thursday night?" I asked then flashed my eyes at him in the rearview mirror.

Spencer squirmed. "Please don't do that. You have no idea how much I hate someone looking at me through a mirror."

"Sorry," I said. And then I knew why Dad did it to him. I had felt that surge of power over Spencer—trapped in a corner as my words lashed him. I now knew I had little restraint over my impulses. If it were up to me alone, I'd have parked the car blocks ago and climbed into the back seat with Ava. We'd see who could rip off the other's clothes the fastest.

But someone would see, and we would be condemned as perverts. It seemed like every day I had to work harder at telling myself no. *Don't. You can't.* It seemed inevitable I'd lose those battles.

Spencer leaned forward and pointed toward an alley just ahead of me. "Take a left there."

I did and saw the front grill of his 1955 Buick Roadmaster backed into a driveway. "I've always loved the chrome boobs on your car, Spencer. I just never understood why until now."

"Oh, my god!" squealed Ava. "They do look like boobs."

"They're called Dagmars," said Spencer, "after the actress who wears bullet bras. Dad used to tease me when he made me polish the chrome. 'That's every man's dream, son. Enjoy it while you can.'"

"Did you?" I asked.

"No. That was years ago. I knew I was supposed to laugh and share a joke with him, but I felt weird. At first he thought I had no sense of humor or was too shy. Then he started shaking his head at me and stopped the comments."

Ava jumped out and ran to Spencer's car where she caressed the Dagmars while looking back at me. I laughed and moved toward her. She stepped toward me, thrusting out her breasts.

"I dare you."

I glanced around then cupped both breasts. Immediately I felt a tingle between my legs. She squealed and we hugged just as Pablo emerged from the back door.

He threw open his arms. "¿Qué pasa?"

Spencer hugged him.

There we were in an alley behind an ivy-covered duplex, happy, maybe in love or at least full of desire, fortifying ourselves before we had to put on a show. I kissed Ava, inhaling her breath, and out of the corner of my eye, I saw my brother kiss Pablo, clutching him like I clutched Ava. More than my passion for Ava, I felt a rush of happiness for my brother.

A car entered the alley from the road, sending jolts of fear through us. Spencer broke away from Pablo and was nearly hit by the car which screeched to a stop.

"Hey, kid!" A rough looking middle-aged man yelled at him through the open window.

"Sorry," said Spencer. "Wasn't looking."

The man shook his head as the car continued down the alley.

"We better go," I said. "Pablo, you're with me."

He broke away from Spencer with "Ándale," and jumped into my passenger seat. "I'm in the shotgun, yes?"

"Buckle up. We need to hurry." I backed up the alley into Rosewood as he clutched my dashboard. A car honked as I whipped into traffic.

"Maybe I should ride with Spencer," said Pablo. "He's not so crazy!"

"We're a couple now. You're going to be driving with me a lot, so get used to it."

"I'll try, but don't kill me."

I grabbed his knee. "Why would I kill my boyfriend? Remember to hold my hand and put your arm around when we're in public."

"Okay. No problema."

I stopped at a light and looked for Spencer behind me. Slow and steady, he'd catch up to me just as the light turned green. He'd smile through his windshield, and I would hear the words in my head that he'd said a million times to me: *"Slow down. Who are you racing against?"*

"Life," I'd say.

"You think you can beat life?"

"No, but I can't stand the thought of letting it push me around. I want some control."

"So you speed," said Spencer, *"and jump train tracks, and challenge every rule you can?"*

"Sums me up, doesn't it?" The light turned, and I sped away, running from a life like my mother's—a prisoner of the patriarchy. Maybe there was another way to escape that future besides running away and scoffing at every limitation. But at the time, I couldn't think of an alternative.

We all walked into the pharmacy as couples, casually holding hands. Mine were sweaty from the nerves firing all over my body. Heads turned as we moved toward an open booth near Eddie's grill. I introduced Pablo to some friends, most of the girls' widening their eyes and blushing a little after hearing his accent and deep voice. I knew he was exaggerating, but he'd convinced them he adored females. Pablo's eyes gleamed as his feet almost danced across the floor.

Ava and I slid into our seats before the guys. The formica table wobbled every time one of us leaned on it. I grabbed a wad of napkins, folded them, then gave them to Pablo. "Stick this under the foot pointing toward Spencer."

He disappeared under the table for a few seconds and bumped his head on the way up. "¡Ay, caramba!"

"Here, let me kiss that and make it feel better," I said while tilting his forehead toward my lips. I glanced around to see if anyone was looking. Yes! Judy and Susan's mouths dropped open. I kissed him three times.

Spencer tightened his lips and whispered, "Don't get carried away, Sis."

I winked at Ava as I backed away from my "boyfriend." Her tongue licked her upper lip.

"Thank you for your concern, Tracy," said Pablo. "That almost makes up for your crazy driving."

Spencer snickered. "Did she scare you? Because she scares me all the time."

"I love her driving," said Ava, looking directly at me with a smile. "Fast and exhilarating." She'd kicked off her shoe and pushed her toes against my leg.

I shook my head at her, trying to hold back a smile. I looked at Spencer and jerked my head toward Ava. He coughed slightly and placed his arm around her shoulders. She snuggled against him, still rubbing my leg.

We ordered hamburgers and cokes.

Pablo watched Eddie add puddles of grease onto the grill before pressing four patties onto the blackened metal. Pablo rubbed his hand down his face. "¡Dios mío!" A few minutes later, Eddie brushed the buns with grease and plopped them near the blackening burgers. Soon the waitress brought our four plates of burgers including a mound of ridged potato chips and fixings—lettuce, pickles, tomato, and onion. The buns sparkled under the naked fluorescent light bulbs where two flies bumped the glass tubes.

Judy and Susan walked toward our table with fake grins. *Here's trouble.* I touched Ava's leg with my toe. She saw them and immediately pulled Spencer's hand from her shoulder to the middle of her chest. Spencer's eyes flashed in alarm. I leaned closer to Pablo.

Judy's eyes moved between Ava and me. "So what really happened during the relay? We've heard all kinds of crazy stories."

Susan folded her arms and tilted her head, her lips pursed in disapproval.

I tried to ignore my stomach flipping. "We both dropped our tooth-picks because Ava turned toward me with a crazy-looking face. I laughed then she laughed, but she caught the candy before it hit the ground. She put it between her lips, I took it from her so our team would win. End of story."

"You didn't really kiss each other?" Susan asked.

"Why would I do that when I can kiss Pablo any time I want?" I lifted Pablo's face and kissed him on the lips.

Pablo smiled at the girls. "Tracy's a good kisser." He brushed his lips against my cheek.

Spencer clenched his jaw. "Any other questions? 'Cause we need to eat."

"Guess not," said Judy. She turned toward the exit, Susan following.

Spencer blew out a breath and said quietly, "That was close."

Pablo cautiously picked up his burger. "It's slippery." He laughed.

"Just take a bite," said Spencer, "and it will slide down easy."

Pablo bit into the bun, causing a stream of grease to dribble onto his plate.

Spencer grabbed napkins and blotted the puddle. "Don't look down. Just chew and swallow."

We laughed and ate. I kept glancing around, hoping we were drawing attention. Mario offered Julie a sip of his shake to pull her gaze away from us. I thought, *Mission accomplished.* Everyone knew we were real couples. So it was time to leave.

Outside on the sidewalk, I realized I wouldn't be driving with Ava. "Save me a seat in class."

Ava grabbed Spencer's arm. "I'm sitting with Spencer. Toodles." I watched them walk away, Ava purposely swaying her butt more than usual.

"C'mon, Pablo. We have to hurry or I'm going to be late for class."

"I'm going to lie down in the back and pray."

And he did.

For the next two days, we performed for the lunch crowd. Spencer and Ava walked to the pharmacy from school while I fetched Pablo. But

I hadn't been able to kiss or hold Ava once since Monday. What was the point of this masquerade if she and I couldn't be together?

On Thursday I'd had enough. I couldn't wait until our movie date to touch her again. "Let's go somewhere else." Ava and Spencer climbed into my back seat, and I sped to Pablo's. Ava leaned forward and played with my hair, brushing her lips along my neck. The only time we could touch each other was in my car.

After Pablo jumped in, I said, "I'm dropping you and Spencer off at Taco Cabana."

"Really?" asked Spencer. "And where are you and Ava going?"

"To the park."

"To do what?"

"Park."

Ava clapped her hands. "Goody."

"It's the middle of the day. You'll be seen," warned Spencer.

"I'll find a good spot."

After dropping off the boys, Ava asked whether she should move up front.

"No. I'll climb back there. I brought a blanket we can hide under. Lie down so no one sees you."

A few minutes later, I stopped on Avenue A near the golf course in a shady area. After scanning for other cars, I climbed between the front seats and found Ava already covered by my blanket. "I'm joining you, so I hope you're decent."

"If you want decent, I'll put my clothes back on."

I pulled back the blanket until I saw her bra straps. She'd unbuttoned her shirt, and her pale skin was dotted with freckles. The sight of the white line marking the beginning of her breasts sucked the breath out of my lungs. I touched her skin and felt dizzy, but then I heard footsteps. "Shhh." I looked across the road and saw a young man jogging. After he left, I looked the other way, my heart skipping beats.

"Tracy, c'mon." She giggled. "Buttons, and zippers, and hooks, oh my!"

I scrambled underneath the blanket, pressing myself against her, but we both couldn't fit on the seat side by side. "One of us is going to have to be on top."

"Be my guest," she purred.

She spread her legs, dropping one to the floor. I hovered over her face, my eyes feasting on her plump lips, before I touched them with mine.

"I forgot the Lifesaver," said Ava. "Sorry." She clutched my neck and sucked my bottom lip into her mouth. "Or maybe I hid it somewhere else."

I pushed my tongue deep into her mouth. "You taste good without the candy."

She giggled. "You should look for it."

"You're a devil." Our hearts beat against each other, pounding through our chests.

"Satan's spawn." She flicked her tongue around my lips.

I pushed my tongue into her ear. "Not there. Maybe the other one." I turned her head and did the same.

She squealed.

"Not there."

I moved lower, peeling her bra off her breasts. She'd placed a candy on each nipple. I sucked both into my mouth.

She gasped. "There's more."

My scalp tingled and my neck throbbed. "I wonder where?" I lifted myself up so I could flip her skirt back from her legs.

"You're getting warm."

I saw her polka dot panties and smiled.

She glanced down. "I wasn't expecting to be doing this today. Otherwise, I would've —"

"I love these." I pushed my fingertips between her skin and the top edge of the cotton then moved my hands slowly toward the middle.

"Warmer," she moaned.

We heard a rapping against the window.

"Shit!" I pulled myself from under the blanket, keeping Ava covered, and saw a police officer's face against the window. He signaled to roll down the window. "Stay under the blanket. Don't move," I hissed then climbed into the front seat, flashing him for sure. I smiled as I lowered the window one inch, wondering if he could hear the pounding in my head.

"What's up, officer?"

He narrowed his eyes, glanced into the back seat then shifted his eyes to me. "This is a no parking area. You didn't see the sign?" He pointed his billy club toward a sign, partially hidden by bushes, red arrows pointing both ways.

"How would anyone see that?" I asked. I started my car.

"Who's in the back?" he growled.

I tried to flash a coy smile as my pulse throbbed in my neck. "My boyfriend. He's pretty shy."

He moved to the back window, placing his hand over his eyes so he could see more clearly. "Boyfriend, huh?" He rapped on the window. "Show your face, son!"

"He's naked. My lipstick is all over his face. And other places. Do you really want to see that, Officer?" I couldn't get enough air into my lungs.

He looked at me in horror. "Naked? My God, don't you teenagers have any guardrails? Any limits?"

I smiled and flashed my brows. "You never made out in the back seat with your girl?"

"Sure, I did, but —"

I fixed my wide eyes on his. "Are you telling me you would've refused her command to strip for her?"

He swallowed. "Command?"

My words dripped with seduction. "When I command, he obeys. You wouldn't have?"

He stared into my eyes, mouth hanging open.

I thought I'd pass out if he didn't back down soon. Ava hadn't moved or made a sound. "We have to get back to school and he needs time to dress. Can I go, Officer?"

He squinted and shook his head. "This time. But don't let me catch you here again. You shouldn't be doing this in broad daylight, Miss."

"Thanks for the advice." I shifted into first and drove away. "Get dressed, Ava. I have to drive fast." I pulled out onto Broadway and raced north toward Hildebrand.

"So what else is new? You were so close."

I looked at her in the mirror as she reached behind her back to fasten her bra. "We were so close to major trouble." The buzz of adrenaline faded, and my body shuddered. *Too close!* "I have to think of something different. There has to be a way we can do this without so much risk."

She buttoned her shirt. "But the risk makes it more exciting."

"We can't get busted."

She leaned forward and pushed her open hand over my shoulder, holding a cherry Lifesaver. "This shouldn't go to waste. Do you want it?"

"I'm not sure where it's been."

She blew on the back of my neck. "In a very warm and wet place. Trust me. You'll love it."

I bent my head and sucked the candy into my mouth. "Yum! Who knew candy could be so sexy?"

"Depends on where you find it."

We barely made it back to class before the bell. I copied notes as the teacher filled his blackboard—and jacket—with chalk, thinking of ways to spend time with Ava with less worry.

From my back row seat, I watched Julie and Mario hold hands when the teacher had his back to us. When he dropped his eraser and bent down to pick it up, Mario reached over for a quick kiss. No one snickered. No one did anything. They'd done it so many times in classes, we'd stopped paying attention.

But no one would ignore two girls holding hands. Ever.

As long as I was a girl, Ava and I couldn't be seen together.

Tingles swarmed up my skin. That was the answer. Disguise myself as a boy when we were away from school, and we wouldn't need to hide under a blanket. We could go to a restaurant or a movie. Anywhere.

I would cut my hair, stop plucking my brows, wear no makeup, maybe even shave my facial hair so I'd get stubble.

And buy some guy clothes.

I looked over at Ava and caught her glance. Would she like me as a boy?

CHAPTER 6

A BOY AND HIS GIRL

During my free period, I drove to Galligaskins, a variety shop close to school on N. Main Avenue. Beads, lava lamps, psychedelic posters, bell bottoms, records, plus "cigarette" papers were available. As well as some "novelties" which Hogan kept in a back room. He was the hairiest guy I'd ever seen. He sported an Afro, though he was very white. His hair was a reddish brown, rising three inches above his scalp. He wore a tribal print shirt with a plunging front which exposed a chest almost as curly and dense as his head. On top of that he wore a long leather vest with fringe hanging to his thighs.

"Hey, Tracy. What can I do you for?"

I took a deep breath and bolstered my courage. "Make me look like a guy."

He came from behind the counter, folded his hands just above his crotch, tilted his head, and stretched his painted lips into a smile. "Which guy? Like me?" He chuckled.

We'd never asked about each other's sexual preference, but we both knew we were different. He'd sold me the Grace Slick poster with the extended middle finger and the signed photo of her exposing her breast I kept hidden in my drawer.

I took a deep breath, trying to slow my racing heart. "I'm going to cut my hair and comb it back. I have a spandex girdle I'll cut in half and wear over my breasts to flatten them out, but I need a pair of men's pants and a shirt."

He squinted his eyes and walked around me, scrutinizing my shape. "Is this for a costume party?"

"It won't be a costume so much as a new me. I'll need to use it pretty often."

"Well, fortunately, you have slim hips. What's your inseam length?"

"No idea."

He grabbed a measuring tape and kneeled in front of me. "Do you mind?"

Hogan had always been kind and polite without being paternal, which was one reason I trusted him. "No, I kinda like you there. It's usually the other way around."

He raised his face to me and smiled. "You seem to have a narrow sexual perspective, Tracy. Guys can eat girls too. And guys do give blow jobs."

"Thanks for that enlightenment."

"You're welcome. If I touch anything I shouldn't, you can kick me in my jewels." He stretched the tape from my heel to just beneath my groin. "Thirty-four inches. My, what long legs you have. But you don't have any jewels, and that's the problem." He stood up and grabbed a few pairs of jeans and cords. "Try these on."

"Couldn't I wad up socks and shove them in my underwear?"

"You could. Or buy a jockstrap and do the same. But I have another option." His eyes twinkled.

"Okay. Be mysterious." I carried the pants into a dressing room and tried them on. I'd worn pants before. We were allowed to wear jeans during Rodeo Week at school. But that day, I felt something different looking at myself in the mirror, trying to imagine myself as a boy. My favorite was a pair of low-cut, flared rusty brown corduroys with two small front pockets. But I noticed the extra bulge of material around my groin. I exited the room and saw Hogan standing in an open doorway behind the counter.

He waved me over. "This is a restricted area. Understand?"

I nodded, wondering what all the caution was about as I followed him.

"One of these will work, I think."

On a glass countertop, I saw three sets of rubber male genitals, all flesh-colored, all with erections. I was mesmerized.

"That look of yours is priceless," he laughed. "Try not to get aroused."

I remembered to breathe. "What . . . why?"

"They are sex toys. Dildos. Technically, I'm not supposed to sell these."

I reached for one. "Can I?"

"Yes."

I picked up the smallest one which still had a four inch boner. "Is this how they look?"

"You've never seen . . . "

"No. It's bigger than I'd imagined." I held it between my legs and wondered how all of it would fit into my pants.

"It's aroused, Tracy. Normally, everything is limp and loose and much smaller. Try it on. I need to change the record. I've got the new Beatles' album." He walked to his other counter in the main room.

I unbuttoned my pants and lowered the zipper. Then I shoved the toy, balls first, into my crotch. *Wow*, I thought. It felt at once strange but satisfying. When I'd imagined how my life would be different as a boy, I'd never considered having a penis. I'd been embarrassed at times about my flat chest and other times wished my chest didn't bulge at all.

How could I walk around with this . . . thing between my legs? I could rebutton my waist easily, but the zipper took some effort. I moved in front of a mirror and stared. My rubber boner was so obvious, the head pushing out against the zipper about two inches below the pant waist. Wouldn't everyone stare at it? Girls looked at boys' crotches all the time. Is that what I wanted?

The opening flutes of "Strawberry Fields Forever" drifted through the store as I walked toward Hogan. His eyes lowered to my crotch then widened. "I know places where you'd make quite the positive impression with that . . . arrangement."

"I can't walk around with a continual boner. Do you have anything smaller?"

"No. The point of a sex toy is the erection, after all."

I pushed the boner closer to my skin. "Maybe I can cut the top off."

He winced and inadvertently covered his jewels. "Don't say that!"

I reached down my pants and pressed the tip into my skin. "Or somehow tape it to stay flat against me. What do you think?"

The door opened and someone walked into the store. I raised my eyes to see Hogan chuckling, holding his hand against his face and a young woman with heavy makeup staring at my groin, emitting a low whistle. I jerked my hand out of my pants, causing my penis to whip forward.

"Personally," said the lady, "I like that look." She lifted her eyes to mine and licked her lips. "Very much."

Then I realized *she* was in drag. We both were in disguise. Or maybe we had left our *disguises* behind. *Wow, this world is going to be interesting.* "Thanks. Just a new look I'm trying out. Hogan, can you bring a couple shirts?" I turned toward the dressing room.

"Yes, certainly."

I closed the door, removed my pants, and held the toy. Charles' must have been bigger than this. To have something this big hanging between your legs had to affect your whole outlook. Did they feel power? Especially when it was erect?

When a girl got excited, who would know? Maybe that's why girls screamed at the Beatles and threw bras and panties at them.

I held it close to my face. Why didn't the real thing excite me? Why did I tingle and squirm when Ava blew the hair on my neck? Kissing her breasts turned me on. Feeling Charles' boner grossed me out.

But wearing this would be . . . what? I needed to find out.

I left the store with the cords, two shirts, and two toys. I knew I would cut and shape the penis and was afraid I'd make a mistake. Besides, I might want the full boner look sometime. My skin prickled with excitement. I wanted to see myself as a full-blown male.

The next day during my free period, I got a pixie haircut—a little shaggy on top with some casual bangs, longer on one side than the other. Everyone noticed when I went to my fifth period class. Ava loved it and couldn't keep her hands off my hair.

When Spencer came by to walk her to class, I chuckled. "Hold her hand and take her away, Bro. She's messing up my pixie."

Spencer's mouth dropped open. "What did you do? Mom's going to freak."

And she did. She covered her face and gasped. "Tracy. Why? Why?"

"I wanted to try something different, Mom. It will grow back."

"But your hair was beautiful. It looked so pretty spread across your back at the piano."

"Yes, but it hampered my emotional connection with the music." I whipped my head around. "Now my head is free to move. I can be more like Spencer. Imagine how my head of hair would cramp Spencer's style."

She wiped her tears and bolted for the kitchen.

That night I experimented. I'd bought a jock strap and pairs of stretch men's briefs. I cut the penis down a half inch at a time until it was about two and a half inches long. I thinned the part that pressed against my pubis so the bulge seemed more natural. I wore the strap under the briefs then worked on my boob flattener, ending with a six-inch band—tight enough to stay put but still allow me to breathe. Once my hair was greased and combed back, I looked almost manly. But when I added a pair of round glasses, tea shades like John Lennon's, I almost didn't recognize myself.

Or had I created a new self?

I put on a pair of penny loafers and a leather jacket I'd bought at Goodwill and practiced walking around my room, feeling more weight in my hips and shuffling my feet. I sat with my legs spread and crossed like a man. I felt good, free, and cocky. What I saw in my mirror was what I'd always imagined myself to be—not a poor rendition of a *pretty* girl, painted, hoping to attract some guy's attention with practiced expressions as I did my makeup. After I stuck a wad of gum into my mouth, I headed for Spencer's room and knocked.

"Come in." He sat at his rolltop desk, hunched over a notebook.

I lowered my voice. "Hey, man. Why don't we walk around the block and you teach me how to smoke?"

He looked up and jumped out of his chair. "What the . . . Tracy, is that you?"

"You can call me Tray." I smacked my gum and walked toward him. "What do you think? Can I pass for a guy?"

"Yes, but why . . ."

"I've got my reasons. C'mon, let's walk. And bring your cigs."

He went down ahead of me, checked for Mom, then signaled me into the foyer. I thought his caution was unnecessary. Frankly, I felt so comfortable with my new self, I felt no fear.

We walked and smoked and talked for thirty minutes about what had happened at the park, my trip to Hogan's, and what I planned to do during our double date tomorrow at the drive-in. I felt loose, grounded, kind of punkish. I spit a few times and blew smoke out my nose. I smiled more and bobbed my head to imaginary music. I listened to the clop my shoes made on the sidewalk. I wanted to feel like that every minute of every day.

But, of course, I had to go back to wearing dresses for school. I already felt I was in disguise there with my real self packed in my gym bag.

On Friday, Pablo and I met Spencer and Ava at the San Pedro Twin drive-in to watch *The Flim-Flam Man*, a comedy about con men with George C. Scott. I wore a dress and tights. Pablo and I climbed into Spencer's back seat. I wanted more room than my little car offered for Ava and me to make out and to change my clothes.

Spencer parked on the end of a row away from everyone, which wasn't hard since most of the spots were empty. Just a field of short poles holding metal speakers.

"Why don't you boys go get us some snacks and drinks," I said. "Should take you about thirty minutes. At least."

"Yes!" shouted Ava as she climbed into the seat Pablo had just vacated.

Spencer hung the speaker on his window. "You want anything in particular?" he asked.

"Surprise us," I said. "With the food. Tap the trunk and wait until we open our doors before peeking."

"So mysterious," said Spencer. "One wonders what we're missing."

"The same we'll miss when it's our turn to walk around."

As soon as they left, Ava asked as she removed her jacket, "What's in the bag?"

"A surprise." I removed mine.

"For me?"

"For both of us. I'll show you once I'm out of these clothes."

"Oooh. Then let me help you strip." She clutched me to her and reached around my back to pull my zipper. "I haven't seen you at all. That is gonna change."

In a frantic fever of kisses and tugs and pulls, she had me naked on the seat in two minutes. Even though it was dark in the back seat, I covered myself.

Ava gently pulled away each of my hands. "Oh, Tracy, you are beautiful." She kissed each breast. My nerves exploded in a heated frenzy, screaming for more.

Headlights slashed across the rear window, and we both dived flat against the seat. We'd just started! *We can't be caught now. Please.*

After a few seconds, I raised my face and watched a car drive along the side road then swing into a row where it parked.

"Clear?" asked Ava.

"Yeah."

"Then slide down."

I scooted along the seat until my head rested on her arm. She licked my lips then dragged her fingers from my chin to my stomach, all the while looking into my eyes. I panted and arched my chest as she explored lower. Soon I was grunting and pushing my head hard against the door, lifting my chin toward the ceiling, straining every muscle until I burst into a moan. I clutched my knees together, trapping her hand between my legs, as a few more spasms jerked my body.

"Ava," I sighed, entirely spent.

"Yes, Tracy?" She played with my hair and giggled. "You have something to say to me?"

"That was wonderful." I pulled on her dress. "Why do you still have clothes on?"

"Started my period today. Sorry."

"Does it hurt? Mine are horrible."

"Sometimes. But this one is okay so far." She kissed my nose. "Was that your first time?"

I sat up and pulled her face to mine. "Yes." I kissed her. "Yours?"

"Oh, yeah." She rubbed my nose with hers.

My stomach fluttered with happiness as I floated in a cloud of hope. Maybe we could actually be together and not have to worry about the scorn of others. Yes, we were hiding in the back of a car at the edge of a drive-in lot, but we were happy. I had shared my orgasm with Ava— something beyond any intimacy I had imagined. Fantasizing was one thing, but the actual experience was precious, fixed in my memory forever.

"What's in the bag?" Ava asked.

"My clothes." I reached for the little duffle and set it between us on the seat. "My manguise." I yanked the zipper and pulled out my shirt and pants then my underwear and finally my trimmed jewels. "You want to play with my balls while I put on my boob crusher?"

Even in the dim light, I could see Ava blush.

She held the toy gingerly, cupping the nuts like she was afraid she'd hurt them. "I don't know what to say."

"In a few minutes, I'm going to take you walking. We're going to hold hands and kiss, and I may even cop a feel."

She pulled my hand to her breast. "Be my guest."

"In public, like guys do all the time. We'll be free like everyone else."

"What happened to the end?" She pointed at the penis stub.

"It was four inches long. It's a sex toy, Ava. I bought it from Hogan at Galligaskins yesterday. I want my crotch to look natural without attracting attention. Girls always notice cocks and balls."

"Some girls do. These balls look so much better without hair."

I gasped. "Have you seen them? Real ones?"

"Henry's bathing suit came off when he dived into the pool at Pam's party this summer. He tried to cover himself, but I saw them. Hairy, limp, and gross. And skinny. Not like this thick one. How do you wear it?"

I pulled on my jock strap and fit the balls inside, the stub sticking out the top a little.

Ava cupped it and pushed it gently between my legs. "Does that feel good?"

"You know it does." She moved it in circles, her tongue tip glued to her upper lip. "Stop. I need to get dressed."

"You have invented the wearable dildo. Every girl should have one of these."

I pushed her hand away and pulled up my underwear then my pants. After buttoning my shirt, I squirted more than a "little dab" of Brylcreem into my hand and rubbed it in. I handed Ava a mirror. "Hold this for me." I swept my hair back with a little flip above my forehead then donned my specs. I grabbed my leather jacket and opened the door. "Come outside. I want to kiss you."

Ava scooted out the door and put on her coat.

I hooked my glasses around my ears and lowered my voice. "Do you like me as a boy?" For just a moment, I feared she would laugh.

"Yes." She moved closer and reached for my bulge. "Hump me while you kiss."

And I did.

I heard footsteps in the gravel and then a knock on the trunk.

"¡Dios mio!" blurted Pablo. "Who is that?"

Spencer carried a cardboard tray of food. Pablo held a box of popcorn. I sauntered over to him, my shoes slapping the asphalt, torso settled into my pelvis, head tilted and chin out. "Who do you think, punk?"

He flinched and leaned toward Spencer. "Where's Tracy?"

Spencer set the box on his hood. "That is Tracy. Damn, Sis, you look real."

"I feel real. And call me Tray." I punched Pablo's shoulder gently. "Jus' pulling your chain, Pablo. This is the new me." I just knew I'd never felt more confident in my life.

He moved closer and examined me closely then turned to Spencer and gave him the popcorn. "I like this Tray." He hooked my arm and started walking. "See you guys later."

"Pablo!" yelled Spencer.

Ava and I cackled while Pablo turned around and ran back to my brother. We ate our food then I grabbed Ava's hand. "Will thirty minutes be enough for you guys?"

Spencer handed me the box of trash. "At least."

"Give me some cigs and your lighter."

He gave me a sly smile, dropped two cigarettes and his lighter into my shirt pocket, then patted my chest. "You're good to go."

Ava coughed a laugh. I tried to breathe.

"Better get used to that, Bro," said Spencer before climbing into the back seat with Pablo.

"He's right, you know," said Ava as I dropped the trash into a can. "Girls put their hands on guys' chest all the time." She put her hands flat against my boobs. "You'll have to learn to ignore it. You have pecs now." She squeezed my shoulders then my biceps. "You do have muscles, but you're skinny for a guy. Maybe you should lift weights."

"Good idea. I'll start tomorrow." I grabbed her hand and walked toward the playground.

"I was kidding!"

"I'm not. Dad has a weight bench in the garage." A couple walked toward us with three kids, leaving the playground. I nodded and smiled. "Good evening."

The woman hugged herself. "It's a little chilly."

I pulled Ava to me and wrapped my arm around her shoulders. "Good thing my girlfriend is warm."

She glanced at her husband behind her, trying to corral the kids. "Lucky you."

The family passed us. After a few seconds, I swung Ava in front of me and hugged her. "Isn't this great? I feel so free. We can hug and kiss and who's to care? We can go to a restaurant. Even dance. Go with me to Teen Canteen. I went with Spencer a year ago. Have you?"

"Once or twice." She laughed as I lifted her off the ground and swung her around in a circle. "But it's dark now. How do you know . . ."

"Then let's get some popcorn."

Her eyes widened. "Are you sure?"

"Yeah. We can do this. We won't have to hide anymore." My spirit soared as a tiny tear ran down my cheek. *We can do this!*

"Okay."

I lit a cigarette as we walked toward the concession stand, each step bringing more light and more people. I smiled and nodded and blew smoke above my head, carried away by a little breeze. The sky was clear, and the stars were bright. We got in line like everyone else and ordered nachos with jalapeños then sat at a table outside.

Someone behind me said, "Hey, buddy."

I turned around. "Yeah?" I swallowed the fear bubbling in my throat.

"Do you have a light?" He held a cigarette to his lips.

Relief warmed my chest. "Sure do." I pulled out Spencer's lighter and cupped my hand to block the wind. He did the same on the other side.

He inhaled until the tobacco glowed red. "Thanks, man."

"No problem. Name's Tray." I held out my hand and held his gaze.

He grabbed my hand with a firm shake that I returned. "Brian."

"Glad to meet you." With the omission of a little "c" in my name, the world became my home rather than my battlefield. *So fucking amazing.*

He nodded.

I reached for Ava's hand and lifted it to my lips. She smiled, laid her head on my shoulder and put her hand on over my breast. I breathed freely in total contentment, my right ankle resting on my left knee, my legs spread for everyone to see.

Such a killer night.

CHAPTER 7

A NIGHT AT THE CANTEEN

A ll of us had tasted freedom and sex and wanted more. Next weekend we couldn't go out again because Ava and I had a tournament that Friday and Saturday. How could we go another two weeks for an encore? None of us wished to wait that long.

But we should have.

When Spencer stopped at my car outside the drive-in, Ava grabbed me. "What can we do tomorrow?"

I was still in my manguise, so I kissed her as other cars drove by. "Would your parents let you go out again?"

"Maybe . . . if there was some special event."

I wracked my brain to think of a concert or performance. Then it hit me. "Dance contest at Teen Canteen."

Ava frowned. "Do they have contests?"

"I don't know, but we can say we heard it announced on the radio tonight. You and Spencer would *have* to enter that. You're great dancers. I'll pick up Pablo dressed like this, and we can meet you and Spencer at 8:00."

"What do Pablo and I do?" asked Spencer.

"Whatever you want. Meet us at Jim's on Fredericksburg at 11:00, and we'll go home from there. Dig?"

"Yes!" Ava grabbed me and fondled my jewels.

"You are so naughty."

Pablo covered his face with his hands while Spencer groaned.

"You haven't seen anything yet," Ava said before kissing me, thrusting her tongue down my throat.

The next night after dinner, I started dressing as Tray in my bedroom. I had just put on the spandex band around my boobs when Mom knocked on my door.

"Tracy, I have some clothes for you."

My heartbeat raced, and my mind blanked out in fear. My corduroys were on the bed, along with my jock strap and dildo. I tossed the pants across the bed to the floor and just sat down on the other items when Mom opened my door.

Her eyes nearly popped out of her head. "What on earth is that around your chest?"

My lungs gasped for air, bringing more attention to my breasts. "I can't stand wearing a bra during basketball. The straps fall down and I get no support at all."

"So you decided to cut up a girdle?"

I tried to smile. "Just trying it out." I saw the dildo poking out from beneath my butt and leaned over on my side.

"Tracy, what's gotten into you?"

"Nothing, Mom." My stomach churned.

"Don't you leave soon?"

"I've got time. Just drop the clothes on the bed. I'll put them up."

"Make sure you do so they don't wrinkle." She dropped her load then stared at my face. "When's the last time you plucked your eyebrows?"

I lurched up, pulling a shirt over the dildo while her gaze fixed on my eyes. "The style is for them to be thicker now."

She tsked. "In the hippie crowd?"

"You know all my friends, Mom. Please tell me which are the hippies."

She shook her head and left my room.

I raced to hang up most of the clothes, then got dressed. Spencer went down the stairs before me and found Mom. As soon as I heard them talking, I bounded out the front door and took off before Mom could see me. Spencer and I would meet at the corner of Shallimar later that night, so he could enter the house first and distract Mom while I ran upstairs.

Pablo and I waited in the lower level parking area at Wonderland Mall. Tom Kelsey rented a dance studio there every Friday and Saturday night to stage his dances and band performances. Teen Canteen was very popular for North Side white teens and their parents who could drop off their kids for the evening, knowing that Tom would chaperone and enforce the rules: no jeans, no shorts, no leaving and returning, 50¢ to enter, no serious necking.

I had my own pack of cigarettes, thanks to Spencer, and I offered one to Pablo.

"Gracias."

"What are you two doing tonight?"

"Spencer wants to go back to the drive-in."

Alarms clanged in my head. "Just you two? Is that safe?"

Pablo flicked his ash. "We saw four or five cars with two guys sitting in the front seat when we got your food. So, Spencer said, 'Why can't we do the same?'"

I cocked a brow. "Yeah, but they were watching the movie."

He chuckled and crossed his arms. "True. I'm sure we'll watch some of it."

I joined his laughter. "I have no idea what that movie was about."

"Neither do I."

Spencer drove up, and Ava jumped out of her door, wearing a short, tight mini dress with go-go boots and red tights. "I was looking forward to helping you dress in the back seat like last night."

A couple of teenage girls walked by, looking at me and Ava, whispering. After they passed, they looked back at me and smiled.

"They think you're a hunk, Tracy. Now you have a choice—either of them or me." She struck a sexy pose with her hand on one hip.

"No contest." I held out my hand. "Ready?"

"Always ready for you. Toodles, boys."

A local band called the Spidels was playing on a small stage at one end of the room. Spencer's class had hired them for last year's prom.

They sounded pretty good playing Rolling Stones songs, despite the poor acoustics in the Canteen. Ava and I walked across the parquet floor, watching ourselves in the wall of mirrors, avoiding the few fluorescent light pools from the suspended ceiling above us.

"Darn," I said in mock disappointment. "We must've been wrong about the dance contest."

"Guess so. Just can't believe what you hear on the radio nowadays." She put her hands flat against my chest. "You know, I can still feel your nipples." She rubbed her fingertips in circles. "Right there and there."

I tried not to flinch as she stroked them, but my nerves tingled and I squirmed. "You are so naughty. Do you plan to do that all night?"

We both saw Mr. Kelsey shine his famous flashlight on the couple next to us. He was a tall, broad-shouldered man with a square face and short, curly hair.

"A little too much, guys," he said in a friendly voice. "Don't make me send you home."

"Sorry," said the boy as he and his girl separated a few inches.

"No problem. Enjoy the music." He walked away.

Ava lay her face against my chest and pushed her tongue against my now-erect nipple.

I tried to back away. "Please don't get lipstick on my shirt."

"Whoops. Too late." She laughed.

"Did you?"

"No. But maybe we should avoid the light." She laughed some more.

We danced fast and slow, enjoying holding each other when we could. We stole a few kisses. She pressed against my crotch, and I rubbed my hand across her breasts, never attracting Kelsey's flashlight.

"I love dancing with you," I said.

"So do I, but I want more." She cupped my breast. "I think I love you."

My legs suddenly wobbled. "I love you too." All I could see were her plump pink lips. I bent down to kiss them.

Her fingers touched my mouth at the last second. "Kelsey's close," she whispered. "We have to wait."

"I don't want to, Ava." My heart hammered my chest. "Maybe we can find a motel."

She pressed her face against my chest. "I'd love to shower with you."

Kelsey cleared his throat, and Ava jerked her head back.

"Want something to drink?" I asked.

"Sure."

We walked to the back where a table sat in front of two ice chests full of pop. I ordered two Big Reds and had just turned around from the table when someone bumped into me.

"Sorry," said Mary Ford, a girl from our school, wearing a mini striped tent dress with orange hose. She was the only freshman on our basketball team.

"Not a problem," I said, keeping my face turned away, feeling my stomach twist and roll.

"Ava? Is that you?" asked Mary.

"Yes. Hi, Mary," said Ava, taking the bottle from me. "Are you here with your brother?" She tried to turn Mary toward her and away from me, but the girl stood like a statue, staring at me, squinting her eyes before they opened wide. My stomach plummeted.

"Tracy? No way! Is that you?"

My chest tightened. "Lower your voice, Mary," I pleaded, glancing around the crowd to see if anyone had turned our way.

"Can you keep a secret?" asked Ava, putting her arm around Mary's shoulders. "Please?"

"Sure. But why —"

"Ava. Your dad." My gaze had been pulled toward the front of the room by someone pushing through couples on the dance floor, his chest pushed out and face contorted in anger.

Ava saw him, her eyes bulging. "Go," she hissed, pushing Mary toward me. "Leave. Now."

"Ava!" growled Mr. Blunt. "Where's Tracy?"

I grabbed Mary's hand and led her to the other side of the room.

"What's going on?" Mary asked.

"Just dance with me." I held her waist and her hand and circled farther away from the shouting.

"Where is she?" screamed Mr. Blunt.

"Tracy's not here. Spencer had to drop off his friend." Her voice shrilled across the room. Ava's eyes bulged as her father stomped toward her. "He'll be back in a few —"

"Liar! The Canteen doesn't hold dance contests!"

The band stopped playing.

"Sir," said Mr. Kelsey, approaching them both. "You'll have to leave."

Couples moved away from the shouting.

"My daughter was here with another girl," barked Mr. Blunt. "They were dancing together. How can you allow that?"

"I don't. Two girls were not dancing here tonight. Please leave. You're ruining the evening for everyone else."

I almost broke away from Mary and confronted the bastard. If I were a real guy, wouldn't I do that for my girlfriend? But I stopped. If I blew my cover, how could she convince him that Spencer brought her there?

The shouts faded as I stood holding Mary. We were alone on the floor. I thought I saw Ava look back just before her father pulled her through the door. I couldn't move or breathe. My chest felt cold and empty.

Quietly, Mary said, "Do you want to sit down?"

The band started playing again and couples slowly gathered on the floor around us until I couldn't see the front door. I remember thinking she might come back. That maybe she'd convince her father Spencer was on his way back to pick her up.

Tears trickled down the side of my face and my heart ached. My limbs were dead weights. We had just confessed our love and now . . . what? Nothing? How could we ever be together again?

Mary hugged me. "I'm so sorry."

I bowed my head and wrapped my arms around her back, my tears dripping onto her hair.

"You dressed like this so you could be with Ava?" asked Mary.

I sighed. "Yes. She was supposed to be here with Spencer." I held her back a little and peered into her eyes. "Mary . . ."

"I won't tell anyone. You must love her a lot to go to all this trouble just to dance with her." She looked me up and down then whispered. "Your disguise is perfect. I would never have guessed it was you except for the mole."

"Mole?"

She beamed. "Yes." She touched the left side of my chin. "You have this cute little mole right there. Well, I think it's cute." She looked at my face and wiped tears off my cheeks. "Boys aren't supposed to cry, right?"

"I can't remember the last time I cried." I rubbed my eyes and took a few deep breaths. "I think if you hadn't bumped into me, Mr. Blunt would've grabbed both of us. Thank you."

"For being a klutz?" She grabbed my hands and squeezed. "Sure, any time. I'm not a star athlete like you."

"You'll get better. You've already improved a lot since the season started. Well, I should . . ."

She moved closer and whispered. "I think you look great as a boy. I mean you look great as a girl, but . . ." She stared at my lips. "Did you kiss her? I'm sorry. That's personal." She looked down then flashed her eyes back up to mine. "When did you know?"

"Know what?"

"That you liked her?" Mary's eyes widened as she backed away from me, looking to my left where Kelsey had appeared. "Sorry. Was I too close?"

"No," said Mr. Kelsey. "You were fine." He looked at me closely. "Are you Tracy? You were dancing with that girl earlier this evening. The one with the crazy dad."

I swallowed. "He is crazy. We go to the same school. So does Mary." I nodded toward her.

She smiled at him, still holding me.

I was lucky the name Tracy was used for boys as well as girls.

He squinted and tilted his head to each side, trying to see through me. "What was all that about?"

I couldn't tell if he knew I was a girl or whether he couldn't convince himself. After all, how could I be dancing with another girl who knew me? Surely there couldn't be three lesbians there that night.

But there were. I realized then that Mary was just beginning to wonder about herself.

"It's a long story," I said. "I better be going."

Mary's forehead crumpled into wrinkles.

"Thanks for dancing with me, Mary. I'll see you Monday." I nodded at Mr. Kelsey then took a step toward the exit.

Mary clutched my hand then pecked my cheek. "Things will work out. You'll see."

"I hope so." I released her hands and trudged to my car, now isolated like I was. Under a wiper blade I found a scribbled note.

Never go near my daughter again!

So much for keeping my cover. I should have followed them outside and . . . what? Fought him? Told him he shouldn't stand in the way of our relationship? I'd just have been a freak to him. A boy wannabe, luring his daughter with my brother to sin.

At least by staying inside, he wouldn't know about my disguise. Unless Ava told him.

During the drive to Jim's, I thought about that word—disguise. I knew I'd feel weird taking it off and dressing as a girl. And all next week at school?

When would I wear it again? If not for Ava, why? My body felt broken into pieces like a puzzle dumped on a table. How could I put it together without knowing what the picture showed?

I went to Jim's at ten o'clock and slid into a booth where I ordered coffee and a slice of chocolate meringue pie. Ava and I should have been squeezed together on this seat, laughing and flirting as we waited for the boys.

After a few minutes, I nibbled the pie and drank a sip, but neither helped calm the storm in my stomach, so I smoked a cigarette.

I was sure I'd never see Ava again.

Unless she ran away.

If that happened, I would run with her.

But I was afraid she'd confess everything to her father who would then tell the school and my parents. I'd seen her crack up before during a game when she was swarmed by defenders as she tried to pass me the ball. She rotated on her pivot foot but couldn't escape the arms and hands mirroring everything she did. Then she screamed and collapsed onto the floor, crying.

Of course, boys in the bleachers laughed. I flipped them off as I ran to help Ava. I was ejected, and we had to forfeit the game. Typical male justice.

But I couldn't flip off Ava's parents. They controlled what would happen next to me. Everything Ava and I had gained was fake. Just like my supposed freedom.

I noticed two girls smiling at me and whispering from another booth. I thought, *Shit, they know I'm a girl. What else can go wrong tonight?* I smiled at them and nodded then sipped more coffee.

A few minutes later, they walked by and dropped a folded piece of paper on my table. I waited a few seconds before opening it to reveal their names and phone numbers. At the cashier desk, one looked back at me and held her thumb to her ear and pinkie to her mouth. "Call me," she mouthed. They both giggled their way out the door.

How easy it would be for a real guy to pick them up, which made my time with Ava all the harder to bear. Would there ever be a time when girls could pick up girls in a restaurant without worry?

I looked around and saw no girls or women sitting by themselves, yet I saw several males on their own. As a guy, I could get away with being alone in public. As a girl, not so much, especially at eleven o'clock on a Saturday night.

Those girls were "looking for trouble," and if they'd been assaulted, many would've blamed them. But I could come and go as I pleased without worry, unless I was recognized or my disguise was discovered.

Come and go, maybe, but not pick them up.

Girls were trapped no matter what they did because they didn't define the rules. That had to change.

It was 11:15. Something must've happened to Spencer and Pablo. What else could go wrong that night? I needed to leave.

During the drive, my chest felt heavier and heavier. Something had happened. There was no other explanation. About fifteen minutes later, I turned off Jackson-Keller onto my street and saw Spencer's car along the curb at the intersection of Shallimar. My mouth filled with a bitter taste, but I couldn't swallow.

I drove over and found him sitting on his hood, smoking a cigarette.

I rolled down my window and saw his half-opened eyes. A chill shook my insides. "Where's Pablo?"

"I dropped him off," he slurred. "What about Ava?"

I turned off the engine and opened my door. "Her dad took her from Teen Canteen."

He flicked his butt onto the street, hopped off his car then wobbled. "Whoa." He steadied himself against the fender. "So we both got busted." He pulled a paper from his pocket. "Did you get one of these?"

"What is it?"

"A ticket for disorderly conduct, which is cop code for humping Pablo." He pulled a pint bottle from his jacket, unscrewed the lid, tilted his head back, and poured the contents into his mouth. Maybe two drops landed on his tongue. "I guess I'm done." He threw the bottle across the road toward the culvert while screaming, "Shit!"

I ran to him. "Hey, not so loud. We don't need a cop out here. Let's get home."

He grabbed me and buried his face into my neck. "I'm done, Tracy. Totally done. Neither of us can do anything right. Pablo's gone. Ava's gone. Fuck it!"

I felt dizzy with the pain of realization. The world had fooled us into thinking we could love and be loved, only to slap us down when we got close. "We'll talk about it at home. You just have to drive half a block." I helped him back to the driver's seat. "Go slow and follow me."

If I could've thought of any other place to go, I would have gunned my car and headed for it. But all I had was a big, empty house where I had to hide who I was. I pulled into the driveway. He hit the curb trying to park in front of our house. I walked across the grass and helped him out of the car.

"Mom will see you," he slurred as we walked up the steps.

"Doesn't matter anymore." We staggered toward our front door. As soon as I inserted my key into the lock, Mom pulled the door open.

"Spencer?" Her voice quavered with fear and love. She reached out to her son with shaking hands. "Are you drunk?"

"Smashed." He stumbled toward the stairs, grabbed the handrail, and climbed a few steps.

Mom turned from him to me and covered her mouth with her hand. "Tracy?"

"Not tonight, Mom. We'll talk tomorrow. Please."

"Mr. Blunt called."

Of course, he did. "Tomorrow."

Spencer had slipped on a step. I rushed to help him up.

In his room, I removed his jacket. "Sit on your bed."

He collapsed and lay on his back. I removed his shoes and socks. "Scoot back to the headboard." As he crawled toward me, I propped up pillows for his head.

After some grunting, he collapsed and stared at the ceiling.

"Tell me what happened."

"We were in the back seat when a flashlight beamed onto us. He was an off-duty cop watching the movie with his wife. He threatened to arrest us and take us to the station. We pleaded. He called us queers and fags and gave us tickets for disorderly conduct so we'd have to go to a judge and at least pay a fine." He covered his face and cried. "Mom and Dad are going to find out."

I put my arm around his shoulders and leaned my face against his head as he sobbed.

He sniffed. "And Mom saw your clothes. We're done."

A cold emptiness spread in my stomach as tears welled in my eyes. But every beat of my heart sent sparks of heat into my chest until a rush of anger surged into my neck and head. I would not grovel or cower or plead for forgiveness. I squeezed my brother, hoping to push some strength into him.

"We're done hiding."

CHAPTER 8
TALES OF TESSA

I slept in my clothes that night. At the time I didn't know why, but now I think I was afraid if I took them off, I would feel like a coward, that the past week would've been nothing more than a phase—a mistake.

But I had come out to myself, Spencer, Pablo, and Ava. Even to Mary.

I'd had sex with a girl and loved it.

Before Mr. Blunt crashed the dance, both Ava and I had felt confident, happy, and in control.

Some would say I felt these emotions because of my disguise, and that the whole situation was fake.

But what made it fake? Wearing pants and no makeup and hiding my breasts? Who had decided that girls couldn't dress like that? Why wasn't wearing a dress and a bust-enhancing bra a disguise?

Taking off my pants and wearing a dress that morning for church would've seemed so dishonest. A capitulation.

I walked outside to fetch our Sunday paper, resisting the urge to hurry. I scanned my block, looking for anyone who might see me. And though my heart pounded, pushing me to return inside, I stood with hands on hips, ready to wave if I saw anyone.

But the yards were empty. I picked up the paper and went to the kitchen to make coffee in our new electric percolator. Mom liked hers black with sugar. I liked cream. I had both cups ready when she made her entrance.

She stood in the doorway with her hand shaking at her throat, eyes fixed on my outfit.

I fought the quiver in my stomach as I carried the cups to the table. "Maybe we should sit down."

"Yes," she said, her voice quavering. "This morning I wondered if I had actually seen those clothes on you last night." She sat down and took a sip of coffee. "Did you sleep in them?"

"I crashed in Spencer's room until he woke me up with his snoring. When I went to my room about two, I couldn't make myself take them off." I sipped my coffee, hiding my face, nervous about what she'd think.

"Because you were too tired?"

"No." I set my cup on the table. "I didn't want to."

She pointed to a spot chest-high on my shirt. "Is that lipstick?"

I tried not to smile, but failed. "Ava's. She tripped over my feet and . . ."

Mom fixed her eyes on mine, her brows raised. "Tripped?"

I lowered my eyes. "No. Do you want me to tell you the truth . . ." I looked at her. "Even if . . ."

She nodded. "Even if."

"Okay. She didn't trip. We were dancing, and she was —"

"I can figure out the rest." She set her cup on the table. "So your dates with Pablo were actually with her, and Spencer's dates with Ava were actually with Pablo?"

"Yes. I'm sorry we lied to you, but we couldn't figure out another way to be with . . . our friends." I couldn't believe she wasn't angry. I wasn't expecting a rage like Dad's, but her calm was unexpected.

"And that's why you wore those clothes?" she asked.

"One of the reasons."

"One?" Her lips trembled.

My heart galloped inside my chest. "The first reason, but not the only."

She lifted her cup to her mouth like a shield. "What's the other?"

"They make me feel . . . happy, confident. It's hard to explain. Like I've always felt nervous dancing, but last night, I didn't. We had a blast. Until . . ."

"Mr. Blunt barged in."

My gut hardened. The hurt and anger and helplessness of last night hit me again. "What did he tell you?"

She pushed stray hairs from her forehead. "Ralph wouldn't stop screaming at me. He accused you of seducing his daughter and demanded I keep you away from her."

My mind replayed the terrified look on Ava's face when she saw him pushing through the crowd. "How did he know we were there?"

"When he came back from playing poker, his wife told him Spencer and Ava had entered a dance contest at Teen Canteen. He called a friend whose kids go there all the time. The Canteen does band contests only."

If we'd left out the *contest* and said they'd wanted to dance, maybe he wouldn't have come. My anger and regret scalded my insides. "Did he say anything about my clothes?"

"No."

"What else?"

She took a deep breath and reached for my hand. "He's pulling Ava out of Adler. You'll never see her again." She squeezed then let go.

My muscles tensed and my breathing stopped.

"I'm sorry, Tracy," Mom said. She took a sip. "What will you do now?"

The phone rang. I shot out of my chair and grabbed the handset from the wall. "Hello?"

"Tracy, I only have a minute," Ava said, her voice scratchy and weak.

I looked at Mom and mouthed Ava's name. My pulse raced, throbbing in my neck. I'd thought I'd never hear her voice again.

Ava sniffed. "They screamed at me all night. They're sending me to Incarnate Word High School and to a psychiatrist. I'm grounded forever."

I clenched my fist. "What can I do?"

Pleading, she said, "Stay away. They almost kicked me out on the street."

I turned from Mom and looked outside. "I would take care of you. We could —"

"No we can't," she hissed. "I'm not going to be a homeless lesbian."

I felt a hot knife slice through my skin. "They're going to make you straight?"

She panted several times before answering, "Maybe."

"Is that what you want?"

"No," she snapped. "I love the situation I'm in." She punched her words with sarcasm. "What about you? My dad says Art will do the same to you. Or worse."

I turned back around and looked at my mother. "Well, he can try, but he's not here. I'm talking to my mom right now."

"Does she know what we did?"

I looked at my mother's red, teary eyes. "Yes."

"And?"

"We're still talking and drinking coffee."

Her breath hitched. "Lucky you." She sniffed and whimpered. "I've got to go."

I coughed, trying to hold the wail inside. *Please, don't hang up on me.* "I'll never see another Lifesaver without thinking of you."

"Don't," she begged then cleared her throat. "I have to forget. So do you."

"Ava, wait. I'll never forget. If there's ever a time you want to see me, just call or send a message through someone. I'll come get you. I promise."

She sobbed. "Goodbye, Tracy."

I clenched my jaw and refused to cry but a few tears leaked onto my cheeks. My throat exploded in pain as I turned around to hang up the phone. My hands shook as I grabbed the counter, trying to keep from collapsing. Then I felt my mother's hands on my shoulders.

"Tracy? I know you hurt now, but in the long run . . ."

I whipped around and crushed the tears in my eyes with my fists. "In the long run, it will still hurt because of the Blunts and Dad and millions more like them who can't accept that a girl can love a girl." My voice rumbled out of my chest. "And *you* have to decide which side you're on because *both* of your kids are gay."

She staggered back a step.

"We didn't try to be. It sure would be easier for us if we weren't." I snapped. "But that's the fucking truth. Will you kick us out? Send us to a shrink? We're still your kids. Spencer's no different today than he was a week ago except he's admitted who he is, and he's scared. You can help him or hurt him. Your choice." I didn't bother to staunch my tears or wipe my face. My rage was too great.

Mom looked to the ceiling as tears filled her eyes. "I don't want to hurt either of you, but I don't want *you* to be hurt. The world can be a horribly cruel place." She wiped her eyes. "I know because I've been there." She walked back to the table and sat down.

You've been there? What the hell?

"Please, come sit. I don't want you looming over me."

I dropped into a chair, my nerves quivering. What was I going to hear?

Mom took some deep breaths. "When I was eight and my sisters were ten and six, my mother took us to an orphanage where we stayed for over a year while she found another husband."

I felt like someone had elbowed me in the gut. "You've never told us this."

"Because I was ashamed. My sisters and I had to live in an orphanage—an *orphanage*, Tracy, not knowing whether our mother would return."

"Grandpa is not your father?"

"No, but he should have been. My actual father lost his land and all his money in 1936 and then left us. We never heard from him again. Mother got a divorce and worked as a secretary, but she couldn't afford us and what she'd have to buy to catch a man. She told us all before she left the most important thing for us to do in our lives was to find a good husband. She'd failed the first time, but she wouldn't make the same mistake twice. She found Father in three months and waited until they were married before telling him about her daughters. After fourteen months and eleven days, they took us to his home. And then when it came time, my sisters and I found good husbands. We all have families and good houses and some security."

"I'm sure that was difficult for you, Mom, but what does that have to do with —"

"Because I had a good friend in the orphanage. A girl named Tessa, two years older than me. If it weren't for her, I probably would have . . . I don't know. I was so depressed." She swallowed and shook her head slowly. "I hated that orphanage. But Tessa and I made up games and stories and snuck outside at night." She smiled as she looked out the window. "She was such a trouble-maker. One night we were lying in the grass, looking for shooting stars, and she kissed me square on my lips. I laughed and said, 'What the hell was that, Tessa?' 'A kiss,' she said. 'Cause we're friends. Did you like it?'

"I laughed and pointed to the sky. 'There goes a star.'" Mom wiped an eye and sighed, "That happened a few times."

My head spun as my stomach flipped. "How many is a *few*?"

"Do you want a specific number? I was eight and didn't know any better. But my older sister, Billie, did. She saw it happen once and told me that kissing Tessa would keep us all in that orphanage forever. So I'd better stop it. When Mother and Father came to take us away, Tessa ran toward me, crying, 'Aren't you going to say good-bye?'"

Mom swallowed and breathed heavily, her eyes shiny. "I knew she would grab me and try to kiss me, so I held out my hand and kept my face strong and firm while I shook her hand. 'Thanks for being my friend, Tessa. I hope you get adopted soon.' I turned around and grabbed Billie's hand as we headed toward Father's car."

The lines in Mom's forehead and around her eyes seemed to deepen as I watched her. Warmth grew inside me. Mom had felt the same kind of loss. I reached for her hand. "What happened to Tessa?"

"I don't know." She sipped the last of her coffee. "I glanced back as we left and saw her flat on the ground. I'm sure she was crying."

"Why are you telling me this?"

"Because my whole life could have been ruined if I'd grabbed Tessa or, God forbid, kissed her."

"You wanted to?"

"More than anything, but I forced myself to be strong." She swallowed and fixed her eyes on mine. "Sometimes you have to resist temptation now for something better. Any relationship with Ava will cause you both problems for the rest of your lives."

"I'm just supposed to forget her? I can't change being gay, Mom. Didn't you miss Tessa?"

She tightened her lips and blinked rapidly. Then sighed. "Terribly."

"Was there anyone else like Tessa later in your life?"

She pulled her hand from mine. "I never kissed another girl, if that's what you're asking."

"Did you ever think about it?"

Her eyes flinched before she blinked. "No."

We both heard Spencer bounding down the stairs and turned toward the open doorway, waiting for him to appear.

His hair was a mess and his shirt unbuttoned, but he sported a huge smile on his face. "I called Pablo. His cousin knows a lawyer who will help us for free. I'm going to pick him up."

He ran toward the front door.

Mom stood. "Spencer?" But he was already gone. She turned toward me. "Why does he want a lawyer?"

I made a snap decision to lie for him. If Spencer wanted her to know, he could tell her. "He got a phony speeding ticket last night from an off-duty cop."

"Why was it phony?"

"I don't know. But the lawyer will fix it, so everything's cool." I wrapped my arms around her. "Thanks for telling me about Tessa. And for not kicking Spencer and me out."

She cleared her throat and hugged me back. "I'm still deciding." She pushed my hair back and smiled at me. "You've always been ornery, so strong-willed. But so kind to Spencer."

"And a trouble-maker, like Tessa. Do I remind you of her?"

She coughed and swallowed, her eyes blinking rapidly to keep tears from falling. "Some."

Maybe that was why Mom had always been more tolerant of me than Dad and why she continued to do so after that day of revelations.

"What will you do now?" she asked.

"I don't know. What do you think?" I winked. "Look for a hand-some pilot?"

She dropped her hands. "There are worse things in life."

"I'm sure there are, but I'd like to try the top of my list first."

"He's been good to me. And to both of you. Don't forget that."

I rolled my eyes. "Maybe in some distant past, Mom. The holidays were pretty much hell for Spencer and me. He won't take this news well. You know that. He will shit a brick."

"Language, Tracy. Please." She took her cup to the sink. "I assume you won't be going to church with me."

"Not today. I need to lift weights."

She turned and almost staggered against the counter. "Whatever for?"

"To build up my muscles, which I'll need to play against the boys this weekend."

She slumped slightly and widened her eyes. "Why would you play against boys?"

I put my cup in the sink. "No Ava, no girls team. I can play at least as well as half our boys' team. I'll talk to the coach tomorrow." I left the kitchen.

Later that night I lay in my bed, thinking about the nest day at school. I would be the gay girl who forced Ava out and killed the Lady Wolves. Was I ready for the fallout?

And I'd have to wear dresses again. I hadn't shaved or plucked or worn makeup for five days. Would I start now?

I'd never enjoyed being glamorous, or trying to be. Why were girls required to paint themselves? The last time I'd worked selling shoes, my supervisor had to tell me to put on lipstick. What would she say if she saw me now? Would I care?

I stood and removed my manguise as I watched myself in the mirror. The body I saw was long and muscular, pale with red bands around my chest from the spandex and several moles randomly scattered from my neck to just beneath my waist. I touched the one on my chin, the "cute" one, according to Mary. My arms were too long, which was great for basketball and even piano, but hardly feminine.

I had no curves or sexy bulges. I had always been disappointed with my body because it wasn't pretty or alluring. Yet I turned to jelly when I saw a girl who was, like Ava. And she'd done the same when I lay before her. She'd called me "beautiful."

Of course, she was horny at the time. She certainly wouldn't pick me out from a lineup of girls to neck with.

But then, what were either of our options? How many lesbians did we know? We had sensed what the other was and taken our chances.

And now, neither of us was going to leave the orphanage and find a good husband unless we hid who we were and played by *the rules*.

Was my mother gay and, like so many other women, had suppressed her feelings because that world was too bleak, too frightening to consider, especially in the thirties? She'd told me her story in hopes I would stand strong against temptation, like she had. All I had to do was turn around and walk away.

But she'd revealed an opposite message—she'd chosen safety over love, and she still pined for Tessa. She'd seen me ache and cry for Ava, and her old wound had split open.

In trying to help me deny who I was, she'd helped me affirm the same.

I stood before my mirror and gazed at Tracy Franks in the flesh.

Somewhere between girl and boy.

Hairy and unpainted.

Strong and gay.

Ready to tell anyone who cared.

And fight the consequences.

CHAPTER 9
TEN BUCKS TO PLAY

My boy's penny loafers clopped up the school's driveway toward the rock wall. I wore my bomber jacket over a short dress and black tights and carried my gym clothes, sweats, and two books in my bag. A few kids glanced over as I sat down and whispered to each other. My stomach felt fluttery and empty. I crossed my legs and shook my foot. Shit would hit the fan for sure. And soon.

After five minutes, I watched Spencer walk toward me with a half smile. We weren't sure whether everyone would assume he and Pablo were a number or just playing along with my ploy to date Ava. Spence hadn't told me what he would say when asked, but I assumed he'd claim he was just helping me. He planned to go to Pablo's house for lunch, regardless.

"The pariah herself," he said, standing over me.

I waved at Judy, who flashed a hard stare before disappearing into the high school building. "I keep watching for Ava." I looked up to him, stifling the hitch in my chest. "Every place on this campus reminds me of a time . . ."

Spencer sat down and draped his arm across my shoulders. "Don't be such a drag."

I leaned into him and pouted. "But the in-crowd hates me."

He play-punched my shoulder. "Just hang tough."

"Get it together?"

He nodded and smiled. "Soon you'll be in fat city again."

"Yup. Rockin' out and having a gay old time."

Our eyes locked, and he grinned. "That's so gay."

"Yes, we are." I wrapped my arms around his neck and hugged his head.

"Not so loud," he said.

"Hey, no PDA on campus," joked Mary from behind us. She plopped down beside me.

"Maybe you shouldn't be seen with me," I said.

Spencer stood up. "I need to cram for a test, so later."

"Last chance to stay cool, Mary," I said, watching my brother head to his locker.

With a firmness I didn't expect, she said, "I'll take my chances."

"What's the word?"

She looked at me with her big, hazel eyes which she'd lined heavily. "Ava's parents pulled her out because you're gay and harassed her. Plus, you killed the team because you couldn't control yourself. Other than that, not much. Have you heard from her?"

Even though I had expected these conclusions, hearing them out loud slapped me hard. "She called yesterday. They almost kicked her out, but instead, they're sending her to an all-girls Catholic school. Which makes perfect sense to someone, but not to me."

With just a hint of sarcasm, she replied, "They'll teach her to fear God and the nuns. Besides, the girls have parties with the St. Anthony boys. She'll be straight in no time."

I coughed a laugh and glanced at her. Some boys teased her for being "chunky," but she had a lot of spunk and wasn't afraid to make space on the court to grab rebounds. She was also a cheerleader, as were all the other Lady Wolves except me. Girls' games were always before the guys', so the squad could change uniforms and grab their pom poms before the boys finished warming up. It was the same at every school we played.

"Do you miss her?" she asked.

I felt a chill. "I keep expecting her to come around a corner or sneak up on me."

"I'm sorry. I guess you won't be going to the tournament this weekend."

"I plan to."

"Just to watch?"

"No, to play on the boys' team." The first bell rang, and I stood.

She leaped up and scrunched her forehead. "Will they let you?"

"I'm pretty sure they'll give me a chance. Well, it's time to run the gauntlet, so to speak."

"Just follow me." She clasped her book to her chest and stomped off.

I walked in her wake as she cleared a path through the first floor then up the stairs toward my locker outside the English classroom. As I passed the principal's office, I heard Mr. Worth call my name.

I stopped in his doorway, my heart fluttering in anticipation of a meeting I knew would happen. Mary turned and frowned.

"Thanks, Mary," I said. "Later." I entered his small, dark office— curtains covering each bay window—and found him sitting behind his desk. His eyes twinkled through his horn-rimmed glasses—a very nice man who always wore a suit and tie. Every student called him "Coach" because that's what he was at previous schools before his brother asked him to open the Adler High School years ago. He wasn't a discipline freak. He liked kids, and we liked him.

"Tracy, would you mind closing the door?"

"Sure," I said. I pushed the door closed as Charles and his entourage walked by, snickering. "Shall I sit?" He'd always been friendly with me, but still I felt nervous.

"Yes, please." He leaned forward, placing his crossed arms on the glass covering his solid oak desk. He smiled. "I hear you had a tough weekend."

"It was great until Mr. Blunt screamed at Ava. I'm sure he called you."

"Yes, he did. More than once." His smile still stretched ever so slightly.

I smiled back. "Sounds like you had a tough weekend too."

He chuckled. "It wasn't my best. He blamed everything on you and recommended I expel you and your brother."

My heart skipped a few beats. I knew this was coming, but hearing it out loud was different than thinking the words in my head. I smiled like he'd told a joke. "Spencer too?"

"Yes, because he was the one who actually picked up Ava. He was part of the homosexual plan."

I raised my brows and tried not to snicker. "Homo . . ."

Coach removed his glasses and wiped them with a handkerchief as his eyes twinkled at me. I realized he wasn't angry. More bemused, like he was waiting to tell me the punch line.

"Yup, the homosexual plan. That's what he called it. He said you were trying to turn his daughter into a lesbian."

I blinked and tried to find my voice. "Turn her into one?"

"Of course, the previous weekend he called me and asked if I'd noticed Ava acting gay and wanted me to keep an eye on her this past week. He told me she forced you to kiss her at your party. So last weekend she was the predator and you were the victim. This weekend your roles reversed." He put his glasses on and pushed back in his chair. "I want to hear your side of the story."

I'd decided I wouldn't deny my sexuality to anyone. But this was the first test of my resolve. My heart skipped a few beats as I leaned forward. "Both Ava and I are gay. We knew we couldn't be together unless Spencer pretended to be her boyfriend."

He bent forward and tightened his eyes. "You *both* are gay? Are you sure?"

I nodded and tried to keep a straight face. "Totally sure. We've kissed . . . Do you want details?"

He blew out a breath. "No." He tapped his desk with fingers from both hands as he frowned at me. "What am I going to do with you?"

All the ideas I had practiced on the way to school that morning lined up on my tongue. "Gays can't attend Adler? Is that written in the Student Handbook? I looked through all the policies last night and found nothing about sexual identity. Neither of us has been accused of inappropriate behavior on campus. Neither of us was arrested for illegal behavior off campus. So what would be the grounds for expulsion?"

Coach frowned and steepled his fingers just below his chin. He cleared his throat. "There is a clause in the handbook which states that whenever the administration believes a student's presence on campus is not in the best interest of the school or the student —"

"Yes, but the publicity of such a move would be devastating."

He pulled on his ear. "Publicity?"

"Certainly." I tried to sound entirely self-assured even as my nerves began to scream. "Spencer and I would go to the newspapers with the story that two excellent students with A averages, both highly respected and well-known pianists in the city, were expelled simply because I'm gay. Spencer's class is the largest in school at twenty-five. My class is sixteen. Your overall enrollment has declined in the past few years. Can you afford to expel two students?"

"Two who cost the school one student already. Tracy, I like you and Spencer. I want nothing but good for you both, but what do I say to parents who worry about their kiddos being . . . influenced by you?"

I rolled my eyes. "I'm not contagious."

"No, but you're very outspoken. Your opinions about the war and civil rights and all kinds of other issues are well known."

"I have no plans to advertise my sexual identity."

Coach seemed surprised. "Really? What if someone asks whether you're gay?"

"I'll say yes, but nothing more. It's not like a club you can join. You're either gay or not. My telling them the truth won't make them gay."

He tightened his jaw and looked hard at me. I could sense the gears turning in his head as I smiled back at him, my stomach twisting and turning.

He folded his handkerchief. "You would really go to the papers and expose yourself and your parents to that humiliation?"

That word stung. My voice turned to ice. "I'm not ashamed of being gay."

Coach squirmed in his chair. "But your parents, Tracy. I can't believe Art is okay with this."

"He's out of town. Mom knows. She'd rather me not be gay, but what can she do? Kick me out of the house like the Blunts threatened to do to Ava? Do you honestly think that would make me want to have sex with boys? What threat would it take to make you want sex with men? Would anything work short of holding a gun to your head?"

He steepled his hands and worked his mouth, like he was trying to get something out of his teeth with his tongue.

"Coach, you said you liked Spencer and me. We haven't changed."

"I know that, and my attitude toward you and your brother won't either. But I know I'll get flak for letting you both stay in Adler."

I held out my hands. "You'll get flak either way. Do you think every parent or student would support you expelling us? I know that's not true, and you do too. Flak will come no matter what you do." I flashed my brows and crossed my legs. "The real question is which side of history do you want to be on? Some parents are scared of changes, but lots want a different life for their kids than they had. You know several girls at this school who want to be doctors and scientists, even engineers. That's a big change that you and this school support. Women's rights and opportunities are growing, and there's nothing anyone can do to stop them. You've had two daughters graduate from here, Coach. Surely you want them to have more options than Mrs. Worth had at their age. Right?"

He lowered his chin and looked over the top of his glasses at me. "That is correct, but I sense you are leading us toward a different topic."

I smiled and leaned forward. "Exactly. You've always been great at reading your students. In a few years time, do you think girls will still be limited to half-court basketball?"

He took a deep breath and sat straighter. "Probably not, especially if there are more girls like you playing. I was looking forward to watching you this weekend."

I locked my eyes on his as my limbs tingled. "I can still play. Talk to Coach Wynn and ask him to let me practice with the boys this week. If he thinks I can help his team, then he can give me some minutes during the tournament."

Coach's mouth dropped open. "Are you serious?"

"Very. I play one-on-one with boys in PE. And sometimes three-on-three. I score on them all the time." I could not stand the idea of retreating to being a girl on the sidelines after I'd felt so much confidence as a boy. I wanted a chance to beat guys at their own game.

"Tracy," Coach said, "I've been to your practices and to Coach Wynn's. There's no comparison. He runs full-court presses and fast breaks every chance he gets. You'll get hurt and wish you'd never asked me."

"Ten dollars says I won't." I opened my bag and pulled a ten dollar bill from my wallet.

He frowned. "Does Art give you that kind of money to throw around?"

"Nope. I have a job and my own bank account, thank you very much." I wiggled the bill and tilted my head. "Ten bucks?"

He grinned. "Betting is not allowed on campus."

I stood, grinned back, and put the bill on his desk. "Then you can keep this, so I don't make any bets I shouldn't. I'll pick it up on Friday—with interest."

"Or not." He slid the bill into his drawer. "So, to sum up, I will talk to Coach Wynn this morning and ask him to give you a chance at practice. You will not find a replacement for Ava among the girls at this school or encourage others to claim they're gay. Or advocate for gay rights on campus."

Even Coach thought being gay was a disease or at least a social anomaly that should be isolated, at best. But I had no choice. "I'm assuming the anti-bullying rules still apply to everyone?"

"Certainly. No one can bully you for being gay, but I think some of the boys will give you a hard time at practice."

"If they grab me, I'll rack them. You think girls never throw elbows?"

He smiled. "I've seen you throw a few during your games."

"Will you be at the tournament?"

"Wouldn't miss it." He pulled out an admission slip pad and started writing. "You'll need this."

A surge of energy filled my body. He agreed! "Everyone in high school already knows where I've been for the past ten minutes."

He signed his name and handed me the paper. "True. But rules are rules. You should consider being a lawyer, Tracy." His eyes twinkled at me.

"Thank you, Coach. It's been a pleasure." I picked up my bag and opened his door.

"Just leave it open."

I walked down the hall to my English class, knocked gently then pulled the door open to see every face looking at me. Maybe they expected me to be in tears or not appear at all because every mouth dropped open when I said, "Hey, guys. Sorry to be so late, but Coach and I were having such a good time talking, we lost track of time." I walked to an empty seat.

During my free period, I found Coach Wynn in his tiny office just outside the boys' locker room surrounded by his team, laughing at something. Wynn leaned back in his chair and clasped his hands behind his crew cut, flat-topped head and smiled. "I understand you'll be joining us this afternoon," he boomed. "The boys and I look forward to it." A few of the guys chuckled. Mario coughed into his fist while saying, "Not." Charles smiled at me, smacking his Dentyne.

I smiled back. "Hey, Charles, what was the score of our last one-on-one match?"

Some of his friends looked at him with raised brows and taunted, "Tell us, Charles."

He pulled out his gum and dropped it into a trashcan. "Don't matter on this asphalt court. Let's see what happens on a real gym floor."

I fixed my eyes on his. "Yes, let's see."

"Boys," said the coach, "y'all need to leave so Tracy and I can talk for a bit." A few muttered as they walked out. He fixed his beady black eyes on me. "I've seen you play, and I know you're pretty good, but you'll have to step up your game to get through my practices."

"No problem. I want to play this weekend."

He lowered his hands and let the legs of his chair hit the concrete floor. "Play? Mr. Worth said nothing about you playing. He said you wanted to practice."

"That's true, but I think after seeing what I can contribute to your team, you'll want to let me play."

"Even if I did, why would the other coaches agree to that?"

I sat down. "They're going to object to you putting a girl on the court? They'll think you're nuts and say, 'Bring her on.' They won't object—until after our first game. Then they'll claim you snookered them."

He chuckled. "You got some cojones, Tracy, I'll give you that."

"Actually, I do." I was so tempted to pull my dildo out of my bag.

"We'll see." He chuckled. "I'm going to run my regular practice today. Not making it easier or harder. If you keep up, then fine. Any time you want out, just tell me."

"Sounds fair to me. Meet at the gym by 3:45?"

"Yeah, suited up and ready to go."

"I'll be there. Thanks." I started to leave.

"Tracy, I heard about you and Ava."

The unexpected punch had hooked my jaw. I turned and saw him standing with folded arms—stocky build, former Army Captain, tough but always fair.

"I just want to let you know that doesn't affect me at all. One of my aunts is a lesbian. I've always liked her. And I won't let the boys pick on you for that."

I breathed and smiled. "Thanks, Coach. I won't let you down."

"Actually, I hope you embarrass a few of them. Make them work harder. Some are a little too cocky."

I coughed into my fist while saying, "Charles."

"Especially him."

"I'll do my best."

After counting the seconds in my last class, I hustled to the girls' dressing room and changed into my gym clothes and sweats. The Adler School had a great science lab but no gym. The girls' team had practiced on the asphalt slab while the boys used a nearby church gym. Every one of our games was away.

I drove down McCullough a few blocks and pulled up next to Rudy, a math genius who wore thick, black glasses. He wasn't the most agile athlete, but he was determined and strong.

"Hey, Rudy," I said. "Are you ready to run behind me today?"

He just smiled, never much of a talker. He could manipulate a slide rule faster to solve equations than anyone else on campus, but he was a plodder on the court.

Inside, several boys were already shooting. Two were pushing brooms up and down the court to remove dust.

I picked a ball from the rack and dribbled a few times.

"A little bigger than you're used to?" Coach Wynn asked.

I palmed the ball.

Coach's eyes popped. "Jesus, I never noticed how big your hands are."

"Actually, I like this ball size better. Sometimes with the girls', I felt like I was dribbling with a softball."

Coach blew his whistle. "Lines!"

Everyone lined up at the end of the court. I knew this drill. Run as hard as you can to the next line, come back to the end, then out to the next line, then back, and so forth. Charles grinned at me like I was a joke. I would not let him beat me.

"Touch the line with your hand, not your foot. First one back gets to sit." He blew his whistle, and we took off, pounding the floor with our shoes, echoing like a freight train off the cinder block walls.

Mario finished first then sat. Gene barely won the next round. On the third, Charles and I hit the end line at about the same time.

"Tracy, sit!" Coach yelled.

"I beat her!" Charles bellowed.

Wynn blew the whistle, and Charles hesitated, forcing him to play catch-up for the rest of the drill.

I lifted my shirt to wipe my face and caught Gene staring. "Does my belly button look different than yours?"

He lifted his brows and smiled then walked away.

Coach Wynn's drills were intense. I knew most of them, but the execution was more urgent, and he allowed no down time. After thirty minutes, he yelled, "Water!"

We all ran to the fountain and lined up. I took one swallow and splashed water on my face. Back then, we were more concerned about getting cramps than staying hydrated.

Before my arrival that day, the team had nine players. During full-court press drills, Coach Wynn would join the offense to break the press. With me on the court, he could stay on the sidelines and yell.

Coach gave me the ball and lowered his voice. "Break the press, Tracy. They're not used to a decent dribbler."

Charles lined up as point on their diamond press, wiping the dust off the soles of his shoes as he sneered at me. I tossed the ball to Doug out of bounds and moved to get open. The point of this defense was to trap the dribbler in either corner. My job was to beat the trap on the sideline or change direction before the trap arrived.

I did both for the first five attempts to stop me. Coach Wynn was livid at his players, ridiculing their effort, but not once did he use my gender to rub failure in their faces. No, "You're letting a *girl* beat you!"

The fact was, I could dribble and I was quick, but I was tired. I needed every day before the tournament to get into playing shape.

Near the end of practice, Coach divided us into two teams to scrimmage, each pressing the other. Charles attempted a cross-over in front of me, but I poked the ball, picked it up behind him, and broke down court. I heard him gaining on me so I started my layup early, leaning forward to keep him on my back, unable to block my shot. He raked my arms with both of his and body-slammed me onto the court.

I felt pain, but when he took his time to get off me, pushing my butt with his hands, I felt rage and whipped my body around, throwing an elbow into his bicep. I was on my feet ready to fight when Coach ran between us.

He glared at Charles, "What the hell was that? You'd be ejected for sure. Guard your dribble, so she can't pick your pocket. Give me five lines right now!"

"Five?" Charles whined.

"Seven! And you'd better hustle on each one." He blew his whistle. Charles took off.

Coach looked at me. "Your chin is bleeding. Somebody get her a towel." Mario ran off. "Are you okay?"

I wiped blood from my face and stared at my fingers, my chest aching to suck in more air. "Great practice, Coach. Did I step up my game enough?"

Mario handed me the towel.

Coach smiled. "Yeah. Same time tomorrow?"

"Wouldn't miss it."

A few minutes later, I pulled on my sweats and drove home—sore, bruised, and wet, but happy as hell. I turned the radio up and beat my hands to Marvin Gaye's "Ain't No Mountain High Enough." Singing and juking in my seat at lights and stop signs, I felt on top of the world. I could fucking do this!

As I walked up our walkway, I heard the sound of Schubert's *Sonata in C Major Duet*, a piece Spencer and I played together for fun. Spencer was good, but not good enough to play both parts.

I opened the door and saw Pablo and Spencer through the Steinway's raised lid. They were both so focused on reading the score, they didn't notice me. I dropped my bag on the stairs and headed for the kitchen where I found Mom setting plates on the table.

"Pablo is staying for dinner?" I asked. After all the trauma and rejections of the last two days, her acceptance of Pablo warmed my heart.

Mom beamed, wearing a full apron. "Yes! He's such a nice boy. How was practice?"

"Rough but fun." I filled a glass with ice water and drank while looking through the pile of mail by the window. One large envelope decorated with large red letters—*Summer Adventures!*—caught my eye. Mom had already opened it. "What's this?"

"We must've been put on a mailing list for camps when we sent you to Interlochen last summer."

Interlochen was a two-week music camp both Spencer and I attended last July. Mom wanted us to go again, but I hoped for something different. I pulled out the brochure and flipped through pages of colored photos and blurbs offering various opportunities—rafting down the Colorado, climbing in Yosemite, horseback riding in Wyoming.

But one stood out to me—a place called Camp Wonder just outside Denali National Park in Alaska. It was founded and run by two women, dressed in jeans, boots, and heavy shirts, both former bush pilots, current conservationists. The huge white mass of Denali stood behind an array of cabins and tents along a ridge.

One picture showed a teenage girl with long, blonde braids, holding an axe on her shoulder, dressed in worn overalls, a flannel shirt, and muddy leather boots. Some blue flowers poked out of her chest pocket. She was rugged and beautiful, and I swear I heard her say, "Come to Alaska. We'd be great friends." A jolt flashed through my body, and I felt an urgency, a hard need.

I found a phone number, grabbed the handset, and nervously poked my fingertip through the holes, wishing the dial would not take so long to rotate back after each letter.

Several rings later, I heard an adult woman's voice, "Hello. Camp Wonder. This is Miki. How can I help you?"

It would be a long time before I actually spoke to the teen in the photo—Jackie—but I swear the voice I heard in my head that day was the same one who seven months later said, "Is anyone in there?" as she knocked on the outhouse I was occupying in Alaska. And then the laughter and apologies chimed like music across a sea of bluebells and lupine.

We would tell everyone we'd met in an outhouse.

CHAPTER 10
BEEP! BEEP!

D uring our conversation, I learned that summer camp guests slept in log cabins and wall tents and ate family-style meals in the main building on most days. But they would also camp inside the park in tents, hike into the mountains, and observe Dall sheep, grizzly bears, wolves, and caribou. Miki and Rhonda carved the camp from the wilderness in 1952 and had spent every summer there since, helping people learn to appreciate nature and protect it.

Two women did this near the end of the ninety-two mile road through the two million acre park. Wow! They were both WASP pilots during WWII, transporting fighter planes across the country.

"How old are you, Tracy?" Miki asked.

I felt a flash of panic. Had I missed something about an age limit? "Seventeen, but I turn eighteen next August."

"Most of our guests are adults, many middle-aged and older. You might be the only teen in the group. Would that bother you?"

I took a deep breath, trying to quell my fear. Was the girl in the photo merely a prop? "I saw a picture of a teenager in your brochure. She looked my age."

I could hear the smile in her voice. "That's Jackie, my niece. She works and lives at the camp. Ever since she was twelve. Most of our workers are in their late teens and twenties."

"Maybe I could hang with them sometimes. Help out with the work?"

"That's possible, but I'd hate for you to pay so much money to do chores."

"I wouldn't care. I just want to be there. The trees and flowers and scenery look amazing. Can you send me more information?"

"Sure."

I gave her my address. "How soon would you need a deposit?"

"We have twenty spots available. Ten of those have been reserved."

My pulse quickened. "How? I just got the brochure today."

"Many of our campers are repeat customers. They reserved their places before they left last summer."

"So I need to send it soon."

"If you're sure you want to join us, then sooner would be better."

I could mail a check or send a wire through Western Union. I hung up the phone and stared at the brochure, lingering over Jackie's photo.

What pulled me to that place? I've asked myself that question many times over the years. The only camping experience I'd had was in a rented motorhome on a family vacation to the Grand Canyon two years before. Hot, dusty, and crowded did not appeal to me. Of all the adventure camps in the brochure, Wonder was the only one founded by women—backpacking, bush plane-flying, tree-sawing women. Rugged and fierce, though Miki sounded kind and patient. Until she was threatened, I imagined, or knocked to the court by an ego-injured male.

And Jackie?

I was attracted, yes. But more than that, I felt a longing, a siren's call —like the voice I heard in my head. Something special awaited me there, I just knew it.

My life would be changed forever by a photo.

And saved by a girl and a mountain.

I was alone with Mom while Spencer drove Pablo home. I showed her the brochure and told her about the women. I said nothing about Jackie.

"Could you have picked a camp farther from home?" asked Mom with an edge to her voice.

"Distance doesn't matter. Dad can get free tickets any time he wants them." Commercial pilots had this privilege back then. We'd flown to England and Disneyland for free. "The cost is nearly the same as Interlochen."

The brochure shook in her hands. "But you'll be in the middle of nowhere with wild animals. And outhouses. Why is that so attractive to you?"

"Because it's different and dangerous, and I want to prove I can do it. Like playing with the boys today. I was so proud of myself driving home. I don't feel that way very often." I looked away.

Her voice shook. "Why? You are so smart and so talented."

I found her pleading eyes and took a breath. "I'm gay and don't fit in where I'm supposed to. Here there's the Woman's World section in the newspaper and frilly dresses. In Alaska, women wear jeans and over-alls and chop wood and pee in an outhouse."

Mom scrunched her brows and shook her head. "That's what you want?"

"More than anything! I have to send a deposit soon."

"We need to talk to Dad about this."

"If I have to, I'll pay for this myself. I'll earn enough money between now and June. I have the cash for the deposit, but it would wipe me out before Christmas, so maybe you can lend me $200?" I touched her hand. "Please, Mom. I can't explain why, but this means everything to me." I held my breath.

After a long pause, she said, "Okay, but we'll have to wait to discuss this with your father. He's already going to be angry about Ava and Pablo."

I breathed and kissed her hand. "Thanks, Mom. When does he come back?"

"Saturday afternoon."

A flash of dread brought bile to my throat. I swallowed and focused on basketball. "I should be playing that evening for the championship."

A smile spread across her face as she chuckled. "You think so?"

"Know so."

"Then we'll drive up and watch you."

I wired Miki the deposit the next day during my free period. I called her and said I'd complete all the forms as soon as I received them.

"Will your parents worry about sending their daughter all the way to Alaska by herself?""Miki asked. "You'll have to catch the train in Anchorage and stay at the Mt. McKinley Hotel for a night. Have you ever done anything like that before?"

Without thinking, I thrust out my chest and stood taller. "No, but I also never played on the boys' basketball team until yesterday."

"Really? Good for you!"

"By the championship game on Saturday night, I'll be one of the starters."

"I can't wait to meet you, Tracy. Good luck!"

During the next several days of practice, I got more bruises and blisters, but I also gained more respect. Coach Wynn tried me at the point position on the diamond press. I stole the ball or forced a tie-up half the time. I filled lanes on fast breaks, and the guys stopped hesitating before passing me the ball.

I even hung out with the team in Coach Wynn's office, laughing at crude jokes and trading insults. We crammed into booths at the pharmacy, three to a side, eating greasy burgers and talking too loud. On Thursday, Judy stopped in a huff next to my booth and said, "I thought you were gay."

Mario slid down in his seat across from me and said, "Uh oh. Cat fight coming!"

"They're my teammates, Judy. Not my boyfriends. Take anyone you want, but treat him nicely. I'm very protective of my guys."

Mario hissed like a cat and clawed the air with his hand. Gene and Buddy leaned into me and wrapped their arms around my shoulders and chest. "We'll protect you too."

Mario sat up and mock whispered, "Guys, your arms are touching her—"

Gene said, "Oh shit!" and pulled his arm away. Buddy did the same. "Sorry," Gene said.

"That's okay." I looked right at Judy. "You can touch them any time."

Judy's mouth dropped open. "You're not gay. You wanted an excuse to be surrounded by boys."

"Why, Judy," I said. "That's the nicest thing you've ever said to me." She stomped off. The guys pounded the table and laughed.

Gene reached over with his arm close to my chest. "I can touch them any time?"

I elbowed him in the ribs. "Any time you want to feel this."

He groaned and everyone laughed again. That was my favorite time at the pharmacy. Ever.

Spencer found me after he returned from seeing Pablo at lunch. The lawyer got the ticket dismissed. The cop was off duty, and he had to shine his flashlight in the car to see the supposed misconduct. Invasion of privacy.

He whipped his pelvis up and side to side, reminding me of his dancing with Ava. He noticed my smile disappear.

"What's wrong?" he asked.

A cold breeze blew and I shuddered. "Nothing. I'm happy for you."

His eyes searched mine. "Have you heard anything about her?"

I shook my head.

At the end of school, Mr. Worth called me into his office and grasped my hand, leaving it filled with two ten-dollar bills.

"You don't have to give me this," I said.

"Yes, I do." He grinned as his eyes twinkled. "A bet is a bet, even if it is illegal. I'm proud of you, Tracy. I'll be cheering for you tonight."

We loaded into the school's 12-passenger van for the hour and a half drive to Medina. Coach let me ride shotgun. Our first game started at 6:30 against the Center Point Eagles. Coach said he'd already called the other teams about me playing. No one had objected. He winked then said, "We'll see what they say after the game."

The boys would stay in two hotel rooms for the night. Several offered to share their bed with me. Coach said he'd pay for another room, but they were all sold out.

"No problem," I said. "Spencer's driving up to watch. I'll ride home with him and back up Saturday morning."

The cheerleaders, including Judy, had made a large sign out of butcher paper painted with our logo and all our names. Mario led the way, breaking through the paper as our fans screamed and stomped the bleachers. The girls' team never experienced this. The surge of adrenaline I felt as I ran around the court was awesome. Mario dribbled the ball toward the basket and bounced it off the board for the next in line to bounce, everyone else keeping it alive until Charles made the layup.

After warm-ups ended, we stripped off our sweats and lined up to be introduced by our coach. Wynn called my name, and I ran toward the scorer's table where I offered my hand to the opposing coach.

He said, "Nice to meet you, young lady."

Before I ran back to the team, I heard, "She's a girl," and "That's one hairy girl!" I hadn't shaved anything since last week. I knew I'd get razzed when they saw my pits, but why did I have to alter my appearance when they didn't?

Before the tip-off, Mary came up with a big smile. "Good luck tonight, Tracy. I'm so proud of you." She gave me a quick hug then ran back to the other cheerleaders.

I started the game on the bench, where I expected to be. Center Point was a tall, thick team but slow in transition, so our fast breaks put us in the lead. Before the end of the first quarter, Charles made a layup then grabbed his shorts and ran toward the locker room. Our cheerleaders were under the basket. Judy turned red and ran toward the bleachers, the other girls following. Coach turned to Ricky, our manager, and asked, "Where's he going? Ricky, take the kit and go find him." Ricky grabbed the medical box and ran down the court. "Time out!" yelled Coach.

Judy had covered her face, the girls surrounding her, asking what was wrong. All of us heard her say, "I saw his dick. It fell out of his shorts. I can't believe I saw his dick!"

All the players who huddled around Coach snickered and laughed. Coach tried hard to keep a straight face, but he blushed bright red. "Jesus, Mary, and Joseph," he muttered. "Tracy!"

I jumped out of my seat. "Yes, Coach."

"Go in for Charles."

I ran to the scorer's table and checked in then ran back to the huddle.

"Tracy will play the point on defense. If we score, set up the press again. C'mon guys, let's run these hicks out of the gym. On three!"

During the last three minutes of the quarter, I stole the ball twice and made lay ups. The Eagles got so flustered from our pressure, they called time out with five seconds left, causing their coach to stomp his foot and throw his clipboard.

We started the second quarter the same way. Soon the Eagles fell back into a zone. "Spread the floor and feed Tracy!" yelled Coach. We did and I made two out of three long jump shots before the Eagles called time out.

"Way to shoot, you beast!" shouted Gene, slapping my ass.

I cocked an eyebrow at him. He lifted his hands. "Just treating you like one of the guys."

I slapped his ass. "Way to rebound, Gene."

Everyone, including Coach, laughed. Then we heard cheers as Charles and Ricky ran back to our bench. We huddled around as Coach asked, "What happened, Charles?"

"My jock strap broke."

Mario collapsed to the floor in laughter.

"Did you bring an extra?" Coach asked.

"No," said Ricky. "I had to tape his dick to his leg."

More screams of laughter.

"That's not in my job description, Coach," Ricky added. "I don't ever want to do that again."

"But I loved it," Charles said with a limp wrist and lispy voice. "You can do that to me anytime, Ricky. Any time you want."

"On the bench," Coach barked. "Now." He got into Charles' face. "What I tell you about gay comments? Maybe you'll play in the second half."

I could have hugged that man.

We huddled again then played like beasts for the rest of the quarter, leading by fifteen at the half.

Coach subbed the five of us out toward the end of the third quarter when we led by twenty-five. Charles played with the second string and made ten points before Coach put the five of us back in with instructions not to press or fast break. We won by twenty.

Mr. Hartman, one of our parents who kept stats for the games, told me I had scored seventeen points, made five steals, handed out six assists, and grabbed four rebounds. No turnovers. Not bad for a first game.

The opposing coach shook my hand afterwards. "I never thought a girl could play like you did tonight. That was something to see."

"Thanks, Coach."

I heard Pablo squeal behind me. I turned and saw him running toward me, arms outstretched. "¡Mierda. Jugaste como una bestia!"

"Thanks, Pablo." We kissed cheeks.

Spencer lifted me up in a bear hug. "Great job, Sis!"

"Tracy!" Coach Wynn yelled.

Spencer put me down. I turned to Coach. "Yeah?"

He shook my hand. "Great game. The ones tomorrow will be harder, so get some rest tonight and be back here at 10:00 am. You hungry?"

"Starving. We'll stop at the Dairy Queen."

"Drive safe," Coach said.

"That's why I'm driving and not her," said Spencer. "Fast on the court. Too fast on the road."

"Beep! Beep!" Pablo laughed. "Like the Road Runner. Yes?"

"Beep Beep. I like that," said Coach. "The girls will like it too."

The next morning we ran through another paper banner full of names and lots of "Beep! Beep!" all around the edges. Coach started me at point on defense, moving Charles to a wing. Every time I stole the ball or dribbled on a fast break, the cheerleaders yelled, "Beep! Beep!" Soon, the crowd joined in. I was faster and stronger every time I heard it.

The coach for the Comfort Bobcats changed to a box-and-one defense, assigning a thick-necked goon to shadow me all over the court. He threw elbows, tried to pinch my boobs, and shoved his hand between my legs. During a free throw, I talked to one of the referees and asked him to watch the guy.

"This is a tough game, girly. Hit him back, or go home to mama."

On the next possession, Charles set a back screen on the goon. As I whipped around him, I backhanded his nuts with my off hand. Goon crumpled, his coach screamed at the referee, who called a technical foul on the coach. As he gave me the ball for my free throw, he chuckled, "Nice job, Beep Beep."

Goon kept grabbing and pushing. I elbowed him in the sternum, blocking out for Gene's free throw. A few plays later, I picked his pocket on the press, but the ball bounced off my knee and headed toward the sideline. I ran after, cupped it in my hand as I leapt out of bounds, turned in the air, and threw the ball as hard as I could at his nuts. The thud echoed through the rafters. He groaned and collapsed onto his knees as the ball rolled across the line. Our possession.

He never returned to the game. We won by ten. I had another nickname—Nutcracker, but the cheerleaders were forbidden to paint that on their banner.

Coach Wynn took us all to Dairy Queen where Spencer called Mom to tell her we were playing in the championship game at 7:00. Mom said she and Dad would drive up.

Our opponents, the Harper Longhorns, had won their games easily, including beating the hometown Bobcats on Friday by twenty points. They had a 6' 7" center—Big Mike— with a wicked hook shot and big forwards. Our center, Rudy, was 6' 3". The Longhorns dominated teams on the board, snagging forty rebounds per game. How could we fast break if we couldn't get the rebound?

"Break off the press," Coach said. "Force turnovers. Press all over the court so they can never set their offense. I want to hear you slap the floor before each press."

Before we broke through the banner, I spotted Mom sitting next to Pablo, smiling and sharing conversation. Spencer and Dad sat stiff as boards on each side away from the other. Shouts of "Beep! Beep!" drowned out the Longhorn cheerleaders.

Coach sat Rudy and inserted Buddy—short but fast—into the starting lineup. As we claimed our spots around the jump circle, the giant Longhorns gazed down at us and chuckled. "Looks like we're playing the Munchkins tonight," said their center. His teammates laughed.

They won the tip, and we trapped the dribbler. He passed and two more of us trapped him. We gave up some easy layups with lobs to their center, but we forced turnovers and made our own layups. We were behind by six at the quarter, but the constant pressing clearly rattled their cages. As they walked off the court at halftime, we heard several players jawing at each other.

We trailed by two and felt pretty good about ourselves. When we sat in the corner for our break, I noticed blood oozing into my socks. I'd ignored my blisters during the game, but now it was hard to focus on anything else.

For the start of the second half, Coach had us switch presses to confuse the Longhorns. After forcing several turnovers, we heard lots of accusations and yelling from their end. By the end of the third quarter, we were ahead by four, and running on fumes and adrenaline. We were gassed.

To start the fourth quarter, Coach Wynn pulled Buddy for Rudy and told him to block out and push their big guy off the block. And to play the middle of our 1-3-1.

Rudy smiled and nodded.

"Half-court press guys," Coach said. "As soon as they cross the line, trap them."

We slapped the floor and yelled, "Wolves," as the Longhorns dribbled up the court. My blister on my big toe had opened up. Another on my heel had started bleeding. I just had to ignore my pain for another five minutes, but each hard stop and sidestep sent spikes of fire up my leg. My yelps and grunts grew louder as my rage burned. This team would not beat us.

Rudy did his best keeping Big Mike on his back for rebounds and pushing him out of the key. The ref called a foul, sending the center to the line. Both shots clanged off the rim.

The guy couldn't shoot free throws!

Coach clapped his hands and yelled to Rudy, "You've got four more. Use them all."

Each second brought more intensity, both teams exhausted, both determined to win. The sound was deafening—soles slapping the wood floor, shoe rubber squeaking, the ball thumping, fans screaming and stomping feet.

With ten seconds left, Big Mike stepped to the free throw line for two shots. He made his first. On his second shot, the ball barely grazed the front of the rim and dropped toward the floor.

Rudy grabbed the rebound, pivoted as I yelled, "Outlet!" and passed it to me. I raced down the court, seeing Charles on my left. A Longhorn forward and guard stopped me at the free throw line, and I fed Charles with a pass he caught in stride then lifted his leg for the layup.

Big Mike leapt high from behind and swatted the ball out of Charles' hands into the backboard. I raced around the forward, picked up the ball, turned, and jumped for a shot. Big Mike lunged toward me, hands high. I switched hands, putting the ball in my left, then under-handed a shot around his body, banking off the board into the net.

Big Mike's body crashed into me, slamming me to the floor.

The gym exploded in noise. I thought I'd heard a whistle but wasn't sure. Then Mike leapt up and held his head while he screamed, "No way!"

The referee had called a foul. I would go to the line, the score tied 62 - 62, with one second on the clock. Charles and Gene pulled me off the floor. Gene smacked my ass. "Fuckin' A, man."

Charles rubbed my head then put his forehead to mine. "Helluva shot, Tracy. Now win this thing."

The teams lined up as I planted my toe just behind the line. The stands rumbled. Our cheerleaders chanted, "Tracy, Tracy she's our girl. If she can't make it, no one will. Go, Tracy!" Then "Beep! Beep!" erupted everywhere, countered with, "Miss it! Miss it!"

I closed my eyes and looked at the Camp Wonder photos in my mind, trying to block the noise. I saw the huge white mountain and Jackie smiling.

A calm flushed through me until I heard no stomping or shouting as the ref handed me the ball. I flexed my knees, dribbled three times while chanting quietly, "Come to Alaska. We'd be great friends." Over and over until I pushed the ball out of my hands with a perfect back spin and snapped my wrist, my middle finger pointing to the big hole in the net.

The ball swished through.

CHAPTER 11
HAIRY PITS & THE MONEY GAME

S creams and stomps thundered off the walls. My teammates crashed into me, hugging, slapping, laughing in my face. I was hoisted onto Rudy and Gene's shoulders, and I floated toward our bench, every nerve quivering. I didn't feel anything when the guys put me down because my head still drifted above the din.

Then coach grabbed my face. "You are one tough son of a gun, Tracy Franks. That was awesome!"

I nodded and asked for water. At least six bottles were shoved into my face. I grabbed one and poured its contents onto my head then raked my fingers through my hair, plastering it to my scalp.

Mario said, "You look like a boy! Look at her."

Gene, Charles, and Buddy agreed. "She does!"

"Thanks, guys," I said with pride.

The teams lined up and shook hands with "Good game, good game," repeated a dozen times.

The Medina principal took the microphone to announce the all-tournament team, which included Charles and me. Five of us stood at center court, sporting medals around our necks. We were about to leave when he said, "Not yet, guys. I have an MVP trophy here." He held it high, showing it to us and the crowd.

"The winner averaged 18.5 points, six assists, five steals, four rebounds, and NO turnovers in our tournament." He walked toward me with a smile. Tears welled in my eyes, but I couldn't let them fall. I was a gutsy player who never quit, and I was afraid tears would ruin that image. I bit the inside of my cheek to focus on something else. By the time he called my name and handed me the trophy, I'd swallowed blood.

The other players patted my back with, "Great tournament," and walked away.

Big Mike held out his hand and said, "You're a winner, Tracy. You refuse to lose."

"Thanks."

He smiled and pointed at me. "But I'll get you next time."

The school trophies were presented then teams posed for photos. The guys put me in the middle with the trophy.

"Hold it high," said Coach.

I raised it above my head, exposing my hairy armpits. Bulbs flashed. Someone yelled, "Look at her pits!" Then peals of laughter.

My teammates turned, stared, and laughed. For a moment, my heart stopped, but then they all had their arms up, showing off their hairy pits, all of us sporting big smiles. Pictures were snapped, but I never saw a copy.

The guys headed for the showers, and I felt a little envious. Soon they would be laughing under a central showerhead that sprayed water in a twenty-foot circle, at least that's what Gene had told me between games that day. A bunch of naked guys totally comfortable wiping soap all over their bodies then daring each other to pop towels. They didn't realize the freedom they enjoyed.

For all I'd done the last two days to prove my belonging on this team, I could never experience that camaraderie and joy. Girls would be covering themselves or wearing underwear or refusing to get wet, trapped in their embarrassment. And if I were there among them, I'd gawk and try not to faint. Maybe someday I could parade my nudity and feel only happiness. But how?

With the game over, I returned to being an oddity—the girl who looked and played like a boy but seemed to be neither one. During the game I was a teammate, trying to defeat a clear enemy without regard to sexuality or politics. But once it ended, I was a bruised and battered queer, waiting for the inevitable condemnation.

I sat on our bench and gingerly removed my shoes. My socks were bloody.

Coach leaned over. "Shit, girl. Doesn't that hurt?"

"It does now." I winced trying to pull off a sock.

"Ricky!" Coach yelled. "Bring the kit and fix this girl's feet."

Ricky scampered over and kneeled in front of me. "Whoa." He grimaced. "These look nasty."

"Better or worse than taping Charles' dick?" I tried to laugh.

"Your feet are worse, but the job is better."

As he gently cleaned and taped my wounds, I saw my parents walk down from the bleachers and stand together, watching me from a distance. Mom smiled and waved. Dad's mouth was a slash across his face. I waved back at Mom, and she took a step toward me, but Dad held her arm. Of course, he did. *What a shit!*

Spencer and Pablo ran to me. Pablo kneeled by Ricky and picked up my right foot from the floor, holding it like a delicate treasure. "It would be an honor to kiss your foot, Tracy Franks, goddess of basketball. May I?"

I laughed. "You may kiss it twice."

He lowered his face to my foot and nearly gagged from the odor.

"Twice," I ordered.

He grimaced and kissed loudly. "And the other?" He coughed.

"Certainly." I pulled my left foot from Ricky's hands and held my toes to his lips. "One for each toe."

Pablo grimaced. "Each toe?"

"Each. Juicy kisses."

Ricky stifled a laugh.

Spencer walked over as Pablo smacked each toe. "Make sure you wash those lips and gargle before . . . you do anything else with them. Especially after kissing her toes," Spencer added. "I know how stinky her feet can get."

Pablo inhaled deeply. "It is aphrodisiac. Yes?" He growled softly and moved his nose up my shin.

I put my hand on his head, stopping his advance. "Toes only," I laughed.

He fixed his adoring eyes on mine. "I think, Tracy, you could make me straight."

Spencer guffawed. Ricky winced.

Pablo stood and grinned. "Or not."

Ricky wiped his forehead and took quick breaths. "Make sure to air out the wounds tonight." He stood.

"Thanks, Ricky." I reached out my arms for Pablo and Spencer to help me up.

"You're welcome," Ricky said. He looked down and shuffled his feet. "You were amazing tonight." He looked at my eyes. "Beyond amazing."

I looked at the short, skinny sophomore with curls on his head, freckles on his face, and what seemed like puppy love in his brown eyes. He'd wanted to play basketball but couldn't get off the bench, so he'd volunteered last year to be the manager. "Thanks," I said. "We couldn't do it without you as manager."

He blushed and walked away.

I moved closer to Spencer. "Looks like Mom told Dad about me and Ava and you and Pablo."

Spencer looked back at our parents. "Yeah, his glare could fry an egg. The Grinch is about to steal Christmas."

"Help me get my sweats on."

Spencer dug them out of my bag. I grabbed Pablo's arm as I lifted my leg to push through the pants Spencer held. After they slipped my top on, I looked over to Mom and Dad, which they took as a signal to approach.

Mom saw me wince as I shifted the weight on my feet and walked quicker toward me. "How badly are you hurt?"

I showed her my feet. "And I've got bruises on top of bruises."

"How did you keep playing so ferociously in all that pain? You should have asked the coach to sit you down."

"If I'd sat down, I wouldn't have been able to get up again. Besides, guys don't quit in the fourth quarter."

"Is that why you have hairy armpits?" Dad barked. "Because you're a guy?"

If he'd wanted to hurt me, he hadn't. "I still have all my female parts. Not shaving hasn't changed that."

"Why did you have to embarrass yourself—and us—by holding that trophy above your head?"

I smirked. Of course, the first thing he'd say to me would be an insult. "You were embarrassed? I'm so sorry. I just wasn't thinking. Next time Coach asks me to lift the trophy, I'll say, 'No. I can't embarrass my family.' Because that's more important than making the winning basket or being named all-tourney or getting the MVP award."

Dad glared and tightened his jaw.

Mom moved closer and hugged. "We are so proud of you, Tracy. The tension was so exciting. During your concerts, I get nervous, but during this game I couldn't breathe at all. Will they all be like this?"

I hugged her back. "I don't know. I'd like a few blowouts here and there." I leaned back and looked into her face. "Thanks, Mom." A surge of love flooded my body, and then the familiar pang of pain followed. How could this woman stay sane with this man? She'd gone from one orphanage to another, except this time who would save her? Spencer and I? What would happen after we were gone?

"You played your heart out, Tracy," Dad said. "And surprised me and everyone else in the stands, but I wish I could've watched this game without having heard about all the crap that happened while I was gone. I talked to Ralph Blunt today. The lying and deception are bad enough, but learning that both my children are queers . . ." He shook his head. "This won't stand."

He glanced over my shoulder and changed his demeanor. "Hello, Mr. Worth."

The Principal patted Spencer's shoulder as he walked toward my parents. "Hello, Art. Alice. Have you ever seen the effort Tracy gave us tonight?"

"We're very proud of her," Dad said.

Mom's mouth dropped open as she turned her head to him.

"I've coached a lot of teams," Mr. Worth said, "but I have never seen a player give more of herself than what we witnessed here." He turned to me with his wide grin and held out his hand. "That was a privilege to watch."

I shook his hand. "Thanks for giving me the opportunity."

"And to think I almost said no."

"You did?"

He nodded. "Made me realize that it's always better to offer encouragement than criticism." He widened his eyes quickly and tilted his head back toward my parents. "Well, I better move on. Good night." He walked toward the exit.

"Hmm," I mused. "Always better to offer encouragement than criticism. I think that can apply to many situations, don't you, Dad?"

Dad folded his arms. "I wonder what he'd say if his two daughters told him they're gay."

"He'd react differently now than he would have a week ago." I tightened my stomach, waiting for the punch I knew was coming. "So you said, 'This won't stand.' Does that mean changing schools and sending us to a psychiatrist?"

"No," Dad said, his face reddening. "I told Ralph he was crazy for wasting his money. Why spend more when your kids have wasted what you've already spent?" He jutted out his chin and thrust his finger at me. "The only reason I'm not sending you to Lee High School at the end of our street is because I paid the full year's tuition at Adler and can't get it back. But I'm not paying for anything else." He slashed his arm through the air. "No music lessons. No clothes. No college. And certainly no Juilliard!"

Each slash stabbed my gut. I grabbed Spencer's arm to steady myself from the nausea whirling inside.

Spencer put his arm around Pablo and pulled him close.

"What the hell are you doing?" Dad snapped.

Spencer yanked his arm away.

"How about food?" I taunted. "Or maybe we should leave dimes and quarters in the fridge and pantry when we take anything."

He pointed his finger at me. "You can move your butt out now!"

"No, she won't," Mom blurted, grabbing my arm, standing between Spencer and me. "These are our children! You will not cut them off."

He fixed his beady eyes on Mom. "You've done a helluva job raising them in my absence, Alice. Maybe you can support them. I'm done."

A flush of panic filled my gut as I thought about Camp Wonder and

Jackie, but anger heated every bit of my skin. I felt like slapping the floor and yelling, "Wolves!" I glared at him like I'd glared at the Longhorn point guard, like Gandalf glared at the Balrog—*You shall not pass!*

I stepped forward, balling my fists. "Did you honestly think that threatening to withhold your money would make us repent and turn straight? Fuck your money!" I marched for the door, trying not to limp, and heard Spencer and Pablo scramble after me.

I heard Mom plead behind me, "Art! How could you?"

"Don't worry," he said with a harrumph. "They'll come around. Now they know who's boss."

The air was crystal clear and cold, seeping through my sweats, and lifting goosebumps everywhere. When we got to Spencer's car, I said, "I'll drive."

Spencer was pale, his eyes pained. Like a ghost he said, "Okay."

"Hey, we'll get through this, Bro. You dig?"

"You sure?"

"Damn right. You two can get in the back and do whatever. I'll turn up the radio. I'm not stopping for food. We're going to eat everything we can find at his house. And drink his beer."

Spencer grabbed my hand and leaned toward me. "Do you think he'll do it?"

"Not if Mom has any say." I wanted to believe this, but Mom had rarely stood her ground against him.

He swallowed. "How would I go to Juilliard?"

"This is exactly how he wants you to react. Remember how you stopped flinching when either Mom or Dad threatened you with a paddle. You said, 'Go ahead,' and stuck out your butt. When the hits stopped affecting you, they stopped hitting. You know how to ignore pressure. You do it every time you perform."

"Yeah, but worrying about money is a different kind of pressure." Spencer opened the back door, allowing Pablo to slip inside. "Please watch for deer. I saw several last night."

"I'll be careful." I slid into the seat and winced when my right foot found the pedal. *Pain is my friend*, I thought. *I cannot flinch from pain. Just slap the floor and keep moving.*

I twisted the key, pulled the shift into drive, and took off for the highway. I saw Spencer and Pablo's heads disappear behind my seat, so I turned on the radio. "Top 40 Hits Countdown" was underway, then playing Gary Puckett's "Woman Woman."

He sang about a girl who had sex for the first time (with him, presumably) and became a woman. As if the only way you could become a woman was to screw a guy. Did I become a woman when Ava made me cum at the drive-in? No. I was still innocent, thinking we could hide forever.

What about that night when I overcame all obstacles and expectations and led my team to victory only to be chastised because of my hairy pits? And then told to leave my home because of . . . what?

Offering to leave quarters on the shelves? No, because I'd baited him. He couldn't stand when I ridiculed him, even though that's what he did to me repeatedly—my political opinions, my lifestyle choices. Basically everything about me.

How could Spencer and I satisfy him?

Agree with everything he said. Never question. Never cast doubt. He provided for all of us, and that should take precedence over any silly ideas we might have had. Like thinking we could be with the person we loved, regardless of gender. Like unashamedly being who we truly were.

Which, of course, led to the obvious conclusion that if we found another source of income, we could ignore him. His ideas and beliefs meant nothing without his money.

We'd heard him say hundreds of times how much he loved to fly and to visit new places. I did not remember him ever claiming he loved to come home to be with us.

Not once.

If I provided for myself, then I wouldn't have to pretend to play his game—shave, pluck, paint, date guys, bite my tongue about the war and civil rights.

He'd hoped we would panic and acquiesce. Instead, he showed us the path forward.

As I rolled up and down hills on a two-lane road through the darkness, The Who's "I Can See For Miles" started.

The singer's lover had deceived him, but guess what? He could see for miles and miles. She'd put the magic in his eyes. Just like Dad had done to me.

My escape to Alaska wasn't killed that night. It was made more urgent.

And for the first time I considered the possibility of not returning. For what? Who? Spencer would be away from home. Mom would always include Dad.

Surely there was a place I could live freely and openly. Why not there?

"Hello Goodbye" by the Beatles started, and I nearly laughed out loud. Whatever I said, Dad said the opposite. Stop! No, I think I'll go.

Something kicked the back of my seat, and I heard a grunt. I cranked up the volume and shouted, "I'll pretend I didn't feel that."

"Sorry, Sis," Spencer called.

"I am so embarrassed," Pablo laughed.

My fingers drummed on the steering wheel. "'There is nothing either good or bad but thinking makes it so,' said Hamlet."

"Great connection, Sis," Spencer said.

I smiled at him through the mirror.

"¿Qué?" asked Pablo.

"Embarrassment is a choice, not a requirement," Spencer said.

"Embarrassment is Dad's primary weapon," I said. "It only works if you agree with his definition of morality."

"So we don't have to stop?" Pablo asked.

I laughed. "No. Carry on." I saw both their heads disappear behind my seat.

My feet no longer hurt. The night sparkled with the Milky Way stretching across the sky as I juked in my seat to "I Heard It Through The Grapevine."

I cleared my head of Mom and Dad just as I'd cleared it of the noise in the gym before my free throw. "Come to Alaska. We'd be great friends."

I'm on my way, Jackie. Wait for me.

CHAPTER 12

FLASH: FIND A NEW LIFE

A fter an orgy of eating every leftover we could find and drinking five of Dad's beers, all of us stood and cleared the table. "They'll be home soon," I told Spencer. "Maybe you should stay at Pablo's tonight. I would."

Pablo widened his eyes and extended his arms. "You wish to stay with me tonight?"

I stacked dishes in the sink. "I'd rather be anywhere than here."

"Then come with us."

I grinned when I saw Spencer swipe his finger across his throat, as in *You'd better not*. "No," I laughed. "You two enjoy yourselves. Pablo, don't you go back to Mexico soon?"

"Yes, before Christmas." He grabbed Spencer's hand, and they shared a sorrowful glance.

"Then don't waste time. Leave now before Mom and Dad get home. I'll clean up."

Spencer grabbed his jacket. "Thanks, Sis." He slapped Pablo's ass. "Ándele."

"Ooh, that felt good. Otra vez, por favor." Pablo wiggled his butt.

Spencer looked back at me and grinned before swatting Pablo again.

"¡Más fuerte!" Pablo leapt forward and stuck out his ass. "Harder!"

I doubled over in laughter and heard this repeated until the front door opened and closed. They both waved back at me as I watched through the kitchen window. What a fun couple! What would Spencer do with himself after Christmas?

I raced to hide our pillaging, grabbed another beer then ran up to my bathroom, desperately needing a bath. I stripped off my clothes in front of the mirror, both scared and fascinated by what I'd find. I guzzled the beer as I examined myself.

My body was full of purple, yellow, and brown bruises. Both my elbows were covered in dried blood, and my knees looked like pulverized alien meat. I set my trophy and medal on the marble counter. Were they worth what my body had endured?

Hell yeah! Every bruise and scrape were medals in their own right.

Something I'd learned about myself while playing sports was how much pain I could stand. If I wasn't hurting, then I wasn't trying hard enough.

Recklessly diving for loose balls, running while my lungs nearly snapped my ribs, standing immediately after being knocked down, ignoring pus and blood-filled socks—all were essential to my self-esteem.

When I won, those signs were proof I deserved the victory. When I lost, I'd wussed out and let the pain stop me.

Only later did I realize I was punishing myself. I simply didn't like me. Or what I thought was me.

But that night I gloried in my injuries, filled the tub, and soaked in simulated embryonic fluid, awaiting my newest birth, feeling a comfortable mix between exhilarated and spent. Two songs competed in my mind: Buffalo Springfield's anti-war song "For What It's Worth" and the Beatles' "All You Need Is Love." The epitome of opposites, the Yin and Yang of the world and of me. I saw the symbol spinning slowly in my mind, the feminine moon—the receiver—and the masculine earth, the giver. In balance only if two opposites filled the circle, a male and female. Spin the symbol faster, and the boundaries disappeared; black and white became gray.

Which was me—blurred with no boundaries, male and female together.

Why did I have to choose one or the other?

I didn't.

I was both.

The next morning I lay in my bed, stiff and sore, hoping that in another minute or two, the pain would be gone.

Dad knocked on the door. "Tracy? Are you awake?"

I thought if I said nothing, maybe he'd go away. I turned over, stifling a groan.

"Tracy, I'm coming in."

I heard the door knob turn. "I'm not dressed. Give me a second."

"Let me in when you're ready."

I fumbled for my robe and tied it closed. "Okay."

He opened the door, flipped on the light, and walked in, working on his necktie. "You don't plan to go to church with us?"

I lifted my head and forced my eyes open. "Remind me again what the church says about homosexuals. I think it has something to do with Sodom and Gomorrah. And one of Paul's letters to the Romans? All condemnation and hell fire."

He pursed his lips and tightened his eyes. "Maybe you should read over those parts. They might be enlightening."

"Like I need another source to tell me how sinful and worthless I am. Certainly not worth investing in or wasting more money on." I looked at him and thought, *The ball's in your court, Daddy. Volley or back down?*

He took a deep breath. "Why don't we start over?"

And then I knew that Mom had forced him to talk to me. Dad would never admit a mistake. "From five minutes ago? Or five years? Pick a date."

He swallowed, gritted his teeth, and looked at the posters of Grace on the walls. "I should have waited until this afternoon to say anything to you and Spencer about Ava." He turned away from the wall and looked at me. "You played a great game, and I should have let you enjoy the moment."

Every single word was stiff, sounding like a bad actor—one who'd had a gun held against his head when he learnt the script. I thought of three great come-backs, but I bit my tongue. "Yes, both Spencer and I would have preferred that."

"Where is he?"

I rolled my neck, trying to lessen the ache. "At Pablo's. I thought it better than him driving back by himself after drinking."

"Why did Spencer start drinking? Is that from Pablo's influence?"

Why did parents always want to blame someone else for their kid's behavior? "Spence is stressed. He's trying to deal with his sexuality. Everywhere he looks, he's told it's wrong, but he likes Pablo and has a lot of fun with him." I relived the butt slapping in my mind and smiled. But how could I describe that to Dad? "They are a riot together. I've never seen Spencer so happy, but Pablo goes back to Monterrey in a week. Then what?"

"Then maybe he can get back to normal."

My anger flared. "Which is?"

He tightened his jaw, almost said something, then turned around. He was trying his best to keep from fighting. "Is Mr. Worth going to let you continue playing with the boys?"

A little panic gurgled in my gut. "Why wouldn't he?"

"I think some of the guys . . . are attracted to you."

What a totally unexpected comment. I rolled my eyes. "I'm doing nothing to promote that."

"True, but still." He folded his arms. "I'm trying to think how my high school teammates would have reacted if a girl joined my team as a pitcher or catcher. Especially one who played as well as you. Guys would have been all over her."

"I'm gay, Dad. They know it."

He winced like he'd been stung then shook his head. "Doesn't matter. They'll think they can convert you. Or that you're claiming to be gay to get attention."

"That's what Judy accused me of at the pharmacy when I ate with the guys."

"Why is that so far-fetched?" He smiled and nodded like he'd revealed a great truth to me.

"That I would say I'm gay for attention?" I shook my head. "Do you have any idea how hard it is to admit to yourself that you're gay, much less admit it to others? I'm pretty much branded for life."

He sat in my desk chair, leaning forward, elbows on spread knees, the same pose that would kill a girl's reputation. "But if you go out with Gene or Charles, all that's over and forgotten."

"Is that what you want me to do?"

He bit his lip, looked at me then away, then back. "Can't you try?" he pleaded. "How many boys have you dated?"

"One or two. I hated it." We had never spoken like this before, and for a moment I thought maybe he would understand.

"And how many girls?"

"Just Ava."

He held out both hands to me, palms up. "Why can't you give more boys a chance?"

My chest felt cold. "Dad, this has nothing to do with quantity or finding the right guy. I'm not attracted to boys. Whatever you felt when you first saw Mom, is what I feel when I see a cute girl. It's been that way since middle school, only back then I thought something was wrong with me."

He leaned back, tightening his lips. "And isn't there?"

I tried to dodge his punch, but it landed square in my chest. "Something wrong? Yeah, but I can't help it." Despite my determination to not let him hurt me, he was getting through. I tried to swallow, but the knot in my throat throbbed. "I'm sorry you're embarrassed by both of us. It must suck knowing your kids are queers. But however much embarrassment you feel, we've felt ten times more."

He stood, his face twisting in disgust. "Then why do you flaunt your . . .strangeness, homosexuality, whatever you call it, by trying to look like a boy?"

I could easily have exploded, but I took a breath and stayed calm. "I feel better about myself . . . I feel tougher. I know this will sound strange to you, but if I paint my eyes and lips, I feel like I'm wearing a disguise. That's not me." I pushed my short hair back. "This is me." I lifted my robe to show my shins. "This is me."

"I might think wearing a beard is me, but I can't do it," he explained like I was five. "My company has regulations. We all have norms we have to abide by."

"Like I have to wear a dress at school, which is entirely stupid. How long will that last?"

"That might change, but that's the rule now, and you follow it. I have to wear a uniform."

"Pants and a jacket and tie, which make you look experienced and solid. What if they forced you to wear a dress? Would you do it?"

"That's crazy . . ."

"Forcing me to wear a dress feels the same for me as what it would feel for you."

"You wore a dress at the party for God's sake!"

I stood and moved toward the door. "I didn't want to, which is why I got the shortest one I could find, just to rebel. And that was before . . . before coming out to Ava and trying to find a way to be with her." My chin quivered, so I wiped my mouth and turned. I had tried to block the memory of that Saturday night, but just then it squeezed my heart again.

"If you did it then, you can do it now. People are saying you're not shaving because you're a freak who wants to change your gender or because you're desperate for attention. Either way, it hurts your future."

A flame lit in my chest as I faced him. "Hurts me or you? Who are these *people?*"

He took a breath like he was deciding what to say. "Kids and adults in the bleachers last night."

"So why didn't you stand up and tell them I'm your daughter and please don't make ridiculous speculations when you know nothing about her?"

"Because I don't know who you are anymore."

The truth hit harder than Big Mike falling on me. "You didn't want anyone to know you're my father. And that's why you waited so long to approach me last night. You held Mom back. You wanted everyone to leave before you got near me."

"Do you blame me?"

Even though I knew this to be true before then, my chest felt hollow and cold. "No, it's what I expect from you." I sat on my bed. He would've let those *people* say anything and done nothing. What about Mom? I was sure she looked at Dad, expecting him to say something, but he probably shook his head. And she obeyed.

Folding his arms, he moved closer and glowered down at me. "Are you going to make an effort to look and act like a normal seventeen-year-old girl?"

"Normal? Define please."

"Shave, wear makeup, stop trying to look like a boy, no more acting gay."

I tried to keep my voice firm, but it wavered. "And if I don't?"

"What I said last night. I won't support this behavior." His voice got colder and mocking. "And that Camp Wonder nonsense? There is no possibility I'm paying for that."

My muscles sagged. Everything felt numb. What I wanted and needed was nonsense to him. "No music lessons. No college. No clothes."

"Exactly," he said with a smug nod and a lift of his brows.

I closed my eyes and tried to steel myself. "So rather than support the kid you have, you'll only pay for the kid you want." My eyes snapped open. "Are you going to tell Spencer the same?"

With a cocksure grin, he said, "Actually, I think Spencer will agree with me. I'm pretty sure I can make him understand what a gay life would do to him." He looked back at Grace Slick wearing white fringe, holding a microphone to her mouth. "Why is this shit in my house?" He thrust his hand toward the edge.

My blood seethed. I shoved my way between him and Grace. "Don't touch that! I paid for it, not you. I will tell the police you destroyed my property. Which is assault, Daddy. Do you want to deal with that?"

He scoffed. "I can't remove an offensive poster of a drug addict in my own house? Since when?" His laugh was sinister as he flattened his lips against his teeth and jabbed his fingers at the poster.

I pulled the knot on my robe and gripped the edges. Every muscle tensed and quivered. "You came into my room in a rage, ripping my poster down and then pulled off my robe."

His eyes twitched. "You wouldn't dare."

I spit out the words. "It's true. You don't know me anymore." I jerked open my robe.

"You little bitch!" He turned around, reached for the door knob, and yanked the door into his face. "Dammit!" Without turning around, he snapped, "I'm not through with you." He stomped away.

My lungs gasped for air. I clung to my dresser, trying to steady my rubber legs. After a minute, I stumbled toward my door and slammed it shut.

The world had shifted beneath my feet. I'd pushed my old life into the earth, forcing up bare rock—looming, shapeless, frightening, staring at me to make something of it.

If I'd been willing to sacrifice Grace, I possibly could have salvaged something with Dad. Just bitten my tongue until he flew away in a few days. But Grace represented defiance to me—against norms and female expectations. Her humor was sarcastic, her love life wild. That's what Dad wanted to rip out of my soul, crushing me like the Blunts had done to Ava.

I'd destroyed any relationship we had. He'd never unsee what I'd flashed, and I'd never forget his retreat.

I'd won, but why did I feel empty and lost?

Perhaps because I was still in that house with the same parents and no foreseeable relief. He'd continue to hurt me and Spencer.

At that moment Alaska became everything to me—a goal, an escape, a burning need to change my life. Two women had built an enclave in the wilderness in full view of the highest mountain in North America where Jackie had worked since she was twelve. The bare rock had loomed for them too, and they'd made something beautiful out of it.

What did I have to do to get there? I sat at my desk and opened a spiral notebook. I wrote "Money?" I had to find another job besides kneeling in front of ladies, doling out compliments for shoes they didn't need. I wrote "College? How?" I'd made good grades and my test scores were high, but now I needed scholarships. So I had to push myself harder, just like I'd done in basketball.

Which now seemed like a luxury I couldn't afford. I'd quit the team after the next tournament.

And what about piano? No more lessons. No more two hours a day in practice.

More time for a job and schoolwork.

And freedom to try writing my own music, something I'd always dreamed of but never had time for.

But job one was "Get to Alaska."

Dad had intended to accentuate my dependence on his largess; in fact, he'd pushed me toward independence, dead set on pursuing specific goals for my future. I should have been any parent's dream kid. Instead, I was the queer pariah, counting the minutes until I could leave.

My clock said 10:30, so I tied my robe and listened at the top of the stairs. They should have left by then. Hearing no one, I crept down a few steps then a few more until I checked the garage. Their Oldsmobile was gone. I had two hours of freedom.

I scrambled eggs and made toast. The coffee pot was still hot so I poured a cup. I sat down and looked through the front page of the newspaper. The Draft Director had ordered local boards to revoke student deferments of individuals protesting induction for "interfering with recruitment." Because any non-violent protest against the war was illegal in the eyes of most adult Americans at the time, including my father. "You either support the troops and the war or you're a communist sympathizer," Dad said frequently.

Another article described a two-year-old boy whose parents had tied to a chair in a closet for at least twelve hours. His limbs were bound with diapers torn into strips. He was frail and starving, too weak to walk, too traumatized to cry or speak. The four other children, however, appeared to be healthy.

How? Why? What could a two-year-old have possibly done to make parents punish him so severely? What would have happened if the policeman hadn't come by the house?

Why had the other children done nothing to help the boy?

I wiped tears from my eyes.

Those parents had to appear the next day at the police station.

But nothing happened to fathers who humiliated sons for being too feminine. Or for dating a boy. Or to fathers who remained silent while others called their daughters freaks. Or ripped posters off walls. Or ridiculed who they loved.

Yet the damage inflicted on those children would be as timeless as what the boy in the closet had endured.

Spencer pulled into the driveway. I stood and watched him shuffle across the grass with hunched shoulders. When he entered the kitchen, I asked, "Do you want some eggs?"

"No, I'm good." He poured himself coffee then leaned back against the counter sipping from his cup, his face pale with dark patches under his eyes. "What did Dad say about money?"

"I'm cut off entirely, but he thinks he can still persuade you to forgo the gay life."

He closed his eyes and whimpered. "I was hoping you could persuade him to . . . change his mind. Oh, man." He pushed his fingers through his hair.

I lifted my feet onto the next seat. "Mom forced him to come upstairs and apologize for screaming at us last night instead of waiting until this morning. I tried to explain things, but he'd already decided. Either we act normal or he won't pay."

"And you said?"

"I threatened to call the police and claim he assaulted me. Then I flashed him."

"You flashed . . . " His eyes bulged. "Jesus, Tracy, why?"

"Because he was about to rip Grace off my wall."

He shook his head and banged his cup on the counter. "You always go too far."

"True, but you're still redeemable." My sarcasm thickened. "Once Pablo leaves, swear off guys, watch football, and all your dreams will come true."

He swallowed, looked at me then away. "Pablo wants me to visit his family."

I leaped to my feet. "Wow. Do it. Would his parents mind?"

His face turned red. "They know he's gay and they don't care. He's going to be a celebrity pianist and bring fame to the family." His eyes filled with pain. "Can you imagine that?"

My stomach fluttered. "What did you say to him?"

"I'd have to think about it."

"Don't you want to?"

"Yes. More than anything, but . . . I know how Dad will react. If I go, I'm cut off."

"Then don't come back."

He threw up his hands. "That's so easy for you to say!"

"No, it's not. But once I said it, I felt free of him. I'll pay for myself."

"How?"

"I'll find a way, Spencer. He knocked me down, but I'm not out. I'm going to Alaska this summer."

"What the fuck is in Alaska?" He stomped out of the kitchen. "You're crazy."

I ran to the doorway. "Do you love him?"

He stopped by Dad's chair, gripping the side wing.

"Do you love him, Spencer? Does he love you?"

He kept his back to me. "Yes and yes."

"If you don't go, you'll regret it for the rest of your life."

He turned around, tears welling in his eyes. "How do I know I won't regret going?"

My heart raced. "You have nothing here except arguments and hiding who you are."

"And you. I'd miss you."

I went to him and kissed his cheek. "I'd miss you too, Bro. But I'd rather you be happy and free than stuck in this madhouse. Besides, I'll be in Alaska by early June."

He scrunched his forehead. "For what? A camp? How long is it?"

"Two weeks." I searched his eyes then lowered my voice. "But I don't think I'm coming back. Please keep that to yourself." I held both his hands. "You need to go home with Pablo. Please. I know you'll both be happy there. You guys are so cool together. He's such a clown. And so good looking."

Spencer blushed. "Thought you're gay and don't like boys."

"He's one beautiful gay boy. You need to follow your heart."

"I want to . . . but I'm scared."

"Just slap the floor and stand your ground. Dad will work on you and try to make you feel guilty and ashamed. Ignore him and think of how wonderful you feel with Pablo."

His cheeks twitched, trying to smile. "I'll try. Thanks, Sis." He squeezed my hands once then turned to walk away. But he stopped and scratched his head. "You *flashed* him? Seriously?"

Heat flooded my face. "Yeah. I was angry . . . that's all I could think to do."

He turned toward me, holding up his little finger. "If I had just one finger's worth of your sass, I could tell him, 'Fuck you' and leave for Monterrey."

"You have enough, Spencer. Use it. Please."

He nodded. "Yeah." He walked up the stairs.

I told him again and again that week.

But he wouldn't go.

CHAPTER 13

THE MASSAGER AND A CLOSET KISS

The sound of chewing echoed off the kitchen walls along with the clang of fork tines on teeth. Mom had cooked a pot roast with potatoes, carrots, and crunchy rolls and filled a bowl with crisp lettuce and croutons. I couldn't imagine a noisier meal to eat in silence. No one had spoken since Dad had ended his prayer with, "And thank you for this wonderful meal and home. They are certainly more than Alice or I had when we were growing up. May each of us show our gratitude to you for this bounty by obeying your commandments and heeding your scripture. Amen."

No one else had repeated "Amen."

The little food I had eaten balled up in my stomach, unwilling to succumb to the intense gurgling of acid I felt beneath my ribs. I set my fork and knife across my plate. "Delicious meal, Mom, but it's hard to eat with so much noise." I pushed my chair back and stood.

"I was enjoying the silence," Dad said. "Quite a change from most Sunday dinners." He mopped up gravy with his roll. "I know you'll both be disappointed to hear this, but I have to fly out Wednesday rather than next weekend. Seems the Defense Department wants us to transport ammunition and weapons to Viet Nam. Next month we carry troops both ways."

I clapped my hands. "Great! Maybe you'll get to fly Spencer in a few months. Wouldn't that be fun?"

Mom dropped her fork, and Spencer choked on his tea.

Dad grabbed Mom's hand. "The war will be over before there's any chance of that. The Reds are losing, and they're getting scared." He chuckled and drank some beer.

"Well, there's always Canada and Mexico if worse comes to worst." I caught Spencer's eye. "I need to study."

"I didn't hear you practice today," Mom said. "Did you do it while we were at church?"

"No need to practice," I said. "Lessons are over. Didn't Dad tell you?"

Mom turned to Dad, mouth agape. Dad glared at me.

I smiled and realized Dad hadn't said anything about our conversation or how it ended. He would never admit to what he saw. "Well, you two can hash it out. I've got to work on winning scholarships."

I went to my room and reviewed my notes on Hamlet for my English final that Wednesday. A few minutes later, I heard a knock.

"Tracy. It's me," Spencer said.

"Sock it to me."

He opened the door and muttered, "Bummer," clearly in no mood for slang games. He slid his back down the wall until he sat on my floor. "He yelled at me for an hour this afternoon."

"And that will not stop until you stand up to him." I couldn't keep the smugness out of my voice. "I bet he never knocks on my door again."

"So I should flash him?"

"Worth a try."

He chuckled briefly then hung his head.

"What's going on downstairs?" I asked.

"They're fighting. About us. What else is new?"

"Will you see Pablo tomorrow?"

"Of course. Why else would I get out of bed?" He forced himself to stand up. "Everything is so pointless," he muttered as he shuffled down the hall.

I almost followed him. His "so pointless" scared me.

He needed Pablo to give him purpose, but he was too scared to commit. I needed Jackie for the same reason and had used her to steel my determination to escape the madhouse. Just then I realized how crazy my plan was.

Chances were high she was straight, and she already had a boyfriend. What would she think about a girl in Texas, often dressed as a boy, who schemed for seven months to see her? I could think of many reactions, and "Oh, I can't wait,"seemed the least likely.

A slight heaviness settled in my chest as doubt seeped through my defenses. This plan could be a fiasco. I knew nothing about Alaska. Who lived there? Why?

I decided to stop by Landa Library the next day and find some books.

I couldn't pin all my hopes on a girl. But I could pin them on Camp Wonder and the two women who'd created it.

Still, I'd heard Jackie's voice in my head, like no other I'd ever heard before. There was such a thing as fate, wasn't there? What would I think about a girl who had seen my picture and worked her ass off for months to see me?

Damn, wouldn't that have been cool?

The next morning at school, I found Mary sitting on the rock wall. I'd decided to slick my hair and no longer pretend to sport a girlish pixie. I still wore my leather jacket, short dress, black tights, and penny loafers. I decided my protest outfit needed leather boots. I'd need a pair for Alaska anyway.

"Hey, Mary." I sat down. "What's happenin'?"

"I talked to Ava."

A shiver ran down my spine. I hugged myself. "How is she?"

"Hard to tell. I'm sure her parents were right there listening, but they couldn't hear me."

"How could you tell?"

"Because I mentioned your name, and they didn't force her to hang up."

Our eyes met for a second then I looked away. "Do I want to know?" I felt a sharp pain growing in the back of my throat.

"I called to tell her we won the tournament and that you were named MVP. She was polite but didn't react like you'd expect Ava to. Normally, she would've screamed and danced around the room. I asked her if she wanted me to send a message to the team or to anyone in particular."

I knew what was coming.

"She said, 'I'm sure they're happy enough without me saying anything.' Then she had to go."

I forced myself to swallow. "That makes sense. Her parents don't want her to communicate with anyone from Adler. I'm surprised they let her take your call."

"That's why they did."

She found my eyes, and I realized the truth. "You'd communicate her lack of interest so no one else would call."

"Yup."

I tried to sound positive. "But we still don't know what she really thinks or feels."

Mary sat up and sighed. "She doesn't feel anything. She didn't react at all, even when I told her about you racking that boy and being called Beep Beep."

Could Ava feel nothing now? Did they cut out her heart, or was she simply protecting herself? "If she had reacted, her parents would've asked her why, and then there'd be a fight. It's easier to pretend to be bored."

"I felt like I was talking to a zombie." She moved her hand along the wall until her pinkie hooked mine. "I'm sorry, Tracy."

I picked up my hand. "Thanks for trying." It hit me then why she had called—to see if Ava had moved on so Mary could deliver a message to me. She was available if I was interested.

Which I wasn't. The loss of Ava was still too sharp for me. Plus, I couldn't afford to start another scandal at school, especially now. But I didn't want to hurt Mary.

"Mary, please keep a lid on what I'm about to tell you. Okay?"

"Sure."

"My family's a mess right now. Dad is cutting me off, so I have to find a better job and work harder on my grades. And I need money to go to Alaska this summer."

"Alaska? Why?"

"Because there's some boss women up there who chop wood and build log cabins, wearing overalls. How bad is that?" I stood and looked down at her gaping eyes. "And use outhouses."

She frowned. "You want that?"

"Duh! So I don't have time for hanging out. Sorry." I squeezed her shoulder.

She sighed. "Okay."

I walked toward the high school building, passing Judy laughing with Charles. I heard her say, "I was so embarrassed, but it was so obvious!"

"Yeah, it is," Charles boasted. "I have to buy extra-large jock straps."

I shook my head and smiled when he winked at me. Charles would make sure she'd see it again.

I heard several calls of "Beep Beep" as I made my way to class, already sounding like distant memories. I found a chair and forced myself to focus on grades, money, and Alaska when all I wanted to do was go numb.

Two days later, I finished my English final at 10:30 and realized I'd left my slide rule at home. My physics final started at 1:30, so I had plenty of time to get it. Mom took Dad to the airport just as Spencer and I had left for school, so I'd have an opportunity to talk to her alone.

I drove into the garage, parking next to Mom's car. As I entered the utility room I heard the dryer going, but as I walked through the kitchen, I heard other sounds. Mom was moaning with little grunts. I bit my lip and felt my skin heat. At first I thought she was hurt, so I took a few quick steps into the den. Then I heard the motor sound, like an Oster barber massager, coming from her bedroom.

Mom was having sex. My skin prickled.

Was someone with her? I listened for another voice, but all I heard was hers.

She was masturbating.

I gasped and almost turned back to the kitchen, but I needed my slide rule. I tiptoed to the stairs and stepped lightly on each tread until I gained the second floor. My room was directly above hers. I walked as gently and rapidly as I could to my desk, grabbed what I needed, then headed back down.

When I reached the base of the stairs, the sounds had stopped. *Shit!* I hurried, but just as I turned into the kitchen, Mom called out.

"Tracy. Why are you home?"

I froze and gritted my teeth while holding out the slide rule. I couldn't face her.

She gasped. "You heard?" She banged against the wall, and I turned to see her gripping her robe tightly around her.

"It's okay, Mom. I should've left the house and come back later. I'm sorry."

With her back to me, she muttered, "I'm so embarrassed."

I went to her and held her shoulders. "I'm sure you are. If you'd caught me, I'd stay in my room for a week." I held her close. "Sorry I interrupted you."

"You didn't interrupt. I . . . heard you walking upstairs when I turned off . . ."

I blurted a quick laugh. "I always wondered whether anyone actually used those massagers for backs or scalps. Slip the thing on the back of your hand, and your fingers become a blur. The first time I saw one, I thought, 'Hmm, what woman wouldn't know what to do with that?'"

Mom buried her head into her hands. "That's why I bought it. Art thought it was so I could massage his back." She lowered her hands. "I'm just a hussy."

"Hey, Mom. Lighten up. You are perfectly normal." I hugged her. "Someday, all I'll have to say is, 'Remember when I came home . . .' and we'll both die laughing."

She finally hugged me back. "Thank you, Tracy. You won't tell . . ."

I laughed. "No one, but only if you let me borrow it." I tried to catch her eyes, but she turned her face away, now bright red.

"I shouldn't be using it at all. I feel like I'm being unfaithful to your father. I was always told it was a sin." She pushed back from me and covered her face.

"Everybody does it, but no one talks about it."

"Do you?"

"Everybody means everybody. That thing is loud."

She cast her eyes down and her lips quivered into a grin. "After a while, you don't notice." She covered her face again.

I squeezed her. "I love you, Mom."

She hugged back. "I love you, Tracy. You . . . you can use it, but how? When? It's so noisy."

I held her face. "Play loud music. Very loud to cover your moaning."

She blushed. "I don't have a radio in my room."

"Then get one. Or a record player. Tell you what, I'll pick one up on my way home tonight."

"I can give you money."

"Pay me back later. It's fine."

She fixed her eyes on mine. "Tracy, I do have money I can give to you and Spencer. I was going to tell you both at dinner tonight." Her voice turned strong with an edge. "I won't let him cut you both off. I won't."

Tears pooled in my eyes as I felt tension oozing out of my shoulders. I hadn't realized how up-tight I'd been that week. "Thank you, Mom." I kissed her cheek. "You can borrow any of my albums, unless you want me to pick up an Andy Williams or Frank Sinatra record."

"No. I like your music. The Beatles, Peter Paul & Mary . . ." She looked deep into my eyes. "Even Jefferson Airplane."

"Cool. Except now every time I hear loud music coming out of your bedroom, I'll know what you're doing." My face stretched into the biggest smile I'd ever felt.

She blushed. "Not every time."

"Okay." We smiled at each other. "I'm kinda glad I forgot my slide rule."

She nodded.

"Well, I better get back. I need to study formulas before my final this afternoon. Ugh! You'll have the house to yourself for the rest of the day. Make good use of it."

"You stinker." She laughed. "Go."

From that moment on, I felt a profound connection to my mother, more than just a secret shared.

That night she told Spencer and me her mother had given her and her sisters one hundred shares each of Johnson & Johnson stock four years ago and signed over oil lease royalties for each of them, courtesy of her husband. Her mother wanted to make sure her daughters had their own source of income, just in case. Since Mom always got the mail, Dad didn't know of her monthly checks which she cashed and kept hidden. She wanted us to keep earning our own money but also know we could get help from her when we needed it. She'd make arrangements to pay Dr. Sorel for Spencer's lessons since he had auditions to prepare for. She'd tell Dad that Spencer took on more students and paid for Sorel himself.

She didn't have enough to pay all our college expenses, but she would do her best. And she could help with the cost of my camp.

Spencer cried and hugged Mom until they were both bawling. Then we played a duet for her.

I stayed up that night until three studying for history and math and writing a note to her explaining how I came into possession of a realistic, flesh-colored dildo and why I wouldn't need it. While Mom made breakfast, I slipped into her room and left the toy and note on her nightstand.

Our basketball practices that week did not let up because we started our first game in the San Antonio Invitational Basketball Tournament on Saturday. Coach Wynn gave us copies of the brackets Thursday afternoon which showed the girls' games as well. I noticed that the Incarnate Word Shamrocks would play two hours before us at Edison High School. I planned to be there. Maybe Ava would attend.

When I came home that evening, Mom did her best to avoid my eyes until Spencer went upstairs after dinner. Finally she looked at me and blushed bright red. "Tracy, what am I going to do with you?"

"Let me know when you want something else."

She took several deep breaths. "I have a special fondness now for Jefferson Airplane's 'White Rabbit.'"

I clapped my hands to my mouth to stifle my screams of laughter as I stomped my feet.

"Shhh!" She rushed over and put a finger to her mouth. "Spencer will hear you."

The next day Spencer finished his last final at 12:30 then brought Pablo back to school so I could say goodbye. I ran to him as soon as he jumped out of the Buick.

"I'm going to miss you," I said in his ear as we hugged. "I tried to convince Spence to go home with you."

"I know," said Pablo. "He's stubborn."

"He's scared." I kissed his forehead. "Take care of yourself until auditions in March."

"Will you drive to Dallas with us?"

"Certainly." I smiled at Spencer. "How else will you two be able to make out in the back seat for five hours?"

"¡Una hermana tan maravillosa!" said Pablo.

"Yes, I'm a wonderful sister. Goodbye!"

He hugged me then jumped into the car. He and Spencer had an hour before the bus left for Laredo.

On Saturday I arrived at Edison High School by 2:00, in uniform and sweats. The place was crowded with lots of people coming and going, so I kept my head on a swivel looking for Ava. My chest heaved. I wanted to scream out her name. A boys' game was racing through its last two minutes. I scanned the bleachers from a corner and found Mr. and Mrs. Blunt by themselves about halfway up.

She's here. But where?

I darted out and looked for the locker rooms. Maybe she was playing with the Shamrocks. Breathless, I followed a girls' team wearing yellow and white warm-ups streaming through a door.

A coach stopped me. "This is the girls' locker room."

"I am a girl. Do you want to see my tits?" I started to lift up my sweatshirt.

She shook her head and stepped aside.

I walked through a locker area and turned the corner. Girls in green and white warm-ups gathered around their coach as she pointed to words on her clipboard. "Rebounds. Run the offense. Hands up on defense. Got it?"

All the girls shouted, "Go Shamrocks!" and stood.

I saw Ava looking at me, her eyes wide open, and no expression on her face. *Please smile at me.*

"Line up!" yelled the coach. "Three laps around the court when it's clear, then two lines for layups."

I watched Ava hold her stomach and grimace then whisper something to her coach as the girls walked through the room toward the exit. The coach nodded and Ava took off toward the toilet stalls.

I followed, my heart jumping in my chest. She kept walking, and I thought she was trying to get away from me.

She moved past the stalls and toward a maintenance closet. Just before she opened the door, she turned, flashed her eyes around the room and ducked inside. I walked as casually as I could toward the door, leaned against the wall for a few seconds and looked around. A girl darted toward an open stall then slammed the door closed just before I heard her retch.

I twisted the knob and slipped inside the closet. "Ava? I can't see anything."

She giggled. "Your eyes will adjust."

Warmth flooded my body. She was still Ava. I smelled her sweat and felt her warm fingertips on my face. I grabbed one and kissed it. Then she pulled my mouth to hers, crushing our lips together. My tongue found hers—hot, wet, urgent. She sucked mine deep into her mouth and slowly pulled away, her warm breath kissing my face.

I reached under her shirt, but she pushed my hands down. "I have to go," she said. "I just wanted one more kiss."

I could now see the outline of her face and touched her cheek.

"Beep Beep?" She moved her pointer finger slowly around my lips.

My legs wobbled. "Crazy, huh?"

"Wish I could've seen it."

"How are you doing?"

She harrumphed. "I'm getting straighter and straighter every day. Can't you tell? I even have a boyfriend."

My body shuddered. "Do you kiss him like you did me?"

"I'll never kiss anyone like I do you."

My face burned. "I wish . . ."

She pressed fingers against my lips. "Shhh. It just can't happen, Tracy. We can't see each other again. Promise me."

I gulped in breaths. "But . . ."

"Promise. No more."

I swallowed. "I promise. I'm going to Alaska this summer."

Her smile stretched slowly across her face. "You'll love it there." She pulled my forehead to hers. "Find someone you can love without hiding." She pushed my face back and wiped a tear from her eye. "You were my first. Goodbye, Tracy." She cracked open the door, peeked through, then darted out.

I leaned against the wall and tried to breathe. Tears pushed through my fingers even as they pressed hard against my eyes. I felt like kicking the door and screaming, but as with most times in my life, I had to stifle my emotions.

Find someone you can love without hiding. I had to. I couldn't go through this again.

I opened the door and ignored two girls gawking at me as I walked by. I started to head toward the court until I saw flashes of green and white uniforms through crowds of bystanders.

I'd promised her.

I turned around and left the gym, heading for my car.

CHAPTER 14
LUCY RIPS HER BOW

We won both games on Saturday. Against Holy Cross on Sunday, we were behind by two in the last thirty seconds. Coach had drawn up a play, knowing they would double-team me. After throwing me the ball, Charles got open in the corner from Mario's screen where I nailed him with a pass. He shot and missed. They got the rebound, we fouled, and they made both free throws. If we'd won, we'd have played St. Anthony's next. I was sure Ava's boyfriend would be in the stands or on the court. Either way, Ava would've been there.

The ache of losing hit doubly hard. If we'd won, I would've had no choice but to play and maybe catch a glimpse of her. Gene saw me wipe a tear out of my eye.

He grabbed my shoulder and pulled me to him. "Can't win them all, Tracy."

I wrapped my arms around him and buried my face in his chest, ready to drop all my defenses and weep. He stopped, and I tensed.

"Tracy, someone who doesn't know you're a girl is going to think this looks weird."

I pushed away, my gut tightening in anger at him and myself. "And your greatest fear is being called a homo."

His eyes bulged. "I didn't say that."

"Weird?" I snapped. "What's that mean?"

He started to say something but stopped and looked away.

I felt my stomach drop. I couldn't tell him—or anyone—the real reason for my tears. A wave of loneliness slammed into my chest. How long before I didn't feel trapped in a closet? I blew out a breath. "It's okay, Gene. Neither of us wants to be called a pussy. For you, that's normal. For me . . . that's my personal hang-up now." I walked away, kicking myself for nearly blubbering like a stereotypical girl in Gene's arms.

We won our next game then lost our last. The Wolves had never been invited to the city tournament before, so everyone was happy with how we did. Adler was the smallest school playing. Both of our losses were close. I should have been overjoyed, but I couldn't escape the pressure I felt to earn money and the ache of my final time with Ava.

Spencer picked me up in a bear hug after the game. "Proud of you, Sis."

I hugged him back. "Thank you." He set me down and our eyes locked. "So now what do we do?"

We were both waiting for something to happen—Spencer's audition and Pablo's return in three months; my escape to Alaska in six. Such a long time for both of us with seemingly nothing fun between now and then.

"Practice," he sighed. "Get a second job. Climb into a social cocoon and practice some more."

I hooked his arm as we walked, an idea forming in my brain. "How much does Alamo Music pay you per lesson?"

"Five dollars."

"Do you think they'd hire me to teach?"

"Maybe," he said. "Go tomorrow and talk to Victor."

I stopped and looked at him. "Does he know you have a sister?"

"Nope."

"You have a brother, if he ever asks."

"Whatever you say, Tracy, but why?"

I tugged his arm to start walking. "Because he's more likely to take a chance on a boy, especially as a salesman."

"You plan to sell pianos?"

"Several."

That night after dinner, Spencer practiced sight-reading for two hours on the piano, with Mom turning pages when he nodded. Dr. Sorel had given Spencer a stack of pieces he'd never seen and told him Juilliard judges expected him to play them perfectly the first time. Spencer struggled in this area, but he was determined to improve, especially since this was one of Pablo's strengths. If Spencer wanted to be with Pablo in New York City, he'd have to push himself for the next several weeks.

I went to my room and slipped the *Sounds of Silence* album onto my turntable. I felt alone, like I was an island, so I dropped the needle onto "I Am a Rock" and listened to Simon & Garfunkel as I looked out my window and refused to cry.

What did I have to protect me? I couldn't bear to read a book at that moment. Watching TV would be difficult with Spencer's piano drowning out the sound, and I didn't want to be like Dad, scooting my chair right up to the screen. I had no one to call.

I could listen to music, feeding my emptiness with sad songs, DJing my own pity party.

But I was restless and angry that I had nowhere to go, no one to be with.

I felt odd, like a mistake, having to hide my love, like John Lennon commanded in his song—"You've Got to Hide Your Love Away."

So many of society's norms had been broken in music. The Stones sang "Let's Spend the Night Together," promoting casual sex. No one could understand the lyrics Jack Ely sang in "Louie Louie," but most thought they heard the line "fuck your girl all kinds of ways." Allusions to taking drugs were everywhere on the radio.

But no one had written a song about girls loving girls. Or guys loving guys.

Because no one would play it.

Unless the real meaning was hidden.

I almost leapt toward my desk to find pencil and paper, scribbling lyrics I heard in my head.

I found your lips in the dark
And tried to touch your heart
Out of sight
From the crowd

I was back in the closet with Ava, feeling a rhythm more than a melody. I needed to find a rhyming dictionary, but that would have to wait until the next day.

I drank your breath like sweet wine
And tried to slow down time
We got caught

And now a clue to the real meaning:

And now we're out

For most listeners, this could be a normal Romeo & Juliet situation where for some reason the two lovers weren't allowed to meet. But gay listeners would hear "out" and wonder. I needed another clue.

Chorus
They say we cannot be together
Straighten up or find a new life
If you cannot be my lover
I will die

I was sure "straighten up" would make the situation clear but still permit deniability.

If they choose who we kiss
And force us to split
We die slow
So very slow
When push comes to shove
We've got to cherish our love

And hold on
Just hang on

Chorus repeat
All we can do
Is run for our lives
Just get away, Baby
And live free
All we can do, Baby,
all we can do
Just run for our lives
All we can do
Just get away, Baby
And live free
Just live free

I'd never felt such a rush of excitement and anticipation. My heart hadn't stopped pounding for the past . . . I looked at my clock and couldn't believe what I saw—two hours of intense, breathless focus had passed in an instant.

I examined my notebook and found potential rhymes climbing up the margins, scratchouts and arrows looping to rejected stanzas. Each line had two or three options, some with circles, others with light Xs through them.

I didn't remember every phrase or word choice or thought process to get to the final wording, but I still felt the fever of creation bubbling in my veins.

Next to an orgasm, this was the most intensely enjoyable sensation I'd ever felt, and it still continued.

Spencer knocked on my door. "Hey, Sis. Can I come in?"

I leapt out of my seat, grabbed the door knob and pulled, then raced past Spencer to the stairs.

"Tracy?" Spence called from behind me.

I bounded down the steps and flew to the piano where I spread my spiral notebook over my brother's music. My left hand found a C7 chord and copied the rhythm of the first lines.

Spencer strode toward me. "What's going on?"

A surge of pride swept through me. "I wrote a song!"

He sat down beside me and squinted at my notebook. "How can you read that? There's words everywhere."

The rush continued. "I'll recopy it later. I need a melody." I built a C, F, G chord progression and used the pentatonic blues scale to match my lyrics. After a few tries, I found a sequence then started singing.

Spencer flinched. "Have I heard you sing before?"

Oh, my god, was I that bad? "Not unless you've been hiding in the backseat of my car. I only sing when I'm driving and alone."

"Why?" he asked. "You sound pretty good."

My face flushed with happiness, but I pretended to be offended. "*Pretty* good? Thanks."

"I mean great. You sound great. You shouldn't keep it secret."

I leaned against him. "Thanks, Bro."

He ripped out my pages, leaving them on the shelf, and took the notebook where he recopied lyrics and added notes as I experimented. After thirty minutes, we'd gone through the entire song. He placed his clean copy over my scribbles.

"From the top," he said.

"I can't decide whether I want it to be hard and bluesy or haunting and pretty." I played C, Em, F, and G and redid the melody. This made my song sound more like Joni Mitchell—full of sweet sorrow.

And then I realized the battle going on inside my head—male vs. female. Joni or Mick Jagger?

If I was going to sing in public, I'd rather be Jagger. I took a deep breath, trying to calm my nerves, then started. Mom walked into the living room during the first chorus, her eyes wide in disbelief, her hands clasped near her heart.

I improvised some blues riffs after the second chorus then belted out the last lines before ending with a glissando and tremolo. Spencer and Mom erupted in applause, and I felt such a rush of warmth spilling through my arms and legs.

"What song was that?" Mom asked.

My chest still heaving, I said, "Mine. But I haven't titled it yet."

"All we can do," Spencer said.

"That works. Or run for our lives."

"Just get away," Spencer said, locking his eyes on mine.

"And run free." We both stared at each other, breathing slowly. "Just get away, baby."

He nodded. "I know. I blew it." He stood up and walked outside. I was sure he'd walk down the street, smoking a cigarette.

"What was that about?" Mom asked.

"Pablo invited him to stay at his house over the holidays. I told him to go, but he wouldn't. Now he knows he should have." I picked up my papers then gave Mom a hug. "Thanks for clapping."

As I broke away, she grabbed my arm. "Aren't you going to practice?"

"No, but I am giving lessons soon."

Her face lost color. "When? Where?"

"Tomorrow at Alamo Music."

"They gave you a job?"

I laughed. "Not yet, but they will."

The next morning I went shopping for dress pants, a white shirt, and striped tie at Gibson's Discount Center, trying to conserve my dwindling funds. Before I emerged from my car parked at Alamo Music on N. Main, I reformed the flip above my forehead with my comb and straightened my tie.

In my lowest register, I spoke to myself in the mirror. "Are you ready for this?" I blew out a breath and smiled. "Why the fuck not?"

I strode to the front door, pulled it open for an older couple exiting the store, then walked inside. A salesman behind the first counter smiled at me. "Good morning, sir. How can I help you?"

I forced the flutters in my stomach to slow down. *Good morning, SIR.* I loved it. "I'm looking for Victor in the piano department."

He pointed toward the back. "Keep walking straight. You can't miss him."

"Thank you." As I approached the piano section, I noticed a placard advertising special financing on Steinway pianos. I scanned the room and saw a man in a suit speaking to a woman near a baby grand piano. No other salesmen were around, so I assumed that must be Victor. A thin, elderly man wearing a hat and cardigan sweater smiled at a young girl as she sat in front of a Yamaha upright and began to play a decent

"Minuet in G." Maybe ten years old with wavy blonde hair past her shoulders, she sat in perfect form in her expensive white dress and tights, punctuated by a bright red bow at her waist. A matching bow rested on her head. She could have been me seven years ago, except my hair was brown, thin, and straight.

Victor ran over to them, spoke for a few seconds then hustled back to the woman, standing near more expensive pianos. That was my chance, and I took it.

With my back straight and my mouth formed into a friendly smile, I strode toward the man and introduced myself. "Hello, I can help you while Victor takes care of his other client. My name is Tray Franks. Are you interested in this Yamaha upright in particular, or could I show you other styles and brands?"

The man chuckled. "Whatever my granddaughter wants to try. Lucy started lessons two months ago and is already playing Bach. Can you believe it?" His eyes twinkled along with the golden tooth revealed in his doting smile.

He'd just given me permission to swing for the fences. "'Minuet in G' at two months is impressive, Lucy." Which was true. Her hands were larger than normal but not freakish like mine. "What piano do you play at home?"

She folded her hands in her lap and smiled up at me. "A Wurlitzer Spinet. We're renting it because my parents weren't sure I'd stick with my lessons."

I nodded and looked directly into her eyes. "Well, you proved them wrong, didn't you?"

She laughed. "I sure did."

"Good for you. Do you have room in your house for a larger piano?"

"They don't," her grandfather said. "I'm Fred, by the way." He shook my hand. "But I do. We live a few blocks apart, and I want a piano for her to play at my house."

"Okay, then." I felt a lightness in my chest as my pulse quickened. I had a plan. "I'm going to show you the difference in sound among pianos. Lucy will be playing at your house for years to come, so you'll want to make sure you give her the best instrument to showcase her increasing talents and abilities." I approached the bench. "Lucy, would you mind giving me your seat so I can play something for you?"

"Certainly." She popped up. "What will you play?"

"Sections of Chopin's *Ballad in G minor*, one of the most beautiful pieces ever written." I sat down and started with the first *agitato* section which allowed me to use most of the piano's range, fast and vigorous. I tore into it, hearing them gasp as my fingers flew across the keyboard. When I got to the first main melody, so slow and achingly enchanting, I spoke above the music. "When I first heard this piece, I fell in love, but I couldn't play many of the parts. However, I could do some of the prettiest sections, like this one. In a few months, you can play this melody."

I stopped and turned to find Lucy with her mouth and eyes wide open.

Finally, she said, "Please don't stop. You're amazing."

Part of me knew I was manipulating them to make a sale, but another part felt my heart skip. The girl's eyes stayed wide, barely blinking, in total awe. *Maybe I can inspire her,* I thought. *She's got spunk. She can be more than a cute, feminine doll to show off.*

I stood. "I'll play some more, but at a better piano. I want you to hear the difference." I looked at Fred. "Can I show you a Steinway?"

"Certainly," he said. "Lead the way."

I looked for Victor and saw him sitting in his office passing papers to the woman. He was closing his sale and would be busy for a few more minutes. I took a deep breath as I moved closer to Fred. "The best gift my father ever gave me was a Steinway Grand." I led him to the B model, just under six feet long. "He bought it for $4800.00 in 1965, and you can see it now costs $5200. Steinways do not lose their value like other brands. My dad will be able to sell that piano for seven or eight thousand dollars in five years if he wants to." I didn't entirely make up those numbers. A salesman had made the same pitch to Dad over two years ago.

I sat down on the bench. "I'll play the same section of the Ballad as I played on the upright. I think you'll hear a difference."

I started and marveled at the rich sound, so much louder in the base and tinkling at the top in this store than in my house. When I got to the melody, I skipped ahead to the octave version where I always felt like screaming in delight as my hands moved in a pounding blur across the keyboard. When I stopped, I heard applause, not only from Fred and Lucy but many others in the store. I stood and waved.

"What'd you think?" I asked Lucy.

"Can you teach me? Please." She grabbed my hand.

My heart drummed in my chest. "If you and your parents want me to."

"They will," Fred said. "When can you start?"

"Any day this week."

Lucy still held my hand. "Can I ever play as well as you?"

"You can do anything you want. Don't ever let anyone tell you differently." I squeezed her hand. "I can simplify the melody, and you can play that in a few weeks. Maybe sooner."

Lucy's chest swelled as her smile stretched across her face.

"When can I have this delivered?" Fred asked.

Lucy clapped her hands and jumped. "Yes!"

My skin tingled with happiness. I remembered feeling the same excitement when Dad finally succumbed to our pleadings and wrote a check.

I hoped Lucy's joy would last longer than mine.

Victor shook hands with the woman then walked toward us.

"Victor can answer that question," I said.

He stood with his hands folded at his waist, smiling at me. "Was that you playing?"

"Guilty."

"You are very talented," he said.

"He was amazing!" shouted Lucy.

"Let me introduce you to Fred and his granddaughter, Lucy," I said. "They want to buy this Steinway."

Victor raised his brows. "Is that right?"

"When can you deliver this to my house?" Fred asked.

"I'll have to check our delivery schedule, but most likely in two or three days."

I found Victor's eyes, locked on then said, "When you're through with them, I'd like to speak to you."

He nodded. "Certainly." Victor led them back toward his office, and just before closing his door, he gazed back at me and mouthed, "Thank you."

I saluted and kept watch for other customers.

I knew then I would both love and hate teaching Lucy. In the coming weeks, I would exit Fred's house after each lesson, feeling more and more apprehension at having to leave her behind when I traveled to Alaska. She learned everything easily, including chord sequences for current songs. Soon, she was trying to write her own. At the end of each lesson, she asked me to play something for her, "Because you inspire me to work hard so I can play as well as you."

I loved that kid.

Maybe because I saw the young girl I once was, so eager and excited about life before I began to realize my difference from everyone else.

By mid-May, I'd sold dozens of pianos and taught students every day, either at the store or in their homes. But none were as special to me as Lucy. I told her about my upcoming trip to Alaska, how I'd be traveling alone and paying for everything. How much I wanted to hike in the mountains and chop wood and look for moose and even bears.

Her eyes and mouth gaped open.

"Would you ever want to do that?" I asked.

"Yes," she blurted, "but how could I?"

"Why not?"

"Because I'm a girl."

A pain stabbed my chest. "Of course you can. Men always tell girls what they can't do. Don't believe them."

She smiled. "You're a man."

I knew I shouldn't say more, but as always, I couldn't control my impulse. "Can you keep a secret?"

She bit her lip and leaned closer. "Yes. What is it?"

Bile rose in my throat as my heart pounded. My brain screamed, "No," but I'd been lonely and so tired of having to be one person at school and another at work and someone else entirely in my room.

As I looked at Lucy, I realized she needed to know. Otherwise she'd grow up believing in all the bullshit limitations her parents and grandfather and the rest of the world had already forced on her.

I breathed a few times and then smiled. "I'm not a man. I'm a seventeen-year-old girl who dresses this way because I want to. My real name is Tracy."

She frowned then shook her head. "You can't be," she whispered.

I showed her my driver's license and a yearbook photo from October before I'd cut my hair. She held each one, staring at me and the pictures, saying nothing. She sucked in her lips, and for a second I thought she would cry or run out of the room, yelling for her grandfather.

Finally, she asked, "Why?"

I took back the license and photo. "Lots of reasons. I think it's stupid girls are forced to wear dresses and to care about makeup and looking pretty. Also, I'm sure my customers would have been less likely to buy pianos from a girl. You never suspected?"

"No!" Her smile widened and she pressed her palm against her chest, rising and falling as she breathed deeply. "Never in a million years. I thought you were a very cute boy."

I chuckled. "No one called me cute when I dressed like a girl."

She blushed. "I've had a crush on you forever." She clasped her hands over her mouth. "I shouldn't have said that."

"That's okay. It's nice to be liked."

She swallowed. "What made you start?"

I shook my head and sighed, knowing I should stop talking and leave, but I felt such a need to share my feelings with someone. I had no one else besides Spencer. "Because I had a girlfriend and wanted to be with her. I dressed like a boy, and we dated."

Her eyes grew wide as words barely escaped her mouth. "You had a girlfriend? Why?"

Clearly she'd never considered this possibility.

"Because I'm attracted to girls, not boys. I've never had a crush on a boy. Lots of girls feel this way, but they hide it."

She stared at me then looked away as she crumpled her brows and forehead. "I never knew."

"I'm sorry I've burdened you with my issues, but I want you to know you're very talented and smart and you can do anything. Don't let anyone treat you like a doll or say you can't do something because you're a girl."

She barely nodded as her eyes met mine.

I stood. "Someday girls will be able to wear and do whatever they want."

"Like go by yourself to Alaska?"

"At the very least."

Her face blushed. "How can you be so brave?"

"I don't think I'm brave. Just scared of the alternative."

She stood. "When do you leave?"

"In about three weeks."

She gasped, her eyes shifting back and forth across my face. "When will you come back?"

I tried to swallow the lump in my throat and stop tears from welling in my eyes. "I won't."

Her chin quivered. "You have to."

"I can't, Lucy. I'm sorry."

She crushed me in a hug. "Please. I want you to teach me."

I wrapped my arms around her and squeezed, my tears dripping onto the bow in her hair. "I wish I could."

Fred walked in behind Lucy and frowned. "What's going on?"

I removed my hands from her back and tried to push Lucy away. My stomach rolled and every muscle tightened.

"Lucy," Fred commanded. "Let go of him."

Lucy squeezed tighter. "She's not a him," she barked. "Tracy's a girl. The bravest girl I know."

"What?" Fred took three quick steps and yanked Lucy's arm, pulling her away from me.

"Let go!" Lucy yelled, twisting herself away.

Fred squinted his eyes at me, trying to see through my skin. "You're a girl?"

"My name is Tracy."

His jaw muscles bulged. "Why were you hugging Lucy?"

"I hugged her first," Lucy barked. "She's leaving for Alaska."

Fred pulled his wallet out of his pocket, rummaged for a bill, and held it out for me to take. "That should cover what I owe you. Please leave and don't come back."

"No!" Lucy screamed, lunging for me. "She still has three weeks!"

I pressed my palm against the back of her head while she convulsed against my chest. "You'll be fine, Lucy. Remember what I told you."

Fred moved closer, his face almost purple in anger. "Take this and leave."

I pulled the bill from his fingers then knelt down in front of Lucy, pushing her back so I could see her eyes. "Be strong, Lucy. Hide your tears or men will think you're weak. You can do this."

She clenched her jaw and wiped her eyes.

I smiled at her. "You're just as brave as me. Yes?"

She nodded and ripped the bow from her hair.

I looked at Fred. "Thank you for the opportunity to teach Lucy. She'll be a great musician. Or whatever she wants to be."

He tightened his lips and said nothing.

Lucy lifted her chin and gave me a firm smile. "Thank you, Tracy. I'll make you proud."

I nodded and took a deep breath. "You already have."

I left the house and part of my heart behind.

CHAPTER 15
YELLOW SOCKS FOREVER

On January 31, 1968, the communists launched surprise attacks throughout South Vietnam with 85,000 troops. Though American soldiers soon regained lost villages and cities, the American public was shocked. Many realized all the optimistic statements by General Westmoreland had been lies. If the enemy were nearly defeated, how could they be storming the American Embassy and fighting in the streets of Saigon?

On the first day of the Tet Offensive, Westmoreland announced we had killed 10,000 enemy soldiers while only losing 249. These lopsided counts had been fed to the American public for years, but in light of what we were seeing on TV, many doubted their accuracy. If we were killing so many of the enemy, why did our military want to send 200,000 more troops?

Which meant more draftees, increasing Spencer's chances of going to the war.

Walter Cronkite, the CBS News anchor whom Dad watched every night he was home because he was a "straight-shooter"and unbiased, went to Vietnam in February and returned to air a one-hour broadcast on February 27 after another 1500 American deaths. All of us watched the show and heard Cronkite declare the war a stalemate whose ending could only be negotiated.

We could not win.

I grabbed Spencer's hand and saw his terrified eyes glued to the television.

Dad cursed Cronkite, jumped out of his chair, and immediately turned the channel. "The media is going to lose this war!"

"Because he's telling the truth?" I said. "I thought Cronkite was 'the most trusted man in America.' Is he a liar now?"

He glared at me. "I guess you and all your anti-war commie friends will be jumping for joy in the streets. Walter Cronkite's on your side now!"

"Art, please," Mom pleaded from the sofa.

My blood boiled. I stood, ready to rush him, but Spencer tightened his grip on my hand. "Do you want Spencer to fight in that war? Do you? Would that make you proud?"

He stood in front of the television, folded his arms, and tightened his eyes. "I'm proud of the soldiers I fly over there, and especially proud of those I fly back to the States. I'd be just as proud of your brother if he were in my plane."

I yanked my hand away from Spencer, who now stared at Dad with such pain in his eyes. "In a body bag or a seat, or does it matter to you? What if he's not on your plane? Would you be just as proud of him?"

Dad tilted his head and smirked. "Do you mean because he dodged the draft? Or burned his card, like your friends do? No, I wouldn't be proud of that."

"You fucking bastard!" I ran toward him.

Spencer jumped up from the sofa and grabbed me from behind. "Tracy! No. He's not worth it."

Dad flinched and raised his hands in fear, turning his face.

"Scared of a girl?" I sneered.

He lifted his chin, as if to affirm his manhood.

"Of a lesbian, queer, gay girl, no less?" I taunted.

"Please, Tracy," Mom begged.

Dad shook his head. "That sums you up, doesn't it? What a daughter to be proud of."

I strained against Spencer's grip. "Surely the big powerful airline captain who flies young men to war wouldn't be scared of me. But maybe so." I was determined to get to him. "All you do is drop them off. You don't have to fight. And you didn't fight in World War II either. Such a little pussy."

Spencer pulled me farther away from him.

Dad bared his teeth and shook with anger. "They had too many pilots!" he yelled. "I've told you a hundred times. By the time I got into the Navy —"

"I know. The war was almost over." I spit the words out. "Such a pity they had to end it before you could prove your manhood. The fact is you're perfectly willing to send others into danger when you never had to face any yourself. When's your next flight to Nam, Daddy? Maybe one of them commies will shoot at your plane so you can brag about your war experience."

At that moment, I thought I couldn't hate anyone more than I did him. But I was wrong. I'd find a new level of hate in four months.

Mom stood and faced me and Spencer, visibly shaking. Her voice quaked. "You two need to leave the house for awhile, so everyone can calm down."

Spencer turned me around and led me out the front door. I headed for my car.

"No, I'm driving," he said. "You'd kill both of us."

He drove down Jackson-Keller to the elementary school and pulled into the parking lot. Gripping the wheel with both hands, he said, "Why do you ask him a question when you know the answer?"

I slumped back against the seat and lifted my feet onto the dash. "I don't know. Maybe I keep hoping he'll surprise me. He does the same to me. Always lumping me with my *commie* friends, as if I have any friends. He hates me just like he hates hippies and demonstrators, even though I've never held an anti-war sign or marched in the streets."

"Why don't you?"

I opened my door. "I don't have time! All I do is go to school, sell pianos, and give lessons." I started walking toward the playground.

Spencer hurried after me. "I hear you playing guitar in your room."

"Yeah, late at night when I'm dead tired but can't sleep."

"Have you written more songs?"

"Some."

"You should play them for me."

I stopped at the swing set. "When? You're always practicing."

He lit a cigarette. "Play them after my audition in two weeks."

I sat down in the swing and gripped the chains. "Are you nervous?"

"Extremely." He pushed his dark hair back with both hands and sat in the swing next to me.

"When Pablo shows up, maybe you can relax," I said. "I think Dad will be out flying then." I leaned back and kicked up my legs to start the swing.

Spencer blew smoke above his head. "I realized a few weeks ago that Pablo's my competition. Juilliard accepts less than ten percent into the piano division. The chances of both of us being admitted are slim to none."

I chuckled as I swung past him. "Do you want me to break his fingers? Or maybe just his thumbs like they did to Paul Newman in *The Hustler.*"

He stared out toward the road and said nothing.

I dragged my shoes in the gravel and stopped. "I was kidding, Bro."

He sighed heavily. "What if I don't get in?"

"Go to Trinity or S.M.U. They both would give you a scholarship."

He shook his head. "It's not the same. Dr. Sorel is good, but he's not Leonard Eisner. Dad won't pay for it anyway."

"He's told you that recently?"

Spencer inhaled another puff then stomped his butt into the rocks. "Yeah. Just before dinner he came to my room for a man-to-man talk. He can't justify spending so much money on a degree that makes me a glorified piano teacher. He said I'm smart, so I should be a doctor or lawyer." He got up and walked to the monkey bars where he reached up to grab each crossbar while walking underneath.

"That's cheating, you know."

"I'm too tall."

"Just lift up your legs. Like this." I grabbed a bar with both hands and bent my legs behind me. I reached out for the next bar and the next, swinging toward him. I straightened my legs and dropped to the ground. "You try."

"No. I've put on weight." He walked back to the other end, grabbing each crossbar. At the end, he stopped and leaned against the post, fumbling for a cigarette in his pocket.

I walked toward him. "Would Dad pay for college if you changed your major?"

His sorrowful eyes found mine and he sighed. "No, not until I put my homosexuality behind me. He said I can't have any career if I'm gay."

"He's full of shit, you know."

"Is he? Name one famous gay, male or female."

I thought a minute. "I can't. Maybe some writers or musicians, but I can't think of any in particular."

He lit a cigarette and puffed. "Okay. Name one professional in San Antonio who's openly gay."

"Hogan at Galligaskins. I think Victor is gay."

He raised his brows. "Professionals, Tracy. Not salesmen." He walked toward the merry-go-round and sat down.

I followed. "Lift your legs, and I'll spin you."

He scooted back. I grabbed a bar and ran to get the platform revolving then jumped on next to him. I lay down and watched the stars spinning around above me in the clear sky. I started singing the chorus of the Beatles' "Fool on the Hill," and felt so lonely. There we were, two gay teens, twirling on playground equipment we'd outgrown long ago, before the truth of what we were had crashed our worlds.

When the spinning stopped, I sat up and looked back at him. "So what does Dad want you to do about being gay?"

He sighed and pushed himself up. "Enlist. He said the military will steer me in the right direction. Make a man out of me."

My blood heated and shot to my head as I leapt off the platform. "Make a killer out of you, he means. And a liar. All the world's major problems are caused by men. Egotistical, tough-guy, always-think-they're-right men. Is that what you want to be?"

He breathed deeply and stared out to the road. "I don't want to be anything right now." He got up and started walking toward his car.

I followed and hooked my arm in his, leaning my head on his shoulder.

He lit another cigarette. "One of my female students hit on me yesterday. I felt embarrassed and stupid. And then there's Leonard, who I think might be gay, but I'm scared to say or do anything. I could get fired or even arrested." He blew smoke above his head. "How do we live like this?" He leaned against his car.

"Be a musician. I think a lot of them are gay."

"Dad won't pay, and I can't afford college on my own."

"Do your best at the audition and see what happens." I grabbed his hand. "Please don't enlist. Promise me."

"I can't promise anything right now." He pulled his hand away and opened his door. "Do you think we can go back yet? I've got homework."

"Yeah." I opened my door and slid inside. "I've spent enough time with my commie friends."

He chuckled. "I must have missed that. Are gay commies allowed?"

"All commies are gay."

"Cool. Bring me along for the next meeting." He started the car and backed up.

Later that night, I sat on my bed doing plucking patterns on my guitar when I heard light knocks on my door.

"Tracy," Mom said. "Can I come in?"

"Sure."

She opened the door and eyed my guitar. "Where'd you get that?"

"From Alamo Music. They had a sale on Martins, and I get an employee discount."

She moved closer. "I never hear you play piano anymore."

"Spencer's on it all the time. Besides, I give two or three lessons every day. I spend enough time on the piano."

"Are you making enough money?" she asked.

"I'll have enough to send my final payment for Camp Wonder by next week."

She sat on my bed. "Tracy, you have to learn to ignore your father."

My pulse quickened. "He started it with his comment about my commie friends."

"No. You started by talking back to him after he cursed Cronkite and the media. You didn't have to say anything."

"But —"

"But nothing. Just let it pass and leave the room. I thought you two were going to throw punches."

I stood and hung my guitar on a wall bracket. "I would have if Spencer hadn't stopped me."

"And what you said about World War II. That really stung."

"I wanted it to."

She sighed and pushed some hair behind her ear. "Please sit down. I don't want you hovering over me."

I sat in my desk chair, purposely spreading my pant-clad legs wide.

"Your father had a first cousin named Dale. They were best friends and both enlisted on the same day. Dale wanted Art to be a Marine with him so they could watch each other's backs, but Art wanted to fly. Dale was killed in Okinawa. Art's never gotten over that. He always felt guilty. Because he chose to fly planes, he never left his base in California until the war was over. But they always needed Marines."

"To stop bullets," I said. "If his best friend was killed, why does he want Spencer to enlist?"

"He doesn't want Spencer to be drafted. Art's worried they'll end student deferments after another year or two."

I searched her eyes. "Do you want Spence to enlist?"

She covered her face. "God, no."

"That's what Dad is trying to convince Spencer to do. And he won't pay tuition for a music degree."

She blew out a long breath. "I know. We've argued and argued."

"He wants the Navy to make a man out of him."

She covered her face and whimpered. "I know."

"Mom, Spencer can't stop being gay. Why can't Dad accept that?"

She wiped her eyes and tried to regain her composure. "Art was the youngest, so he had to wear hand-me-downs. His father brought home new yellow socks one day and gave them to Art. They were a few pennies cheaper than regular white socks, and pennies were important during the Depression. Art had to wear them and was teased every day. Boys called him all kinds of names, including homo. Art claimed he fought his way to and from school every day until he outgrew the socks. He never forgave his father for that."

"Not forgiving seems to run in our genes."

"From his side of the family. Your father is worried that Spencer will be bullied and teased, and he won't be able to cope. He thinks being in the Navy will help him get over . . . being gay."

My jaw tightened. "You know that's ridiculous. Spencer can't be around a bunch of naked yahoos on a ship. They'll tear him apart."

"I know," she whispered.

"The truth is that Dad is ashamed of Spencer. He wants to tell his pilot buddies that his son didn't run from the war. By God, he joined the Navy! He sure doesn't want to tell them his son is a gay pianist." I sat next to her. "Is that yellow sock story supposed to excuse him?"

"No. He's told me several times and then again after you two left the house. In his mind, what he went through explains his attitude. But tonight I asked him, 'Imagine if you could never outgrow those socks or take them off?'"

"What did he say?"

"He probably would have killed himself."

We looked at each other, knowing what each was thinking. I pulled her to me, and she shuddered.

"I'm so worried, Tracy."

"I am too."

Two weeks later, Spencer and I drove to the bus station to pick up Pablo. They hugged but refrained from any other display of affection until they disappeared in the back seat as I drove them home. Dad was on the other side of the world, and Mom allowed Pablo to stay with us that night. After dinner, Pablo gave Spencer pointers on how to sight read then blew us all away playing a Stravinsky piece adapted for piano he had never seen before. His hands flew over the keyboard, never missing a note.

Spencer sat stupefied on the sofa when Pablo finished with a flourish and a scream of joy. "That was pretty good, no?"

"You played that better than I do," Spencer said, "and I've been working on it for months." He stood and grabbed Pablo for a hug. "You are fucking amazing!"

I knew Spencer was dying inside even as he complimented Pablo. If Juilliard's judges had to choose between Pablo and Spencer, he knew who their choice would be. The only hope was that Spencer was better than everyone else besides Pablo.

The next morning we left early for the five-hour drive to an auditorium on Southern Methodist University's campus where the auditions would be held. We sang along with the radio and tried to keep our conversation light and silly, but the underlying tension was still obvious during the silences.

The lobby was small and a little dingy with blue cushioned chairs spaced along a wall. Four other student musicians looked up at us when we found our seats. After an hour's wait, Pablo went first and came back elated. He said one of the judges had given him a standing ovation for his Liszt performance.

A man called Spencer's name.

I kissed his cheek before he left us. "Just have fun playing."

He looked terrified but nodded then hugged Pablo.

Both of us pushed our ears against the doors, trying to hear Spencer play, but the sound was muffled, so we gave up and sat back down. After forty minutes, he returned with a little smile on his face. "I think it went okay," he said.

"What about the sight-reading?" I asked.

"I made mistakes but maintained my tempo and kept reading ahead. Probably the best I've done."

"Yahoo!" Pablo shouted before kissing him on the lips. None of the others waiting to be called cringed or commented about the gay display.

One raised his fist in the air and shouted, "Right on!"

Spencer needed to be with a group like this. He could actually live his life and have fun.

I noticed a girl staring at me. She wore black pants and shoes, a pink dress shirt with a black tie, and black jacket. Her long black hair was tied in a ponytail, revealing a round face of dark skin. Her eyes were small and dark. I wore my salesman outfit, complete with dildo and oiled hair.

I walked over to her. "Are you auditioning?"

"Yes," she said then stood.

I noticed a hint of lipstick and mascara around her eyes. "Are you the only girl?"

"I think so. It's hard to tell sometimes." She tilted her head and laughed. "So you are a rebel too?" She looked down at my pants, focusing on my crotch.

I had the strangest feeling she knew it was fake. "Yeah. I just wanted to wish you luck."

She stared at my lips. "We could meet somewhere later."

My heart skipped a beat as my mouth dried. I cleared my throat and licked my lips. "I have to drive the two lovebirds back to San Antonio." *She thinks I'm a guy and is hitting on me.*

"Pity." She leaned closer. "I think we'd have fun."

She stared at my lips, and I stared at hers. She picked a hair off my shirt right where my nipple was. "You are gay, aren't you?"

I felt dizzy. "Yes. How did you know?"

"I think we have a sixth sense."

A man opened the door to the lobby and called out, "Kim? You're next."

She lifted her hand and waved slightly. "Wish me luck with a kiss?" She offered her cheek.

"Good luck, Kim." I barely touched my lips to her skin.

"Thank you." She walked past me, toward the boys, then disappeared into the auditorium.

I went back to Spencer and Pablo, who stared at me with wide eyes. "What's wrong?" I hooked their arms and moved toward the door.

Once outside, Pablo said, "Kim had a huge boner. Did you know you kissed a guy?"

I stifled my surprise and tried to keep cool. "Certainly. He's gay. He knew I was a girl dressed as a boy, and I knew he was the opposite."

"That's bullshit, Sis. He thought you were a guy, and you thought Kim was a girl!"

Pablo laughed and pinched my cheek. "Tell us the truth."

"Okay, okay. I thought she was a lesbian. She . . . he wanted to hook up later."

"That would've been interesting," Spencer teased.

Pablo coughed a laugh. "I would've paid anything to see Tracy's face when he pulled down his pants." He cackled all the way to the car.

We had a fun drive home. I didn't see them in my mirror for hours from Waxahachie to Austin. Mom tried to ignore their kisses and jokes at dinner, but she blushed many times. The next morning we drove Pablo to the bus station.

"Call me when you get your acceptance letter," Pablo said.

Spencer smiled. "You do the same."

On Thursday, May 2, Mom gave Spencer a thin letter from Juilliard as he entered the house. I wasn't there because I was making a sale at the store. When I finally got home at 8:00, I found Mom crying on the sofa in the living room.

Spencer had been rejected and left the house. She didn't know where he'd gone.

I ran outside to my car and took off. I found him lying down on the merry-go-round as it spun. He held a bottle in his hand as he sang the lyrics to "Fool on the Hill"—his own version.

"And nobody seems to like me, they know what I want to do, and I can't hide my feelings, but the queer on his back, sees the world spinning away. . . "

Tears streamed down my cheeks. A gust of wind blew, kicking up a paper bag and an empty cup, rattling them across the asphalt. I felt a few drops of rain.

He ranted. "Round and around the loser goes, where he stops, nobody knows."

"Can I join you?" I called.

He struggled to sit up. "Join me doing what? Singing or drinking or both?"

"I just want to hug my brother."

He grabbed his head and started bawling. "I didn't get in."

My heart breaking, I moved next to him and pulled him to me. "I know. I know. We'll figure something out."

He wrapped his arms around me and pushed his face against my neck, wailing so hard I thought he was choking.

"I don't want to be a queer. Why do I have to be? What did I do? I want to die! Just let me die."

I clutched him, blubbering as rain began to fall. "C'mon, Spencer. Let's go home."

"Why? I'll just open my mouth until I drown." He flopped onto his back and flung out his arms.

I grabbed his shirt and pulled him up with a grunt. "Goddammit, Spencer. You're not drowning on my watch. I need my brother, so get the fuck up!" I pushed him to stand and led him to his car. "Can you drive?"

"I don't think so."

I opened my car and pushed him into the passenger seat. Then found his keys in his ignition and locked all his doors. When I got back to my car, he was asleep. I drove home and parked in the garage. Mom and I struggled to pull him out of the Mustang and into the house. Mom draped towels on the den sofa before I laid him down. We covered him with a blanket and stood over him while he snored.

"What did he say?" Mom asked.

My legs felt like rubber, and I could barely think. "He wants to die and doesn't want to be a queer. I know how he feels."

Mom grabbed me into a hug. "I love you both, no matter what."

I felt her tears against my cheek. After a few minutes, she led me into the kitchen.

"You must be starving." She made a quick ham sandwich and offered it to me.

I tried to take a bite but could only dent the bread with my teeth. "I'll sleep on the floor next to him. I don't want him wandering off somewhere. When does Dad come home?"

"Tomorrow," she whispered and clasped her hand to her mouth, stifling a whimper. "Maybe we should drive somewhere for a few days."

I stared at nothing. "Alaska? Vietnam? Take your pick."

She collapsed into a chair.

"I think he needs to see a doctor," I whispered. "Maybe check into a mental health hospital. I'm afraid he's going to kill —"

"Don't say that," she cried.

"That's right. Dad will make him feel all better." My lethargy was overrun by anger and then hate. "If he starts into him about enlisting, I swear I'll kill him."

She looked at me with blood-red eyes.

"I am not kidding," I said.

Later that evening, I brought pillows and a blanket from my bed and stretched out on the floor along the sofa. During the night, I had horrible dreams, flashes of boys screaming in the jungle and Mom crying, plus crazy, dissonant piano playing. I tossed and turned and thought I never got to sleep.

I awoke when Spencer wiggled his toe around my nose.

"Wake up, sleepy-head. I made coffee."

I forced my eyes to open and saw him fully dressed, standing over me.

He offered his hand. "Grab it. I'll pull you up."

I took his hand and stood. "Are you okay?"

"Never better." He smiled and walked into the kitchen where Mom was cooking breakfast. "I almost stepped on you this morning. Guess you were afraid I'd do something stupid."

"Based on last night, yeah. Don't you remember?"

He nodded, and I saw a flash of pain flit across his eyes. "I was a wuss last night. Sorry. It won't happen again. I called Pablo early this morning. He got into Juilliard. He wants me to visit him as soon as I graduate." He sipped his coffee.

"Do it." I moved toward him and grabbed his arm. "Please. Don't make the same mistake twice. What did you say?"

"I told him I needed to weigh my options and talk to my dad." He looked out the window. "Also, that I wasn't going to live as a homosexual anymore."

Mom turned her head toward me with strained eyes and a wrinkled brow. Cold gripped my core. "What do you mean?"

He stood with his back to us. "I mean what I said. More than half of life is pretending anyway." He turned around and met my eyes with a cold stare. "How many times have you told your students they're getting better when they suck? Your whole sales spiel is a game to take your client's money. Everything is fake. I can fake it too."

The world spun in front of my eyes. "Our love for you is real," I said. "I don't think your feelings for Pablo are fake."

He tightened his lips. "What would you know? You kissed a guy, thinking he was a lesbian. He got a boner, thinking you were a guy." He cackled. "Everything is fucking fake. I don't need Pablo. I'm sure I can get a boner with a girl, just like everyone else." His chest heaved, sucking in quick breaths. "Hurry up and eat, Tracy. You've got to drive me to my car." He strode out of the kitchen and then pounded up the stairs.

Mom and I stared at each other with furrowed brows and open mouths.

"He's going to crack up," I said. "Please talk to Dad before Spencer comes home tonight."

"I will, but Spencer says he can't wait to talk to him."

I shivered with fear. "I'm more scared now than I've ever been."

CHAPTER 16
SPENCER GETS PHYSICAL

The next afternoon Mom presented Spencer with three letters as he entered the kitchen—one from Southern Methodist University, another from Trinity University, and one from Selective Service. Spencer told me later he nearly fainted when he saw his draft notice.

Dad had returned that afternoon and sat at the table, looking proud with a slight smile. "You should open the most important one first, son."

Spencer sat down and watched Mom wipe an eye as she stood behind Dad. He opened the letter. He was to report for induction on June 17, the day I was supposed to arrive in Camp Wonder. Spencer said he tried as hard as he could to control himself. He bit his lip and took deep breaths, but then his head exploded in pain. He yelled, "Fuck!" and ran up to his room.

When I arrived, Mom gave me a plate of food and told me Dad had been talking to Spencer for over an hour. She showed me the letter, and a whimpering moan leaked out of my mouth before it burst into a scream. "God damn this fucking war!" I pushed my plate away and stood. "He's going to college! He'll get a deferment."

Mom pressed her lips against her clasped hands as tears dripped down her cheeks.

I noticed the other two letters on the Lazy Susan. "Why didn't he open these? He was accepted to S.M.U. and Trinity."

Mom cleared her throat. "Because he ran upstairs."

I ripped open both envelopes and read the cover letters. A jolt of joy lifted my spirits. "Each school has offered him a music scholarship. Trinity added an academic award. All he has to do is choose one offer and bring proof of pending enrollment to the induction office. Problem solved!" I gave the letters to Mom.

Her chest heaved as she tried to smile. "Art says he's heard the deferment is going to end."

"Heard from whom? I think he's lying so he can push Spencer to enlist."

"Why would he do that?"

I spit out the words. "Because he wants to brag about his Navy son!" I grabbed the letters and the envelopes and ran out of the kitchen, meeting Dad as he turned from the stairs. "He was offered scholarships to both schools. Don't you care?"

He tightened his eyes. "Yeah. How much of a scholarship?"

"Two thousand from S.M.U. and three from Trinity."

"Leaving hundreds more to pay—books, boarding, and fees. We still have some issues to take care of before I make that kind of investment."

"Can you ever be proud of him?" I snarled, resisting the urge to push him against the wall.

"I'm hoping to." He walked away.

I ran upstairs, knocked, then flung open his door. Spencer lay on his bed, hands crossed under his head, blank eyes pointed to the ceiling. I sat next to him. "Both schools offered you scholarships, Bro. How about that?" I tried to smile.

Barely moving his lips, he said, "I'm excited."

"What did he say?"

He stared blankly. "He wants to take me to a recruiting station tomorrow so I can learn how great opportunities are in the Navy and what steps I need to take."

"You were more excited to talk to him this morning. What happened?"

He turned his moist eyes toward me. "I wasn't expecting a draft notice." His lips barely moved. "I thought I had more time."

I bit my lip. "Neither of us has time. I'm leaving for Alaska in six weeks." I grabbed his hand. "Maybe you should come with me."

He stared straight ahead. "Money, money, money. Everything is money."

I nodded and smiled, trying so hard to lift his spirits. "I've got money. That's all I've been doing for months is making money."

He took away his hand to scratch his nose. "What would I do in Alaska?"

"There was a big oil discovery there in March. Should be lots of jobs available."

"Cool. Except I have to report for induction June 17."

My chin trembled. "Don't go," I pleaded. "We could find a cabin in the woods." I reached out to touch him but saw my hand shaking. I pulled it back. "How would they find you?"

He harrumphed and sat up. "That's fantasy land, Tracy. I'll go with Dad tomorrow and see what's up. Maybe he's right." He pointed at his dresser. "There's a flask in the third drawer on the left. Can you bring it to me?"

My heart sank. I found the flask and tossed it to him. "This is not a solution."

He smiled. "No, but it deadens the problem." He took a drink.

I wrung my hands and felt my heart race. "With your scholarship from Trinity, I could help you make up the difference, so Dad wouldn't have to pay anything."

He stopped mid-drink and raised his brows. "You'd do that?"

"If I had to," I pleaded. "I don't want you enlisting or being drafted. Remember that tomorrow when he tries to sell you macho world."

"Thanks, Sis." He held out the flask as a salute before taking another drink.

I had to work all day Saturday at the store and give lessons. The house was empty when I got home. A note on the kitchen table said, "Went to see *Guess Who's Coming to Dinner*. There's a plate in the fridge." My stomach clenched.

What hit me first was that Spencer's day with Dad must have gone well. The Navy recruiter had done his job, and Spencer had been receptive. So the family went out to celebrate. And that's what slapped me second—*they* were now the family. I felt I was seeing the future after I'd left. The world spun around, and I had to sit down.

I know what would've happened if I'd gone with them to see that movie—a big argument with Dad. Why should a white girl bringing home a black man to meet her family make a story? The only way white society would accept such a premise would be if the brilliant doctor were played by Sidney Poitier. Mom and Dad, and maybe even Spencer, would walk away feeling good about themselves. They'd have been tolerant too in those circumstances. Who wouldn't?

But no casting or director's tricks would sell the story of the girl bringing home her girlfriend. I would've brought that up, and the fireworks would've become bombs.

Maybe I was the cause of all the family discord. Maybe when I called Spencer from Alaska, he'd say, "Yeah, funny thing, but everyone's getting along fine. We haven't had an argument in weeks."

The possibility sent pangs to my chest.

But by the time I'd have called, Spencer would've been in boot camp, taking group showers like those he feared at school.

If he made it that far.

I could see no way the façade could continue.

But that night it did. When they came home, Spencer and Dad were laughing and joking while Mom smiled at them both.

"Good movie?" I asked as I walked through the kitchen.

"Actually, it was," said Dad. "But I'm sure you would've ruined it for all of us."

Mom gave me a warning glance, and I smiled. "Then it's best I stayed home." I poured a glass of water. I could tell Dad was itching to pull my chain. He had a gleam in his eye. Something was up. What could it be?

Dad opened a beer and smiled. "You'll be happy to know that your brother is scheduled to take the ASVAB on Tuesday. That's the Armed Services Vocational Aptitude Battery. The higher your score, the more jobs you're eligible for in the Navy."

My stomach froze, but I was determined to show no surprise or anger. "I know about the test. The highest score is a 99.5." I looked at Spencer whose eyes pleaded for understanding. "I'm sure Spence will score at least a 99."

Dad took a sip of beer and cocked his head at me, trying to figure out what my game was. I realized we fed off each other. Outside of confrontation, we had no other relationship.

I kissed Mom's cheek. "I'm going to bed. I have a long day at the store tomorrow."

"How much money are you making?" Dad asked.

I smiled as sweetly as I could. "Enough to take me away from here. Good night, everyone."

An hour later, Spencer knocked and entered my room.

"So the Navy it is," I said, sitting on my chair with my guitar.

He collapsed onto my bed. "Or Air Force." He laughed. "When I mention that as a possibility, he goes nuts. It's fun to watch."

My chest tightened. "You're really going to do this?"

"All I agreed to was the test. I'll take it and go from there."

I strummed the guitar hard and felt my face heat. "Right into the showers with all those naked men."

He snapped up. "Stop it, Tracy. You're not helping."

"I'm not trying to help!" I barked. "I don't want you to do this."

He blew out a slow breath. "I've got to try."

I closed my eyes and attempted to calm myself. "There's another way. Go to the induction center on June 17 and tell them you're gay. That's it. No war. No death. Simple. Then go to college."

"I can't —"

"Yes, you can!" I shouted. "I've already told you how. We don't need Dad for tuition."

He sighed. "Do you know who else got a letter?"

I looked up, frightened. "Who?"

"Charles. Same date and everything."

Shit, I thought. "What's he going to do?"

"He's not sure yet, but he's not running away." He nodded and stuck out his chin as if he admired Charles. "He thinks the war is necessary, and if he needs to fight, he'll go fight."

I rolled my eyes. "Because he's a man, and that's what real men do." I strummed through four chords—Am, C, F, and D7—and established a hard, rocking rhythm. "I wrote an anti-war song. You want to hear it?"

"Sure. Title?"

"It's a Great War." I strummed a four-bar intro then sang.

> Little boys in the sandbox moving their soldiers
> Planning sneak attacks, can't wait till they're older
>
> Joey gets a new gun and itches for a kill
> The bird bleeds out, such a freakin' thrill
>
> Once in the Nam, he searches and destroys
> Killing Viet Cong, we're so proud of our boys
>
> Burn a village to the ground even if it's friendly
> Only way to save it from the stinkin' commie
>
> It's a great war
> like a party in the jungle
> Such a gung ho war
> And it ain't much trouble
>
> It's a bad ass war
> wouldn't want to miss it
> Love my M16
> Keeps me feeling mean
>
> It's a lovely war
> USA is something special
> It's a great war
> Wouldn't wish it on the devil

I picked a few more notes then stopped. "I have more verses, but you get the idea."

"That's really good, Tracy." He scrunched his brows. "Were you being sarcastic? I couldn't tell."

I punched his shoulder, and he laughed.

I leaned my guitar against my desk. "Charles will fit right into the gung ho mentality."

"Yup. I'm sure he'll walk around the barracks comparing his dick to everyone else's."

I bored my eyes into his. "The Navy is full of guys like Charles. You can't hide what you are."

Spencer tried to chuckle and averted his gaze. "Says the girl who wants everyone to think she's a guy."

"True, but I can walk through a men's locker room without a problem. I could even take a group shower with girls, and if I can keep myself from staring or fainting, no one would know I'm turned on." I leaned over him. "But you, Bro, have a penis, and you can't control it."

He looked up to the ceiling and sighed. "Yeah." He stood and scratched his ear. "I have some practice tests to look at, so I should go study."

I grabbed him in a hug. "You're going to drink in your room, like you do every night. Which is fine with me because they'll probably check your breath or blood on Tuesday for drugs and alcohol."

"For real?" The tendons stood out on his neck, and I could see his pulse.

"According to what I've read. You'll have to find something else to keep your demons away."

He rubbed his hands as beads of sweat gathered on his forehead. "What do you do?"

"I write songs, and I've started a journal."

"Does that work?"

I pulled my gaze from his. "If you mean get rid of my fear and anxiety? No. Nothing works for that." I swallowed and saw the walls spiral around my face. "But it gives me something else to focus on when I'm alone."

He bit on his bottom lip then hugged himself. "Well . . . I should go." He slowly left my room.

I sat on my bed and pulled my legs to my chest, watching a blurry movie in my head of what was likely to happen in the next few weeks. Spencer would ace his test, Dad would be ecstatic, so proud of his son.

More trips to the recruiter. Then the crack-up. Maybe during the physical or during a night out with other recruits. I wasn't sure what would happen, but I knew a crash was in the offing.

What I didn't expect was a girl trying to screw my brother at a graduation party.

At the ceremony on Friday, May 17, Spencer was named the Salutatorian, but more importantly, his nearly perfect score on his ASVAB test was announced, along with his scholarships. Afterwards at Charles' party, Dad threw his arm around Spencer's shoulders and walked him over to everyone, claiming his son could choose any job he wanted in the Navy.

Spencer beamed under the spotlight of his father's attention and praise. He'd never felt it before then. Neither of us had. And if it had started for Spencer under different circumstances, I would have been happy for him.

I hooked arms with Mom as we watched the spectacle. "Dad's in love," I said. "Maybe all this happened for a reason, and it's for the best."

Mom turned to me with a severe frown and half-whispered, "That's bullshit, and you know it."

I feigned shock. "Language, mother. You don't have to be crude."

"I'm just warming up for when I get Art home. At every one of Spencer's concert receptions, Art stayed in a corner, never wanting to be seen as his father."

I felt her muscles tense.

She clasped my hand and lead me to the bar. "I need some wine, and I'm sure you do too."

Charles' house was a mansion in the King William District, larger than our high school building, with chandeliers and high ceilings, decorated with elephant tusks and hides from his father's latest African safari. Carrying our wine glasses, we sauntered back toward the main room where we saw Spencer and a girl sitting at the baby grand piano. He was playing an enhanced version of the Beatles' "Yesterday" as she draped her arm over his back and leaned her head on his shoulder. Her fingers wandered around his jacket as he played. Dad appeared behind us with a whiskey on the rocks.

"That's Charles' first cousin," he said. "Cheryl is a beauty."

We heard a crescendo of applause as Spencer finished the piece and stood. Cheryl threw her arms around him and kissed his cheek. Spencer looked back, caught my eye, and smiled like a cat who'd caught a bird.

Dad sipped his drink. "I told him that opportunities like this are rare, so he shouldn't let it go to waste. Especially when the girl is a knock-out." He drained his glass.

"You want Spencer to get laid?" I asked.

"Far worse things could happen to the boy." He chuckled.

"Did you ever have such an opportunity, Art?" Mom asked, tapping her foot.

"You were my opportunity, dear." He leaned in to kiss her cheek.

She backed away. "I think we should go home. We have some things to talk about. Tracy, will you stay here and drive him home, if necessary?"

"Sure." I leaned toward her cheek. She met me halfway then kissed me back.

Dad clenched his jaw, looking at us both. He offered Mom his elbow. "Shall we?"

On the way out, they stopped for a minute to speak to Charles' parents. Afterward, Mom pulled her arm away from Dad and stomped ahead through the front door.

I found Spencer and Cheryl holding glasses of wine. I watched at a distance as she laughed at whatever Spence said, touching him at every opportunity. By the time the glasses were empty, her fingers had hooked his belt. She drew him closer and said something. Hand-in-hand, they climbed the winding staircase, my stomach dropping farther with each step.

While looking up at the disappearing couple, I hadn't noticed a girl move close to me.

"Where do you think they're going?" said the girl in a tight, red dress.

"To someone's bedroom. I guess my brother's in for a treat."

"That's your brother? He's cute. But not as cute as you." She winked as she raised her wine glass to her full, red lips.

I knew my eyes had flashed wide upon seeing her, and that she had seen them. The girl was gorgeous.

She held out her hand. "I'm Liz."

I shook her hand and smiled. "I'm a girl." I had rented a black tux, much to Dad's consternation, and slicked my hair almost flat against my scalp. Mr. Worth had breathed in sharply when he saw me at graduation but decided he wouldn't make a scene.

Much to my surprise, Liz did not jerk her hand away. "Oh, that's interesting. Cheryl and I go to Columbia University in New York. Are you trans or lesbian or both?"

I stared at her, open-mouthed. I sensed no condemnation. Merely interest. We sat down. "I'm definitely lesbian, but I feel more comfortable in men's clothing," I told her.

"Well, if I were lesbian, I'd be pulling you up those stairs right now, but I'm not so we'll just have to talk."

And we did for the next hour, much to my amazement. Music, politics, my plans for Alaska—everything except Spencer and what I was afraid would emerge from upstairs.

Liz stood to bring us both more wine then noticed Spencer and Cheryl walking down the stairs, arm-in-arm. "Your brother."

His face looked strained, his smile stiff and his eyes searching. She seemed abnormally prim, showing none of the overt gestures she'd used to get him upstairs. My stomach gurgled with worry. I needed to get him out of there.

"They both look a little scared," Liz said.

"Hey, it was great talking to you," I said, "but I need to take him home. If you ever come to Alaska, look me up." Spencer seemed relieved when he saw me approach. "Ready?" I asked. "Some of us have work in the morning."

Spencer froze, starting to introduce me to Cheryl then stopping.

I smiled at her. "Liz is waiting over there for you." I pointed. "She's a great girl. I enjoyed talking to her."

Cheryl swallowed, smiled, and squeezed Spencer's hand. "Good night, Spencer. Congratulations!" She almost ran to Liz, grabbed her hand, and led her toward the back of the house.

"Does she have a story to tell?" I asked Spencer.

He hooked my arm. "Let's go."

As soon as I started driving, he banged his head against the window. "Stupid! So fucking stupid!"

My heart ached for him. "You want music or not?"

"No." After another five minutes he said, "I tried everything." He began to cry. "I thought about Pablo. I kissed her hard. I let her . . . but . . ." He covered his eyes and wept.

I drove on while the growing pain in my throat gagged me.

He sat up and hugged himself. "She thought it was her fault, that maybe I didn't like her. She started crying. I told her I thought she was beautiful, but I was tense because of my draft notice. We agreed to tell everyone we had a great time."

"Dad encouraged you, didn't he?"

"No shit. He said, 'That girl is hot to trot, Spence. Go get her!' Then he slapped me on the back."

I almost asked him why he cared what the bastard thought, but I knew why. For the first time in many years, he'd attracted Dad's attention, and a floodgate of stifled desire for approval had broken inside him. Kids want their parents' love.

Though I felt no such need from him. He'd hurt Spencer too many times, and I could never forgive him. I seemed to not care what he'd done to me.

Or maybe I didn't want to look too closely at my own pain.

The next day after work, as soon as I stepped through the door, Dad bellowed, "Tracy! We need to talk."

Mom stopped in the hallway just outside her room and looked at me with teary eyes before running up the stairs. *Spencer?* My chest clenched and I almost followed her.

"Tracy!" Dad boomed.

I moved toward the kitchen where I found Dad standing by the sink with his arms folded.

"Sit down," he ordered.

I stood, my anger at him and fear for my brother wrestling with each other in my gut. "What happened to Spencer?"

"After nearly killing himself and me, he's a little shaky, but he'll recover."

The *and me* kept me from running upstairs. "He tried to kill you?"

His top lip curled back from his teeth. "She says with such excitement."

"What happened?"

"We were driving to see the recruiter, and just before the train tracks on Woodlawn, he sped up, said, 'Hang on, Dad,' jumped the hill and then panicked after landing. He took his hands off the wheel as we were headed for the palm tree. I had to jerk the wheel hard right to avoid a crash."

"That's the same hill you jumped every day with us. What caused him to panic? Did you yell at him?"

"Damn right, I yelled at him! After we finally stopped, I asked him what the hell he was doing." His face turned red as he glared at me. "He said you told him to jump that hill when I was in the car."

"That was months ago after the concert in November. I told him to do the same thing I'd done to you in your Volkswagen so he'd stop being afraid of you."

He sneered and puffed out his chest. "What else have you told him? Let's see." He held out his hand and flipped up a finger for each item. "One, don't enlist. Two, don't take the test. Three, go to college because you'll pay for it. Four, don't have sex with Cheryl —"

My throat tightened. "What? I never told him —"

"Yes, you did, which is why he couldn't . . ." He sucked in his lips and growled.

My head felt like it would explode. "He couldn't get an erection because he's gay! He didn't talk to me before she pulled him upstairs."

"That's not what he said."

I was panting and trying to make sense of what I'd heard. He must've asked Spencer how it went with Cheryl or made some crude joke, and Spence was too nervous to claim he'd laid her.

I tried to calm down. "Look, Dad, Spencer can't take the physical. He won't be able to stand with a bunch of naked men without getting an erection."

"That's bullshit. You keep telling him he can't so he'll get nervous and run out. That's what he told me. You keep telling him he's gay. My God, how sick is that? All these years you've convinced him he's as screwed up as you are. It isn't enough you have to be a fucked up queer running around in men's clothes, but you have to turn your brother into one too? You're a monster, Tracy." His face was purple, and his entire body was shaking in rage. "You've stolen any relationship I could've had with my son until now. Until NOW! You're not doing more damage to Spencer. He nearly killed us both today, all because of you!"

I grabbed the back of a chair to keep standing. My body felt beaten, but nothing hurt more than my brain. I knew Spencer had been badgered until he'd said what Dad wanted to hear, but how could my brother blame me? Or Dad misconstrued everything Spencer told him to fit into his own reality. My mind was exhausted trying to follow his rant.

Everything hurt and I had trouble breathing. I pushed myself back up and tried to stay calm. "Both Spencer and I are gay. Neither of us wants to be. Spencer cried all the way home last night because he couldn't get an erection with Cheryl. He wanted to more than anything, but he couldn't. Look, I know you hate me and want to have a normal relationship with your son, but he can't change. Please let him go to college for a year. I'll do anything you want. I'll shave and pluck and wear makeup. I'll never wear guy's clothes again. I swear I'll do this if you send him to college instead of the Navy."

Dad twisted his face in disgust. "The last thing Spencer needs is to be in a college music department with fags everywhere."

Every one of my nerves electrified. "Please. He'll kill himself."

"Only if you talk him into it." He folded his arms and slowly shook his head. "You're a witch."

A molten river of rage shot up from my feet. I pushed myself away from the chair and out of the kitchen before I could launch myself at him. I walked up the stairs, trying to calm down, trying to think of something to say to Spencer. When I entered his room, I found Mom sitting on his bed, holding his hand. He dropped the arm draped across his eyes and looked at me. His breathing quickened and he grabbed his forehead, twisting the skin and whining.

"I'm sorry, Tracy," he blurted.

I ran to him and took his hand in mine, kissing it over and over. "It's okay, Bro. I still love you."

"What did he say?" Mom asked.

"I'm a witch. I made Spencer gay. I'm the cause of all things he hates."

She stood and wiped her eyes.

"How do you stand it?" I asked her.

She tried to look at me but couldn't keep her eyes on my face. "It's getting harder." She turned away, mumbling, "I'll try to talk to him." She left the room.

I touched Spencer's face. "Are you going to take the physical?"

He looked away. "I'll try."

I felt like someone was thumping my solar plexus, sending nauseating pain through my gut. "When is it?"

"Tuesday at 1:00."

"Can I drive you? I'll wait outside."

"You have school."

"Fuck school. I want to drive you."

"I'll be fine. Charles has his at the same time. We plan to go out afterward."

The thumping had turned into punches. "Will you call me? I'll be at home. You have to call me. Good or bad. Promise me."

"I'll call."

Two days later I waited by the phone in the kitchen. Mom wouldn't drive Dad to the airport, so he took a cab after flashing a thumbs up to his son. Spence had smiled back.

Before Spencer left the house, he said, "Hey, you two. Lighten up. It's just a physical." He chuckled.

"Let me drive you, please," I begged.

He chuckled again. "I'd like to get there in one piece. I'll call. Don't worry."

Mom and I hadn't stayed still since he drove away. We paced and listened to the clock while each tick stabbed our hearts.

The phone rang twice before 4:00. Mom had grabbed one and barked, "Spencer?" A salesman started to speak and she slammed the handset down.

I'd grabbed the other. "Hello?"

"Hi, this is Cheryl. Can I speak to Spencer?"

What the hell? "He's not here, Cheryl. Can I help you?"

She paused. "I . . . just heard a rumor and wanted to talk to him. Can you ask him to phone me? Please."

"Sure," I said. "I'm expecting him to call, so I need to hang up. Good-bye." What else could the *rumor* have been except that he was gay?

More ticks. More pacing until I felt a tiny tremor in my mind. I looked at Mom and found her startled eyes. She'd felt it too.

"We should go," Mom said.

"But what if he calls and we aren't here?"

"Something happened. You'd better drive fast."

I avoided school zones by racing through residential streets until I could access the expressway and head toward downtown. I exited at Woodlawn.

"Why did you leave IH10?" Mom asked. "You should go to IH35 to get to Fort Sam Houston."

"I need to check the hump first." I couldn't stop thinking—*What if he'd tried to call while I chatted with Cheryl?*

I screeched to a stop at a red light on Blanco.

Mom's hands grabbed the dashboard. "Please, Tracy. Slow down."

I looked ahead and thought I saw flashing lights about two blocks away. "No!" I screamed as fear squeezed my chest. I saw a gap to race through the traffic and dashed into it. A police car had turned sideways before the tracks, blocking traffic. I pulled over and parked. "C'mon, Mom."

We raced toward the hump, ignoring the officer's commands. From the tracks, we saw Spencer's car crushed against a palm tree. Medics were moving a covered body on a gurney into the back of an ambulance.

Mom screamed and ran.

A spiraling emptiness filled my chest, sucking all warmth into a pit of stinging cold. I tried to take a step but fell to the road, unable to make a sound.

CHAPTER 17
A SONG AND A JOURNAL

H ours later, we trudged into the house—numb, haunted, empty. We'd wept in each other's arms until our throats made no more sound, until our skin felt like husks in a dry wind.

I'd never felt such pain, such hopelessness. I would have been sucked into the hole where my heart had been and disappeared if not for Mom. She was totally broken, and I couldn't bear leaving her in such misery.

Spencer's body was at Porter Loring Mortuary. A very kind man told us we would need a closed-casket ceremony due to the injuries. Visitation would be Friday evening with a Saturday afternoon church service. I'd called the airline company so they could contact Dad.

At that moment, I was too spent to think about him, but I feared the depth of my rage when I could feel again.

I called Mr. Worth and asked him to announce Spencer's passing at school the next day so we wouldn't have to call everyone. He cried at the news and told me not to worry about school or finals. He asked the awful question—How? I said, "Spencer had a car accident. He was born at the wrong time and place and wanted to find something better."

I think that's when my last tear fell.

A kettle whistled on the stove. Mom placed two cups and saucers on the counter and added tea bags. I watched her hands shake as she lifted the kettle to pour. I rushed over to hold her.

She dropped the kettle into the sink as dry heaves convulsed her body.

"We need to get food and water into our bodies, or we're both going to pass out." I helped her to the table and sat her down. After a few minutes, I brought us soup, crackers, and cheese. We ate in silence.

"Why don't you take a warm bath, Mom? I'll start the water for you."

She nodded.

After she closed the door to her bathroom behind her, I walked upstairs to Spencer's room. Maybe he'd left a note or something. I also wanted Pablo's number.

His bed was a mess, as always. But his roll top desk, usually just as messy, was clean.

Why? Did he know he wasn't coming back and wanted to hide something? Or did he expect me in his room and wanted to make sure I'd look through his desk?

I found nothing in his cubby holes or decorative drawers. His bottom side drawers wouldn't open. I reached back along the desktop until I found the slot where I could jam my fingers down to push a lever. Spencer had shown me this trick years ago. I pulled open the drawers on one side and did the same to the other.

A couple of drawers contained gay novels and a gay magazine. Another held a few nude photos of men. Then I found a spiral notebook —his journal.

He'd printed in large letters across the first page. *I'm sorry Pablo!*

At the bottom, I found a numbered list.

1) I was angry you got in and not me. I blamed my rejection on you.

2) I accused you of getting me drunk our first night together so you could take advantage of me.

3) I said the only reason you wanted me in Monterrey and then in New York City was because you wanted a live-in whore. You just didn't want to search for new dick every night.

On the next page, Spencer wrote *I fucked up! I didn't think you'd forgive me so I never called you back. I wanted to come see you after my graduation, but Dad got in the way.*

Why didn't I think to call Pablo? After Spencer had said that crazy shit Friday morning about everything being fake, I should have thought to call him. Maybe Pablo would have tried one more time to talk sense to my brother.

I thought I couldn't feel more guilty about Spencer's death until then. I'd already blamed myself for jumping the hump back in November and for not hanging up on Cheryl. He'd needed me, and I had failed him.

I found another passage, dated Friday, May 17. He wrote this after the failed sex with Cheryl.

I have a crazy idea. Tomorrow I'll drive Dad to the recruiter to get more info. I'll race over the tracks then pretend I've lost control after I land. At the last moment, I'll swing the wheel hard left so his side crashes into the tree. I'll probably be hurt, but it will be worth getting rid of him.

Then beneath it, this:

Fucked up again. Dad had to grab the wheel. Now Tracy's mad at me for what I told him. I tried to tell Mom the truth, but she was already so upset. I didn't want to hurt her more.

I'm just a fucking coward.

If I had any balls at all, I'd beat the crap out of Dad and go to Alaska with Tracy.

But I don't.

I know what will happen on Tuesday, but I'll go anyway. Like a lamb to the slaughter.

All I ever wanted was for Dad to be proud of me, and now that he is, I realize I can never be who he thinks I am.

I could never keep the fireflies in a jar.

Or burn ants with a magnifying glass.

Or shoot birds with my BB gun.

Or pop girls' bra straps.

Or tell dirty jokes.

Or love working on cars.

Or want to fly airplanes.

All the things Dad did and wanted me to do.

I filled his life with so many disappointments, the biggest being I'm not even a man. I'm the lowest thing on earth in his mind—a goddamned queer, a cock-sucker, a homosexual who didn't want to be.

But at least I'm not him, and I take some comfort in that.

All I wanted to do was play piano on a stage for a cheering audience, like Van Cliburn. And I did that, more than once. So that's enough for me.

I can be at peace whatever happens.

My tears dripped onto the paper. I thought my head would burst from the pain.

I flipped through every page, trying to see through drowning eyes, looking for more from him, until a scrap of paper fell out from inside the back cover.

Dear Tracy,

Don't tell Pablo. He'll just feel guilty, thinking he should have done more. I know you feel the same. Please don't. Nothing you could have done would have stopped me.

I was destined to do this. I couldn't keep the thoughts out of my head for a long time.

I love you, Sis.

"I love you, Bro," I whispered.

The cold pain in my chest burned with the heat of rage. *You were not destined to do this! You were driven!*

My first thought was to take Dad's pistol he hid in his top dresser drawer and shoot him when he next entered the house. Or maybe force him to read the journal as I held the gun to his head, waiting for his reaction.

But what could he possibly say or do to atone for how he'd treated Spencer?

Maybe genuine tears and regret, but I'd never seen him display either. Shooting him would prevent any chance of him suffering remorse. At some point surely, he'd have to realize his mistake.

Such was my anger that I discarded the option of murder because the pain would end too soon.

I put Spencer's gay novels and photos in a garbage bag and dropped it into the trashcan in the garage. Afterward, I found Mom in the kitchen, wrapped in a robe.

"Would you like some coffee?" she asked.

"Yes, please." As I watched her scoop the grounds, I tried to decide when to show her the journal. Or if. How could she stay with Dad after reading it? Would it be enough to overcome her fears in the orphanage?

If she stayed, she'd be more miserable than ever with no kids around to take her mind off him. And how could she be totally alone in this house with both Spencer and me gone?

Mom readied the cups and cream as the machine percolated. "What will you do?" she asked.

"When?"

"After the funeral."

"Go to Alaska."

She closed her eyes. "I can't lose both of you." She hitched several breaths then looked at me through watery eyes.

My pity for her was not strong enough to stifle the anger boiling in my gut. "I can't live with Dad. He caused this. You know it."

She covered her eyes. "Maybe it was an accident!" she cried. "We don't know what Spencer was thinking."

I held her weeping face and struggled with telling her the truth so she'd hate Dad too or letting her keep her fantasy.

She wept in my arms, her muscles clenching tight against the pain then succumbing to more agony when she let go. I'd touched and squeezed her more that day than I had in all our years together. Yes, she was a soft and huggable woman, but her shoulders and back and thighs were thick and strong. Her body wasn't fragile, just her mind and spirit.

I didn't have the heart then to shatter them more.

"We'll get through this, Mom. I'll help you as much as I can."

"I love you, Tracy."

"I love you, Mom."

Later that night, I sat in my bed, reading his journal over and over. I decided he'd written it all Monday night. He'd said nothing about Cheryl or graduation or jobs in the Navy. He was justifying his plan, telling himself he had no other choice.

Yes, he'd wanted me to read it. Why?

So I'd know exactly why he'd killed himself? He must've known I would have no doubts about his motives.

But Mom and Dad—especially him—would avoid the truth.

Why hadn't he written them letters? Why couldn't he tell Dad what the bastard had done to him?

Because even in death, he held back. He'd never confronted Dad, told him off, or screamed at him.

Spencer was leaving that to me. He gave me a journal and the decision to use it or not.

The next morning, the phone ringing down the hall woke me up. I'd needed sleep and hadn't set my alarm. Clutching the robe around me, I grabbed the handset. "Hello?"

"Tracy? This is Charles. Can you talk?"

"Yes. Hang on." I carried the phone to my room and closed the door. My breathing was quick and shallow. I needed answers. "Okay."

"Mr. Worth just told us about Spencer," Charles said, his voice cracking. "God, I'm so sorry."

"Did you see him leave Fort Sam?"

"Yeah." He sniffed and cleared his throat. "We were standing in line to be weighed and measured, talking and laughing, and he just bolted away."

"Were you in your underwear?"

"Yeah."

"Did anyone say anything before he left?"

"Some guys behind us had just been ordered to drop their underwear for the digital exam. They had to bend over. One guy talked like he was gay."

"And said what?"

"Something like, 'Oooh, Doc, I hope that's your finger.' We turned around and laughed. Some of the guys bending over straightened up. The doctor yelled at them to get back down then said to the guy he'd poked, 'Maybe you'd like two fingers, asshole.' The guy squealed. Everybody was laughing. That's when I saw Spencer running out of the room."

Fucking gay jokes! Can't guys ever get over them? "That happened around four o'clock?"

"I think so. I thought maybe he was sick and had to puke, but he never came back. I tried calling your house after I finished, but no one answered. I guess by then he'd already had the wreck. Why did he leave? Do you know?"

Did he suspect suicide and wanted me to confirm it? Or did he honestly have no idea?

"I don't know, Charles. Cheryl called to speak to Spencer just before Mom and I left the house yesterday to look for him. She mentioned something about a rumor. Do you know what that was about?"

He hesitated.

"It's okay, Charles. Tell me what you know."

"Liz told Cheryl that you're gay so maybe Spencer is gay too. She asked me, and I told her about that Mexican kid who you were supposedly dating months ago, but that was just so you could hide your relationship with Ava. Anyway, that's what Spencer told us. I thought at first maybe he ran out because of the digital exam incident, but there'd already been a bunch of comments like that, and none of those affected him. So it had to be something else."

Bro, what do you want me to say? Do I confirm you were gay so everyone can make fun of you? Or hide the truth?

Before I could think everything through, I found myself saying, "Spencer wasn't sure about enlisting. Our father wanted him to, but Mom and I didn't. He must've decided to go to college instead. Just changed his mind."

"What about the wreck?"

In my mind I saw myself in my car with Spencer, telling him, *Just a little jump. Please. You'll love it. Trust me.* The image spun faster and faster until I saw his car crumpled against the tree. I could barely breathe. "It was just an accident. Dad used to jump those tracks when we were kids. Spencer did it and lost control."

"Man." He sighed. "I'm really sorry."

"Thanks for calling, Charles. Will we see you Friday?"

"Yeah. All of us are coming."

"Goodbye." I hung up and leaned against the wall. *Oh, Spencer, I miss you.* After a minute, I tied my robe and walked downstairs. I heard some clattering from the kitchen and thought Mom was up.

But it was Dad, drinking coffee in his pajamas, staring out the front window. He turned his head to me briefly then jerked it forward. I stared at his back, unable to move, feeling my face turn to fire.

His neck tensed. "Is this where you say, 'I told you so'?"

My voice was cold. "I wish I'd been wrong. Don't you?"

Still facing the window, he rubbed his face. "I'd hoped . . ." He cleared his throat. "I thought he could —"

"Could what?" I barked. "Put up with guys comparing a digital exam to ass fucking? I just talked to Charles who was with him at the physical. Spencer had to hear macho men demean queers for hours. He couldn't take any more, so he ran out, got into his car, and rammed a tree."

He turned to face me. "Does Charles think he left because of gay jokes?"

"No," I said bitterly. "His secret is safe. I'm still the only queer in this family. I told him Spencer had doubts about enlisting. You wanted it, but Mom and I didn't. He simply changed his mind."

He nodded and looked at the wall. "I think that's best." His eyes turned to me. "I'm surprised you covered for your brother."

"I figured if Spencer wanted to out himself, he would've told the recruiter he was gay." I couldn't stop the tears pushing out of my eyes. "Dad, all you had to do was love him for who he was. Why couldn't you? He was sweet, kind, funny, smart as hell. Why wasn't that enough?"

He clenched his jaw, blinked, then rubbed his left eye. In a raspy voice, he said, "I know all those things. But I knew how he'd be treated unless he changed." He tried to swallow then breathed deeply a few times. "He had to change."

"Why do you think that's possible?"

He lowered his chin and gave me his authoritative voice. "A pilot friend of mine has a nephew who claimed he was gay. They took him hunting and fishing and got him into boxing. Got him interested in, you know, men's activities. And it worked."

"It worked how? Because he makes out with girls in his truck?"

"Yeah, basically. The kid is fine now."

"That's bullshit," I snapped.

"How do you know?" he shouted.

"Maybe your dad and uncle could badger you into kissing guys, but that wouldn't change who you are."

He slammed his cup onto the counter. "What are you . . . Why would my dad make me kiss a guy?" He threw out his hands and snarled. "Sometimes I think you're crazy!"

"Please," Mom said behind me in the doorway. "Please don't fight. I can't take it."

I held her close. "I'm sorry, Mom. I won't fight with him any more. I promise." The man was simply ignorant. No one whom he disagreed with could get through to him. Ever.

The phone rang. Dad answered quietly and turned toward the window.

Mom stroked my head. "Why does the phone keep ringing?"

"People are calling about Spencer. They want to tell us how sorry they are. It's going to be like this for the next several days."

She cried into my shoulder.

Dad and I avoided saying anything to each other until late Friday afternoon when I came downstairs in my new black suit, wearing Spencer's favorite tie, the paisley Dad had questioned at our party months ago.

"You're wearing that?" he asked.

"You look very nice, dear," Mom said with a smile. She hooked my arm and led me to the car.

That night was long and full of tears, but also some laughter. Gene, Mario, and Charles relived the Medina Tournament. Ricky asked about my feet.

Mary asked me what I was doing that summer. I told her I was moving to Alaska. Her face paled as a sigh whimpered from her chest. I gave her a long hug.

"I wish," she said then swallowed. "You know what I wish."

"I know." I kissed her forehead. "You'll find her."

Cheryl made the rounds, sniffling, telling everyone she'd just started a wonderful relationship with Spencer and then he died.

Mr. Worth held my hands and asked whether he'd see me next year. I laughed and said, "Sure, if I can dress like this."

Tears welled in his eyes. "I'd fight like hell to let you."

I knew he was serious. "I have no doubt, Coach, but I'll be in Alaska."

His eyes widened as he sighed and said, "Alaska. I always wanted to go there. Will you finish school?"

I'd been worried about how I'd manage school and make money. "I don't know. I'll be on my own and need to work."

He lowered his chin and looked hard at my eyes. "Tracy, you need two credits—English and government—to graduate. When you're settled you call me. You can finish those classes quickly through correspondence. I'll help make the arrangements. You finish those any time before next summer, and I'll send you a diploma. You hear me?"

I felt a surge of affection for this man. "Yes, sir. Thank you. I'll send you a postcard."

He nodded, wiped his nose, gave me his wide, thin grin, said, "Good luck up there," then turned away.

Dad spent most of the evening with his pilot friends, talking about Spencer's excitement to join the Navy, his ASVAB score, how quick he was to learn how to change the oil on his car—everything except his piano playing.

Mom was surrounded by kids, talking about Spencer's dancing at the parties and his DJ skills. She shed many tears, but she also laughed. They asked her if she liked their music. Yes, she did, very much, especially Grace Slick's "White Rabbit." She winked at me.

I had hoped Ava might appear, but she didn't.

The next day I came downstairs with my guitar case.

"What's that?" Dad asked.

"My guitar. I called Pastor Wright yesterday and asked if I could sing a song during the service."

Dad's mouth dropped open. He looked at Mom then at me then back to her. "Did you know about this?"

Mom smiled. "No, but I think it's wonderful."

"What song?" Dad asked.

"One I wrote for Spence."

"Since when do you play the guitar and write songs?"

"For months, Art," Mom said. "She's excellent. You should pay more attention."

Once again, she hooked my arm and led me to the car.

After our choir director sang a solo of "Amazing Grace," the pastor called me to the stage and set a stool by the microphone. I sat down and strummed a D minor chord.

"Everyone here knows my brother could dance like Mick Jagger and play piano like his idol, Van Cliburn. But there are some things you don't know. When we were kids, on summer nights we'd chase fireflies around the neighborhood, catching them in jars. When we got home, I'd ask him, 'How many did you catch?' He showed me his empty jar and said, 'I let twenty-two go.' So I let mine go too. I never saw him hurt anything or anyone on purpose. But he received his draft notice nevertheless." I started picking the chords. "This song is for him."

> He was
> Too sweet to live,
> too soon to die
> Too quick to forgive
> And too gentle to fight
>
> He was
> Too blind to see color
> Too bright for the dark
> Too nice to be cruel
> With too big a heart
>
> Yet they called him to war
> to fight overseas
> when he wouldn't keep fireflies
> overnight in a jar
>
> He was
> too hip to be lame
> too cool to feel hate
> too boss to bomb
> too wild to go straight

Yet they called him to war
to fight overseas
when he wouldn't keep fireflies
overnight in a jar

When the good guys die
The songbird cries
The tooth fairy steals
and the angels make deals

It's time to make the world better
For brothers like Spencer
Make the world better
And love every Spencer

I could barely sing the last line and stopped in mid-strum, but the gap of silence was very short. The applause started quietly like people were deciding whether it was proper to clap at a funeral. Then I heard Pablo's voice.

"¡Magnifico, Tracy!"

I saw him stand, clapping and shouting. Others did the same. I felt a surge of warmth power through my skin, and tears wet my face. I stood and blew him a kiss. He moved to the aisle and walked toward me. We met in a fierce hug.

"Oh, Pablo, I've missed you. I'm sorry I didn't call. How did you know?"

"It's okay, Tracy. Dr. Sorel called me."

I held his face in front of mine. "I wish Spencer had . . ."

He bit his lips and nodded, tears filling the dark circles under his eyes and the deep creases of agony on his cheeks.

"Come," I said as I led him to my pew. "Sit with me."

Mom hugged me as I sat down. "Tracy, that was beautiful. Thank you." She reached over and squeezed Pablo's hand.

Dad moved over and kept his gaze toward the pastor. I clutched Pablo through the rest of the ceremony.

When it was time for Mom, Dad, and me to approach Spencer's

coffin, I squeezed Pablo's hand and whispered, "He loved you to the end. He wanted me to tell you he was so sorry for what he said to you."

He kissed my cheek and walked back to his family. I held Mom's hand as we stood before Spence, the pain still raw and sharp.

Mom leaned against me and whispered, "How do I live?"

I kissed her head and put my lips to her ear. "With me."

She turned her face slowly to mine. "How?"

"We'll talk."

We moved to the side of the pews and waited as friends and family approached Spencer then came to greet us. When it was Pablo's turn, he wailed and hugged the coffin, kissing it several times. His mother and father helped him stand and walked him to us, showing no embarrassment. They mirrored the pain Pablo felt. He kissed and hugged me again then introduced his parents who had so wanted to meet Spencer. Their son had spoken so highly of him. Pablo crushed Mom with hugs and kissed her hands. He stood straight in front of Dad and offered his hand. As Dad shook it, Pablo said, "I loved your son from the bottom of my heart. I would have taken care of him and lived with him forever, if he'd given me the opportunity. You were very lucky to be his father."

Dad's face had turned red as he struggled to keep tears from flowing. His voice croaking, he said, "Thank you for being his friend."

Pablo nodded firmly and left. Dad turned around and walked a few steps away. I heard him blow his nose. When he returned, his eyes were puffy, and he had trouble stopping the hitch in his breaths.

Nothing I could have said to Dad would have had as much impact as Pablo's words. Faced with real love for Spencer, he had to realize how paltry was his own.

I looked back at the line approaching the coffin and saw Ava holding hands with a handsome boy. My stomach dropped to the ground as she looked at me and smiled.

Her friend escorted her close to Spencer and stopped. Ava walked the next steps and clasped her hands in prayer. She walked toward me with a twinkle in her eye, her boyfriend following.

Standing before me, she reached out her hands. I took them and felt her slip a lifesaver into my left palm.

"I know how much Spencer meant to you," she said. "I'm so sorry."

I could feel sparks between our hands. "Thank you for coming."

She bent forward, placing her cheek against mine. "You know where it's been."

I bit my lips to keep from laughing. She leaned back with a sly smile and a lifted eyebrow.

"This is Eddie," she said as he offered his hand.

"So pleased to meet you, Eddie." I squeezed his hand especially hard. "Be nice to her or I'll come after you."

Ava barked a laugh and Eddie frowned. "When do you leave for Alaska?"

"Soon." We locked eyes for several seconds. So much pain and regret and affection flowed between us.

"Goodbye, Tracy."

After they walked away, Dad turned to me. "Looks like Ava changed."

I held out the lifesaver and smiled. "Really?" I held it to my nose and breathed in the sweet, pungent aroma. *Yes, I know where, Ava.* I waited a few seconds until she looked back. I dropped the candy into my mouth and chewed. She smiled and looked away.

That night I was restless and couldn't sleep. I wandered down the hall into Spencer's room and turned on the light. I nearly screamed when I saw a body sleeping in the bed. Mom turned over, covering her eyes.

"I couldn't sleep," she said.

"Neither can I."

"Turn it off and climb in."

I scampered to the switch and flipped it. Crawling under the covers, I found her warmth.

She touched my face. "Just like when you had bad dreams."

"Except this isn't a dream."

"I know." She touched my forehead with hers. "Earlier you said I would live with you. Does that mean you're not going to Alaska?"

"No, I'm going early, but I want you to join me."

She clutched my shoulder. "How can I? How would we live?"

"I have plans. On Monday, I need to get books and talk to some people. When does Dad leave?"

"Tomorrow afternoon."

"We'll talk after he leaves." I rubbed her cheek. "I love you, Mom."

She pulled me close. "I love you."

We held each other all night.

As Dad waited for the cab the next day, he looked out the kitchen window while I read the paper. The day had been strained since neither Mom nor I wanted to talk to him. The weight of awkward silence must have forced him to speak.

"When do you leave for that camp?" he asked.

"Would've been June 15, but I'm going to leave sooner." I kept reading.

"When do you return?"

"I don't."

He said nothing for a full minute. With no apparent emotion, he asked, "You're going to live in Alaska?"

"That's my plan."

"Why?"

"Because I can dress and act like I want without being considered a freak." I put the paper down and looked at him. "And I can't live here with you."

He nodded and checked for the cab. "Does your mother know?"

No anger? No defensiveness? "Yes, she does. When do you come back?"

"On the 11th."

"I'll be gone by then."

"I didn't know that."

"You haven't cared to know."

He folded his arms and checked for the cab.

I tossed the paper onto the Lazy Susan and leaned back in my chair. I should have ignored him or left the room. All he wanted was to get back with his buddies where he was Captain Franks, a great guy with funny jokes, and fly around the world. He hated being home, and I couldn't help but want to aggravate him one more time. "A week ago you had two kids. After you walk out the door today, you'll have none. That plan to cut us off worked out pretty well, didn't it? Guess you'd make the same choice again?"

He lifted his brows and folded his arms, as if he would lay some wisdom on me. "You make choices and live with them, Tracy. You don't get do-overs in life."

"True." I stood. "But sometimes people change their minds when they realize they're wrong. Did that ever happen to you?"

A cab pulled up along the curb. He glanced outside then back to me.

I leaned on the chair, squeezing the oak back as hard as I could with no effect. Just like talking to him. "You cried after Pablo talked to you, but you hid it. Do you ever cry when you're alone?"

"I've got to go." He moved past me and picked up his bags in the foyer. I watched him walk out to the cab, say something to the driver to make him laugh, then climb into the car. He never looked back.

I tried to feel something—pain, joy, anger, anything—but the closest emotion I could identify was dismay. How could someone lose his children and not seem to care? Perhaps he was tired of the drama and just wanted to leave.

But the drama wasn't over yet.

We'd talk again.

CHAPTER 18

CHASING THE SUN

For the next several days, I read everything I could find on Alaska, living in the wilderness, and backpacking. I bought a tent, sleeping bag, cooking equipment, and a Kelty frame pack. The salesman taught me how to use everything and helped me pick out my leather boots. He'd always wanted to go to Alaska.

I showed everything to Mom—gear, maps, photos, including the one of Jackie. "I can't wait to meet her," I said.

"Why?"

"Because she's my age, dressed in overalls like that's no big deal. She has an axe and a guitar. And I love her smile."

Mom touched my arm. "Tracy, you're not infatuated with her, are you?"

I touched Jackie's face in the photo. "She's probably as straight as an arrow. But there's got to be lots of girls like that up there. Maybe one or two are queers like me." I didn't tell her I'd heard Jackie's voice in my head many times.

"How much money do you have?" Mom asked.

"Over three thousand dollars. Plus, I'm going to sell my car next week."

She opened her purse and found Spencer's wallet.

My fingers tingled. "I didn't know . . ."

"I've had it since last Tuesday."

I touched the leather and still felt a pang. But lately I'd been recalling more good memories and feeling less pain.

Mom opened the wallet. "Art never even asked about his personal effects." She pulled out cash. "This is for you." She handed me the money. "Three hundred dollars, mostly from graduation presents. And I emptied his bank account. So here's a little more than five hundred."

I put my hand over hers. "You need to keep some."

"Why?"

I locked onto her eyes. "So you can buy your plane ticket to Anchorage and train ticket to the park. You're going to meet me at the McKinley Hotel when I leave Camp Wonder on June 28." *Please say yes.* "Then we'll take the train north or south and find a place to live."

She looked at the table. "Tracy, I can't just walk away . . ."

"Yes, you can. You'll be miserable the rest of your life if you don't."

"But what will we do for money?"

"I can sell pianos—anything, actually. And give lessons." My words tumbled out. I'd been full of ideas and wanted to share them. "There are hundreds of things I can do. And you're the best cook, and you can sew. Besides, we'll start off with a good-sized stash after you sell the piano."

"Why would I sell —"

My skin quivered with excitement. "Who's going to play it? I've already talked to Victor. Half of everything here is yours, Mom. There's no reason you can't walk away from him with your share."

She looked up and grabbed her head, trying to catch her breath. "I made vows —"

"So did he." I dropped Spencer's journal on the table. "You need to read this. Spencer wrote it Monday night before he died. I found it in his desk where he knew I would look."

Her hands slowly moved to the notebook. She looked up at me, her chin quivering.

"I'll be in my room," I said before I left her.

An hour later, I heard Mom knock and cry out, "Tracy!"

I ran to my door and pulled it open. Her hands clutched each side of the jamb, her arms tense, chin pushed forward and lips tight around slightly open teeth. We stood looking at each other for several seconds. She was beaten but angry.

She took a shaky breath. "I'll call a lawyer tomorrow. I honestly don't know what I would have done if I'd read that while Art was here."

"You'll come to Alaska?"

"I don't know, Tracy. I need to calm down and hear what my options are." She moved forward and hugged me. "When Art was here, how did you keep from . . ."

"It was hard."

During the next few days, I sold my records to Hogan and my car to Mario. I changed all my money into traveler's checks except for two hundred dollars. All my posters and photos went into a cardboard tube which I stuffed into my pack, along with canned chicken and Spam, pasta, rice, oatmeal, coffee, tea, bags of peanuts mixed with raisins, peanut butter, and my Stanley two-quart thermos. Somehow I found room for my tent, bag, and cooking gear, plus the rest of Spencer's cigarettes and his flask.

Mom bought me an Instamatic camera and rolls of film.

My life was contained in my duffle bag, pack, and guitar case. I would wear my clunky boots on the plane because I couldn't fit them anywhere.

Mom still wouldn't give me a definitive answer about her plans. Some days she was determined and angry; others, she was scared, haunted by memories of her life in the orphanage.

I had to accept the possibility of leaving Mom and living alone thousands of miles away from anyone I knew. The night before I left, she peppered me with questions about what I was bringing, where I would stay and what I would do. I promised to call her on Sunday afternoon, the 16th, the day before the Camp Wonder cars took me ninety miles into the wilderness. We drank wine and slept together one last time in Spencer's bed.

On Monday, June 10, I checked my duffle and carried my pack and guitar to my flight gate. Mom waited with me.

Two young kids, probably brother and sister, walked over and asked where I was going.

"To Alaska."

"Wow," said the sister. "What are you going to do there?"

"Camp and hike and meet new people," I answered.

The brother squinted his eyes at me. "Are you a boy or a girl?"

"Does it really matter?" I said.

"Well, sure it does."

I smiled. "Tell me why."

He frowned and thought. "I don't know."

"Exactly." I nodded. "Remember that as you and your sister grow up."

An adult came over and took the kids away, muttering, "Sorry."

Boarding started. Mom and I stood and grabbed each other. I tried to swallow the monster lump that had grown in my throat but could only cough.

"I need you, Mom. And you need me."

She nodded as she cried.

"I'll call you Sunday."

"You're so brave, Tracy. I don't know how you do it."

"I'm scared shitless, Mom, but I can't think of anything else to do." Tears poured down my cheeks. "I can't stay here." I wiped my eyes. "I just have to put on my game face and hide behind this disguise until I don't need it anymore."

"I believe in you, Tracy. You can do anything."

"Thank you." I kissed her lips and walked into the jetway, leaving my old life behind, looking for a better world.

I sat by the window next to a large man who smelled like an ashtray. As soon as we reached altitude, he lit up, spread his legs, and covered my arm rest.

I pushed myself closer to the wall and watched the rolling hills north of San Antonio disappear in the clouds. My stomach felt heavy and cold. After a minute, I realized I was scratching my arm from shoulder to elbow as I hugged myself. The loneliness was crushing.

What the hell had I gotten myself into? I knew no one. Whenever people looked at me, they saw someone who didn't exist—the cool dude with a guitar and pack who'd rather be alone in the mountains than in an airport. Except the pack was in perfect condition, as were my boots. I'd set up the tent once in my backyard.

No longer my yard.

I was heading to a state which was always omitted from maps of the U.S.A., never included in national weather reports. Hoping to find something to help me leave the past and maybe someone to find a future with.

Right then, the idea of Jackie and Camp Wonder seemed ridiculous to me, and I shivered at the fear flashing in my gut. I'd bet everything on this venture, even begged my mother to follow me.

What if Alaska was a bust? Then what? I felt like the last brown leaf on a tree as the wind began to blow.

I pulled out the brochure from inside my shirt and stared at Jackie—happy, totally real, strong. Her rolled-up sleeves revealed thick forearms. I still heard, "Come to Alaska. We'd be great friends."

"That your girlfriend?" the man asked then sucked the last smoke from the butt before dousing it in his spent cup of Coke.

"No. Just a girl who works at a camp I'm going to."

"Where's that?"

"Alaska."

He coughed. "She looks kinda rugged. Guess the girls got to be tough up there." He chuckled. "Don't think I'd want to mess with her carrying that axe." His laughter devolved into a coughing spell.

"Why would you have to *mess* with her at all? She chops wood for the cabins. She's not carrying an axe to defend herself." I almost added, "from assholes like you," but shut my mouth.

After landing at Love Field in Dallas, I walked to another gate and watched a few soldiers return to happy families. One was in a wheelchair, missing both legs. The girl pushing him was about my age, maybe his sister. The proud parents walked beside him, his mom holding his hand. At least the young man was alive.

Spencer's death wouldn't be listed among the war's casualties, but it should have. How many families whose sons never deployed had been ripped apart by the war? Thousands never counted or listed in history books. Where were their stories? Who would ever know about them?

I saw the crew approach—four dashing men in dark uniforms followed by four pretty ladies in suit dresses, all pulling bags in small carts. The man in front was the captain with four gold stripes around his coat sleeves, smiling, chatting happily, the stewardesses responsive to his every word and gesture.

Maybe his gay son had recently committed suicide, and his gay daughter had run away while his wife was debating whether to leave him or not. Who would ever guess? Dad would be acting the same way.

I'd seen it myself. On our trip to Europe two summers ago, we flew on his plane as he took charter groups to London and Berlin. Despite arguments between Dad and me and frequent tension in the privacy of our hotel rooms, he was always smiling in public, the perfect professional whom everyone adored, while with us, he was often cranky and sullen and embarrassed.

I pointed out the Jekyll and Hyde routine to Mom. She said, "With them, he's Captain, their boss. Their careers depend on his evaluations. They don't argue back."

"Which version is the real Art Franks?" I asked.

"You, Spencer, and I are the only ones who know there are two."

On the flight from Dallas to Seattle, I decided to stop thinking about the past and focus on the future I wanted. Through my window, I watched the green land become table flat with occasional canyon gashes, then turn yellow-brown before erupting into tendrils, leading to a wall of mountains.

This landscape was continually interesting with twisted rock and high, hidden valleys. Snow capped the tallest peaks and frosted the ridgelines.

Always ahead, just above the horizon was the sun. I would chase it to Seattle, where it would pretend to set. Actually, it would move north to Alaska, dip just below the horizon at about 10:30, but shine light into the sky until it officially rose six hours later.

By the time I arrived in the park, daylight would never stop. No more darkness until the end of July.

I could live with that.

I opened my journal and began to write phrases for a song.

> I chased the sun until I found you
> Out of the darkness and into your light
> Such happiness I never knew
> You got me feeling all right

Maybe a little cheesy, but not if it turned out that way.

After the plane landed, I had to change airlines, so I rode the loop train from Terminal A to C. I had two hours to kill and an empty stomach. I bought the cheapest sandwich I could find and found an empty row of seats by a wall of windows. Though I had plenty of money, I had no idea when I'd be adding to my stash, so I needed to be careful.

After eating, I pulled out my guitar and worked on chords and a melody for my song, softly singing a few lines.

Ten minutes later, I heard, "Hey, that sounds good. What song is that?"

I looked up and saw bare legs, long and muscular, topped by a pair of short white shorts. I tried not to gasp, but some sound emerged. By the time my eyes lifted past her University of Seattle sweatshirt, bulging at the chest, to her round, freckled, beautiful face, she smiled and stared at my lips.

I cleared my throat, "Something I'm working on."

"What's a cute boy like you doing sitting in a corner? You should be out in the crowd, busking for tips. I'm Greta." She reached out her hand.

"Tracy," I said, grabbing her hand briefly.

She sat down. "You write songs?"

"A few."

"Can I hear one?" She swung her left leg over her right and turned toward me in her seat, so her sandal touched my leg. Her gaze flicked between my eyes and mouth, her lips slightly parted, touched by her tongue. She cocked a brow. "I'll make it worth your while. I've got over an hour before my plane boards."

This gorgeous girl was hitting on me, thinking I was a boy. Maybe I should have said something then, but I played along. "Do you normally search for musicians in the airport?"

"Only good-looking ones." She touched my arm. "Sing me a song, dammit. I'm bored."

"Okay." I started strumming the chords for Ava's song, and sang.

I found your lips in the dark
And tried to touch your heart
Out of sight
From the crowd

Her eyes widened, and she sat up. When I finished the song, she clapped, along with a few others nearby.

"That was good! Who'd you write that for?"

"A girl I left behind in Texas named Ava."

"Why'd you leave her?"

"It's complicated."

She tilted her head and flashed me a smile. "Well, if your guitar case were open, I'd throw in some bills, but since it's not . . ." She leaned forward, puckering her lips.

I could have kissed her so easily, but warning lights flashed in my brain. I touched her cheek to stop her advance. "Greta," I whispered. "I'm not who you think I am."

She frowned. "What?"

"I'm not a boy."

She flinched backward and stared hard at my face then spit out, "What kind of game are you playing, freak?"

My heart pounded, and I knew I was in trouble. "I'm not playing a game. You're the one who was hitting on me."

She jumped out of her seat and leaned forward, snarling. I thought she would rake my face with her nails.

Her freckles disappeared in her reddening skin. "You're the one crossdressing trying to lure innocent girls. I'm finding a cop, you freak." She stomped off.

I turned around and saw others giving me looks. One guy chuckled. "I'd find another terminal, if I were you."

Half of me felt hot rage heating my chest; the other half, a cold fear. I didn't want either, so I steeled my nerves, calmly gathered my gear, and headed for a bathroom.

When I found the entrances, I hesitated, looking at the men's and women's symbols on opposing doors—one with pants or with a dress. I'd used the unisex stalls in the plane, so this was the first time I'd had to make this decision. I knew if I went through the women's door, someone would panic. But if I went into the men's, was I committing a crime? Could women impersonate men and walk around, watching men pee in a trough?

A door opened to my left, and a woman pushing a stroller emerged. The sign designated this bathroom for families. I rushed inside and locked the door. Was I breaking some law using this restroom? I had no family.

My shirt suddenly felt scratchy, my skin sensitive to every fiber and seam. I splashed water on my face and flinched—the water seemed so cold.

Normal people didn't think twice about which bathroom to enter. They'd donned the approved uniform and stayed in their separate lanes. Anyone outside these were freaks, subject to arrest. But what these people couldn't fathom was my fear of police was less than the panic I felt upon realizing I had no door, no line. The basic function of going to the bathroom was denied me.

The entire purpose of separate facilities was to hide your privates from the other gender. It was fine to grunt and fart and tinkle among other women, but certainly not among men.

Or queers.

Greta would have been angry even if right after she said, "Cute boy," I'd told her the truth. Why? Because she'd already shown attraction, and she couldn't handle getting hot over a lesbian cross-dresser. She couldn't wrap her binary mind around me.

What should I have done? Did I need to do anything?

Yes. There would be more Gretas.

What was I willing to do?

I reached into my jeans and pulled out my dildo.

Did I want people to believe I was male or to accept me for who I was?

Obviously, I wanted the latter, but that wasn't possible in San Antonio. It had to be in Alaska. I pulled out my Camp Wonder brochure and looked again at the photos of Miki and Rhonda wearing pants, standing by a cabin with the mountain in the background.

And, of course, there was Jackie.

I stuffed the penis into my pack where I found a small bottle of shampoo. I washed my hair in the sink to remove the Brylcreem then wiped it with paper towels.

Someone knocked on the door. I said, "Hang on. I'm almost done." I looked in the mirror. What was I? Something in between male and female in appearance and spirit, but I wasn't impersonating anyone.

I gathered my pack and guitar and left, heading back toward the gates. After a few steps, I stopped and thought maybe I should walk somewhere else for an hour until Greta had boarded her plane.

Screw that, I thought. *I'm a girl wearing jeans. Is that a crime? I'm not at Adler anymore.*

I found my gate, kept my guitar in its case, pulled out my journal and tried to finish my song. No one bothered me.

When we took off, the sky was dark and clear with just the tiniest glow in the northwest. I slept for about an hour until a dim light tickled my eyelids.

I could see enormous white mountains below, stretching out for miles. Glaciers undulated like rivers through their own valleys, broadening against the ocean, forming pale blue cliffs.

No town, no buildings, no lights. Just endless snow and ice.

The sky revealed no stars. The sun at the horizon cast a pale yellow light flat across the landscape, throwing shadows across the surface.

I had to remember to breathe. My brain seemed frozen, unable to decide whether to be awed, afraid, or fascinated.

Was there any life down there? How could there be?

After another twenty minutes, I saw faint orbs of yellow light, a few clumped together, others isolated. Tiny dots of humanity almost lost amidst the vast land.

The plane turned then began its descent. Soon I could see trees, millions of them, closely packed, occasionally separated by rivers.

No highways lined with street lights like Seattle. No roads at all.

Then wide mudflats, soon drowned by the ocean.

The plane descended more rapidly until it crossed banks of runway lights. The thud of landing followed.

I was in Alaska, what seemed like an alien land.

As I exited the jetway, I wondered whether I'd see people or creatures or some combination.

At one o'clock in the morning, I saw an empty, dingy terminal which could have been anywhere. We followed signs to Baggage Claim where we were greeted by polar and grizzly bear mounts. Some passengers posed for pictures with them, but most stood silently, a little wobbly from fatigue. A warning horn sounded, startling some who had nodded off while sitting on the edge of the carousel, and the oval belt started moving.

As people grabbed bags, many moved purposely toward car rental booths or outside. Others were greeted by men holding signs. A few looked dazed and started walking, heads swiveling from one sign to another.

My body felt heavy as I looked to the floor and sighed in disappointment. Why did I come here?

I shouldered my pack, grabbed my duffel and guitar, and walked toward a bank of phones for hotels. A man near me exclaimed, "That much? Outrageous!" He slammed the handset down.

The woman next to him said, "We have to sleep somewhere."

"Half the night is gone, and they want a hundred dollars." The man looked over at me as I scanned the advertisements. "Hey, Bud, where do you plan to stay?"

"I think I'll sleep at the train station." I walked away, hearing them argue behind me. If Mom came up, what would she do?

I found a taxi and headed toward the depot. Anchorage was larger than I'd expected, with hotels and bars and people wandering the streets, some very drunk. The city snuggled against the Chugach Mountains—tall, wild, lush with trees, but downtown looked seedy, like many I'd seen in the Lower 48.

After paying the driver, I walked into the brightly-lit depot where wooden benches hugged the walls and formed squares around support posts. Nothing was open. I checked the departure schedule and learned that my train would leave at 8:20 in the morning. Half the benches were occupied with sleepers, leaning together or alone under jackets. I saw no women without male companions.

I sat on an empty bench and ate from my bag of peanuts and raisins, again wondering about Mom. I knew tomorrow I'd feel excitement on the train, but right then I wasn't very enthused about Alaska.

My last thought after leaning against my pack to sleep was, *Maybe this isn't Alaska. Not yet.*

CHAPTER 19
A BATHROOM & A YURT

My alarm was set to buzz at seven, but activity in the station woke me sooner. Lines had formed to purchase tickets. I gathered my gear and got behind a couple in their twenties with large backpacks. *Finally, another woman dressed like me.*

After we purchased tickets, the woman asked, "Are you by yourself?"

"Yes."

She raised her eyebrows. "Cool. Meet my brother."

We shook hands, and I felt a pang in my chest. Spencer and I could have been them. How different would everything have been?

She flicked a wisp of her auburn hair out of her face. She wore a tie-dye band around her forehead. "Charlie wouldn't let me go alone. Now he's stuck with me for two weeks in the wilderness. But he gets to carry my camera gear."

I noticed a tripod tied to her pack and a soft-sided case hanging from his fingers.

"You're a photographer?" I asked.

"Yes. Freelance for now but hoping this trip will fix that. My girlfriend wanted to come, but she's taking a summer class at U.C. Berkeley."

Charlie flinched, and his eyes darted around.

A smile flashed across my face as a rush of warmth surged through my body. "I'd rather come to Alaska than take any class."

"Yeah, right!" She looked at her brother, then said softly, "Charlie doesn't want me to mention her in public. He believes in the patriarchy, and a man's role is to protect the ladies."

Charlie cleared his throat and shook his head at her.

"Then why did you?" I asked, my pulse racing.

"Because I knew you'd understand." She smiled and winked.

I felt my face heat up. "Is it that obvious?"

"To me. I have yet to meet a straight woman backpacking alone. I'm Emily. You hungry?"

"Yes."

"There's a bakery around the corner. Charlie can watch our stuff."

I nodded. We carried our gear to a bench where Charlie would stand guard.

"Coffee? Bagel? Danish?" Emily asked her brother.

"All of the above," he said.

During our quick breakfast, I told Emily my life story. I didn't realize how much I'd needed to talk about the last several months. Words spilled out as well as tears. Emily held my hands and cried with me. As we walked back, I said, "So it's possible to have a normal girl-girl relationship where you live?"

"Not really. There are always dickheads. It might actually be easier up here because people are so spread out, except for Anchorage."

She gave Charlie his breakfast.

"Where are you going?" I asked.

"Seward, with stops along the way. We leave tomorrow morning. You?"

"North to McKinley Park. I leave in ten minutes." I gave her a hug. "Thanks for listening."

"Write to me when you're settled. I'll write back. Promise."

I shook hands with Charlie and walked toward my train, feeling hopeful, excited, and so much better than yesterday. I checked my bags, hanging on to my pack's top pouch with my thermos, bagels, butter, and cream cheese.

The train moved away from the station, and my real Alaskan adventure began.

During the next eight hours, I couldn't sit still, trying to see everything on both sides of the train. At most stops, I left my car and walked around outside, breathing the fresh, clean air, intoxicated with the aroma of lush trees and shrubbery. Every breath I took seemed to fill my lungs more deeply.

The views were grand and endless—mountains, glaciers, bridges crossing deep gorges, broad passes and narrow canyons. And for the most part, I saw no people, few dwellings, and not a single fence. The land was empty yet supremely verdant.

I couldn't believe some passengers slept. Did they know what they were missing?

What I never saw, however, was Mt. McKinley's summit. It stayed hidden in every view I had. I saw glimpses of its massive face, but never very much at one time. Like a slow striptease behind clouds, revealing random parts in no particular order. Its size seemed to grow in my mind with each icy wall I detected, but the top remained elusive.

When an animal was spotted, people sprang to a window with long lenses, snapping repeatedly. I looked through my Instamatic viewfinder and realized I'd have to be nose-to-nose with a moose or caribou for it to be larger than a dot in my frame. A good excuse for chasing after the beasts when I saw them.

We left Broad Pass and a view of the cloaked mountain near Cantwell and entered a series of canyons twisting along the Nenana River. Just before entering the park, we crossed a high, long steel bridge across the river, stopping just below the hotel.

Of all the views I had seen, this spot was one of the least impressive with hills tight around us, affording a limited view. But this is where I would camp and cook for myself for the next six nights.

After another hour, I had paid my fees and set up my tent in a spot overlooking Riley Creek, which looked more like a rushing river to me. I was surrounded by spruce and birch trees, suffusing the air with a sweet, sharp, cleansing smell. I breathed it deep into my lungs and felt calm, almost weightless. The sound of water and the breeze shaking the leaves emptied my mind, and for the first time in forever I felt at peace, totally in tune with each moment, unhindered by memories or aspirations or worries.

I stretched my arms behind me along the picnic table and leaned my head back toward the sky, the sun's rays keeping the chill of fifty-degree air at bay. I sat for half an hour in that blissful state until my stomach rumbled for food.

Regretfully, I sprang to action, organizing my gear to make a dinner of rice and fried Spam with hot tea, which for a first meal I'd cooked outdoors myself tasted pretty damn good.

Nature called, and I wandered toward the restroom where I found a man standing outside the women's bathroom door. He looked me up and down and frowned.

"You sure you're on the right side?" he asked.

"Are you?"

He turned his head slightly. "Hey, Hon, are you decent? Someone wants to come in."

A young woman laughed from inside. "Let her in, Tony. I don't care."

"My wife is washing up," he explained. "Just wanted to make sure . . . well, you know."

"I don't really, but whatever." I moved toward the door.

"Just don't fling it wide open," he said.

Totally confused and curious, I opened the door just enough to let me in. Standing naked in front of one of the sinks was a woman with a towel draped around her shoulders.

"Hey!" She looked at me through the mirror as she wiped a soapy washcloth across her ample chest. "Don't mind me."

My eyes darted from her breasts to her butt and legs. "No problem," I gasped. I tried to stifle my nervousness and walk casually to a stall, but I stumbled against the toilet and then hit my face with the door trying to close it. I peed and tried to take my time, thinking she would leave, but her humming never stopped.

Finally, I flushed and left the stall, moving toward the other sink. She was bent over hers with shampoo in her hair, the towel now hung over a window latch. She held out a plastic cup.

"Would you mind pouring water over my head?"

I swallowed and said, "Sure," as I took the cup, trying not to stare at the goosebumps all over her light pink skin. I filled the cup. "This water is cold."

"Yes, it is. But I can take it."

With a shaking hand, I poured the water over her head as she pushed her fingers through her hair. Her breasts hung freely, swaying to her movements. I poured three more times until she shivered, twisted her hair, and reached out her hand.

"Towel?"

I removed it from the window and gave it to her. She rubbed her hair vigorously, forcing her breasts to jiggle and her butt cheeks to shake. My heart pounded so loud I thought she would hear it.

I pulled my eyes from her body and looked out the window. "Well, I'd better get back to my tent."

She wrapped the towel around her head and turned toward me. "Can you grab me some paper towels?"

I pulled out several and handed them to her, trying to keep my eyes averted. "Don't they have showers to buy?" My muscles twitched I was so nervous.

She wiped her chest and arm pits, which were at least as hairy as mine. "Sure, but they cost fifty cents, and I'd rather spend that on beer. Besides, why is everyone so scared to look at a human body? We all have the same basic parts. You see one, you've seen them all." She wiped the paper towel wad between her legs then tossed it into the trash. "I think all the fuss about showing too much skin is what leads to pornography. I can't understand it."

"Women aren't used to it, I guess. Men are naked around each other all the time."

The woman laughed. "Yesterday, my husband walked into the bathroom, and a naked biker was lifting his scrotum into the sink so he could wash it."

I kept my eyes fixed on hers and chuckled. "What did your husband do?"

"He took a shave right next to him. He said they had a good talk." She looked at herself in the mirror, grabbing a wad of her stomach fat in each hand. "I know some will say I'm pudgy and need to lose some weight, but I'm happy with how I look. It doesn't matter to me what others think. If they like what they see, then fine. Otherwise, look somewhere else." She pointed at a long-sleeve t-shirt hanging from the other window. "Can you hand me that?"

"Sure." I gave her the shirt, which she pulled over her head, the cloth clinging against her large nipples.

She reached behind her for the sweatpants hanging over the stall wall next to her. "Your first job is to be happy with yourself. Because if you aren't, who else will be?" She pulled her pants up her legs.

Though I was still nervous, I admired her spirit. "I think you look great, with or without clothes."

"Well, thank you . . . what's your name?"

"Tracy."

"I'm Sharon." She gave me a hug. "Thanks for not screaming and running out of the building like the mother and kid did before you came in." She laughed. "That's why I told Tony to stand there." We walked outside.

Tony said, "Sounds like you ladies had a good talk."

Sharon hooked my arm. "Yes, we did. Where are you staying, Tracy?"

"In the green tent three sites up."

"We're right across from here in a red truck camper." She pointed through the trees. "Come by anytime and we can drink a beer together."

"I think she's too young," said Tony.

She punched his shoulder. "Like we never did at her age. See you later, Tracy."

They walked away, him complaining about her punching too hard as she laughed. I went back to my tent and climbed inside, thinking about what she'd said. I had always been disappointed, hell, ashamed of my body. Never once in my life did I like looking in a mirror. Maybe that's why I didn't like makeup because I needed to stare at myself for too long.

Could I ever be so comfortable that I could be nude around others, or even one person? I was naked with Ava in the back of a dark car for a few minutes having sex, nervous as hell.

Sharon stood naked with me for at least fifteen minutes, not caring what I thought about her.

I needed to like myself more. I took off my shirt and removed my spandex band, revealing red creases in my skin. I hadn't really looked at my breasts for months. Showers were always quick, and I realized I always looked at the wall when I washed my face and torso.

I held my boobs and squeezed gently. They had grown a little. I found my little camp mirror and stared at them. My nipples had turned from small, dark circles like a boy's to be much wider and puffy. They were cute. And when I shook my chest, they actually jiggled.

I pulled off my jeans and noticed blood in the crotch of my panties. I'd started my period. *Crap!* I didn't want to be cramping while I hiked. I poured water on a cloth, wiped myself, and inserted a tampon.

Maybe one reason I didn't like being female was having periods. They made me weak and tired and embarrassed. I hated them.

I had to change my thinking. They're part of me, and my first job is to like myself. If I could play basketball with bloody feet, I could damn well do anything else with a bloody vagina.

I washed out my underwear and found another pair. I put on my pants and shirt and climbed out of the tent with the spandex wadded in my hand. After I threw it in the trash can, I laughed at the prospect of some kid seeing it before dumping food scraps. "What the hell is that?"

What the hell was that? Something I didn't need or want anymore.

I drank a beer with Sharon and Tony that night while sitting around their fire. The next night I brought my guitar and sang some songs. Soon, we had a sizable group bellowing loud enough to cause the ranger to shut us down.

I took the shuttle to Savage River and scampered up the Alpine Trail until I reached an overlook fifteen hundred feet above the road where I could gaze across the broad valley between me and the Alaska Range. The view cleansed my mind and filled it with wonder. The mountain still played hide and seek.

I found other trails and fought my cramps, eventually declaring victory at Mount Healey's summit, three thousand feet above the road. I was alone and pulled off my shirts. With arms raised against the blistering, cold wind, I shouted, "Hello, Alaska! I don't care what you think about me. I'm here to stay!"

I pulled on my long-sleeve t-shirt and carried my top shirt in my hand, not caring that my boobs were obvious to anyone who looked.

On Sunday at noon when the campground was almost empty, I decided to wash up in the bathroom. I took a deep breath and walked from my tent in my thin tank top and sweatpants. Once inside the building, I tried to pull off my top, but couldn't. I pushed the wet washcloth under my shirt, along my arms, and over my face.

I dropped my pants and stood in my underwear. Again, I couldn't remove more. I washed under my panties then my legs and feet. I bent over to wash my hair, filling a cup and pouring it over my head. Just after I sudsed up, Sharon walked in.

"Hey, Tracy. I was getting ready to do the same."

I held out the cup. "Can you rinse me?"

"Sure, Hon." She poured three cups over my hair before I couldn't take anymore.

I stood up shivering and pulled the towel from the window, draping it over my head.

"What are you doing with clothes on? They're all wet." She pulled off her shirt. "You have to get naked and love it." She removed her pants and scratched her pubic hair.

I rubbed the towel quickly over my head. "I tried, Sharon, but couldn't go further than this. But that's a lot more than I would've done before meeting you, so thanks."

"Well, you're welcome." She looked me over and raised her brows. "You look good. Don't you think?"

I pulled the towel around my chest and shivered. "Pretty good. I'm getting there."

She held a large bowl of warm water between her legs, dipped in a cloth, and wiped. "Mmm. Warm water feels nice. When do you leave for that camp?"

"Tomorrow at noon. I'm going to call my mom now." I pulled on my pants, collected my things, and walked toward the door.

"You going to come by tonight?"

"Sure."

After I dressed in my tent, I walked to the hotel and found a pay phone. It would've been 4:30 in the afternoon in Texas. I called collect and waited to hear her voice.

"Tracy? Are you okay?" Mom said, her voice strained with worry.

"I'm fine, Mom." I felt such a rush of excitement. Everything was going to work out. "It's beautiful up here. You wouldn't believe the scenery." I hesitated, my stomach twisting. "Are you coming?"

She paused and said stiffly, "I'm glad you're having a good time."

Panic hitched my breath. "Mom, answer me."

"Oh, that sounds amazing!" she gushed.

"He's standing right there, isn't he?"

"Yes. We're both so happy you're having fun and meeting wonderful people."

"Can I call back later?"

"You'll be at Camp Wonder until when?"

Tears trickled down my cheeks. "Until the 28th, but I need to know what you're doing before then, and I won't be able to call you after tomorrow morning."

She paused and spoke more softly. "I don't know. Maybe when you get settled I can mail it to you."

Mail what? The journal? "Has he read Spencer's journal?"

"No, I don't think he's read that article." Her voice quavered. "Could be just a local story."

I tightened my fists. "Let him read it," I snapped. "See how he reacts and ask yourself whether you can live with him for the rest of your life."

"I think that's a good idea, Tracy. You should keep a journal."

"Mom, if I have to do this by myself, I will. But I'd rather you'd be with me. I love you more now than I ever realized. If you do come, after you land, take a cab from the airport to the train depot. It's safe, and you can sleep on a bench just like everyone else there. Your train will leave at 8:20 on Thursday morning going north. They alternate directions each day. So you have to fly to Anchorage on Wednesday. Got that?"

"Yes . . ." she stammered. "Yes, dear."

"Stay in the hotel Thursday night. I'll be there between 11:30 and noon on Friday." I sniffed. "I love you."

"I love you too."

I hung up. She wasn't going to come. She was too scared of the unknown, and I foolishly had made everything sound complicated— sleep on a bench, come a day early, alternating trains. I lit a cigarette and walked back toward the campground.

Women like Mom had been trained to believe they were helpless. Men opened their doors, helped them sit and stand, and on and on. I'd seen Mom wait in front of a door for five seconds until Dad pulled it open. Yet when he was gone, she'd open every one herself.

Charlie had insisted he accompany Emily into the wilderness because she couldn't do it on her own. She needed his protection.

What men considered politeness and putting women on a pedestal was actually a ploy to keep them helpless without men.

I fucking got up here by myself, Mom. You can damn well do it too!

I ground out my cigarette and tossed it in the trash.

But she wouldn't.

I had to resign myself to being alone in Alaska. I knew I could do it, but being with her would've been so much easier. And less lonely for both of us.

After dinner, I sat at my table with my guitar and notebook, feeling dejected. I'd barely eaten and found myself staring blankly at the trees. I felt hollow and trapped in an ass-backward world.

I worked on my song as I took sips from Spencer's flask. By the time I was finished, I was a little drunk. Maybe more than a little when I sang out loud.

> Like a bird that won't sing
> Or a mind that can't think
> Like a heart that can' feel
> Or a wound that won't heal
>
> What's the point?
> Yeah, Babe, what's the point?
>
> Like a joke that hurts
> Or a clock that won't work
> Like a lie to yourself

And a truth you can't tell

What's the point?
Yeah, Babe, what's the point?

Like a friend that won't share
Or a God who doesn't care
Like a girl who's a toy
And never equal to a boy

What's the point?
Yeah, Babe, what's the point?

You say
It's just the world we were given
Maybe it's the one we made
How can this be living
I'd rather walk away

Time to make a change
Or what's the point?
Time to rearrange
Or what's the point?

I finally understood why Spencer drank himself to sleep. I crawled into my tent and barely zipped my bag before I crashed. No thoughts. No worries.

Oblivion.

The sound of people breaking camp woke me up. After a rushed breakfast, I heated chicken soup and rice for my thermos—something to eat during the long drive to Camp Wonder.

I hoisted all my gear and trudged up to the hotel where I stood near the bus stop along with some others. After a few minutes, we realized we were waiting for the same thing and began to introduce ourselves.

All of them were at least thirty, several in their sixties. They were amazed I was seventeen and traveling alone—a girl no less. They'd spent the night in the lodge and couldn't believe I had camped for the past six days.

Of course, if I'd been a boy, they wouldn't have been so surprised, but they meant well.

I immediately loved talking to Hallie and DeLacie, twin black sisters in their 40s with beautiful round faces and sparkling eyes who had always wanted to come to Alaska.

"How come you're so skinny, girl?" Hallie asked. "Were we ever that skinny, DeLacie?"

DeLacie laughed with the biggest smile. "I know I was, but you, never!"

Hallie pretended to be offended. "That hurts me to the quick."

"I don't think you have any quick." DeLacie laughed, squeezing her sister's plump arm. "At least I haven't seen it in years."

They both laughed hard then hugged each other. I laughed with them until my sides hurt. I couldn't remember being so happy.

One woman stood away, wrinkling her nose at us—at the twins, mainly. She looked to be in her late thirties, hair in a ponytail, the only woman in our group wearing a dress—long over boots, almost like the pictures of pioneer women sixty years ago.

"Are you always this much fun to be around?" I asked.

"Always," Hallie said, her cheeks pushing hard against her eyes.

"Actually," DeLacie added, "we're holding back a bit because we're among strangers. But not for long!" She pulled me to her and squeezed. "I like you, Tracy. I think we're going to be good friends. Do you play that guitar?"

"Yes."

"And sing?"

"I try."

"We can't wait to hear you."

Two dark green Land Rovers headed toward us then parked. Miki hopped out of one, her long hair braided down to her waist. She looked exactly like her picture in the brochure. "Welcome to McKinley Park," said Miki. "I think we can fit all of you in these Rovers. Climb in and get close to your neighbor."

A skinny, younger and taller version of Paul Newman emerged from the other car and waved.

"Ooh, he's cute," Hallie said. "Let's ride with him."

The twins walked over and gave him their bags, which he hoisted up to the metal rack on top of the car. I followed.

"Hey, I'm Jeff. Is it okay if I put that guitar on top?" His crystal blue eyes sparkled in the sunlight.

"Yes," I said. His face was almost too pretty, especially under his head full of blonde curls.

He smiled, revealing impossibly white teeth. "We've never had a guest bring a guitar before. You'll have to play for the crew."

"I'd love to." I sat in the front seat. Just before I closed the door, the woman with the dress grabbed the outside handle.

"Can I sit here? All the other seats are taken."

I scooted over next to Jeff. "Sure. I'm Tracy."

"Glenda. Thanks."

She slid in next to me, overwhelming my nose with her perfume—vanilla, rosewood, and something else, bitter and stifling. Jeff rolled his window all the way down.

A high school teaching couple from Florida and a retired couple from Montana squeezed together in the back.

An older man named Jake tried to slide into the seat with the twins after apologizing for bothering them. All the other seats were taken.

Hallie pushed against her sister. "DeLacie, suck it up, so this man can sit down."

"Suck what up?"

"Your butt, girl."

"You suck it up," DeLacie said.

"I'm not going near that thing!"

"Well, if this man is gonna have a seat, you better get near it."

After more laughter and shoving, the man finally wedged in.

"Sorry my sister is so plump," Hallie said. "But she got the fat gene."

"We're twins!" DeLacie shouted. "We have the same genes."

Hallie folded her arms and lifted her chin. "Don't forget, you weighed one ounce more than me at birth. Taking up more than your fair share even in the womb."

"Well, we both got the bubble butt gene."

"That's for sure."

I could barely breathe I was laughing so hard, and my face was wet with tears. Glenda hugged herself and stared out the window, unaffected. Jeff handed me some tissues.

"Thanks," I said. After wiping my face, I took some deep breaths. "Hey, Jeff, do you know Jackie?"

"Yes. Do you?"

"No. Her picture is on the brochure." My stomach fluttered. "Miki told me her name. Does she play guitar?"

He nodded. "She's really good. She'll probably do a singalong once or twice while you're here. She writes her own songs."

"Really?" My body flushed with excitement. "Cool. I do too."

"Yeah, she'll be up in the middle of the night, plucking on her guitar. It's hard to sleep sometimes."

A tingle of fear rose in my throat. "You can hear her?"

He smiled and looked at me, almost winking. "We share a yurt, so it's pretty hard not to."

I stopped breathing. As I stared out the windshield, my head started spinning. My stomach felt cold and empty.

They shared a yurt.

Shit!

Jackie is straight.

CHAPTER 20

AN OPPORTUNITY OR A NUISANCE?

J ust before we crossed the bridge at Savage River, Jeff braked and
pulled over behind Miki. I was vaguely aware of excited murmurs
behind me.

"Tracy," Jeff said. "Moose." He pointed toward the willows
outside the window. "Tracy? Are you okay?"

I turned toward him and felt like his face was at the wrong end of a
telescope—forehead deeply creased, mouth half open. Cameras clicked
behind me. I couldn't speak. My brain was spiraling into a hole. I had
told myself many times that Jackie was probably straight. The chances of
being gay were what? One in ten? In twenty? Still, my disappointment
was crushing.

"Have you ever been inside a yurt?" he asked then reached over to
hold my wrist. "I'm sure Jackie would like you to visit."

Hearing her name must have been a lifeline because I could feel my
breaths again and my heart beat. "I've never seen a yurt. What is it?"

He smiled. "It's a round frame house covered with vinyl. It's really
cool."

A tiny feather of warmth tickled my cheek. "I'd love to see it."

His eyes fixed on mine. "Tracy, don't worry. Okay?"

I searched his face, trying to understand what he meant, but nothing came to me. "Okay. Thanks." I looked out the window and saw a giant moose moving away, disappearing through the willows like a shadow.

Glenda handed me two developing Polaroid photos before rolling up the side window. I watched as the massive animal appeared in my hands.

Glenda leaned against me. "I didn't want to wait until I got home to see my photos, so I bought this Polaroid Land Camera. You can keep one of those if you want."

"Thanks." I tried to show more enthusiasm, but couldn't summon the energy. I put one in my pocket and gave the other to her.

"You're very welcome." She flashed a smile with her bright red lips.

"My God," Hallie bellowed. "That moose was as big as a bus! Is that their normal size, or is he a runt for Alaska?"

"That's a good size," Jeff said. "Probably a seventy-inch spread. If you're outside a vehicle, you should stay at least seventy-five feet from them, and if they charge, run." He started the car and followed Miki.

"You hear that, Hallie?" DeLacie said. "When that beast runs at us, you turn around and wave your arms."

Hallie blurted, "He said to run!"

"You know we can't run, so you need to distract him. You've always said you're prettier than me."

"True," Hallie said. "For attracting men, dear sister. *Your* face, however, is a moose magnet."

I exploded in laughter.

Hallie continued, "Bullwinkle will fall in love and drag you back into those bushes. By the time he's finished with you, I'll be safe in this seat."

DeLacie swatted her sister's arm. "That's disgusting, Hallie. Remember, we have a youngster in this car."

"If she can come all this way by herself," Hallie said, "she knows a thing or two about the motivations of Bullwinkles. Tracy, as pretty as you are, how'd you keep all those men between here and Texas from coming after you?"

My mouth spoke before my brain could stop it. "I disguised myself as a boy."

Both their mouths dropped open.

"Not a single boy hit on me," I said while seeing Greta's long legs in my mind. Out of the corner of my eye, I saw Jeff flashing me a coy smile. "Of course, I'm skinny and can get away with it. Not every girl can."

Hallie looked down at her bosom. "Not this girl," she said with a harrumph.

"Or this one," added her sister.

The male teacher in the back row said, "You're lucky some guy didn't think you were gay." He chuckled like he'd told a joke.

My muscles quivered and my hands balled into fists. "Because if he thought I was gay, he might hurt me? Or because he might hit on me?"

He hesitated. "Well . . . I guess either one. But it would be creepy to have a guy show interest in you when you were disguised."

I turned my head and glared. "What are gays supposed to do? Hide their feelings? Pretend they're not attracted?"

"Well, personally, I think that would be best." He chuckled. "Or disappear. There's too many as it is."

The man from Montana said, "Amen."

The Montana wife rolled her eyes while the teacher wife folded her arms and stared down her nose at me.

Heat roiled my gut—two know-it-all males passing judgment because they could. "You both got your wish three weeks ago." I spit the words. "My gay brother killed himself because of bigots like you. *You* should disappear." I glared at them hard before turning around.

For the next fifteen minutes, the only sounds we heard were tires biting gravel and the squeak of springs as we bounced over ruts. After several sweeping turns through a thick forest, Jeff followed Miki into the Teklanika Rest Stop. As soon as he parked and Glenda had left the car, I bolted outside and walked across a deck overlooking the river.

Is Alaska going to be like everywhere else?

I watched braids of shallow water rush toward a bridge in the distance where the road crossed into Igloo Canyon. I had studied maps of that park for months and knew the major features from the hotel to Camp Wonder.

A lone caribou trotted along the river. I wished I was down there with him.

"Hello, Tracy," Miki said from behind. "I didn't get a chance to say hi earlier."

I turned and saw her extend a hand, which I shook. It was strong and thick. "Hi, Miki." Her face was tanned, and her lips chapped. She moved like an athlete in her high-rise leather boots. "You must like driving this road. There are so many things to see."

"Yes, there are, but I try to minimize my impact on the park. Cars kick up dust and interfere with animal movements, so we limit our trips to the hotel to no more than two per week." She took a deep breath and looked to the hills across the river. "When you're out there far away from the road, then you'll see something."

"Will we do that?"

"Not as far as I'd like. We're limited by the group's abilities. But you could go anywhere. Maybe you and some of the crew would like to hike out for a day."

"I'd love that."

Her eyes twinkled. "By the way, did you become a starter for the boys' basketball team?"

My chin jutted out and my chest filled as those moments from December filled my brain. "Yes, I did. I was named MVP of the tournament."

She clapped her hands. "You don't say." She touched my shoulder with her fist. "Way to show those boys what fer. Good for you!" She walked back toward the cars and hollered, "Five minutes 'till we leave!"

I took one last glance at the river before walking toward the car. Halfway there, the two couples converged on me, heads down, looking contrite.

"I'm real sorry for my stupid comments," said one of the men.

I'd forgotten their names and had no interest in asking for them again.

"We're sorry about your brother," said the other man.

Both women looked down and said nothing.

What did I feel then? A mixture of pity and disgust for their ignorance. Then I remembered what Mom had said to me about egging Dad on. I could have said nothing when the teacher made his first comment.

Just turned around and looked outside. But then there would be no chance these people would learn anything.

I nodded. "I appreciate your apology, but you'll still tell queer jokes to your friends and be *creeped-out* when you see two guys or two girls kiss. My brother was a wonderful, talented, loving person. If he'd been loved in return by others, he'd still be alive. Think about that the next time you show hate to a homosexual. I don't want to talk about this again."

I walked toward the car but saw Jeff smoking a cigarette by a tree. "Can I bum one? Mine are in my pack."

"Sure." He pulled his box out of his shirt pocket and shook it, raising one above the others.

I pulled it out, and he flicked his lighter.

"Did they apologize?" he asked.

"In their way." I blew smoke above my head.

He looked toward the car. "How long ago?"

My chest tightened. "May twenty-first. Dad wanted him to enlist in the Navy. Queer jokes during the physical pushed him over the edge."

I watched Jeff's facial muscles twitch and tense like he was going to say something but couldn't quite get it out. Finally, he said, "You still came up here."

"Nothing to stay for except Mom, but she's with Dad. I hope she leaves him and flies up, but I don't think she will."

His eyes caught mine. "No boyfriend?"

I shook my head slowly, wanting to tell him the truth but afraid to do so. *Too soon.* "Nope. Nobody back there. I thought maybe someone in Alaska would pop up."

He smiled and nodded. "That happens up here. We better go."

We hustled back toward the car. Glenda stood by the passenger door, and when I was two steps away, she moved toward me with her arms out for a hug.

"I'm so sorry about your brother, Tracy." Her arms wrapped around my back as she pulled me close.

I was too shocked to react. My arms hung down at my side.

After several awkward seconds, she leaned back and said, "If there's anything I can do for you, please let me know." Her eyes searched mine then she touched my cheek. "You're so brave, coming all this way dressed as a boy, no less."

The same warning lights I had seen with Greta flashed bright in my brain. I nodded, and she made sure she entered the car first. I sat close to the window.

Soon we were moving through Igloo Canyon just starting to make our ascent up to Sable Pass when the couples in the back shouted, "Bear!"

Jeff looked in his mirror and stopped the car.

"They're babies!" said the Montana woman in wonder.

Through the side mirror, I saw two dark brown cubs play with each other like puppies in the road. A blonde grizzly sow waddled out of the bushes and crossed behind them, paying us no attention. I sucked in a quick breath. *I am truly in the middle of nowhere. Wow.*

Glenda passed me her camera and asked me to photograph the cubs. I leaned out the window and took one, handing the print back to her. At one point, both cubs stood on their hind legs and swatted each other. I took two more and sat back down.

"Did we ever do that?" asked Hallie.

"Every damn day," DeLacie chuckled.

Just like me and Spencer. I hitched a breath but smiled at the memories.

"These are wonderful," said Glenda, her photos resting on her dress spread wide across open legs. "You're quite the photographer. Take this one. You deserve it."

She handed me one of the prints. Her right leg pressed against mine.

The bears disappeared in the drainage on the other side of the road, and we drove on. Patches of snow covered much of the pass, providing some respite from the flies bothering the caribou. On our way to the Toklat River, we saw a fox, ptarmigan with white feathers remaining from their winter camouflage, and grizzlies high up a slope, digging for ground squirrels.

Climbing up Polychrome Pass, we could see the three sources of the Toklat emerging from hidden glaciers in the peaks to the south. Glistening, silver braids of water swept across the rocky valley before merging into a single torrent of water tumbling under the bridge. Brilliant white

Dall Sheep with golden, curled horns sat on the slopes just below us as we passed. The road was single-lane, a scratch across the scree which extended a thousand feet below us.

The colors of the land were rich, like an earthen paint palette—ochre, orange, deep green, crystal blue, white, yellow, and red. As clouds moved and lighting changed, hues brightened or dimmed—a living, breathing portrait.

My mind and emotions were overwhelmed with awe. My breath stalled and despite the cool temperature, my skin flushed with heat.

Coming down from the pass, we saw a white wolf in bushes just off the road, lifting his bloody muzzle up to look at us before bending down to eat more of the hidden animal it had killed. Later we saw two wolves trotting near the road with huge paws and bodies three feet tall at the shoulder and six feet long.

We should have been able to see the mountain as we moved toward Stony Dome, but a lid of gray clouds hovered at about eleven thousand feet. I had seen photos of Mt. McKinley from that viewpoint, dominating the valley between there and Thorofare Pass, looming over the thread of road undulating toward it. The mountain in the photo was breathtaking. That day, it was generating its own weather and preferred to hide.

Eilson Visitor Center perched hundreds of feet above Thorofare Gorge. Dark canyons slithered away from hidden glaciers, feeding water to the west where it merged with the McKinley River. Farther down the road, we could see the Muldrow Glacier, spilling white from its gorge in the mountain, then partially covered in gravel as it turned west before ending in massive lumps of green tundra. Jeff said some years it surged but had been stationary for a decade. Dozens of beaver ponds filled the rolling landscape before we drove around Wonder Lake where hundreds of photographs had captured the mountain's reflection. Just past the lake we stopped at a sign for Camp Wonder with a phone in a box. We were supposed to call before ascending the one-lane road carved into the ridge to ensure another vehicle wasn't descending.

This was a dedicated line. We were truly cut off from the rest of the world, but people from outside brought their own issues and agendas.

By the time we had reached the main lodge, all of us were hungry and eager to stretch our legs and get settled. Jeff and another crew member, Johnny, set our luggage on the ground as Miki pointed to various log cabins assigned to each of us.

As soon as she called Hallie, DeLacie, and Glenda's name to share Cabin C, I knew trouble was coming. The twins walked excitedly toward their new home, arguing about who had first choice of bed. Glenda stood with her mouth open, face drained of all color, staring back at Miki, who pointed me toward Cabin F.

I heard snippets of a tense conversation behind me as I opened my door to find a double bed, wood stove, sofa, chair, and desk. Though the place was tiny, it was much nicer than I had expected. I had just set my gear on the bed when I heard a knock before Miki entered.

"Tracy, I have a problem. I hope you can help me."

"Sure, whatever you need."

"Glenda refuses to stay with Hallie and DeLacie." She lowered her voice. "She claims they're loud, and she didn't come to the wilderness to have to listen to them all day and night."

I folded my arms and shook my head. "Did she also notice they're black?"

Miki rolled her eyes. "I didn't ask, but I imagine so. These cabins are for my special groups and now they're full. I have a wall tent down the hill a little. It's not near as nice as this, but it's private —"

"I'll take it. No problem at all. You're putting Glenda in here?"

"Yes." She flashed me a wry smile. "Or you could stay with her and share the bed. She said she wouldn't mind."

I remembered the hug and the leg pushing against me and realized she was hitting on me. "Hmm. Sleep with a racist or have my own place where I can play my guitar? Hard choice." I picked up my gear. "Point the way."

"I'm telling the twins I made the change so they'd be more comfortable not having to share a bed."

I looked at the mattress and tried to imagine both ladies trying to fit. "They'd fight and laugh all night."

"Exactly. Thanks, Tracy. I owe you one."

Two weeks later, I remembered that comment. She never paid her debt.

We walked outside where Glenda stood between the cabins, lips tight, head bowed, like she expected someone to yell at her. Miki showed me the path to follow, and off I went.

My tent was at the very edge of a steep slope, thirty feet from everything else. The frame was 2 x 4 lumber, covered in white canvas. I had a metal bunk bed, wood stove, small table, and a chair. I loved it.

I set my gear on my mattress and walked outside, looking for an outhouse. I saw a little wooden sign by a narrow path which seemed to disappear over the hill. After a dozen steps, I found a very nice wooden structure, elevated above the ground. I walked up two steps and found a toilet lid over a hole in plywood with toilet paper on one side and a sign on the other telling me to not throw trash into the pit.

I turned around and started to unbuckle my belt when I realized there was no door. How cool was that? The view while sitting on the seat was amazing and totally private—no road, no other structure, just lush willows and alder all the way down to wherever.

I peed and stood up with my pants at my ankles and didn't worry about anything or anyone. *Fucking amazing!*

I hiked back up the hill toward the lodge where we were supposed to meet for dinner. For the past few nights, I had dreamed of meeting Jackie. How it would go. Where? When? How nervous I would be.

But after Jeff's revelation, it seemed less important. We could be friends, even play guitar together, but we couldn't be more. I wondered how I would feel being near her while Jeff held her hand or . . . I tried to think of something else but had trouble.

Then I saw Glenda waiting for me just outside the lodge. *What now?*

She reached for my hand. "Tracy, you didn't have to move on my account. Where'd she put you? I watched you walk from halfway down this ridge."

My first thought was, *That's creepy.* My second thought was I'd never use that word again after teacher-man's comment. "I love the walk. Love my wall tent and especially love my outhouse." I walked past her and found our group moving toward a dining area, a large room with a kitchen in one half and tables and benches in the other. Miki led us to a long table where we picked up plates, utensils, and cups of water from the end before sitting down. Platters and bowls of food were spread evenly over the surface.

Miki picked a piece of bread from a platter near her and handed it to Jake. "Take what you want and pass the dish to your neighbor. We eat family-style here."

Jake passed the plate to Glenda, who sat on the other side of the table, catty-corner from me.

I was beside the twins. For the next five minutes, we passed and grabbed and ladled—sliced ham, macaroni and cheese, bread and butter, chicken noodle soup, green beans with bacon. The aromas were heavenly.

I faced the kitchen area where another long table full of people ate. Through gaps between the Montana and teaching couples, I glimpsed Johnny then Jeff with his arm around Jackie. They were laughing.

Her hair was golden, parted in the middle with long braids hanging over each ear. When she laughed, her cheeks flushed pink beneath large, brown eyes. I felt breathless, every nerve on edge.

Hallie noticed my long stare and whispered to me, "That Jeff sure is cute. I saw y'all talking at that rest stop." She laughed and pushed her elbow against my arm.

I snapped back to reality. "Yeah, he is."

"You need to eat, girl. You haven't touched your food. It's delicious."

I took a bite of ham and a spoonful of soup under Glenda's steady stare. When the Montana couple leaned close to each other, I saw Jackie laughing and putting a piece of bread in Jeff's mouth. When my view was blocked, I saw Glenda crane her neck to see the people behind her. That woman was freaking me out.

"Everything is so good," DeLacie said. "Miki, who cooked all this for us? It is so scrumptious."

Miki gestured toward the other table. "Cooking crew, stand and be recognized."

Several teens and young women stood up, including Jackie, wearing an open flannel shirt over a tank top. Miki called out their names. Jackie waved at us, her right breast shaking as she lifted her arm. She caught me staring, raised her brows above a tiny grin, and spread her shirt wider before sitting down.

That sucked the air out of my lungs. She did exactly the opposite of what I'd expected, as in, "You like that one? Here's the other."

I joined the twins as they stood and clapped, mainly to get another chance to stare at Jackie. Jeff caught my eye and waved then said something to Jackie, who raised her eyes and smiled at me, burning her face into my eyes forever. I had to force myself to look at others before sitting down.

I tried my best to eat everything on my plate, but my stomach already seemed full. Every place I looked seemed to have her afterimage.

After scraping and stacking our plates, we gathered with Miki in the main room of the lodge. "Breakfast is at eight," she said. "Tomorrow we won't drive anywhere. You can explore our surroundings, even walk down toward the lake if you want. At noon we'll gather in here before lunch and talk a bit. Feel free to read any books while you're in this room. It's always open. Most are about Alaska history and wildlife and flowers. Any questions?"

"Where's Rhonda?" I asked. "I was looking forward to meeting her."

"She's in Fairbanks for some medical needs. Nothing serious. She'll arrive on the train the day you leave. She'll be happy to meet you then."

Hallie picked up an animal skin. "What is this? It's so soft."

"Beaver. There's also wolf, bear, and moose hide. Plus labeled rocks. This room is like a park museum. Look and touch all you want. Just leave it for the next person."

As everyone else wandered around the room, I made my exit, needing to be alone with my thoughts.

From my wall tent, I could see the northern tip of Wonder Lake and glimpses of snow-covered mountains beyond, but they paled against the image of her face still blazoned onto my mind. Inside, I found a kerosene burner, porcelain cups, tea bags and sugar, ground coffee in a jar, a small percolator, and a pitcher of water. A wood stove sat near the center of the tent. Nearby stood containers of kindling and newspaper. Directions for using everything were tacked to one of the studs.

Soon I had coffee brewing. I took out my guitar and notebook, found the verse I had started on the plane, and made some changes.

I chased the sun until I found you

Out of the darkness and into your light
A smile so bright I never knew
Could steal my eyes
And see only you

I tried different chord progressions and melodies until my coffee was ready. I poured a cup and watched Jackie and Jeff at the table in my mind—laughing, playing, feeding bread. She was already his.

But then I saw her eyes on me. I'd felt a connection. How could she not?

And I realized what Jeff had never said—"Jackie's my girlfriend." They *shared* a yurt. He didn't say, "We live together."

Something didn't add up.

Or I was desperate for even a little hope.

I heard footsteps then a knock on my door. For a few wild seconds, I thought Jackie had come to meet me.

"Tracy?" Glenda asked. "Can I come in? I brought you something." She opened the door and beamed—her lips glossed, eyes lined, and cheeks rouged. A breeze at her back filled my tent with her perfume.

My neck stiffened, and I rubbed my head to stop the ache rushing toward it.

She held out a small plate containing a piece of chocolate cake. "The girls brought out dessert just after you left. I thought you might want it since you didn't eat much dinner."

I pointed toward the table. "I'll eat it later. Thank you." I felt a flame of anger tickling my throat, but I swallowed and tried to remain polite.

She looked around the tent, tightening her shawl around her shoulders. "They put you at the edge of the wilderness, didn't they? Five more steps and you'd fall off a cliff." She laughed.

"I love it here."

She smiled at me, her chest heaving like she was short of breath. "I heard you playing and singing some. Your voice is lovely. What song was that?"

Not looking at her, I played a few notes. "Something new I'm working on."

"'A smile so bright I never knew could steal my eyes and see only you.' Such lovely lyrics." Her voice changed, taking on more of an edge. "Whose smile?"

I stopped playing and looked at her. "What?" How long had she been listening outside my tent?

"Whose smile are you writing about?"

I saw desperation in her eyes. The flame burned hotter in my throat. I put my guitar on my bed and stood. "Glenda, why are you here?"

"What do you mean? Here in your tent? I told you, I —"

"No, in Alaska, at Camp Wonder. Of all those in our group, you seem the least likely to want this kind of trip."

Her voice became more defiant. "I came here for the same reason you did."

I was beyond confused and couldn't respond.

She folded her arms. "I wanted to find something I couldn't get at home. A new start." She sucked in her lips and stared at mine. "Maybe someone to be with. Your brother died." Her chin trembled. "My girl-friend left me."

My stomach soured and a stab of fear slammed my temple. "You're twice my age at least."

She raised her brows and smirked. "I notice you didn't say you're not gay. You wore men's clothes. You don't want your face to look feminine at all. And you were practically swooning over that girl, one of the cooks." Her top lip curled back as she spit out, "Jackie. But she's hooked up with Jeff, so where does that leave you? Please." She took a step toward me.

I raised my hand. "Stay back, Glenda. This ends now. You need to leave."

Trying to sound sultry, "You're so handsome when you're angry. We'd be perfect together."

"Except I'm not a racist and you are."

She shook her head. "I wanted to share a cabin with *you*, not them."

"Especially not them. How can you show prejudice to the twins when others have shown it to you? They can't help being black any more than you can help being gay."

Her face reddened and her lips tightened. "I have to live with them in Dallas all the time. You'd think I could escape them in the middle of Alaska." She spit the words, "Why are they allowed here?"

I shook my head and couldn't stifle the disgust burning my throat. "You're nuts and you're smelling up my tent. If you ever bother me again, I'll report you to Miki. Now leave."

Her eyes narrowed. "I don't like being scorned."

"I don't like being assaulted and stalked." I pulled the Polaroid prints out of my pocket. "These are yours." I held them out for her as my pulse pounded in my neck.

She yanked the photos from my hand. "Life is hard for women like us, Tracy. You have to learn to take advantage of opportunities as they arise."

"This isn't an opportunity. It's a nuisance. And take the cake. I'm sure Miki wants her plates left in the lodge."

Glenda grabbed the plate and stomped toward the door. She turned back with a red face, ready to say something but could only emit a snarl before she charged outside and up the hill.

The release of tension left me dizzy, forcing me to grab one of my bed posts and lean my head against the top mattress.

What just happened?

After a minute, I held my door open as I stepped outside so my tent could release her scent. I heard slow footsteps to my right and turned to look but saw no one. Glenda? No, it had to be someone else. I looked up the hill to my left and thought I saw Glenda walking near the lodge.

I knew this wasn't over. People like that don't expose themselves and let a rejection slide away. But what could Glenda do?

Watch me. Watch Jackie.

Okay. So what?

I had no idea how far she would go.

CHAPTER 21

MOONSTONE

T rying to sleep that night was rough. I worked on my song, but couldn't keep my focus, my mind drifting back to the fight with Glenda or replaying the looks Jackie shot me. I had weird dreams—people and events from San Antonio shattered into random sequences and fused together in frightening loops. I woke at 2:00 am, my mouth dry and head aching. I thought I was dehydrated so I drank several glasses of water. The white canvas of my wall tent glowed with light from outside, enough to read by, much brighter than what I had grown accustomed to in my little green tent.

By 6:00 I was shivering and gave up pretending to sleep. After a few minutes and several matches, a fire burned in my stove. I curled around and gave it an air hug until I could move my fingers. A cup of hot tea made me feel human, and I ventured away from the stove to my door. Clouds still covered the mountains, but the morning light shimmered against the flowers—blue bells, sundews, asters, daisies, purple lupine. The view was gorgeous.

I finished my tea and felt a sudden urge to pee. I scrambled back to my bed for my sandals and raced outside, barely planting my bare butt on the toilet seat before a long, powerful whoosh threatened to fill the deep hole. The release was heavenly. From my perch, I watched ravens squawk at each other in the sky and a pika scamper across the ground.

I stood, kicked off my sandals, and pulled off my shirt and sweatpants, flashing the world. The sense of freedom was intoxicating. Who wouldn't want to stand nude in the wilderness without a care or worry? I rubbed my hands across my skin, feeling my goosebumps, my breasts and tight nipples. My eyes followed clouds as my right hand reached between my legs. I rubbed for five seconds then heard footsteps.

Glenda? She won't check here. I'm safe. She'll knock at the tent, call my name, and leave.

I waited, making no sound.

I heard a handle clanging against a metal container and a thump onto the stoop outside my tent. Then more footsteps—coming closer to the outhouse.

Shit!

"Hey, is anyone in there?" The voice I'd heard in my head so many times. Jackie!

"Y-yes!" I said much too loudly. Adrenaline shot through me, tensing my muscles.

I'm naked!

"Give me a second." I scrambled to put on my clothes. I pulled on my tank top then realized it was backward. So off it came then I couldn't fit one arm through the strap. My elbow banged against a wall. All the time I was trying to slide into my sandals. I succeeded with one but the other flew out and landed near a willow. I had to scramble over rocks to fetch it while trying to muffle my squeals of pain. Finally, I climbed back up to the trail.

Jackie laughed, her mouth wide open, cheeks bright red, each peal sounding like merry bells. "That's the most noise I've ever heard coming from an outhouse that wasn't a fart. What were you doing?"

"Trying to put my sandal on." I knew my face was blushing purple by then.

Her eyebrows crushed her forehead into wrinkles as she laughed some more. "Do you always take off sandals in an outhouse?"

I paused, considering whether to tell the truth or make up some obvious lie. But this was the girl I wanted to have as a friend. I needed to tell the truth. Otherwise, how would I know her or she know me? I took a deep breath. "Only when I take off my pants."

She looked directly into my eyes and smiled. "You were naked, weren't you?"

"Would you hate me if I said yes?"

She shook her head slowly, her eyes wandering down my thin top to the wide gap between it and my pants. "No. I've done it too."

My scalp tingled. "In the outhouse?"

"No. There's a place up behind the camp where a platform of rock is surrounded by willows except for one side. I go there sometimes when the sun's out."

"Cool. I thought I was the only pervert who wanted to flash the world."

She chuckled. "There's at least two of us. And the perverts are the ones who think we should be ashamed of our bodies and hide them."

"Maybe you can show me." I couldn't help watching her lips.

She half-smiled, revealing cute dimples. "My body or the rock?"

I so wanted to say, "Both," but bit my tongue. I cocked a brow and said casually, "The rock, of course."

She licked her lips. "Why would I show you my secret hideout?"

"Because secrets are meant to be shared. Otherwise, they gnaw at you."

She nodded. "Do you have secrets?"

"Too many to count." I had a weird feeling she was playing with me as much as I was with her. "Do you always check who's in the outhouses?"

"Only before I clean them." She lifted her bucket. "I brought you some more wood."

"Thanks. Do you need any help?"

"Are you serious?"

"Yes. If you haven't noticed, everyone in my group is at least two or three times my age. It would be fun to hang with you. Besides, I'm going to live in Alaska, so I need to know about outhouses and axes."

Frowning, she said, "Where in Alaska?"

"I don't know yet. I'm starting here then will decide where to go next Friday."

She pursed her lips. "You're either brave or kinda crazy."

"One implies the other, don't you think?"

She flashed me a smile and slowly nodded her head. "Okay. Follow me." She led me toward the outhouse. "I hope you didn't leave anything embarrassing. You wouldn't believe what I find in these things." She pulled on thick rubber gloves.

"Such as?"

"Playboy magazines, women's panties, oh, and a bottle of baby oil."

We walked up to the toilet.

"Speaking of which . . . " She picked my pink panties off the floor. "Look familiar?"

My face heated and I coughed a laugh. "You scared the shit out of me, and I rushed to put everything back on. Except these." I grabbed them from her fingers and shoved them into my pocket.

"We're getting to know each other real fast. First I see your panties, then," she lifted the toilet seat, "I see your pee, though there is a lot of shit down there."

"Not mine!"

"So you say." She sprayed the seat with Lysol and wiped it with folded toilet paper. She pulled a container from her bucket. "I sprinkle some lye over the contents. When you fill up your ash bin and set it outside, I'll sprinkle that down the hole." She set a new roll of toilet paper in the corner. "All done." She pulled off her gloves.

"Cool. Thanks. When do you chop the wood?" I looked for any sign of exasperation. I didn't want to come on too strong, but dammit, I'd waited seven months to meet this girl and only had two weeks before I would leave.

She tilted her head and smiled. "After lunch."

"Can I help? I don't want to be a pest, so if you'd rather not, just tell me."

"Jeff told me you play guitar and sing."

"So do you. Maybe we could . . . "

"Exactly my thoughts." She headed back to my tent. "Bring your guitar to the yurt at 10:00."

"Where's the yurt?" I asked, following her, tingling with excitement.

"Behind the lodge. There's only one. If you're good, I'll show you how to chop."

My stomach dropped. "What if I'm not?"

"I'll still show you. You'd help me finish sooner. I'm not fond of chopping wood. Besides, you are very good. I was walking last night and heard you." She lowered her eyes. "That secret was gnawing at me, so I had to tell you."

The footsteps last night were from her! Then it hit me—she must have . . . "Did you hear Glenda?"

"Some. Don't worry, I'm not inviting *her* to my yurt." She blushed and almost winked. "Hey, I need to make my rounds. Nice talking to you." She lifted the handles of her cart, full of kindling and toilet paper. "Why don't you eat with Jeff and me at breakfast?"

"I'd love to. See you then."

I watched her push the cart to the next wall tent then disappear down another trail with her bucket. I bolted inside and silently screamed, "Yes!" She was amazingly cool. I loved talking to her, and she seemed to have fun being with me.

Even if we couldn't be more than friends, I'd love her company. I lit the burner to reheat the percolator and sat on my bed, realizing I'd sit across the table from her and Jeff and have to watch their love play.

And then leave both of them in ten days.

To where?

I had no clue. Maybe they could give me some ideas.

Or maybe I could talk Miki into letting me stay and work for meals.

But if I did, how would I know whether Mom left Texas and was waiting for me at the hotel?

I poured more coffee and drank. *Jackie heard some, if not all, my encounter with Glenda, which means she knows Glenda thinks I'm gay. Jackie heard me sing about her, though she probably didn't realize that. She knows I stripped in the outhouse, and even after all that she still invited me to her yurt.*

What did all that mean?

Maybe she's desperate to play guitar with someone else.

Maybe she doesn't care that I'm gay.

Or maybe . . . I couldn't finish the thought. I told myself to not get my hopes up.

Just go with the flow and see what happens.

I pulled out my guitar to practice, watching the clock until 7:45 when I jumped up and headed for my door, only to remember I still had panties in my pocket and a thin little shirt on top. I threw my arms into a flannel shirt and ran toward the lodge.

Just as I stepped onto the porch, I heard, "Good morning, Tracy," from Glenda sitting in a rocking chair.

I glanced over and did a double-take. She was wearing khaki riding pants, a white shirt, and a safari hat.

"Oooh, look at you," she said then stood up, staring at my exposed stomach.

I fastened two buttons on my flannel. *She's not giving up.* "Good morning, Glenda." I walked inside. That little encounter made me more determined than ever to avoid activities with my group and find ways to be with Jackie and Jeff and their friends.

The twins were posing with a bear skin while Jake took pictures. "Good morning, Tracy," Hallie said. "Come join us. We'd like a picture of you."

"Maybe later," I said as I walked to the door separating us from the dining room.

"Miki said they'd call us when they're ready," DeLacie said.

I cracked the door open and saw Jackie, Jeff, and others setting tables. "Can I help?"

Jackie looked up, smiled, and waved me in. "Fill those cups with water."

"Sure," I said. I used two pitchers to fill about thirty cups.

Platters of hot biscuits and bowls of sausage gravy filled the room with a heady aroma, forcing my mouth to water and my stomach to ache. I was starving.

Jeff placed a tray of butter dishes onto a table. "Hey, Tracy, spread these out for me."

"Can I eat one first?"

"Absence makes the heart grow fonder."

"It's not my heart I'm worried about." I pulled plates from the tray and set them two feet apart on every table.

A scowling woman wearing an apron and a hair bun emerged from the kitchen, scanning the tables. "Is that everything?"

Jackie walked in, wiping her hands on a towel. "Think so."

"Who are you?" the woman asked me, pushing her fists into each hip.

"Tracy," I answered. "I'm just helping out."

"She's cool," Jackie said. "We're friends."

"Okay," the woman said, rubbing her hands with a towel. "I'm Helen. Did you wash your hands?"

"Y-yes. Back at my tent," I stammered, glancing at Jackie, who smiled and shook her head at me.

"Next time, come back to the kitchen and wash before you touch anything."

"I certainly will."

"Okay," Helen said, "call them in."

One of the girls opened the door, and the horde streamed in with exclamations about the aroma. Other workers entered from the kitchen, including a family with kids.

As I watched Jackie, waiting for her to take a seat, a hand touched my shoulder.

"Where are you sitting, Tracy?" Glenda asked, too close to my ear.

"With us," Jeff said, grabbing my hand and pulling me toward the end of their table.

"You're a life saver," I whispered. I sat across from him and Jackie. As we grabbed biscuits and passed plates, I said, "Just so you know, I'm helping with every meal and sitting with you guys."

"Because you like us, or you're avoiding the predator?" Jackie teased.

"Both," I replied.

For the next few minutes, I concentrated on eating fluffy biscuits with gravy, blueberry and raspberry jam—from local bushes, canned last year—and honey. Not once did Jeff or Jackie feed or touch each other.

Once I was full, I asked, "How'd you two get these jobs?"

"Miki's my aunt," Jackie said, looking around for possible eavesdroppers then leaned closer across the table. "I wanted to work in Fairbanks this summer, but I had no choice."

"You'd rather live by yourself?"

She raised her brows. "I might have had a guest."

"Jeff?"

He laughed and she coughed.

"No," she said. "Jeff has a tendency to snore."

I looked at them both and knew they were hiding something. "Jeff, how long have you been working here?"

"Two summers."

"Did you two share a yurt last year?"

"No," Jackie answered, "the yurt was reserved for teen girls."

"Including you?"

"Yes." She drank water.

I looked at each of them, trying to see what they were hiding. "Where'd they go after Jeff moved in?"

"You ask a lot of questions," Jackie said with a grin.

"I'm sorry, but there seems to be so much unsaid in y'all's answers."

"Y'all? Are you serious?" Jackie asked with a snort.

"I'm from Texas. And that's what we call changing the topic."

We stared at each other with half-grins until Miki walked over. Jeff draped his arm over Jackie's shoulders and pulled her close.

"Tracy," Miki said, "I see you've found new friends."

Jackie smiled at me as she held Jeff's hand.

"Yes, I have," I said. "We're going to play guitar together later on."

"That's wonderful. Maybe you can join Jackie when she does her singalong for our guests."

"I have to audition first," I said. "To see if I'm worthy."

Jackie actually kicked me under the table, and a flood of memories filled my mind—Ava rubbing her foot against my leg at the pharmacy as we both tried to convince the world we had boyfriends.

And then I realized Jackie was doing the same thing. For the same reason.

Miki chuckled. "I'm sure you're very good, Miss MVP on the boys' basketball team. We'll look forward to hearing you both." She walked away.

Jackie's eyes widened. "MVP?"

For the rest of breakfast, I told them about my brief glory in basketball before I quit to sell pianos.

They didn't touch each other for the remaining thirty minutes.

After breakfast, Miki took us to the shed where men and women alternated days for communal showers. Three heads emerged from plastic-covered walls. The water was heated for two hours each evening. We could use the shed any other time during the day or night, but the water would be cold. That night was open to women.

As we left, Hallie asked her sister, "When's the last time we showered together?"

"Maybe when we were five," DeLacie laughed. "After that, we both couldn't fit in the shower any more."

"I think we can fit in that one. We could relive our childhood."

"I know you want to see me naked, Hallie, but I'm not taking a shower with you."

"If all I wanted was to see you naked, I'd look in a mirror. I wish we'd brought squirt guns. Remember how we used to . . ."

"Yes!" DeLacie cackled.

They walked toward their cabin, laughing. I stopped and noticed the others standing several feet behind me. The other women looked pissed, watching the twins. Glenda glared, shook her head, and stomped toward her cabin.

They obviously didn't want to share their shower with the twins. I didn't want to share with any of them. I wondered what Jackie did? I decided I'd ask her later.

I changed into jeans before I walked to the yurt and stood outside her door, wondering what I'd see inside. A double bed?

I heard the opening fingerpicking of Dylan's "Don't Think Twice, It's All Right," a difficult piece, but Jackie played it effortlessly. Once she started singing, I had to see her. I knocked once and pulled open the door. She sat in a chair, smiling as she sang. I pulled out my guitar, found another chair, and strummed the chords—C, G, Am, F, C, G—as she picked. I started singing with her on the second verse.

She let me take the main melody while she harmonized. We smiled at each other for the rest of the song.

"Shit, that was fun!" I shouted.

Jackie nodded. "We sound good together."

I couldn't take my eyes off hers. "I loved your picking. How long have you played?"

"Eight years. You?"

"Since January."

"Of this year?" she asked. "Wow."

"Yes. Before then it was all piano."

"Are you good?"

I nodded. "Playing classical stuff, yeah."

"Cool. The closest piano is at the McKinley Hotel, so I'll have to wait to hear you."

I looked around the yurt. Single beds evenly spaced along the circular wall, only two slept in recently on opposite sides.

"Where's Jeff?" I asked.

"Taking a leak and a smoke. He'll be back. Play me one of yours."

I'd thought about what I'd sing for her. Since I hadn't finished the one about her smile, I'd decided to play Ava's song then maybe Spencer's.

I started my strumming then picked a few licks, bending the notes.

I found your lips in the dark
And tried to touch your heart
Out of sight
From the crowd

I drank your breath like sweet wine
And tried to slow down time
We got caught
And now we're out

I heard the door open during the chorus and figured Jeff was behind me. During the last verse when the lines repeat, Jackie joined me, singing harmony.

All we can do, Baby,
all we can do

Just run for our lives
All we can do
Just get away, Baby
And live free
Just live free

We repeated that stanza several times. I loved our sound—her voice high and lyrical, mine lower with an edge. The rush I felt after we finally stopped was beyond anything a drug could induce. Her skin glowed, and I could tell she'd felt it too.

"That was righteous," I said. "If that word means anything, it's what we just experienced. I love, love, love singing and playing with you."

Jeff applauded. "I came back and saw everyone standing outside and wondered what the hell was going on. You've got fans."

"They'll have to wait," Jackie said. She took a breath and searched my eyes hard with hers. "Who was that song about? It sounded real. *Who* got caught?"

This was the moment of truth. I knew she wouldn't believe me if I told her a boy's name, but still, I was nervous. My mouth dried up and butterflies hatched in my stomach. I said quietly, "Me and Ava."

A slow smile began to grow on Jackie's face. "Ava. What happened?"

"I dressed like a boy and we went dancing. Her father caught her."

"And you wanted to run away with her?"

"At one point, but she wouldn't. She went to another school and now has a boyfriend." It seemed so distant, and surprisingly, I felt no pain sitting there with Jackie.

She set her guitar on a floor stand. "Miki caught me with Lisa in my room in March. She blew up and threatened to kick me out. I told her I'd stop. Lisa's dad got transferred, so they left the state in May. We weren't in love or anything. When we got to camp two weeks ago, she moved the other girls out of the yurt, claiming she couldn't trust me. Then Jeff and I got together."

I almost felt giddy. "Ava pretended to date my brother, while I pretended to date his boyfriend. You're doing the same thing?"

Jackie looked at Jeff. He nodded.

She said, "Yeah."

Everything made sense—Jeff telling me not to worry on the drive to camp, their displays of affection when Miki would see them. I took a deep breath and exhaled my worries.

Jackie was like me.

"Does Miki suspect?" I asked, resisting the urge to hug her.

"I think she did at first, but we made sure we kissed in public so guests would see. Some complained until Miki told us to tone it down." She laughed. "She warned me about getting pregnant, and I pulled condoms out of my pocket. She rolled her eyes and walked away muttering about kids these days."

"According to my father," I mimicked his voice, "homosexuality is a sexual preference, so just prefer not to have sex. Simple solution."

Jackie leaned forward, her elbows on her thighs. "Even without sex, we'd still be gay. I just want to touch someone I love and not be worried who sees me."

"The only way I could do that was by wearing my manguise. Then I got hit on by Greta in Seattle. Now Glenda hits on me here."

Jackie flashed me a coy smile. "You don't like girls hitting on you?"

"Not if their names start with G." I winked. "But I've always loved names beginning with J—Joni Mitchell, Judy Collins . . ."

Jackie shook her shoulders. "How about beginning with M?"

I was loving the tease until her question blanked my mind. "Who?"

"Moon Jacqueline Dust."

I blurted, "Is that your name?" I jumped up. "Moon Dust? I love it!"

"Too much teasing in school which is why I go by Jackie."

Jeff laughed. "You never told *me* your real name. Guess you like her better, huh?" He winked.

I put my hands on her chair's arms and leaned close to her. "I particularly like to be hit on by girls named Moon, especially after they moon me."

Her face cracked into a smile. "You wish."

"Yes, I do."

Our eyes roamed each other's faces until she blushed and broke the trance. "What's your last name?"

"Franks, but I want to change it to my mother's maiden name —Stone."

She stared at my lips. "Do your parents know you're gay?"

"Yes. Mom accepted my brother and me, but Dad never did. What about your parents?"

Jackie leaned back and looked to the ceiling. "Dad was killed in Vietnam three years ago. Mom was a Beat poet and teacher who dropped me off with Miki for quote 'just a day' until she could get her quote 'head straight.' I don't know if she's alive or dead." Her eyes gazed at distant memories as her voice wearied over old pain. "I've been with my aunt ever since."

I reached out with my hand. "I'm sorry about both of them."

She held my fingers and rubbed the back of my hand with her thumb. "Jeff told me about your brother. I'm sorry."

Feeling her skin stirred every nerve in my fingers. Our hands fit together even though mine was long and narrow while hers was broad and thick. We watched our fingers caress then our eyes met.

She smiled. "Maybe you should play something else." Slowly, she pulled her hand away.

I positioned my guitar. "I wrote this for Spencer."

He was
Too sweet to live,
too soon to die
Too quick to forgive
And too gentle to fight

Jackie lifted her guitar and began to pick the chords I played. When I got to—

When the good guys die
The songbird cries
The tooth fairy steals
and the angels make deals

—she said, "Oh, I love your lyrics. Sing that again."

I did and she sang the harmony. Our eyes locked at the end.

"You guys need to go on the road," Jeff said. "Seriously, you could be Simon & Garfunkel in drag."

Jackie frowned at him. "Have you ever seen me in a dress?"

"Okay, overalls." He snapped his fingers. "You could be Tracy and Moon."

She snapped her fingers, mocking him. "Or Jackie and Tracy."

I jumped up. "How about MoonStone? Just one word. It's a combination of our names, but it's also a crystal. It's supposed to have healing properties."

"Wow. Perfect," Jackie said. She reached out her hand. "MoonStone."

I held it and sat down on the floor near her chair. "If we did play," I asked Jeff, "where would you be?"

"Managing," said Jeff. "Keeping track of your money. I was a business major, after all."

"You *were*?" I asked.

Jeff sat on one of the beds. "I got my draft letter two years ago when I entered college, so I had a deferment." He picked at his fingernails. "My family found out I'm gay and cut me off, which was great timing," he scoffed. "Last summer I came here to make money and to get off the grid. Then last fall I enrolled at the university in Anchorage, but couldn't make enough progress to maintain my deferment and keep my job. I dropped out and disappeared for months then came back here."

"Why don't you tell the draft board you're gay?" I asked.

He stood up and paced around the yurt. "Because that doesn't always work. I've heard some doctors won't accept checking one box on a form saying you have 'homosexual tendencies.' Some demand you produce signed affidavits from men you've had sex with. And if they do declare me 4-F, that can ruin job prospects." He blew out a breath. "Nobody in government knows where I am. Even Miki doesn't know my last name."

"Does she know about your draft status?" I asked.

"Yes. She hates the war. I do odd jobs for her, including keeping her accounts straight. She pays me in cash."

I squeezed Jackie's hand and thought, *So much old pain in this yurt.* I looked at Jeff. "Don't you get lonely out here?"

"Yes, but on days off I go to the park campground at Wonder Lake." He winked. "Sometimes I get lucky."

"And sometimes," Jackie said with a smirk, "he gets punched in the face."

"That happened once last summer. I avoid Brits now." He laughed. "The French and Spanish are the best prospects, though they never bathe."

I turned to Jackie. "Do you use the shower shed?"

"Not since Miki forbade me."

"Doesn't she think you're straight now because of Jeff?"

"Maybe, but I'm still a pervert in her eyes. So no showering with anyone else."

"What do you do?" I asked.

"I heat up water and sponge off in a small, metal tub I keep under my bed. Sometimes Jeff helps me with my hair."

I sighed. "I guess I'll do the same. Maybe I can borrow your tub?"

"Or use it here. Jeff won't look."

I turned to her with a grin. "And you?"

She half smiled. "Whatever you want me to do."

Jeff snorted. "You guys are going to bust this arrangement. We're all going to be exposed."

"Why you?" I asked.

"Because as soon as they catch you two, they're going to know I'm not straight."

I threw my arms out. "We haven't done anything."

"Yet," Jackie added.

I hooked her arm. "We're working together on songs to sing to the camp."

"And for our new band," Jackie said. "What's wrong with that?"

Jeff folded his arms and looked at us like we were fools. "Because sooner or later, you'll get caught."

Jackie pulled her arm away and pointed at him. "And you won't at the campground? Someone's going to do more than punch you in the nose. Besides, I'll be eighteen in six days and can do what I want. I'm tired of hiding who I am."

Jeff shook his head. "She'll kick you out."

Jackie pushed her chair. "Or I can kick myself out. Tracy did."

The idea that Jackie might leave camp before me slapped my face. I understood her anger and frustration, but we needed time. "All we're doing is working on our music. We can give a quick performance in a day or two, so Miki will believe us. Everyone in my group is much older than me, so why wouldn't I want to be with you guys, especially since Jeff will be our manager."

Jackie rolled her eyes and sat down. "We're not going to be Simon and Garfunkel."

"No, we're going to be MoonStone." I grabbed her hand. "Don't ever underestimate me, Jackie. I've played basketball with bloody feet and won games against boys. I made thousands of dollars on my own so I could come here and make my own life. All we have to do is work on our music, behave in public, and hide anything else for a little longer."

"Hey, we need to get to the kitchen," said Jeff, looking at his watch.

"I'm coming with you," I said.

Jackie hooked my arm. "Yes, you are." We exited the yurt. "Thousands of dollars?" she whispered. "How?"

I hooked Jeff's arm as we walked toward the lodge. "Selling pianos and giving lessons. All so I could I meet you."

She stopped, pulled her arm away, and stared at me. "Are you serious?"

"Yeah. As crazy as that sounds. I'll tell you more when we're chopping wood after lunch."

Her eyes searched hard for any sign I was toying with her. After a few seconds, she nodded, hooked my arm and started walking. "And we'll practice more songs in the yurt after the wood is done."

"Yes. And again after dinner."

She squeezed my arm. "MoonStone rocks."

"Yes, we will."

CHAPTER 22
MY HOPE, MY JOY, MY ROCK

At one point during lunch, Jackie sat in Jeff's lap, her arms hugging his neck while he and I laughed. I felt a twinge of what? Jealousy? It was foolish, but emotions are fickle. We were honestly having fun with each other, though we knew what message we were sending—I was friends with both of them who were a pair. Once we announced our new band and played for everyone, we thought we could hang out in any combination and not raise questions.

After finishing our chores, Jackie and I stood outside the kitchen on the porch, looking toward the mountains. "This Mt. McKinley thing is a hoax, isn't it?" I asked. "How many people travel to this park and never see it?"

"Most don't," Jackie said, working a toothpick into her teeth.

"Then why do people come here?"

She gazed into the distance. "The thrill of anticipation. The possibility you might see something others haven't. When it's partially hidden, your mind plays tricks and makes the mountain seem larger than it actually is. I've known people to be disappointed when it finally appeared because they thought it would be higher."

I watched gray clouds fade, revealing slabs of blue ice. "Is that the summit?"

Her grin spread wide. "Certainly not. It's got to be higher than that. Otherwise, why would they name a park after it." Her tongue moved the toothpick around her mouth.

"You're playing with me."

"Could be." She sat down on the porch and put the toothpick above her ear.

I looked higher and found what may have been part of the mountain—something white behind gray swirls. Or was it just more clouds? I sat next to her, our legs touching. "You've seen it, right?"

"Lots. I like it best at dawn when it's covered with pink alpenglow. If you get up between 3:30 and 4:00, it might be open."

"If it stays covered for much longer, I might try that. I'm not leaving this park without seeing it."

"That's the value of the tease." She set her hands on the porch behind her and leaned back, causing her tank top to stretch tighter across her chest. "If it were out all the time, it wouldn't be as exciting. But keep its true size and shape a mystery, and it becomes alluring. Like boobs."

She caught me staring at hers and smiled.

"Show some cleavage," she said, "or make them push out your shirt, maybe throw in a nipple bump, and they turn you on."

Hers were doing exactly what she described. I tried to pull my eyes away.

"But if we walk around nude," she continued, "all the supposedly sexy parts become like fingers and noses and lips."

I flicked my eyes around, looking for eavesdroppers. "I see your lips all the time, and I still find them alluring." I stared at hers and licked mine.

Her eyes fixed on my lips. "I like yours too."

Tingles crawled up my legs. "Doesn't that ruin your theory?"

"Maybe *ruin* is too harsh. *Complicates* would be more accurate."

"So you're saying if we took off our shirts while talking together and playing music, seeing each other's boobs would have no effect on us?" I shook my head. "Fat chance, Jackie. I also love your button nose and your cute little ears." The sunlight intensified, revealing tiny flecks of gold and green in her large, brown irises. "I get lost in your eyes."

"Yeah, but they don't turn you on."

I lowered my voice. "I'm actually pretty wet right now."

Jackie bit her lips and looked away. "Me too. But that actually proves my point. Attraction should be based on familiarity, not mystery. Sex shouldn't be a groping discovery. That's what it was with Lisa and me. Quick, hot, and ultimately meaningless."

I thought about Ava. The only times we weren't grabbing for each other were when I was disguised. We couldn't work up to a deeper relationship because we were always hiding.

"What do you want?" I asked.

She sat up and looked at me. "More than an orgasm. I want a deep bond of friendship and trust, a long, all-consuming warmth that lingers after the touch. I want my need to be constant, not just at the moment I see a bare breast."

"You don't want nakedness to be the cause of your attraction."

She nodded. "Exactly."

"So you want to check me out before you have sex with me."

She cackled and pushed my shoulder. "You're purposely missing the point."

"I didn't miss it." My gaze wandered over her face—the bushy blonde eyebrows, pale skin that blushed in random spots, her thick lips and wide mouth, perfectly curved ears with a tiny lobe, and freckles splashed across her nose. "You want love, not a quickie."

She gazed in return. I wished I knew what she saw as her eyes moved from my face to my neck. Did she react to me as I did to her? Always that question and always the same answer—she couldn't possibly be as fascinated with me as I was with her.

"Is that okay?" she asked.

"Yes. Now that you've got me all worked up, I need an outlet."

She stood. "The best cure for being horny is chopping wood. Different activity, but same result—sweaty and exhausted."

We laughed as we walked toward the wood yard behind her yurt where the scent of spruce almost overwhelmed. I asked, "Was that photo of you in the brochure holding the axe taken before you chopped or after?"

"That was posed. I never chop with a shirt on." She took off her flannel. "You should take yours off too."

I did and we stared at each other's nipples through our tops. "So far I'm not cured."

She handed me leather gloves.

"Do what I do." She bent over and pulled a 14 x 14 inch section of log from a stack under a roofed platform and stood it inside an old tire on the ground.

I did the same inside another tire.

She handed me an axe. "This is an eight pound maul. You want to hit the log more on the edge than the center. Lift it straight above your head with your feet spread and bring it down hard. The tire will keep the wood in place as you strike it several more times."

She whacked the wood, causing a split. Eight more hits and the round was in pieces, which she stacked under another roof.

I held my maul directly above my head, arms fully extended, and paused, smelling the sweet release of spruce sap and hearing the repeated claps of Jackie's blade through the wood. I pulled my maul down with all my strength, resulting in a ragged split across my log. I screamed in delight.

Jackie looked over with a big smile. "Having fun?"

"I have so looked forward to this." I lifted my axe again and struck, feeling the catharsis of destruction. "What do you imagine your log to be before you strike?"

She wiped pieces of bark from her forehead. "Every frustration I've ever felt."

"Is there enough wood to get through them all?"

"Before today, it seemed like I'd need to split a forest. But now, maybe not so much." Sweat dripped from her chin as she smiled at me.

"Cool."

I tried to keep up, but her stack was twice the size of mine. Eight pounds doesn't sound like much, but after lifting that above my head dozens of times and carrying rounds and stacking wood, I was pooped after thirty minutes.

"You're doing pretty good," she said, wiping sweat from her forehead. "You'll be sore tomorrow."

"I'm sore now."

She laughed. "Wait 'till tomorrow."

Our tops were soaked, like we had entered a wet t-shirt contest. She saw my gaze and shook her shoulders.

I gasped. "Until now, I was cured. You are so wicked."

We put away the gloves and mauls and picked up our flannels. I started to put mine on, but she said, "Keep it off until after we wash up."

"Where do we do that?" I asked.

"In my yurt, of course."

"Where's Jeff?"

"He and Johnny are finishing a new cabin. He'll be busy until dinner."

Once inside, she tossed her flannel onto a chair and pulled out the tub from under her bed. She filled tea kettles with water and lit her burners then handed me a pitcher and a bucket. "Go fill these at the spigot."

Our eyes met, and I knew what was coming. "Is this when the mountain comes out?"

"Yes. Don't worry, Tracy. We'll be great friends."

I felt dizzy. The floor seemed to shift under my feet. "That's what I heard you say in my mind for months."

Her eyes widened. "That sounds really crazy or really cool."

"It's both." I swallowed and left the yurt. As I filled my containers, my mind raced with excitement and worry—hell, fear. No one had ever seen me nude in the bright of day, taking a bath no less. For a brief moment, I thought about walking back to my tent, but I wanted to trust this girl. And yearned to be great friends with her.

I carried the water back and opened the door. Jackie stood naked in the tub, her back to me, unbraiding her hair. The kettles whistled, and I closed the door.

She turned around, separating her hair, sporting a mischievous grin. "We're not going to comment about each other's bodies, if that's okay."

I nodded, trying to get enough air into my lungs and keep my eyes fixed on hers. She was so beautiful, like Botticelli's painting of Venus standing in the shell, but with no modesty.

"Turn off the burners and bring one kettle here with a bucket."

Thankful I had an excuse to look at something else, I did what she asked.

"Pour some water from the bucket into the tub then from the kettle."

I watched her wiggle her toes as the temperatures mixed.

She kneeled, lifted a washcloth off the rim, and rubbed it with a bar of soap before handing it to me. She pulled her hair off her back and leaned forward. "Would you wash my back?"

I tried to calm my breathing as I rubbed soap over her beautiful skin, dipping the cloth in the water several times.

She pushed up a little and wiggled her butt. "Please, don't stop. It feels so good."

I dipped the cloth and added more soap. "I thought feeling good wasn't the point."

"It's stimulating in a calming way. You'll know what I mean in a few minutes."

I hitched a breath and pushed the cloth around her bottom and between her cheeks. After a while, I added more water to the tub.

Her eyes fixed on mine as I carefully washed her face and neck. She lifted her arms so I could wash her hairy pits and closed her eyes as I squeezed soapy water down her chest before softly scrubbing her skin. She raised up on her knees and spread her legs.

I hesitated. "Don't you . . ."

"Just wash mine like you do yours."

I barely touched the cloth to her vulva.

"I won't break, Tracy."

I closed my eyes and imagined myself in the shower then cleaned Jackie as if she were me.

Soon she stood. "Add the other kettle water to the bucket and use that for rinsing me."

I dipped the cloth into the clean water and squeezed it over her flesh until all the soap floated in the tub.

"I haven't been bathed since I was four. That was glorious." She pointed toward a towel hanging on a chair, and I brought it to her. After she dried off, she kneeled over the tub and flung her hair into the water, getting it wet before adding shampoo.

"Do you want me to rub your scalp?" I asked softly, kneeling beside her.

"That would be heavenly."

I pushed my fingers through her hair until she groaned. "That sounded sexual to me," I teased.

"I know. I couldn't help it. Do it some more."

"Okay, but don't complain later." I dragged my fingers over her head until she whimpered.

"I'll get you back," she said, gasping.

"Promise?"

"Yes. Okay, that's enough. Rinse."

I poured the rest of the water through her hair. She twisted it over the tub, pulled the towel off her back, and wrapped it around her hair.

Standing naked before me, her waist at my face, she smiled and said, "Your turn." She pulled on sweats and a clean t-shirt then lifted one handle on the tub. I lifted the other and we carried it outside to dump before setting it back inside the yurt.

I filled the kettles with water from the pitcher and lit the burners while Jackie filled the bucket outside. I removed my sandals and pants and took deep breaths before pulling everything else off. As she opened the door, my hands flinched and almost covered myself, but I stood steady and met her eyes with mine.

She bit her lips and half-grinned as she set the bucket near the tub. "Kneel, Tracy. I'll get a fresh cloth. Do you want your own bar of soap?"

My heart raced. "No. We can share." I sat on my legs, waiting for the kettle to whistle.

She kneeled beside me and touched my hair and my back with her fingertips, sending tongues of heat through my skin. "I didn't know I could touch you without the cloth," I gasped.

"Maybe next time we'll just use our hands and the soap. That's how I normally bathe."

"Me too."

Once the kettle steamed, she mixed the cold and hot water in the tub. She rubbed her wet hands with soap. "Yes? I won't linger or try to arouse you, I promise."

I searched her face for any hint of mischief. "Okay, but go fast. I don't think I can take it otherwise."

She nodded and went to work, sometimes with a little too much vigor, perhaps to keep her mind focused on the job. Except when she washed my feet and between my toes. I squirmed and laughed, and she decided to torture me until I nearly tipped over the tub with a scream. She washed my hair slowly, pushing her fingertips from the top of my head down to my neck, forcing shuddering moans from my throat.

After rinsing me, she insisted on drying. Closing my eyes, I raised my hands above my head and let her. My muscles relaxed and my breathing slowed as every touch of the towel cleansed my mind. I had never known such peace, such tranquility.

I finally noticed she had stopped drying me and opened my eyes. When I saw her gaze exploring my body, I did not flinch. My skin flushed with warmth.

"You're not nervous anymore," Jackie said with a smile. "You don't care that you're naked."

I lowered my arms and realized I felt no need to hide, no worry about what she thought. "Not with you. Thank you." I had never felt so happy with myself. "Can I hug you?" I reached for her.

"I've been wanting to." She pressed herself against me gently, our warmth and affection flowing between us.

In her arms I felt comfortable, secure, and refreshed.

We held each other's faces in our hands, almost touching noses. Amazingly, I felt no desire to kiss her.

Two great friends.

"Same time tomorrow?" she asked.

"Yes, please."

"Cool. Get dressed and let's clean up. Then we need to practice. I think we should sing something at dinner."

We rinsed out our tank tops and hung them up to dry. As soon as I pulled up my pants and slipped into my sandals, I heard footsteps approaching the door. I glanced at Jackie. "Jeff?"

She frowned and shook her head quickly. She put her guitar in her case and signaled for me to do the same. Just as I snapped it shut, we heard knocking.

"Jackie?" Miki asked. "Are you in there?"

Jackie carried her case to the door and opened it. "Yeah. What's up?" She walked past Miki.

I followed right behind.

"I was wondering where Tracy was," said Miki, her eyes tightening. "Where are you two headed?"

Jackie replied, "To Tracy's tent to practice. We want to play during dinner."

"Great!" Miki said with forced enthusiasm.

Jackie and I walked a few steps before Miki added, "Tracy, did Jackie make you chop wood?"

"No, I volunteered. It was fun," I answered, wondering why she cared.

Miki folded her arms. "You both look pretty clean for doing such a sweaty job."

Jackie glared at her aunt. I half expected her to say, "That's because we bathed each other."

Just before Jackie spoke, I blurted out, "Looks can be deceiving. Don't get too close. We both stink." I laughed and pulled Jackie's arm as we walked down the hill toward the lodge, leaving Miki behind.

"Do you think she suspects?" I asked.

"Sure she does." Jackie kicked a rock along the path. "She'll probably peek inside the yurt and find our shirts hanging above the tub. She's all but accused me of being a sexual predator and a pervert. She probably thinks I'll have sex with anyone or anything."

I put my arm around her waist. "I'm sorry."

"Once this summer is over, I'm not living with her in Fairbanks."

"Where will you go?"

She stopped near one of the cabins. "I don't know, but I can't live with someone who thinks I'm wicked."

I pushed some hair out of her face. "How about with someone who thinks you give amazing baths?"

She half grinned. "Only because you're wicked too."

"At least we're clean devils."

She looked at me then to the mountains, blinking rapidly. "Only on the outside. Inside, we're foul and depraved."

"Is she religious?"

She sighed and started walking along the path toward the wall tents. "Very. Which is ironic. She's very much into protecting animals and the environment, helping the poor, respecting every race and culture, even women's rights. All of that. But sex is only for procreation and between a married man and a woman. Since lesbians can't get married or have children, they defy God's plan."

I was surprised about Miki. I thought she'd be more accepting. "Has she ever married?"

"No."

"Why?"

"She says she was too busy exploring the outside world to settle down with one man."

"Rhonda?"

"Yes, to a backcountry ranger, so he's gone a lot." She stopped and leaned against a tree in the shade.

I set my case on its end and draped my arms over the top. "When I first read the story of the two women who opened this camp, I assumed they were lesbians. Do they live in separate cabins?"

"Not in Camp Wonder. Same cabin but different bedrooms." She tightened her lips. "When we fought about Lisa, I accused her of being a closet lesbian. She slapped me. I told her I had heard her and Rhonda having sex in Miki's bedroom last summer, that she was displacing anger at herself onto me." A sardonic laugh rose in her throat. "What do you think she did then?"

"Slapped you?"

Jackie cocked an eyebrow. "She threw a right hook at my face. I ducked under it and left the house. When I came back later, she cursed her sister for abandoning me." Her eyes were red and moist.

"Do you miss your mom?" My mind flashed to holding Mom just before entering the jetway to board my plane. *Will that be my last image of her?*

"Yes, I do," Jackie said, "but I'm still angry at her."

"Would she have reacted the same way to you and Lisa as Miki did?"

Jackie looked away. "I don't know, but she dumped me before I did anything, so what does that say?"

I held her hand. "Maybe she thought she was saving you."

"I know. I've always thought she killed herself. She doted on Dad." A long sigh rattled out of her chest. "He was everything to her."

My heart ached. "To you too?"

"Yeah," she wiped a tear. Her chin began to quiver. "I miss him."

I pulled her to me and felt her body shake with weeping. "Cry all you want," I whispered in her ear. "I'll hold you for as long as you need."

She set down her case, clutched my back, and pushed her face against my neck, her tears flooding my shirt and skin.

I heard footsteps trudging up the road and raised my eyes to see the twins, the teaching couple, Glenda, and others from my group round a corner then stop to stare at Jackie and me.

Hallie called, "Tracy, is everything all right?"

Jackie flinched and jerked her head around. "Jesus Christ!" Her wet eyes met mine just before she picked up her case and trotted toward my tent.

I moved toward the group, trying to keep my heart from pounding through my shirt. "Jackie lost her father in the war three years ago. We were talking, and some bad memories came up. She'll be fine." I flashed a warm smile. "We're going to sing for you at dinner."

The twins' eyes brightened. "That's wonderful," DeLacie said.

Hallie added, "And you tell Jackie that we're all sorry about her father. Such a shame."

Glenda's eyes squinted in anger, her lips tight against her teeth. The teacher wife pursed her lips and shook her head.

"I will." I turned and walked away. I found Jackie sitting on my bed with her guitar, still wiping her eyes and nose.

She looked up at me, still hitching breaths. "Now the rumors will start. I'm sorry."

"For what?" I sat in a chair across from her. "You're allowed to miss your parents."

"It's been a while since I've cried about them." She wiped her eyes.

"I know the routine. That's what we do when we're alone—pretend nothing can get to us. 'I am a rock,' as Paul Simon says. But now we have a friend, and it's okay to cry." I held her hand.

She squeezed me back. "I'm glad you came."

Her gaze seemed to look for my soul, and I felt a warm hug inside. "Me too." After a few seconds, I pulled out my guitar. "I started this song on the flight from Seattle and added more this morning. Maybe you can help me finish it."

> I chased the sun 'til I found you
> Out of the darkness and into your light
> A smile so bright I never knew
> Could steal my eyes
> And see only you
>
> I heard your voice before I saw you
> Changing the noise to music so clear
> A sound so warm I never knew
> Could steal my ears
> And hear only you
>
> You are my hope my joy my rock
> The foundation of every thought
> The notes in my tunes
> The words in my songs
> Every beat of my heart
> Is a chorus to you

As I sang, I watched her face change from surprised to awed to teary. I stopped the repeat of the chorus and knelt before her, holding her legs. "Tell me."

"I can't be her. I can't be your rock when I'm drowning in my own tears."

I kissed her hand. "You stole my eyes." I kissed her other hand. "You stole my ears. You can't deny either of those."

She held my face, her breathing slower. "You did the same for me."

"There's another verse." I held her hands and sang to her.

Before you now I am naked
Every fault and scar you can see
All my life I have yearned and waited
For a friend who believes in me

"I can do that," she said. "I can believe in you."

"Then the rest will come."

She bit her lips and nodded. "I love the song. Maybe tonight we can finish it."

I stood. "Your place or mine?"

"Maybe in the lodge where everyone can see us."

"That's a great idea. We've got nothing to hide. Well, we do, but appearance is everything. What do you want to play tonight?"

After dinner, we sang "Don't Think Twice, It's Alright," "I Am a Rock," "Leaving on a Jet Plane," and "Spencer's Song." Jackie played all the picking parts while I strummed. I sang the lead while she harmonized on top of me—which she claimed she would do for real in our bed one day. We got a standing ovation and even smiles from Miki.

We announced our plans to form MoonStone, with Jeff as manager, and play wherever we could after we built up a repertoire of new songs and covers during the summer. After dinner, we found a corner on the porch and worked on "A Chorus to You," changing a few words and adding another verse. Jackie was brilliant at developing the harmony between our guitars and voices.

Hallie and DeLacie sat near us reading books, but watching us compose. When we finally sang the song in its entirety, the twins cried and hugged us both, declaring us geniuses.

Hallie mused, "You are my hope, my joy, my rock. DeLacie, wouldn't you love to have someone write that song about you?"

"I'd die on the spot," she declared. "Who's that song about, Tracy?"

Jackie and I glanced at each other then I said, "Someone we hope to meet someday."

After that night, Jackie and I were able to spend every minute of the day with each other to no one's concern. We worked all of Jackie's chores together, gave each other baths, and played our music. As we walked together around Camp Wonder, people would ask us what we would play that night. I skipped all of my group's outings, including the three-day camping trip near Igloo Mountain. When they returned, they couldn't wait to hear what we had composed during their absence. They had missed our performances!

Jackie and Jeff played girlfriend and boyfriend at the appropriate times. I even slept over in the yurt a couple of nights on the excuse we had worked too late. We cuddled each other in Jackie's bed, but we never made love or even kissed.

That changed when Jackie took her birthday off, and she took me to her secret rock. I carried my pack with food, water, a stove, and a blanket. We had planned to lay naked in the sunshine, rubbing each other with suntan lotion. But as soon as we reached our play area, rain fell, at first as a mist and then as wet missiles. We stood under a tree in our ponchos, huddling close, shivering, our stomachs growling from hunger.

She lifted her wet face to me, hair plastered to her skin, her lips almost blue, and said, "Can I kiss you?"

I grinned. "Yes, but why now? Does the rain turn you on?"

"No, but I thought what if lightning strikes us, and I'd never kissed you? I've wanted to for days. And my lips are cold."

"Let's warm them up."

We pushed back our hoods and pressed our lips together, gently at first while water streamed down our faces. The heat in our mouths was intense, our tongues like torches licking every surface inside and outside our lips. I felt a bond between us, welded by passion on the outside but also fused deep inside, like each of our nerves clasped together.

We pulled each other closer, trying to feel flesh through layers of wet plastic and cloth. Steam rose from our faces. Our kiss ended gently, both of us touching the other's cheek, our gaze locked to the other.

"I think lightning struck," I said, touching her bottom lip with my thumb. The downpour increased.

Jackie grabbed my hand. "Let's hurry back to the yurt."

We scrambled down through wet shrubs and over slippery rocks, trying to balance our desire to kiss again with our fear of hurting ourselves. Despite the torrent and having to fight our way through thick, wet brush, we laughed like children, even stomping puddles to splash the other.

When we burst into the yurt, Jeff jumped off his bed, laughing, as we stripped down to our t-shirts and panties before clutching each other in another kiss.

He directed us away from the stove so he could add wood. Neither of us realized he had hung our ponchos and clothes to dry until later.

Panting against each other, she said, "If lightning strikes now, I wouldn't feel it."

"I know. Like a mosquito bite after the bear mauls you."

"You're a helluva kisser," Jackie whispered. "Think I'd like more of those."

"Would thousands be enough?"

"Maybe not." She pulled my head to hers. "You are my hope, my joy, and my rock."

"Every beat of my heart is a chorus to you."

CHAPTER 23
THE MOUNTAIN IS OUT

After breakfast the next day, I asked Miki if I could speak with her. As we walked outside the lodge, I told her about my parents and how I hoped Mom would meet me at the hotel on Friday. "I'd like to stay here at the camp and work for meals so Jackie and I can play our songs."

She stopped and faced me. "Is that the reason?" Her voice was cold and surly. "To play songs or to be with Jackie?"

I tried to hide my reaction with a smile. "Obviously, both. We have to be together to play, and we're friends."

She looked hard at me, as if trying to see behind a mask. "And Jeff is going to be with Jackie?"

I bounced with fake joy. "He wants to be our manager."

Miki raised her brows above a bitter grin. "You and my niece have been very clever."

She knows. "We're going to have to be clever to be successful, don't you think? If I'm able to stay here beyond Friday, we can continue to entertain your guests. They like it, and I'd think you'd want happy clients."

"If I let you stay past Friday, you two couldn't arouse suspicions."

I wanted to say, "Maybe you and Rhonda can give us tips," but I held back. "Suspicions? About what?"

She folded her arms. "You two spend an awful lot of time together. Seems like Jeff would object."

"The better Jackie and I get, the more money he'd make managing. I think he understands that."

She chuckled. "True. I'm sure that's what he's thinking."

She obviously didn't believe a word I was saying, but I pretended not to notice. "My problem is I need to contact my mother to see if she's flying to Alaska. I need to know if I should drive out on Friday to meet her."

"And what if she's there? What then?"

"She can come back to camp and live with us in the yurt. She's a great cook and would love to help Helen."

Miki harrumphed. "That yurt's getting crowded. You don't think Jackie and her boyfriend would mind losing their privacy?"

"I've already talked to them both. They're cool with the plan."

"'I'll bet," Miki said. "How do you know your mom would be?"

"That's why I need to call her. Is there a way for me to contact her from here?"

Miki shook her head. "Nope. The closest phone is at the hotel."

How can it be ninety miles away? "What if someone has an accident here at the camp? What would you do?"

"We'd radio the rangers, and they'd send an ambulance. To call your mother, you'll have to go to the hotel, but we're not driving there until Friday."

"If my mother is there," I asked, "can she come back with me?"

Miki stared at me for several seconds with cold eyes before saying, "I'll have to make that decision Friday. There's no point in worrying about it now since you don't know whether she's coming."

She'd not been friendly to me once during the entire conversation. "Does Jackie seem happy to you? Or have you noticed?"

"You both seem very happy," Miki said, obviously displeased.

"Is that not a good thing?"

"Depends." She tightened her eyes. "People can be happy for the wrong reasons."

This game had become tedious. My gut knotted while heat filled my chest. "And unhappy for the right reasons? Who decides which reasons are right and wrong? You? God?"

She folded her arms and shot me a stern look. She pursed her lips then sucked them in like she was fighting with herself about what to say. After half a minute, she said, "Tracy, I've got other things to do now. I'm obliged to your parents to take you to the hotel on Friday. I can't say what happens after that."

I felt my face heat up. "Why to my parents? They didn't pay for my trip. I did."

"That's very impressive, but you're still a minor. They expect you to be at the hotel on Friday."

"I'm not returning to Texas, regardless of whether Mom flies up or not. If Jackie lives in Fairbanks, that's where I'll be. Do you care whether Jackie stays at Camp Wonder all summer?"

Miki smiled smugly. "It's up to me whether she stays and up to her whether she goes. She's eighteen now."

"Which means your sister's burden on you is over. You must be very happy. The question is whether that happiness is for the right or wrong reason." We locked eyes for another few seconds then I walked away toward my tent. I felt like I'd been in a boxing match, ducking and weaving, trying to avoid the knockout punch. I had, but my body still ached from her disdain.

I knew then that Miki would not let me stay. Jackie was right—her aunt wanted her gone.

Before I opened my door, I looked to the mountains. As always, they were obscured by clouds. My need to see McKinley had waned. I'd asked myself how my life would change if I saw it and couldn't think of an answer. My heart felt heavy with disappointment.

I sat on my bed and grabbed my notebook. I couldn't allow myself to succumb to self-pity. The one blazing sun in my life was Jackie. I had to focus on her.

Thoughts about a new song had flashed in my head since yesterday's kiss. I'd written two lines and had the beginnings of a melody.

When I kissed you that first time

I saw colors rich and bright

Our first meeting was in an outhouse, and our first kiss happened under a tree during a downpour. Indicative of what? We didn't know yet, but we'd always have those stories to share as needed to add humor to a conversation—or possibly inspiration. If a relationship could start in those circumstances and survive, I thought that boded well for our future. Opportunities snuck up on you. You either grabbed them or let them slip away.

I'd just started on the second verse when I heard a knock and Glenda's voice. "Tracy, can I come in?" She tried to sound friendly, but I detected a little desperation.

"No."

"I have something to show you. Please."

I put my guitar on the bed and walked outside. "Why are you here, Glenda?"

"Because this is the first time I've been able to talk to you alone. Can we go inside?"

"There's no reason to. Look, I'm busy."

She stared at my lips then obviously licked hers.

I tried not to laugh. "You said you wanted to show me something?"

She stepped back two paces then pulled a Polaroid photo out of her jacket pocket. She turned it around to show me. "I took this —"

Heat filled my neck. "I know when you took it." The picture was of me holding Jackie the day she cried about missing her father. "Why is this important?" I realized she'd stepped away to prevent me from snatching it.

"I thought Miki should know, so I showed it to her before breakfast." She gloated. "She was very interested and quite upset."

"Because there's something wrong with me hugging a friend who's crying about her father killed in the war?"

Her face reddened. "Because you are obviously trying to steal Jackie away from Jeff. You two hiked off by yourselves yesterday on her birthday."

I clasped my hand to my mouth to hide my smile. "Jeff's day off is Thursday. He knew where we went. Why is this your business, Glenda?"

She panted. "We're leaving here in three days. I can help you with your career. I'm a public relations specialist. You're very talented, Tracy, and you write such beautiful songs. I could make you famous." She pushed the photo back into her pocket then moved closer and reached her hand out to touch my face.

"Do not even think of touching me, Glenda. You've shown me your precious photo and made your offer, which I decline. Now you need to leave."

"I could make both of you famous." The cords in her neck bulged. "Bring Jackie with you. You both can stay at my house." Her chest heaved.

That offer surprised me, but I realized she'd offered a reason for Jackie and me to disagree. Maybe she hoped to drive a wedge between us.

Perhaps sensing an opening, she continued, "I just want what's best for you."

"I'm sure that's true, Glenda, but no thanks."

Her lips quivered then tightened into a slash. "I guess I'll have to show this to Jeff. He might be interested in knowing what you two are doing behind his back."

I couldn't stop my laughter though I'd clenched my jaw. "You do that."

"Or better yet, I'll make my offer to Jackie. Maybe she'd like to leave the wilderness and see a big city for a change. We could have a blast together."

I didn't know what she expected me to say or do in response, but I was so shocked all I could do was stare at her.

Her lips pouted. "Well?"

"It's worth a try, Glenda. Now I'm going to worry all night. Good-bye." I slipped into my tent and stood by the door until I heard her stomp away. I thought two things.

That photo was at least partly responsible for Miki's attitude toward me after breakfast.

And Jackie and Jeff's ruse had been successful. Even Glenda was convinced they were a pair.

What Glenda didn't know was that Miki already knew Jackie and I were real, and Jeff would laugh when he saw the photo. I made a mental note to tell him what was coming.

I picked up my notebook and tried to focus on my song. After a few minutes, I wrote two more lines.

When I kissed you that first time
I saw colors rich and bright
I tasted wind-blown ocean waves
My soul danced in pure delight

All I had to do was replay her kisses in my mind, and the words flowed.

Your lips were soft and full
as I breathed you like a drink
In the beauty of your eyes
I lived between each blink

I soon had a chorus.

Chorus
You were springtime
Covered in flowers
You were sunshine
lifting the clouds

You were music
playing my high notes
With a heartbeat
pounding so close

And I knew
That I loved you
And hoped you'd love me too

In a better world
In a beautiful world

In a perfect world
You would love me

I sang the first two verses slowly, working on chord changes. Then I tried some ideas for the chorus, but where my mind wanted to go, my voice couldn't. This would be a perfect song for Jackie's voice.

I heard footsteps and thought Glenda had returned.

"That's pretty," Jackie said. She opened the door. "You wouldn't believe what Glenda asked me."

"To go with her to Dallas?"

She scrunched her forehead and came inside. "How did you know?"

"Because she asked me first. What did you say?"

"Nothing. I held my fist to her nose and drew it back for a punch. She ran away."

"Damn. Why didn't I think of that? I have a new song. Listen." I sang as best I could. Before the end of the chorus, Jackie had covered her mouth with her hands and collapsed in my chair, her eyes red and chest heaving.

"Tracy. God, you are so amazing."

My heart danced in my chest. "So you like?"

"I love it." She dropped to her knees and crawled to me. "And I do love you." She puckered her lips.

I was so shocked, I couldn't move.

Jackie widened her eyes. "That's your cue to move the fucking guitar."

I did and fell to my knees in front of her for a kiss—deep, warm, slow. Neither of us wanted to stop.

Afterward, I said, "Now that the experience is fresh in your mind, help me write more verses."

She sat next to me on the bed. "Is that really how our kisses make you feel?"

"Better than that, but there's no words. So I have to use these."

After another twenty minutes, we had two more verses.

When I kissed you that first time
I rose high into the clouds

Lightning flashed across the sky
But I could not hear a sound

Your hands softly found my waist
And pulled me into you
A flutter deep and strong
Begged me not to move

Then we repeated the chorus and added one more line:

In a better world
In a beautiful world
In a perfect world
You would love me

Like I do you

Jackie changed the melody a little, making it more beautiful, then added a four-bar, picked intro. And as always, she set the harmonies. We decided to sing it that night.

Jackie put her guitar down and gave me a wry smile. "Miki said we both could live together here for the rest of the summer. Right?"

"How did you know?" I teased. "No. She claims she'll make a decision on Friday, but we both know what it will be."

"I'm leaving with you. Will your mother . . . will she be okay with us together?"

"If she shows up, she'll be your best friend. If she doesn't, we'll make the best of what we have."

Jackie swallowed. "I don't have much money. Miki is supposed to pay me ten dollars a day, but who knows what she'll do?"

"Don't worry about money. I have plenty to get us started."

"You don't mind?"

"Only if I can't be with you."

Later that morning, we talked to Jeff in the yurt about our plans.

"Would you come?" I asked. "We could live together. If you found a boyfriend, you both could stay with us."

His brow furrowed while he blew out a long breath. "I'd love to, but I'm safe here. The draft board could find me in Fairbanks."

"But once we go," Jackie said, "your cover is blown."

"Not really," he said with a grin. "I could be heartbroken you left me. For a lesbian, no less." He fake cried and wiped an eye.

On Thursday after breakfast, Jeff headed toward the Wonder Lake Campground. He'd heard about a group there from the university in Fairbanks doing research and thought he might score.

At lunch, Miki announced we would join the group after dinner and enjoy a bonfire, s'mores, and hot chocolate. She also said, "And maybe Jackie and Tracy will grace us all with a singalong." Everyone cheered when we agreed. Miki also told my tour group to pack before dinner since we would be leaving Camp Wonder by 6:00 am the next day.

Jackie and I spoke with Miki after lunch about us both leaving on Friday.

"Well, I'm not surprised," Miki said from behind her desk.

"And certainly not upset," Jackie said. "Your camp will be free of the wicked." She glared at her aunt, daring her to start an argument.

"Where will you stay?" Miki asked.

"We'll find a place when we get there," I said.

"Do you have money for rent?" Miki asked.

"Speaking of which," Jackie said, "you owe me $270."

Without emotion, Miki opened a drawer and pulled out an envelope with Jackie's name and the amount of cash inside written in marker. "Yes, I do." She tossed it toward her niece.

Jackie smirked. "I was leaving tomorrow one way or another, wasn't I, Aunt Miki? I'll need to get the rest of my stuff from your house once we find a place. And, yes, Tracy has money for rent."

Miki folded her hands beneath her chin as she leaned back in her chair. "You know where the key is hidden. I trust my house and my things will be in good order when I return in September."

"I will make sure of it," I said. "You won't know we were ever there."

"I'm sorry we can't remove all your bad memories of me living with you," Jackie said, "but everything else of mine will be gone." Her smile was tight and bitter. "Maybe after we're settled and you've returned, we can invite you to dinner at our place."

Miki tightened her mouth and returned Jackie's icy stare. We left the office and headed for the yurt.

"Shit. Why can't any of my departures from an adult be friendly or kind?" Jackie pleaded.

I held her hand as we walked down the steps outside the lodge. "Will you miss working here?"

"Yes, actually. I've grown up with many of the crew. But I knew when we came back in June, this would be my last summer." She turned to me outside the yurt and held both of my hands. "I was sad thinking about leaving then, but I'm not now because of you. First thing we're going to do in Fairbanks is take a bath together in a real tub."

"At Miki's house?"

"Where else? We can live there for almost three months, rent free. Miki can't do anything about it, and she knows it." She pulled me close. "And then we're going to make love in my bed after a nice dinner and some of Miki's wine. I'll let you choose the music." She kissed my cheek.

"Do you have records?"

"Lots." She kissed my other cheek.

"Jefferson Airplane?"

She kissed my neck. "One of my favorite groups."

"I know just the song." I kissed her on the lips. As we opened the door, we saw a little girl with her mouth open, looking at us.

"Hey, Ruthie," Jackie shouted.

The girl shook her head then ran away, yelling, "Mom! Mom!"

Jackie slumped against the door frame. "I held her as a baby. Her mother and I have worked here together for six years." Jackie sighed and pushed away from the door. "We're not hiding anymore. What can anyone do to us now?"

I helped Jackie wash clothes and pack. Then we walked to my tent, holding hands, and organized my stuff in my pack and duffle. We decided we'd bathe one last time in her tub after the bonfire at the lake.

Though the trip to the campground was only supposed to be for the tour group, Jackie jumped into the front seat with me in the Land Rover Johnny would drive. Glenda opened the front door, saw us together, and gasped.

"Hey, Glenda," I said. "You get in the middle, and I'll sit on Jackie's lap. She won't hit you."

"Speak for yourself," said Jackie. We slid out and Jackie lightly touched her fist to Glenda's shoulder. "Just kidding."

We let Glenda scoot in. I sat on Jackie, who wrapped her arms around my waist.

"Where's Jeff?" Glenda asked.

"He's already at the campground," Jackie said. "We'll probably see him sometime tonight. Maybe he'd like to go to Dallas with you."

I coughed a laugh. Glenda crossed her legs and folded her arms—a statue of scorn.

As soon as we arrived, we pulled our guitars from the luggage rack. Before we headed down the hill toward the lake, Jackie gazed at the mountain and said, "I think tonight's the night."

I looked and still saw clouds covering the summit. "Why?"

"Because the ceiling is lifting and the clouds are thinning." She flashed her brows at me. "This is a 'get up early and check' night for sure."

Near the bonfire on the edge of the lake, we found about twenty college students and faculty plus other campers, some speaking a foreign language. Jackie said it was German. They had formed a half-circle around the fire sitting on picnic tables and camp stools. Those from Camp Wonder stood in the gaps or found space to sit down. A wall of trees rose up behind them.

A man with a beard and a cowboy hat shouted, "Do y'all play guitar?"

"Do y'all want to hear us?" I asked with a grin. "I'm from Texas. Where are y'all from?"

"Louisiana. Shreveport."

"I'm Tracy and she's Jackie. We just formed a band called Moon-Stone, and we'd be happy to play for you."

"Great! I'm Steve and this is my wife, Sally. Why don't you sit in our chairs?" He and his wife jumped up and sat at a nearby picnic table.

"Thank you!" Jackie said as she sat down. "We're going to play everything we know or until you get tired of hearing us, whichever comes first. We play lots of tunes you've heard before and some originals. When you hear something you know, don't be afraid to sing along with us."

We started off with Simon and Garfunkel's "Homeward Bound," followed by Seeger's "If I Had a Hammer." Our audience loved us. They all started singing Dylan's "Blowin' in the Wind" and Seeger's "Where Have All The Flowers Gone?" We followed with my anti-war song, "It's a Great War."

Someone shouted, "Play more of your songs."

So we did—everything we'd written, ending with our latest, "You Would Love Me." Amazingly, they gave us a standing ovation. Even Miki and Glenda smiled and clapped.

We took a break to drink some hot chocolate. Lots of people gave us kind words. An older woman in boots and a long skirt handed us her card. She owned restaurants in Fairbanks and wanted us to give her a call once we were in town.

"I love your songs and your sound," she said. "We need more girl bands."

"Yes, we do," I said, trying not to jump up and down. "We're leaving tomorrow and should be in Fairbanks Saturday night."

"Call me Monday."

We were just about to start another set when a big man dragged a stumbling, beaten Jeff behind him toward the fire. In a thick German accent he asked, "Who runs that camp up on the hill?"

Jackie and I ran to Jeff and helped him stand.

"Let him go!" I demanded.

"Who are you?"

"We're his friends. Get your hands off him!" I ripped his hand from Jeff's shoulder as heat flushed through my body.

Jackie and I each took a shoulder around our necks to walk him away.

"Did you do this?" I asked, my muscles tense.

"Nein. My son's friends."

Miki walked over to the man and spoke quietly before moving away. We helped Jeff up the hill away from the crowd and sat him at a picnic table.

"I'll get our guitars," Jackie said then ran back to the fire.

I checked his bloody lip and nose. "What happened?"

"This guy and I were hooking up in his tent when someone came by. Fritz got scared then yelled for help, saying I was raping him. Others ran up, pulled me out of the tent, and started hitting me."

"Is anything broken?" He had dried blood in his curly hair.

"I don't think so."

I remembered Spencer and asking him to come with me to Alaska. How different his life would've been. Maybe he and Jeff . . . I wiped tears from my eyes. "Live with us in Fairbanks. Jackie and I are leaving tomorrow."

We both watched Miki, Johnny, and Jackie walk toward us.

Miki's words were cold and clipped. "Johnny will drive you three back to camp. Jeff, get packed and be ready to leave tomorrow morning. I'll have your money ready then." She turned away.

"Thanks for asking how I am!" Jeff yelled.

We climbed into the back seat, Jeff sitting between us, and said nothing during the drive. Once back at the lodge, Johnny went inside for a first aid kit while we helped Jeff back to the yurt. Jackie heated water for tea as I wiped Jeff's face with a wet cloth.

"We'll be living at my aunt's house for a few weeks," Jackie said. "We have three bedrooms. If Tracy's mother comes tomorrow, she can stay in Miki's room. Tracy will stay with me, and you can have the guest room. We don't want you on your own."

"Please?" I asked. "You're like my brother. I can't lose another one." We stared at each other, both of our eyes filling with tears.

"Yes. Thank you."

Johnny came in with the kit and doctored Jeff while Jackie and I stacked his clothes on the next bed.

After fifteen minutes, Johnny said, "I need to get back. I'm going to miss you guys. Miki is being a bitch." He gave each of us a hug then walked out.

We packed, we drank tea, we talked about our future, and we laughed. Finally at about eleven, we decided to crash. Jackie spooned me in her bed.

"I'm going to check the mountain at 3:30," she said, brushing her lips against my neck.

"If it's out then, won't it be out at five when we have to get up?"

"It won't be pink then." She kissed my ear. "If it's out, we're heading to the lake. I have a plan." She moved her hand under my shirt and held my left breast.

I dreamt of applauding crowds and Miki's stony face and Mom. God, I wanted her to show up. Could one adult in our lives love any of us and not be afraid to show it?

I woke up shivering, alone in bed. I sat up just as Jackie opened the door.

"It's out," she whispered. "Get dressed."

I pulled on my pants and shirt and boots as Jackie found two towels.

"Why towels?" I asked while putting on my jacket.

She giggled. "We're going to fuck the mountain."

We left the yurt and trotted to the road.

Then I saw it—massive, dark pink, with just a wisp of cloud near the top. And the moon! Full against a beautiful cyan sky. "I need my camera."

"It's on the way."

We stayed on the road for a bit then detoured left to the trail to my tent. I grabbed my camera and found Jackie standing near the cliff edge, staring at the most beautiful thing I'd ever seen. I snapped three pictures.

"We need to hurry before it turns yellow," she said. "C'mon!"

We ran back to the access road and down the ridge until we reached the main road. After a few more curves, we found the northern end of the lake, two miles from the campground and bonfire. The water was perfectly still, revealing a mirror image of the mountain, a bright magenta now.

I snapped several photos.

Jackie ran to a dock and began to remove her clothes.

I followed. "What are you doing?"

With a mischievous grin, she said, "Stripping. We're going for a skinny dip. Take off your clothes."

I pulled off my jacket. "Won't the water be ice cold?"

"Yes. Your nips will likely freeze and break off." She pulled off her pants and panties.

"And I was just getting used to having decent boobs. Have you ever done this before?"

"Nope. But always wanted to. The mountain's real name is Denali, the Great One, and she's female. When we dive into her image, we'll make love to her."

"Says who?" I pulled off my panties.

"Says me. We are going to ravish her and be ravished."

"We're going to drown with hypothermia."

"The orgasm will heat us up. Trust me." She reached out her hand for mine and pulled me into her. "I love you, Tracy. Beyond words or thought. You are the best thing that ever happened to me."

"I love you, Moon Jacqueline Dust. And if I have to jump into this lake to prove it, I will."

"She wouldn't have shown herself tonight," Jackie said, "if she didn't want our embrace."

"Or our dead bodies."

"Ready?"

"Fuck!"

We dived in. My skin burned. I thought I'd died. *How can my body be on fire?*

I thrashed my arms to reach the surface and found Jackie's head above water, facing the mountain. "Don't you burn?"

"Yes! That's the orgasm."

"That's death!"

"Same thing. When you cum, don't you feel like you're going to die? And the pain feels so good." Somehow she rose out of the water to her waist, her body slick and shiny in the pink light. Our movements had sent ripples through the reflection, blurring it. As if it shuddered in our presence.

"Hold me." I reached out to her and discovered she was standing on a mound beneath the water.

She hugged and kissed me again. "We will always remember this night."

"If we survive." My teeth chattered.

"We're going to thrive, Tracy. Who the hell else would've done this with me? You're coming up here was fate all along. God, I love you."

Even though I was freezing and my skin was on fire, I felt my core warming up. I loved her more than anything. Tears flowed from my eyes. "Jackie, you saved me. The only thing that kept me alive after Spencer died was you."

Headlights flashed behind us.

We turned and saw a car pulling off the road.

"Shit." I said. "How do we get out of here without being seen?"

"We don't. Denali's out and so are we. They can look all they want to. Let's give them a show." She started swimming toward the shore.

I followed.

When we reached the dock, several people from the campground stood at the bank, taking pictures. One yelled, "You ruined the reflection!"

We both hoisted ourselves up and smiled at them.

"Whoa!" someone said. "They're naked."

"That's disgusting!" another yelled.

Another car drove up—Miki's Land Rover. She must have brought some to the lake who wanted pictures of the reflection.

I started shivering. Jackie came to me for a kiss—a long, sensuous, open-mouthed kiss, warming both of us.

I saw flashes from cameras through my eyelids. Amazingly, I felt no embarrassment. I was nude in front of people, and I didn't care. Jackie flashed a smile and pushed out her chest—she didn't care either.

No longer burdened by limits or worries or fears, I felt I could fly.

We reached down for our towels and dried off. Then we picked up our clothes and shoes, held hands, and walked through the crowd— some muttering disapproval but most silent—until we found a table.

More flashes.

We dressed and started walking toward the road where we found Glenda holding her Polaroid camera, smirking.

"Jeff will definitely be interested in these," she said. "I already showed them to Miki."

Heat roiled my belly. "Jeff is recovering in the yurt," I said, "from being beaten by a bunch of assholes. So no, he won't be interested." I reached out my hand to her. "You will give me every photo you took of us naked. I'm seventeen, a minor. Those pictures are child pornography.

If you don't, I will report you to the rangers and to police. I don't believe a public relations specialist can survive such a disgusting accusation."

She lifted her chin in defiance. "You wouldn't dare."

"Try me." I moved my hand closer to her.

She hesitated, snarled, then thrust her hand into her pocket, removing several prints. She glanced at the top one then handed it to me. I showed it to Jackie. We were kissing. Glenda handed over another. We were walking hand in hand.

"That's all," Glenda said after riffling through the others.

"Nope. I saw more than one flash while we kissed. Hand it over."

Glenda looked through the others. "Oh. I must have missed this one." She gave it to me.

"Thank you, Glenda." I handed all the prints to Jackie. "We're very glad you showed up. Now we have these amazing mementos. You're the best."

Jackie and I walked toward the Land Rover where Miki leaned against a door.

"Do you have room for us?" I asked.

"Afraid not, girls. You'll have to walk."

We moved past her.

From behind us, Miki shouted, "Aren't you embarrassed at all?"

We stopped and turned to face her.

"No," said Jackie. "We are totally open about who and what we are. You should try it sometime."

After another thirty minutes, we slipped inside the yurt to find Jeff standing naked in the tub, squeezing water out of a cloth over his body. "Hey, girls. Don't mind me."

Jackie plopped onto her bed, watching him. "The mountain's out."

"Cool." Jeff dropped the cloth and rubbed a towel through his hair.

"This must be National Gay Nudity Day," I said. He looked like Michelangelo's statue of *David* except Jeff was circumcised. "You're beautiful."

He faced me, drying his chest. "Thanks. No one's ever said that to me. Why aren't you a guy?"

"I've asked myself that many times," I said. "But now I know the answer." I sat next to Jackie. "If I were a guy, I'd never have met and loved Moon Dust or jumped naked into Wonder Lake."

"Or made people laugh and cry with our songs," Jackie said.

"And missed all the other amazing things we'll experience together. So I'm happy to be who I am. But if I ever want babies, you'd be my first choice for daddy."

"Mine too," Jackie said, holding my hand. "Will you?"

"What?" he asked while pulling up his pants.

"Give us babies, if we ever want to have them," Jackie said.

He smiled. "Sure thing."

"We're serious, Jeff. Promise?" I asked.

"Yeah." He looked at each of us. "I'd be honored. I promise." He smiled as he pulled on his shirt.

He did father our children.

His last name was Lake.

CHAPTER 24

THE MOONSTONE GIRLS

We left Camp Wonder a little after 6:00 am and drove toward a brilliant white Denali, anchoring a clear, turquoise blue sky. Jeff, Jackie, and I sat in the front seat, while the twins filled the second row. The Montana couple paid Miki to stay an extra week now that the mountain was out, giving room in the back seat for Glenda, Jake, and the teaching couple, who had seen us swimming in the lake earlier that morning.

Miki stopped a few times to allow everyone to take photos. I gave Hallie my camera and asked her to shoot Jeff, Jackie, and me with Denali in the background.

"Sure, I will," Hallie said.

With Jackie in the middle, we all threw our arms around each other as she shot the first one. For the second, Jackie and I pressed our cheeks together as we faced the camera, holding each other's waists. Jeff sat on the ground in front.

Hallie scowled. "Are you sure that's the pose you want?"

"Yes, please," I said.

She shot it.

"One more!" I shouted. Jackie and I faced each other and held each other's face with our hands as we kissed.

"No way!" shouted Hallie. "What's wrong with you girls this morning?"

"We love each other," I said.

Hallie shook her head. "The Devil snuck into your place last night. You all need to repent."

"Amen," added her sister.

Jeff jumped up and took the camera from Hallie. "Say cheesy lesbian," he commanded just before snapping the photo.

Before we entered the car, I approached the twins. "So all the good times and laughter and songs we've shared mean nothing now because we're gay?"

DeLacie lowered her eyes while Hallie's stayed fixed on mine as she said, "They don't mean nothing, Tracy, but what you and Jackie are doing is a sin. You should pray."

"Love thy neighbor as thyself only if she's straight? Otherwise, you're free to condemn? That's why I won't pray."

For the rest of the trip, the twins scowled and tsk-tsked us, especially when I played with Jackie's hair, or she leaned against me for a nap.

At our last rest stop, *the three homos*—we'd heard this epithet a few times—stood together on the deck overlooking the Teklanika River.

Jeff lit a cigarette. "Will your Mom show up?"

"I don't know," I answered. "It depends on who wins the battle between fear and love."

Jackie wrapped her arms around me. "She'll be there. I feel it in my bones."

I didn't feel anything except my stomach churning.

I started to bite my fingernails until Jackie grabbed my hand and kissed each finger. "You need those, Baby. Chew on gum." She handed me a piece.

We turned to leave and saw the twins standing in a group— including Glenda—judging us from a distance. The same people who had criticized the twins behind their backs now joined them in prejudice. Perhaps it was easier to unite in hate and fear than in love.

As we got closer to the hotel, I couldn't sit still. I felt random itches, and my breathing varied from a panicked gulp of air to a series of pants to forgetting to breathe at all. Jackie rubbed my face and kissed my cheek and pushed her fingers through my hair, forcing more sounds of disapproval behind us.

We drove past the dog kennels and a view of the big bridge across the Nenana until we saw the lodge. As soon as we parked at the train depot, I popped the door open and jumped outside, shifting my gaze frantically, looking for Mom.

I didn't see her. My insides quivered until Jeff said, "Tracy, take your guitar." I caught it and set it on the ground.

Jeff was pulling bags off the roof, handing them to their owners. Once all of ours were in a pile, I grabbed Jackie's hand and asked Jeff to keep watch while we searched. We quick-walked toward the lobby, our heads on swivels, the knot in my throat growing with each person we passed who wasn't her.

A man held a door open for us to move inside where we searched every corner. I was about to approach the man behind the counter when I saw phone booths along one wall. I decided to call home. I asked the operator to make a collect call and waited for the rings to stop.

Dad answered the phone with an angry, "Hello?"

"Will you accept a phone call from Tracy Franks?" asked the operator.

"Yes," he snapped. As soon as the lady disconnected, he yelled, "Where the fuck is your mother?"

My head pounded. "She's not there?"

"Like you don't know, you little bitch. I just got home and found a note about her leaving for Alaska to join you and the phone number of her lawyer. Her *lawyer!* You have totally destroyed this family!"

I couldn't think. Maybe she left but ran into a problem and didn't arrive on time. Or maybe she'd been hurt. My eyes jerked around the lobby, desperately searching while my father screamed incoherently into the phone.

"Dad, what does the note say?"

He kept screaming. I heard something about the piano being gone and money taken out of his bank account. I squeezed my forehead, trying to think. Then out of the corner of my eye, I saw a woman push open the lobby doors and yell, "Tracy?"

Jackie pointed. "Is that her?"

Warmth surged through me. I dropped the phone and ran to her, Jackie close behind. "Mom! I'm here."

She opened her arms wide, and my heart hammered against my chest. I grabbed her off the ground and spun around. "You came. You came. Goddammit, you came!"

When I set her down, we were both blubbering. I wiped tears from her cheeks. "I love you, Mom."

She kissed my cheek and pulled me to her. "The girl. Is this the girl?"

I turned around and grabbed Jackie's hand. "Mom, this is Moon Jacqueline Dust, the most amazing girl in the world, my best friend. I love her."

Jackie wiped her tears and smiled. "Hello." She reached out for Mom's hands. "I'm sorry. I don't know your name."

"It's Alice."

"Can I call you mom?"

"Certainly."

Jackie spread her arms, and Mom moved into them. Soon we were all hugging each other.

"I called home," I said. "Dad was screaming."

"That's his forte," Mom said. "He's had lots of practice."

It finally dawned on me she was wearing pants, a shirt, and a light jacket full of pockets. "Mom, your clothes."

She raised her arms and turned around. "Do you like them? It's a safari outfit. I brought only one dress with me." She swallowed. "I also altered some of Spencer's clothes so I could wear them."

I grabbed her hand. "You look great. We searched everywhere for you."

"I got lost trying to find my way to the back exit, which was supposed to be a quicker route to the depot. Somehow I went out a side door and couldn't see anything but trees. So I looped around and saw a young man sitting on a bag next to two guitars. One of them had to be yours. He told me where you'd gone."

"I can't believe you did it," I said as I squeezed her.

"I almost didn't, I was so scared," Mom said, "but then I told myself your spunk and bravery had to come from somewhere, so I had the same stuff in me if I'd just look hard enough. And I did, dammit, I did."

I felt weightless and warm. "I'm so proud of you."

Jeff stood up smiling when he saw us approach.

"This is Jeff," I said. "He's our friend. We've asked him to stay with us."

Mom reached out her hand. "My, my, but aren't you handsome."

Jeff shook her hand and blushed. "Thanks."

"Are you gay?" asked Mom with a smile, still holding his hand.

He took a breath. "Yes."

"Wonderful. So was my son, Spencer. I miss him so much. Do you have family?"

Jeff's face turned red. "Not anymore."

"We can be your family." Mom opened her arms.

Jeff's eyes flooded with tears. They pulled each other close. Jeff wept as Mom stroked his hair.

I clutched Jackie. "You were right."

She kissed my cheek. "I love your mother already."

"She's something, isn't she?"

Jeff and Mom separated, both wiping their faces.

I lifted my pack. "Well, we should find a campsite."

"We don't need to," Mom said. "I kept my room. We can all stay there. There are two double beds and a sofa."

"Isn't it expensive?" I asked.

Mom flashed a wry smile. "Your father insisted."

"Well then," I said, "when have I ever refused Daddy when he insisted?"

Mom's eyes twinkled. "This might be the first time you complied."

Another group of tourists had filed into the two Land Rovers, now loaded with bags on top. The train taking Glenda and the twins and everyone else in my tour group had already left for Anchorage. Despite cheering at all our performances during the past two weeks, none had said anything to us before they left.

I saw Miki laughing with a tall woman wearing a baseball hat, standing outside the car Jeff had driven. Rhonda looked just like her brochure picture—tall, blonde, lanky. Miki held the woman's face in her hands for a moment as they both smiled at each other. Then they embraced for a strong hug. When Miki broke away, she saw me watching her, and walked toward us.

As Miki approached, I asked, "How's Rhonda? Looks like you two missed each other."

"Certainly, we did." Her look was ice cold. "We've been friends for thirty years. Is this your mother?"

"She certainly is," I replied, curious about Miki's motives.

"Mrs. Franks?" asked Miki.

"Only until I change my last name back to Stone. And you are?"

"Miki. I'm one of the owners of Camp Wonder." She thrust out her chin and looked down her nose. "You do know your daughter is homosexual."

Mom didn't miss a beat. "Yes, I do, and I'm so proud of her. It's very difficult living in a world where people condemn you for being gay. That is so ridiculous, don't you think?"

I wanted to scream, "You rock, Mom!" but had to hear what happened next.

With a frown, Miki added, "Jackie and Jeff are too."

Mom's smile stretched wider. "I'm so happy Tracy will have such great friends. Thank you for delivering them all safe to me."

Jackie folded her arms and gave her aunt an evil grin. "The mountain came out today, Miki. Maybe you should too."

Miki's gaze was hot and her smile cool. "I'm always out. I have nothing to hide."

"And neither do we," I said, putting my arm around Jackie. "We're proud to be gay and free. I've never been happier—for all the *right* reasons. I hope someday you can accept all of us."

"Goodbye, Miki," said Mom. She turned around to face us. "Have we got everything?"

Each of us picked up our gear.

"Yes, Mom."

"Yes, Mom."

"Yes, Mom."

Mom gasped and took a second to compose herself. "Then let's drop all this off in our room and get some lunch. I bet you're starving."

Thirty minutes later, we were feasting on crab cakes, halibut and fries, and shrimp salad.

I wiped my mouth with a cloth napkin. "You showed Dad the journal?"

"Yes, I did. He accused you of forging it and claimed that Spencer would never write such things. No remorse or regret." She shook her head in anger. "He wouldn't have recognized Spencer's or your hand-writing because he never bothered to read anything you wrote past elementary school. That's when I knew I had to leave." She clenched her jaw. "He left on a trip. I cashed in my stock, had my royalty checks sent to my lawyer to forward to me when I'm settled, called Victor to sell the piano, and took half of the amounts in the savings and checking accounts. My lawyer will handle all the details of a divorce. I'll never have to see Art again."

I covered her hand with mine and felt such pride. "I know it was hard, but you're free now."

Jackie covered Mom's other hand.

"Jackie's father was killed in Vietnam three years ago," I said, "and she hasn't seen her mother since. Miki kicked her out of the camp for being gay. Ditto for Jeff, whose parents also kicked him out years ago."

Mom sighed. "I'm so sorry for both of you. Families tear themselves up for such stupid reasons. I promise to be kind and fair while I learn to love you both. And I hope you can learn to love me."

Jackie kissed Mom's hand. "I already do."

Mom kissed Jackie's cheek. "Oh, Jackie. When Tracy first showed me your picture, I knew she was hooked. I told her she was crazy, but I was wrong. I so want to hear you two play together."

"You will tonight," I said.

Our waiter came by, asking if we would like dessert. I had seen the upright piano across the dining room.

"Who plays the piano?" I asked.

"Sometimes one of our guests. Sometimes we hire a pianist for the weekend."

"Can I play it?"

"Please," Jackie begged. "I've never heard her."

"Certainly," our waiter said.

"Would you like coffee and cake?" Mom asked.

"Yes, please," I said, rising from my chair.

"Good," Mom said. "It will be waiting for you."

Jackie and Jeff followed me. I sat at the Yamaha and played a quick scale. It was in tune, and the action was decent. I played a few arpeggios to warm up. A few of the guests in the restaurant applauded. Then I started playing Chopin's *Fantaisie-Impromptu in C-sharp Minor*, a beautiful piece with a lightning fast beginning that leads to one of the sweetest melodies ever written. It ends with speed and depth, always passionate and heart-breaking. This was the piece I'd played last November when Spencer performed with the symphony. He always loved to hear my *Fantaisie*. I could see his enraptured expression in my mind even then.

When I finished, I turned around to loud applause, most everyone standing at their tables, and Jackie gasping for air, her cheeks red and wet.

Jeff hugged me then Jackie. I felt such a rush.

"We need a piano for our house. I want to hear everything you play," Jackie said.

We walked back to the table arm in arm, guests still applauding, throwing out compliments.

Soon a man in a suit approached us. "Hello, my name is Adrian. I am the manager of the hotel." He looked at me. "Your Chopin was exquisite. Would you be interested in playing for our guests during dinner? I would be happy to comp your meals."

"Jeff?" I said.

He was rising from his chair. "Already on it. Hello, Adrian. My name is Jeff. I'm the manager for Tracy and Jackie."

Adrian raised his brows. "They both play?"

"Yes. They're known as MoonStone, and they've just finished gigs at Camp Wonder. Why don't we talk over here?" He led Adrian toward an empty table near a window.

We played two sets that night to enthusiastic audiences, especially Mom, who loved watching her "children" perform. Adrian comped our room and meals with an option to book us through the weekend, depending on how we did that evening. After our performance, he hired us for the next two days, including lodging, meals, and a hundred dollars. When we finally boarded the train on Monday to Fairbanks, we carried contracts to play four more weekends that summer, including Labor Day.

During the four-hour ride, we wrote our namesake song—The MoonStone Girls—one we would use to open every set.

From a lake of wonder two teenage girls emerged
Trying to wash away a past that neither one deserved
A mountain rose above them in the dawning light
With a mother's love it helped them find a better life
Find a better life

In these wicked times when too many live to hate
And pick and choose who loves and who should separate
We formed a bond and band to make a better world
Each other's joy and hope we are The MoonStone Girls
We are The MoonStone Girls

Born to sing
Born to love
And to raise our voice above
The din of indignation
And the screams of accusation
To change hypocrisy to harmony
And noise to a soothing melody
to a soothing melody

During our lives together, Jackie and I repeated that song over a thousand times before we lost count. After our emergence from Wonder Lake, we felt cleansed and renewed, unafraid of who and what we were. We honestly believed we were born to sing together and to love each other, and everything that had happened before our meeting at camp was forever behind us.

We raced forward, hardly ever looking back.

But Jeff was still tied to his past.

During our first winter in Fairbanks, he slid into another car while driving our truck through an icy intersection. The police took his license and ran a name check, discovering he was wanted for failure to report to his draft board. After another month, he was sent to boot camp. By November of the next year, he was in the jungles of Vietnam.

We wrote at least once a week and panicked when a month passed without a response.

But he survived, though much of his spirit had been crushed during the war.

Jeff returned before Christmas in 1971 with a bronze star and PTSD he never discussed. He moved back into our house and more firmly into our hearts. Mom's love and patience and sympathy were boundless, but they weren't enough to help Jeff keep his demons at bay. He disappeared for weeks then returned. Once he brought another young man home with him, but their relationship didn't last, and Jeff was gone again.

By that time, Jackie and I took courses at the University of Fairbanks while playing on live radio, restaurants and clubs, music festivals, and special events. We ran out of time each day, trying to juggle all our duties, but we always found our deepest comfort with each other every night. The all-consuming warmth Jackie had described the first day we met lingered through every hour of every day.

By 1975, Jackie and I had completed our degrees and found jobs— she as a middle-school music teacher and me as a reporter for the local paper and a contributor to various magazines.

Jackie and I had talked about wanting children. When we mentioned it to Mom, she lit up. She was so keen to become a grandmother.

We had some money saved from the sale of recording rights for three of our songs, and another was used as a background for a commercial. MoonStone had been our most consistent means of support through college.

The next time Jeff came home, we reminded him of that night in the yurt when we declared him the future daddy of our kids.

Laughing at our request, Jeff said, "Give me a turkey baster. When I'm done, I'll bring it to you."

Jackie moved close to him, brushing her breasts on his arm, her lips grazing his cheek. "No, that's not what we had in mind."

Blushing, he asked, "Why can't you use a sperm bank?"

I moved to his other side and pushed my hands under his shirt. "Single women and lesbians aren't allowed to be inseminated. We want to have real sex with you, Jeff. At least, our own version."

We both kissed his cheeks.

"We want to do this together," pleaded Jackie.

I touched his golden locks. "You're beautiful and kind. Please make children with us."

He pulled our heads to his and whispered, "You're the only women I've ever loved. Let's try."

We scheduled two different weeks with him, coinciding with our ovulations. We bought *Playgirl* magazines, incense, and massage oils. When Jeff came into our room the first night, he found us dressed in sexy lingerie, entirely shaved and painted. He laughed as we slinked toward him, but he got an erection. We helped him ejaculate into a baster while Jackie and I made love. Just as I came, she pushed Jeff's sperm inside me. I did the same for her.

Our nights together were amazingly fun. But more importantly, we could honestly say our children were conceived in love.

Eight weeks later we learned we were both pregnant—much to our surprise and joy. We thought we'd be lucky if one of us conceived. Jeff had once again disappeared, but he returned to town shortly after the births of Abigail Lake Stone and Thomas (after Jackie's father) Lake Dust. He held his children in awe, though somewhat clumsily. He said he'd never had siblings or been around babies before.

"I'm scared to be a father," he told us many times.

"You gave us these precious kids," I told him. "Anything more is icing on the cake. Enjoy them when you can."

"What will you tell them about me?" he asked as if he were already gone.

Jackie hugged him. "That you were the best and kindest man we knew, a war hero, and so fucking sexy that two lesbians couldn't keep their hands off you."

He laughed and threw his arms around us. "I love you both. I wish .

. . I wish . . ." He choked on his tears and never finished his thought. He soon disappeared and never returned.

We learned later he ended up in San Francisco where he died of AIDS in 1981.

Our children never knew him. When they were old enough, we told them he'd died of cancer and that we'd both loved him, which was why their mothers lived and slept together. We'd done the same when he was alive.

And why Grammy lived with us because she'd loved Jeff like her own son.

He'd told us many times we were the only lights in his life, and he couldn't bear to see the pain *"my fucked-up head"* would cause us.

Or his children.

Were it not for the sweet love Abigail and Thomas shared with us, Jackie, Mom and I might not have survived his passing.

So we kept looking forward and not back into a past of pain and heartache.

We raised our children to be tolerant of others, that different races and cultures enriched our lives, that all sexual identities were to be embraced and loved. Jackie and I were a loving couple in front of our kids, but like most parents, we limited our displays of affection to hugs and kisses on the cheek.

When Abigail was twelve, she asked me if Jackie and I were lovers. "Yes, we are and have been since June 1968."

Her big brown eyes bulged. "So you're lesbians?"

I couldn't stop touching her French braid Mom did for her each morning. "Yes. Is that okay with you?"

She frowned. "Yeah." She sucked in her lips and she couldn't keep her eyes on mine. "Does that mean I'll be a lesbian?"

Her worried look made my throat ache. "So far, no one's found a gay gene, so the sexuality of your parents has no effect on you. By your age, though, I'd begun to realize I was different from other girls."

Her face brightened. "Like preferring to look at Michelle Pfeiffer and Madonna instead of Tom Selleck and Bon Jovi?"

We should've talked about this much earlier. Damn! "Something like that. I was obsessed with Grace Slick at seventeen."

Her face flushed. "Cool."

"So who do you like?"

"Girls," she said without hesitation. "But I'm scared, Mommy."

My chest tightened with worry. "Why?"

"Because yesterday Natalie was called dyke and homo and butch."

"Oh no. Who did this?"

"Mostly guys, but some girls too." She lowered her eyes and sighed. "Thomas was one of them."

Her brother too?

My heart seemed to shrink, and I felt dizzy. Jackie and I had waited too long to share all of our stories. We thought our children were too young, but we didn't realize that age twelve in 1988 was like age sixteen or older in 1968.

That night and over the weekend, Jackie and I told them how we'd met at Camp Wonder and why we had to leave with their father. All of us had been hated because we were gay. Though Jeff had never told us the actual events, we'd surmised from some of his comments that he'd been harassed about his sexuality in Vietnam and had earned his medal to prove them wrong. He should have died in the jungle, he'd told us.

But he hadn't because he'd made a promise to Jackie and me.

Thomas and Abigail were proof that love could defeat hate. Through no fault of their own, their parents were gay and loved each other and them beyond words.

The world didn't need more hatred.

Thomas cried and apologized and wrote a beautiful letter to Natalie, who became a frequent visitor to our house.

Life went on with its normal ups and downs, but I thought this issue would no longer cause problems. Abigail experimented with boys and girls, but by her sophomore year in college, she seemed to stick with boys. At least, they were the only ones we saw with her. By twenty-four, she'd married a wonderful man, Alexander, in Anchorage and had her first child a year later. Thomas found his love at twenty-two and had his first child six months later with Nicole.

For a while it seemed Jackie and I were the only gays in our family. But we had lots of friends in the LGBTQ community in Fairbanks. We performed at the Blue Loon during drag week and supported gay theatre groups and publications. Since moving to Fairbanks, we'd never hidden who we were, and for the most part, we hadn't suffered discrimination. How could anyone disapprove of two very talented women singing great songs? Being MoonStone brought us love and acceptance.

Of course, many fought hard to keep the world safe for straight people at the expense of everyone else. After years of efforts throughout the country to restrict marriage to a man and a woman, a District Court judge in Anchorage ruled Alaska's law unconstitutional on October 12, 2014. One week later, Jackie and I were married and changed our last names to MoonStone as we slipped moonstone rings onto each other's fingers.

Yes, we did.

Our families returned to Fairbanks to celebrate with us at Christmas. Thomas, Abigail, and their spouses helped Mom cook enormous meals, while Jackie and I brought out our guitars and amazed our grandkids They called us old hippie rockers.

Abigail seemed especially jazzed about our marriage, which made me curious at the time, but I didn't say anything. However, her eldest daughter, Emma, peppered me with questions about my past, especially when did I know I was gay. Later, Jackie told me of Thomas's concern for his son, Tyler. He'd caught him wearing makeup recently.

Within the next six years, Abigail had divorced and moved in with a girlfriend. Emma had come out as bisexual. Tyler wanted transition surgery. And Thomas' youngest daughter said she should have been a boy.

Thomas and Nicole and Alexander thought their world was coming to an end with . . .

The din of indignation
And the screams of accusation

Jackie and I tried to explain and to comfort, making frequent trips to be with our precious children and grandkids. We tried to tell them to love unconditionally, like Mom had done for us.

Then Covid hit in 2020, and we hunkered down. The MoonStone

Girls were then seventy, and Mom was ninety-three—a grandmother of two and great-grandma of six.

It was long past time for me to look backward and face all the old pains once again and share them. I decided to write this book and give it to everyone in our families.

A history of love and hate and prejudice and acceptance.

Of great joy and great suffering.

Of redemption and resilience.

Of discovering who you are and finding comfort in that knowledge.

Of the time when the mountain came out for The MoonStone Girls and never again disappeared.

EPILOGUE

A HEALING STONE

The book I gave to our kids and grandkids on Christmas Day 2020 ended with that last sentence. I added a little more before I published for the general public.

Mom's health declined precipitously in May 2021, but she still Face-Timed members of her family and her many friends almost every day. She was happy with the life she'd lived since moving to Alaska. She asked me to contact Dad after she passed and send him my book. "It's time to heal," she said. I promised I would.

Mom died fifty-three years to the day from when she found us at the hotel on June 28. Jackie and I held her hands during her last hours, talking about the good and bad times we'd shared together. All of us knew we had saved each other's lives—three women who found their collective strength in the wilderness and carved out a life of love and joy from MoonStone. Just before the end, Jackie and I sang her favorite songs. She closed her eyes and smiled.

After much anxiety and arguments with myself about why I couldn't fulfill my promise to Mom, I decided to call Dad the next day. With a dry mouth and a fluttering in my gut, I pressed the numbers I somehow remembered. When a woman answered the phone, I thought he had moved or possibly died.

"Hello, I'm looking for Art Franks. Does he still live there?"

"Yes, he does. Who is this?" Her voice was kind.

I had to bite my lip to keep my breathing steady. "I'm his daughter, Tracy. We haven't spoken in over fifty years."

"Oh my. I'm Elizabeth. I married your father in 1972."

I didn't ask if he'd mentioned me or Spencer. "The reason I'm calling is to tell him my mother died yesterday, his former wife, Alice."

"I'm so sorry."

"Thank you." I cleared my throat. "She was the rock of all our lives. I want to send Dad a book I've written. My name now is Tracy Moonstone. It's a novel about what happened in our family in '67 and '68. He needs to read it, and maybe you should too. If he does and wants to contact me, my number and email address will be inside the cover. I'll send it tomorrow. You should receive it in two or three days."

"Okay, Tracy. I'll look for it."

I thought I wouldn't care about him. Frankly, I thought he would've passed by now, but my heart tugged me toward a path I realized I should have followed long ago. "How is his health?"

"Not good, I'm afraid. Congestive heart failure and cancer. His doctor wants him in the hospital, but he's stubborn." She offered a tiny laugh. "But I'm sure you know that."

Memories of our arguments flashed in my mind, and I felt a knot of sorrow in my chest. "Yes, we both are. If he can't read it himself but wants to, will you read it to him?"

"Yes, I will."

A month later I received a text from an unknown number. *Can I call you?*

Yes, please.

A few seconds later, I sat down and answered the phone with Jackie standing at my side. "Dad?" My hands trembled.

"Just a minute," Elizabeth said. "We're putting this on speaker. Okay?"

"I'm on speaker too." I put the phone on the table. My heart skipped beats as Jackie rubbed my shoulders from behind.

In a thin, quaking voice, my father said, "Tracy?"

Tears poured from my eyes, and I couldn't hide my crying. "Yes, Dad, I'm here." Jackie pulled me close.

"I'm surprised you'd want anything to do with me." He sniffed and stifled a whimper.

"We're both too old for grudges, Dad. Life's too short."

"Not for me. It's been too damn long, Tracy."

I smiled and blew out a breath. "I'm not going to argue with you."

"That's the first time I've heard that from you." He tried to chuckle.

"I'm sure it is, Dad. But our arguing days are over." I grasped Jackie's hand and held it against my chest.

"Well, you've never heard me say what I'm about to tell you." He coughed and wheezed. "Alice had every reason to leave me, and I've known I was the reason for . . ." He coughed again and cried then pulled in several raspy breaths. "I know I treated you and Spencer horribly. And it's been gnawing at me all these years. I'm sorry, Tracy. So very sorry." He broke down crying.

I wept into Jackie's stomach and I couldn't speak.

"Tracy," Elizabeth said. "Take your time. We're still here."

I tried to get enough air into my lungs. "Thank you, Dad. Hearing you say that means everything to me. And I know I was difficult —"

"No, you weren't," he blurted. "You did what you should have done. What you had to do under the circumstances. Elizabeth helped me understand so many things. And I'm proud of you." He fought to control his weeping. "That's a helluva book, Tracy."

"Thank you, Dad."

We both cried quietly into the phone.

"Someday," he said, "I'd like to talk to Jackie."

"She's right here." I got up and let Jackie sit.

"Hello, Mr. Franks," Jackie said.

"So you're the one who got Tracy to jump naked into that freezing lake."

"I'm afraid so." She clasped my hand. I knelt beside her.

"You sound like the perfect match for her."

"I try to be. She keeps me on my toes."

I kissed her hand and held it to my cheek.

"I'll bet." He cleared his throat and started to speak but stopped.

"Ask them," Elizabeth whispered.

"Could you send me pictures?"

"We'd love to," I said.

"And recordings of your songs?"

"Yes, we'll send you everything," I said, my scalp tingling. "It won't be tonight but maybe by tomorrow I can send you a link to a Dropbox."

"Okay. Elizabeth should know what to do." His laugh was thin, like spent aspen leaves rattling in a September breeze. "I can't even play Candy Crush." He muttered something then blurted, "Oh! I love the name MoonStone. So much better than Flintstones!" He tried to laugh at his joke but coughed instead.

My heart almost burst with hope. "Dad, thank you. Maybe now we can talk more often. I'd like that."

"So would I, Tracy. Thanks for still caring enough to give me another chance." He coughed some more.

"We better hang up now," Elizabeth said.

"Okay," I said. "Take care of him." I still heard coughing.

"That's what I do. Goodbye."

I buried my head in Jackie's lap and cried until I had no more tears. "Why did he change?" I asked.

Jackie kissed my hands. "He said Elizabeth helped him. Plus fifty-three years of regret and bad health. And your book."

"Our book."

Jackie squeezed my hands. "You wrote it."

"You made that possible. And Mom. I wish she could have heard him."

"I think she knew what would happen. That's why she wanted you to contact him."

That evening we collected and captioned photos and chose songs to include. There were so many we decided to send a partial group the next day and more later.

We heard nothing back. The day after, we texted. *Were you able to open the files?*

An hour later we received a text from Elizabeth. *I took Art to emergency a few hours after your phone call. He slipped into a coma yesterday and passed this morning. His last words were, "Tell Tracy that I'm finally at peace, and I hope she is too." Thank you for contacting us. He had been nervous about dying, but after speaking with you, he had no fear.*

MoonStone was conceived in a yurt at 11:00 o'clock on Tuesday, June 18, 1968.

It grew every day since then, feeding the bond between Jackie and me and Mom.

And among our children and their families.

It represents new beginnings and strength, love and inspiration, success and good fortune.

It is also a healing stone.

With the power to cleanse and restore.

And bring peace to our hearts.

May this book do the same for you.

THE END

APPENDIX

MoonStone Songs

All We Can Do

I found your lips in the dark
And tried to touch your heart
Out of sight
From the crowd

I drank your breath like sweet wine
And tried to slow down time
We got caught
And now we're out

Chorus
They say we cannot be together
Straighten up or find a new life
If you cannot be my lover
I will die

If they choose who we kiss
And force us to split
We die slow
So very slow

When push comes to shove
We've got to cherish our love
And hold on
Just hang on

Chorus repeat

All we can do
Is run for our lives
Just get away, Baby
And live free

All we can do, Baby,
all we can do
Just run for our lives
All we can do
Just get away, Baby
And live free
Just live free

It's a Great War

Little boys in the sandbox moving their soldiers
Planning sneak attacks, can't wait till they're older

Joey gets a new gun and itches for a kill
The bird bleeds out, such a freakin thrill

Once in the Nam, he searches and destroys
Killing Viet Cong, we're so proud of our boys

Burn a village to the ground even if it's friendly
Only way to save it from the stinkin' commie

Chorus
It's a great war
like a party in the jungle
Such a gung ho war
And it ain't much trouble

It's a bad ass war
wouldn't want to miss it
Love my M16
Keeps me feeling mean

It's a lovely war
USA is something special
It's a great war
Wouldn't wish it on the devil

Spencer's Song

He was
Too sweet to live,
too soon to die
Too quick to forgive
And too gentle to fight

He was
Too blind to see color
Too bright for the dark
Too nice to be cruel
With too big a heart

Yet they called him to war
to fight overseas
when he wouldn't keep fireflies

overnight in a jar

He was
too hip to be lame
too cool to feel hate
too boss to bomb
too wild to go straight

Yet they called him to war
to fight overseas
when he wouldn't keep fireflies
overnight in a jar

When the good guys die
The songbird cries
The tooth fairy steals
and the angels make deals

It's time to make the world better
For brothers like Spencer
Make the world better
And love every Spencer

What's The Point?

Like a bird that won't sing
Or a mind that can't think
Like a heart that can't feel
Or a wound that won't heal

What's the point?
Yeah, Babe, what's the point?

Like a joke that hurts
Or a clock that won't work
Like a lie to yourself

And a truth you can't tell

What's the point?
Yeah, Babe, what's the point?

Like a friend that won't share
Or a God who doesn't care
Like a girl who's a toy
And never equal to a boy

What's the point?
Yeah, Babe, what's the point?

You say
It's just the world we were given
Maybe it's the one we made
How can this be living
I'd rather walk away

Time to make a change
Or what's the point?
Time to rearrange
Or what's the point?

A Chorus To You

I chased the sun 'til I found you
Out of the darkness and into your light
A smile so bright I never knew
Could steal my eyes
And see only you

I heard your voice before I saw you
Changing the noise to music so clear
A sound so warm I never knew
Could steal my ears

And hear only you

You are my hope my joy my rock
The foundation of every thought
The notes in my tunes
The words in my songs
Every beat of my heart
Is a chorus to you

Before you now I am naked
Every fault and scar you can see
All my life I have yearned and waited
For a friend who believes in me

You are my hope my joy my rock
The foundation of every thought
The notes in my tunes
The words in my songs
Every beat of my heart
Is a chorus to you

<u>*You Would Love Me*</u>

When I kissed you that first time
I saw colors rich and bright
I tasted wind-blown ocean waves
My soul danced in pure delight

Your lips were soft and full
as I breathed you like a drink
In the beauty of your eyes
I lived between each blink

Chorus
You were springtime
Covered in flowers

You were sunshine
lifting the clouds

You were music
playing my high notes
With a heartbeat
pounding so close

And I knew
That I loved you
And hoped you'd love me too

In a better world
In a beautiful world
In a perfect world
You would love me

When I kissed you that first time
I rose high into the clouds
Lightning flashed across the sky
But I could not hear a sound

Your hands softly found my waist
And pulled me into you
A flutter deep and strong
Begged me not to move

Chorus
You were springtime
Covered in flowers
You were sunshine
lifting the clouds

You were music
playing my high notes
With a heartbeat

pounding so close

And I knew
That I loved you
And hoped you'd love me too

In a better world
In a beautiful world
In a perfect world
You would love me
Like I do you

The MoonStone Girls

From a lake of wonder two teenage girls emerged
Trying to wash away a past that neither one deserved
A mountain rose above them in the dawning light
With a mother's love it helped them find a better life
Find a better life

In these wicked times when too many live to hate
And pick and choose who loves and who should separate
We formed a bond and band to make a better world
Each other's joy and hope we are The MoonStone Girls
We are The MoonStone Girls

Born to sing
Born to love
And to raise our voice above
The din of indignation
And the screams of accusation
To change hypocrisy to harmony
And noise to a soothing melody
to a soothing melody

Playlist

In order of appearance

- Pyotr Tchaikovsky— *Piano Concerto No. 1 in B flat Minor*
- Claude Debussy— *L'isle Joyeuse*
- The Rolling Stones— "19th Nervous Breakdown"
- The Beatles— "Sgt. Pepper's Lonely Hearts Club Band"
- Sam the Sham— "Lil' Red Riding Hood"
- The Association— "Along Comes Mary"
- Simon & Garfunkel— "Scarborough Fair/Canticle"
- Simon & Garfunkel— "The Sound of Silence"
- The Association— "Cherish"
- Percy Sledge— "When a Man Loves a Woman"
- Jefferson Airplane— "Somebody to Love"
- The Turtles— "Happy Together"
- Ludvig von Beethoven— *"Pathétique" Sonata 1st Movement*
- Jefferson Airplane— "White Rabbit"
- Aretha Franklin— "Respect"
- The Beatles— "Strawberry Fields Forever"
- Franz Schubert— *Grand Duo Sonata in C Major*
- Marvin Gaye— "Ain't No Mountain High Enough"
- Gary Puckett— "Woman, Woman"
- The Who— "I Can See for Miles"
- The Beatles— "Hello, Goodbye"
- Marvin Gaye— "I Heard It Through the Grapevine"
- Buffalo Springfield— "For What It's Worth"
- The Beatles— "All You Need Is Love"
- Simon & Garfunkel— "I Am A Rock"
- The Rolling Stones— "Let's Spend the Night Together"
- The Beatles— "You've Got To Hide Your Love Away"
- The Kingsmen— "Louie Louie"
- Johann S. Bach— "Minuet in G"
- Frederich Chopin— *Ballade No. 1 in G Minor*
- The Beatles— "The Fool On The Hill"
- The Beatles— "Yesterday"
- Judy Collins— "Amazing Grace"
- Bob Dylan— "Don't Think Twice, It's All Right"

- Peter, Paul & Mary— "Leaving On A Jet Plane"
- Simon & Garfunkel— "Homeward Bound"
- Peter, Paul & Mary— "If I Had A Hammer"
- Bob Dylan— "Blowin' In The Wind"
- Peter, Paul, & Mary— "Where Have All The Flowers Gone?"
- Frederich Chopin— *Fantaisie-Impromptu in C-sharp Minor*

MoonStone Band Logo

ACKNOWLEDGMENTS

In June 1968, a month after turning fifteen years old, my father flew from JFK airport in New York City by himself to Anchorage, Alaska. He took the train to what is now known as Denali National Park and spent two weeks in a place much like Camp Wonder, living in a wall tent with a wood stove.

And, yes, his outhouse had no door, but he claims he never flashed the nearby hills and shrubs. I have doubts, however.

He chased after caribou to get a picture with his Instamatic, always beat everyone else in his group to the top of mountains (of course, everyone was at least three times his age), stomped on dead branches to make kindling for camp fires, and saw the pink mountain appear at 3:30 am on his last day before returning to civilization.

He also spent a wonderful day exploring the area with a 17-year-old teenage girl who worked at the camp. They found an old cabin and food caches on stilts, scrambled up steep slopes for grand views, and eventually drank tea in the yurt she shared with others. He was too young and inexperienced to recognize whether she had any interest in him. But he does remember that he reeked because he refused to take a group shower in the shed. He didn't think to ask the girl whether she had a metal tub under her bed.

All in all, this was one of the most formative experiences of his life. He returned to Denali Park when his children were old enough to carry a pack, camping at Wonder Lake dozens of times, often waking up early to see the pink alpenglow reflecting from the mountain.

Because of his whimsical decision to choose a camp in Alaska and his parents' desire to get him out of the house for two weeks, his life and eventually mine changed forever. This book would not exist otherwise.

I have been very fortunate to find excellent beta readers and editors. Before my last book—*Crystal's House of Queers*— was published, I sent a few special readers the bare bones of an idea which would become *The MoonStone Girls*. Their support and suggestions kept this baby growing one chapter at a time over the summer of 2021 until birth in early October.

Jerrica McDowell has helped me with all my novels, each from initial idea to completion. It is amazing to send out a chapter or two and get immediate, meaningful feedback. As always, my guide through the meanderings of imagination.

Ruth Torrence has worked with me on three novels before the age of nineteen. Always honest, kind, and enthusiastic, she contributed much to this book even before I wrote the first sentence.

Emily Wright, a newly published author herself (*Tamara King*), has been very helpful to me for two novels. Her enthusiasm for this story in particular kept my spirits high and my determination strong.

Rhiannon Joseph, Jade Visos-Ely, and Bianca also helped develop my story with great insights and attention to details.

Jessica Seevers, Alyssa Kegel, Oskar Leonard, Flor Propato, Bree Ric, and Amber reviewed the final draft, and each offered actionable suggestions and great support.

Cherie Chapman (ccbookdesign.com) has designed all my covers, each one perfect for the book's themes and catching a reader's eye. But she outdid herself with this cover.

Many aspects and events of the late 60s nearly broke this country apart, but the music and slang of that period were the baddest of all time. You dig? The playlist is guaranteed to make you smile.

ABOUT THE AUTHOR

Brooke Skipstone is a multi-award winning author who lives in Alaska where she watches the mountains change colors with the seasons from her balcony. Where she feels the constant rush toward winter as the sunlight wanes for six months of the year, seven minutes each day, bringing crushing cold that lingers even as the sun climbs again. Where the burst of life during summer is urgent under twenty-four-hour daylight, lush and decadent. Where fish swim hundreds of miles up rivers past bear claws and nets and wheels and lines of rubber-clad combat fishers, arriving humped and ragged, dying as they spawn. Where danger from the land and its animals exhilarates the senses, forcing her to appreciate the difference between life and death. Where the edge between is sometimes too alluring.

The MoonStone Girls is her fourth novel. Visit her website at brookeskipstone.com for information about her first three novels—*Crystal's House of Queers, Some Laneys Died,* and *Someone To Kiss My Scars.*

CPSIA information can be obtained
at www.ICGtesting.com
Printed in the USA
LVHW032240250122
709251LV00006B/35